MURDER IN
HINDSIGHT

Mysteries by Anne Cleeland

Murder in Hindsight

Murder in Retribution

Murder in Thrall

MURDER IN HINDSIGHT

ANNE CLEELAND

KENSINGTON BOOKS
http://www.kensingtonbooks.com

KENSINGTON BOOKS are published by

Kensington Publishing Corp.
119 West 40th Street
New York, NY 10018

All Kensington titles, imprints, and distributed lines are available at special quantity discounts for bulk purchases for sales promotion, premiums, fund-raising, educational, or institutional use.

Special book excerpts or customized printings can also be created to fit specific needs. For details, write or phone the office of the Kensington Special Sales Manager: Attn. Special Sales Department. Kensington Publishing Corp, 119 West 40th Street, New York, NY 10018. Phone: 1-800-221-2647.

Kensington and the K logo Reg. U.S. Pat. & TM Off.

Library of Congress Card Catalogue Number: 2014953096

ISBN-13: 978-0-7582-8794-6
ISBN-10: 0-7582-8794-1
First Kensington Hardcover Edition: April 2015

eISBN-13: 978-0-7582-8796-0
eISBN-10: 0-7582-8796-8
First Kensington Electronic Edition: April 2015

10 9 8 7 6 5 4 3 2 1

Printed in the United States of America

For Judge Bauer, who loves the law; and for all others like him.

CHAPTER 1

DETECTIVE SERGEANT KATHLEEN DOYLE WAS FRETTING; FRET-ting and stalling until Detective Chief Inspector Acton could make an appearance whilst she tried to appear calm and composed in front of the Scene of the Crime Officers. As a newly-promoted DS, she should maintain a certain dignity and display her leadership abilities, even though she was longing to bite her nails and peer over the hedgerow toward the park entrance.

The various Scotland Yard forensics personnel were impatiently waiting because Acton was delayed, and Doyle had a good guess as to why he was delayed. One of these fine days, someone else may make the same guess, and then the wretched cat would be among the wretched pigeons—although the mind boggled, trying to imagine Acton being called on the carpet by Professional Standards. Pulling out her mobile, she pretended to make a call just to appear busy.

"I'll lose the light soon, ma'am." The SOCO photographer approached, cold and unhappy, and small blame to her; Doyle was equally cold and unhappy, but with better reason.

"Ten more minutes," Doyle assured her, holding a hand over her mobile so as to interrupt her pretend-conversation. "Then we'll move forward—whether DCI Acton makes it or no." She wanted Acton to have a look before the corpse was processed and removed, but she could always show him the photos.

The woman immediately plucked up. "No hurry; we can wait, if the DCI is on his way."

Has a crush on him, the brasser, thought Doyle. Join the club, my friend; the woman probably had some private photographs she'd be all too happy to show Acton in her spare time.

The SOCO photographer used to treat Doyle with barely-concealed contempt, but her attitude had improved remarkably after the bridge-jumping incident. A few months ago, Doyle had jumped off Greyfriars Bridge into the Thames to save a colleague, and was now a celebrated hero. All in all, it was a mixed blessing, because Doyle was not one who craved the spotlight and now she was perceived as some sort of a female version of St. George—except that she'd rescued the dragon, instead of the maiden, when you thought about it.

Irish by birth and fey by nature, Doyle had an uncanny ability to read people, and in particular she could recognize a lie when she heard it. This perceptive ability had launched her career as a detective, but it also made her reclusive by nature—it was no easy thing, to be able to pick up on the currents and crosscurrents of emotion swirling around her. The SOCO photographer, for example, was lusting after the vaunted chief inspector, but bore Doyle no particular ill-will for being married to him, since she was the heroic bridge-jumper and thus above reproach.

With a nod of her head, the photographer gestured toward the victim, being as she didn't want to take her hands out of her pockets until it was necessary. "Is there something special about this one, then?"

There was, but Doyle did not want to say, especially before the loose-lipped SOCOs, who were notoriously inclined to blather in their cups—it came from wading knee-deep in guts all the livelong day. So instead, she equivocated, "There are a few details that are worrisome, is all. I wanted the DCI to have a quick look."

As it appeared to be an ordinary case of a bad 'un coming to an only-to-be-expected bad end in this part of town, this pronouncement would ordinarily hold little water, but because the photographer was anticipating a chance to bat her eyes at Acton, no demur was raised. Doyle was reminded that on the aqueduct case, this particular photographer had withheld evidence at Acton's request, and wondered at such foolish devotion. Then she recalled that it was a case of the pot and the kettle—Doyle herself was an aider and abettor, after all—and so she tempered her scorn. Although she was married to him, Acton was in many respects a mystery to her as few were; he abided by his own notions of justice, and was not above manipulating the means to achieve the ends he desired—not something one would expect from a well-respected DCI at the Met. But the fact that no one would expect it was—ironically—the very reason he got away with murder on certain memorable occasions; his reputation acted as a shield. Any suggestion that the celebrated Lord Acton was running illegal weapons, dispatching villains, or manipulating evidence would be met with disbelief and derision, as well he knew. In the meantime, his better half was left to hang on to his coat tails and try to curb his wayward ways—it was no easy task, and Doyle reluctantly rang off from her pretend-conversation so as to decide how best to proceed without him.

After peering over the hedgerow yet again, she blew into her hands because she'd forgotten her gloves, and reflected that the cold was actually a blessing, because the recently departed wouldn't be further decomposing whilst they cooled their heels—she truly shouldn't delay for much longer, or the evidence officer might think they'd all gone for a pub crawl.

"Here he comes, ma'am," the photographer chirped happily, and with a great deal of relief, Doyle looked up to see that Acton was indeed approaching; his tall, over-coated figure emerging from the evening fog. In such a setting he appeared larger-than-life, and small wonder that female underlings harbored a crush, or that the younger detectives at the Met called him "Holmes" behind his back. He was a local legend, which only made her fret all the more whilst she entertained the bleak conviction that the whole thing was about to come crashing down around their heads.

"DS Doyle." He nodded to her. "Have you an ID?"

"I do indeed, sir." They kept up a professional façade when they were dealing with each other at work, but she met his eyes and felt the chemistry crackling between them like an electrical charge. No one could fathom why the great Chief Inspector Acton had married the lowly likes of her, and literally on a moment's notice. She could fathom it, however, and did—sometimes twice a day. Thus far in their short marriage they were very happy together, despite the occasional crisis.

She continued, "He's twenty-three years old with a record of petty thefts and drug-dealin'—nothing major—but he was a suspect in an arson homicide about eight years ago." She paused significantly, and Acton met her eyes with interest. He then stepped carefully over to the body, lying next to the hedgerow, and she followed to crouch down beside him and contemplate the victim's remains for a silent moment. The victim had been shot in the back of the head, and there were no signs of a defensive struggle. "No sign of robbery, and he was armed—had a .38 revolver tucked into the back of his belt." That it was illegal went without saying; guns were carefully controlled in the UK, but the black market flourished, particularly among the criminal classes. Lowering her voice, she indicated with a finger, "The entry wound is angled, and there's no visible residue, so it's at mid-close range—no more than a foot or so. Another shot from behind, but not a professional hit."

He began to pull off his leather gloves by the fingers. "Allow me to lend you my gloves."

"You mustn't," she warned. "I'll never learn, else."

"Your fingers are white."

"Are you *listenin'* to me?"

"Yes." He glanced up at her. "He used a different weapon, this time, and shot from the opposite side in an attempt to obscure his identity."

"I think so," she agreed, mollified that he was paying attention, and had come to the same conclusion that she had. "He's trying to disguise it, but it's the same killer. And the victim has another cold case connection."

They rose, and Acton stood next to her, his breath making a cloud in the chill air. In a low tone, she ventured, "Perhaps you should button your coat, my friend—and try not to be breathin' on anyone."

There was a pause. "Is it so obvious?" he asked quietly.

"Only to me," she assured him. "Was it completely wretched?"

"I've been admonished not to discuss it with you, but the answer is yes."

"Grand," she observed dryly.

He continued in a neutral tone, "I am asked a great many questions about my mother and about you."

"Whist, Michael," she scoffed. "As if that has *anythin'* to do wi' it."

He chuckled, which was a good sign, and she chuckled with him, not caring what the impatient SOCO team would think to see the CID detectives amusing themselves over the remains of the decedent. Acton had begun therapy for an obsessive condition, the object of his obsession being her fair self. He'd developed a fixation for his first-year colleague, and by the time Doyle had become aware of it, he'd convinced her to marry him—which she had, in a pig's whisper, which only spoke to the state of her own mental faculties. To make a try at a normal life, he was seeing a therapist, hoping to learn techniques to control his symptoms without necessarily disclosing the reason. Apparently, the therapist had not been misled.

"So you've been servin' yourself some self-help," she concluded. After his sessions, Acton would drink impressive quantities of scotch. He was not one to refrain, even under normal conditions, but it seemed to Doyle that the therapy was only making matters worse.

"We're losing the light, sir," the photographer ventured from a respectful distance.

Thus reminded, Acton called the SOCO team over and began giving instructions; particular care was to be given to physical evidence at the site, although there was little to hope for, with the ground so cold. Because the killer was using a variety of murder weapons to disguise his involvement, any footprints or trace evidence they could scrounge up might provide a means to link this murder to the others; by all appearances, they were dealing with a serial killer.

While they watched the forensics team go to work, Acton lifted his head to survey the area, and observe the placement of the CCTV cameras. "Tell me about the cold case that is connected to this one."

"Unsolved double-murder by arson. Our victim here was the chief suspect, eight years ago, but there was little evidence, and he had a lot of sympathetic press coverage, bein' so young." There was a pause. Doyle's working theory was that they were dealing with a vigilante; someone who was murdering earlier suspects who'd gotten away with murder.

"Eight years; a strange sort of vigilante, who abides for such a length of time."

"Aye, that," she teased solemnly. When Acton drank, his tone and language reverted to House-of-Lords, and so she reverted to hardscrabble Dublin so as to counter him.

Amused, he turned to meet her eyes and said sincerely, "This was very good work."

She shrugged, nonetheless pleased by the compliment. "Lucky, more like. And give yourself some credit; it all came of you throwin' me off the cases." Acton had been concerned— and rightly so—that Doyle was in danger when they were investigating the Kempton Park racecourse murders. He had taken her out of the field, and instead placed her on thankless and uninteresting cold case duty, locked in the CID basement and looking through dusty boxes of unsolved homicides. Thoroughly frustrated and resentful, she had nevertheless used the time to review and index Acton's cold case files, and had noticed a link between a recent string of apparently-unconnected murders and some of the unsolved cold cases. Her intuition came to the conclusion that someone was murdering killers who had previously escaped justice—a vigilante was at work. This latest victim would appear to confirm her theory.

A PC who was monitoring the cordon came over to have a word with Acton. "Sir, there is a reporter who would like to have a word."

Doyle caught a quick flash of annoyance from her husband, but there was nothin' for it; if you tried to avoid the pests, it would only make them think you were hiding massive police abuse. Cooperating with the fourth estate was a necessary evil, especially in this day and age, but on the other hand, Acton was not one to suffer fools. This attitude worked only to enhance his standing with the public, who followed his career with avid interest—not that he cared or noticed.

He signaled for Doyle to accompany him, and so she followed him as he went to address the reporter, a woman who stood with her arms crossed against the cold despite wearing a fine cashmere coat—reporting must pay well. She was from the *London World News*, a paper that had often been critical of the Met. Recently, however, an uneasy truce had been achieved, and the detective chief superintendent had cautioned them that the Home Secretary desired as much cooperation with the press as possible. Doyle was nervous; Acton was very self-possessed and she doubted that anyone else could tell that he'd been drinking, but if the interview did not go well, she'd have to create some sort of distraction—perhaps another pretend phone call.

The reporter seemed a very competent woman in her midthirties, brimming with confidence, Doyle could see; someone who would never forget her gloves on such a day. Holding out a hand to shake his, she threw Acton a friendly smile that held a touch of flirtatiousness, not an uncommon occurrence, as the SOCO photographer was also attempting to sidle up next to him on the pretext of waiting to be discharged. You're not his type—neither of you, Doyle thought; his type was shy redheads who nonetheless tended to fly off the handle on occasion. She was resigned, though; Acton was titled, handsome, rich, and unattainable, a combination that was apparently fatally attractive to the general female population. Male, too, she amended, remembering Owens, the detective trainee who had harbored an unhealthy obsession for him. She was lucky Acton was literally crazy about her; there was a lot of temptation lyin' about.

Acton didn't introduce her, and so Doyle stayed back, monitoring the conversation between the two and wondering if she had the wherewithal to step in, if the need arose. Judging by the questions, however, it didn't appear that the reporter was yet aware of the pattern that pointed to a serial killer, and so Doyle relaxed a bit. Because the scene had been cordoned off in a public place and there had been a delay in waiting for Acton, no doubt the press had merely caught wind of it, and had come to see if there was a story. Serial killers were tricky; although there were times when the public should be warned there was such a killer afoot, in cases like this, when it seemed unlikely the killer was aware they'd twigged him, discretion was the better option—all the better to set up a trap and seizure.

In a provocative gesture, the reporter threw back her head and laughed at something Acton said, which inspired the photographer to interrupt with barely-concealed jealousy. They were both making a dead run at him, but he appeared completely oblivious to it, which was commendable, being as his wife was making a mighty effort not to interject a smart re-mark. Instead, said wife comforted herself by recalling that she'd carried off the palm, and thus managed to curb the urge to knock both their heads together.

At this point, the reporter deigned to notice Doyle. "Why, you're the bridge-jumper, aren't you?"

Doyle acknowledged that indeed, she was the bridge-jumper.

The woman shook her head. "I have to say—I don't think I could have done it."

Doyle remembered that Kevin Maguire, the reporter who had interviewed her from the same paper, had told her it was a great human interest story because everyone who read it would pause and wonder if they would have run such a risk. Apparently, he was right. "Please give my regards to Mr. Maguire," she said; the man had done her a favor, and Doyle was grateful.

"Will do," the woman agreed, and with one last glance under her lashes at Acton, she left.

After giving instruction to close down the scene, Acton and Doyle walked back toward Acton's Range Rover, parked a block away. He was quiet, and she broke the silence. "You should probably go straight home, my friend."

"Come with me."

She could see that he was in need of the cure—it was her ex-perience that a good, hearty serving of ungentle sex tended to bring him out of the dismals. "I can't," she explained regret-fully. "I'm slated to help at the clinic, and I'm past due already."

He ducked his head for a moment, and then looked at her with an expression she knew very well. "Don't stay late."

"I won't. Don't be startin' without me."

"Not a chance," he replied.

CHAPTER 2

*T*HE CHARITY MEDICAL CLINIC WAS LOCATED IN AN AREA OF LONdon near high-rise housing projects that were teeming with recent immigrants and other members of the population who were hard-pressed to make ends meet. One of Acton's oldest friends was Dr. Timothy McGonigal, a well-respected surgeon, and it was the information that Timothy volunteered at the clinic two days a month that had inspired Doyle to volunteer her own services, such as they were. She'd never had an opportunity to engage in charitable work—being as up to now she'd been struggling to keep her head above water, and the devil take the hindmost. Then she'd married Acton—or more correctly, he'd married her—and her life had undergone a dramatic change that made her feel a bit guilty, truth to tell; as though she were masquerading as someone else, and at any moment she'd be found out. Therefore, she'd jumped at the opportunity to help the less fortunate, and as an added blessing there was little doubt that as a result of her involvement, Acton would unlock the vault to meet whatever financial needs the clinic presented. Doyle had no idea how much Acton was worth, only that he seemed steeped in ancient wealth and bore a title that went back to the Conquest. It was something neither of them spoke about; she guessed that he was doing his best to suppress any information which

would make her feel even more unworthy, and she was like-
wise afraid to make any inquiries for fear of what she'd discover.

After assessing her talents, the director of the clinic had determined that Doyle should be put to work accompanying the
visiting nurse as she conducted follow-up visits to the surgical
patients, particularly as Doyle was a police officer, and some
of the patients lived in questionable neighborhoods. Thus
far, Doyle had managed to gloss over this aspect of her duties
when she spoke of it to Acton, knowing that he would feel it
was too dangerous, and intervene with Timothy. She also left
her mobile phone behind when she made these visits, because Acton kept track of her through its GPS system. In
truth, she was ashamed of this subterfuge, which arose as a result of the subtle tension in their relationship; he tended to
be over-protective and she tended to resent this tendency,
and the unfortunate result was this semi-defiant secrecy, which
was rather childish and not—she acknowledged honestly—
very good for her marriage. She would have to ask to change
her role at the clinic after today; she and Acton should have
no secrets from one another, and it was true that she tended
to be a calamity magnet, if the past few months were any indication. Perhaps instead she could help clean up in surgery—
she was well-used to blood spatter, after all; as long as she
didn't have to interact with any needles.

At the clinic, Doyle greeted the director, a very capable
doctor from East Africa, who gave her a list of three patients
who required follow-up visits—all three in the nearby housing projects. List in hand, Doyle went to gather up the nurse,
but first stopped to greet Nanda, a young Rwandan woman
who'd been given a job at the clinic through Acton's generos-
ity. Upon seeing her, Doyle had to suppress a wrench of grief;
Nanda's husband had been Doyle's friend, Aiki, and after his
murder, Acton and Timothy had arranged for her job at the
clinic as a means to support his widow and baby.

Nanda smiled, and exchanged pleasantries with Doyle in her heavily accented English; Doyle asked after the baby, and was assured he was exceptional in every way. With some surprise, Doyle realized that Nanda was very content, considering the recent tragic events. On the other hand, the young woman had a baby and a new job and life went on—Doyle wondered how she'd manage without Acton, and shied away from the very thought.

Nanda explained that the visiting nurse had been called home to tend to a sick child, and that Nanda herself would accompany Doyle on the rounds, if Doyle would just wait until the end of Nanda's shift.

"Oh—I can handle it, Nanda," Doyle assured the woman, reluctant to wait so long, with Acton no doubt pacing the floor at home. On the previous visit when she'd accompanied the nurse, the former patients were either not at home or too suspicious to open the door, and in any case, Doyle had an illegal gun in her ankle holster, courtesy of Acton. It was not so late as to make the visit foolhardy and she was a police officer, after all.

Doyle navigated her way toward the first address on her list, crossing the street and glancing back over her shoulder—she had a vague sense that she was being followed, but didn't see anything to raise alarm. It happened, sometimes, when she walked along a crowded sidewalk—it seemed to her there were more people than there really were. Paranoid, is what you are, she thought. Comes of knowing Acton would slay you if he was made aware you are knocking on doors by yourself at the projects—you should have brought one of the orderlies along. Hesitating, she considered this idea, but then forged ahead, promising herself that if there was the slightest whisper of trouble, she'd retreat; after all, she was a flippin' sergeant now and should act like one. I wonder why I'm worried, she thought and glanced over her shoulder yet again; it was not as though there'd been any problems on the earlier visits.

Her footsteps echoing on the bare metal, Doyle ascended the graffiti-sprayed stairwell until she came to the appropriate door and knocked, announcing that she was from the clinic and was there to check on the former patient. The door remained locked while muffled voices assured her all was well, and with a small sigh, she moved on.

At the second address, her knock was met with silence, although her instinct told her there was someone on the other side, peering through the peephole as a baby cried in the next flat over. She glanced behind her; the hallway appeared deserted, yet again she had the feeling she was being watched, and there was no crowd this time to cross up her wires, so to speak. Ignoring it, she knocked again. "I'm from the clinic and I'm here to see how"—she checked the name—"how Leticia does." The patient was a seven-year-old girl who underwent an emergency appendectomy the week before.

The door suddenly opened a crack, and Doyle was faced with a very serious young man pointing a very serious gun barrel at her. "What do you want?"

Faith, thought Doyle; moral dilemma. The weapon was undoubtedly illegal and she should make an arrest, but she was here on an errand of mercy and it didn't seem in keeping. "I'm from the clinic," she began again. "I'm here to check on your"—gauging his age, she took a guess—"little sister."

"You don't look like a doctor." The gun did not waver.

"No, I'm not. But the clinic did send me." Best not to mention that in her other life she was a police officer.

He looked her over in a way Doyle could not like, and then the gun was lowered. "Right, then; come in."

Doyle, however, was not a fool. "Do you think you can send Leticia out, so I can examine her out here?"

"You don't trust me," he accused with a scowl.

"No," she agreed. "Recall that you have a gun."

He thought this over, and apparently saw her point. "I'll get her."

In short order, a nervous little girl emerged, her dark eyes wide. Doyle crouched down and smiled in what she hoped was a reassuring manner—she had little experience with children. "May I see your tummy, where the operation was?" She didn't know much, but certainly she could check for signs of infection. The girl dutifully lifted her shirt, and as Doyle examined the incision, the man pointed his gun to Doyle's head. "Hand over your drugs and be quick about it."

Mother a' mercy, she thought; if I manage to get out of this alive, Acton will *kill* me. "I have no drugs," she protested, speaking in a calm tone as she carefully closed her hand around her own weapon in the ankle holster, and released the safety. "I'm only tryin' to make sure Leticia—"

"Now," he demanded, gesturing with the weapon as he took a quick look down the deserted hallway. "Come inside."

Although it was almost superfluous at this point, her intuition was doing the equivalent of flashing red lights in her face, and so there was nothing for it; her own illegal weapon would have to make an appearance. Therefore, with a swift motion, she leapt up and grasped his wrist, bending it back and holding her gun to his head. "Police," she announced. "Drop it."

He stared at her in stunned silence and dropped his gun.

"Go into the flat, Leticia," Doyle instructed the little girl, who looked from one adult to the other with no real surprise, which seemed a sad commentary. As the girl obediently slipped through the door, Doyle pondered her next move; she had no flex cuffs, as she was off-duty—best enlist a neighbor to call for backup.

"On the ground, facedown," she commanded, and as he dropped to his knees, she kept the weapon trained upon him but looked up along the hallway to see if anyone had been curious enough to open a door. Her assailant saw his opening, and lunged at her legs with his body as his hands reached to close around the wrist that held the gun. Off-balance, she struggled to remain upright as he yanked on her arm and threw her backward, forcing her to release her weapon at the risk of breaking her arm.

"Oh no! Leticia—watch out—" she gasped, and when the man turned to look toward his door, she slammed a fist across his jaw and scrambled to escape. Enraged, he reached at the last moment to grasp at her ankle and she went down headlong, hard. Frantically, she kicked at him as he yanked her leg toward the doorway, calling her a vile epithet and detailing his intention to make her pay for her actions. As she tried to brace against the doorway, she fought a sick sense of panic—she was ovulating, and utter disaster loomed. Turning her head, she shouted for help but the sound only echoed against the walls—even the baby in the next flat had been silenced. Her assailant reached to unpeel her fingers from the doorjamb and while he was left vulnerable for a moment, she managed to kick him in the groin with all the leverage she could muster. He let go of her hand and bent over, cursing in pain whilst she twisted to get away, but he did not relinquish his grip on her ankle, and rose to his knees with a cocked arm and the evident intent to punch her into submission. He did not succeed, however, because another man suddenly appeared behind him, yanked back his head by the hair, and knocked him out with one efficient blow.

Doyle stared in gratified astonishment as the man held out a hand to her. "Come, come." He had an accent.

Taking his hand, Doyle scrambled to her feet, her heartbeat pounding in her ears as she stepped over her fallen assailant. As her rescuer bent to gather the weapons from the floor, she managed to gasp, "Do you have a mobile? I should secure the area—"

"No." He began to walk swiftly toward the stairwell, jerking his head briefly to indicate she was to accompany him. Un-willing to linger in this hostile hallway without her champion, she followed him, quickening her pace as they nearly ran down the stairwell—he was obviously interested in vacating the area as quickly as possible. Only when they had cleared the next building over did he stop and allow her to lean against the wall, gasping to recover her breath.

Doyle had already made a very shrewd guess as to his role in these affairs, and offered with all gratitude, "Thank the saints and holy angels Acton is an over-protective knocker; I was never more glad to see anyone in my life."

The man watched her impassively. He was medium sized; wiry and strong, with close- cropped blond hair and a narrow face that featured a slightly crooked nose, as if it had been broken. "You fight well, but he was too strong for you." He said it with a trace of sympathy, as though he was trying to make her feel better for needing help—and there was the ac-cent again. Doyle was not good with accents, and could not immediately identify it.

"I'm not ashamed to say I was flailin', my friend. Thank you again for ridin' to the rescue." She smoothed her hair back from her forehead with a hand that still trembled from reac-tion, and gave him what she hoped was her most beguiling smile. "I suppose there's nothin' I can say that would con-vince you not to report this to Acton."

His gaze did not waver. "I do not know this Acton."

She stared at him, the smile fading as she realized that she was once again in a precarious situation with a strange man, only this time he had her weapon in his pocket.

Reading her aright, he shrugged. "Do not be afraid; I will not hurt you."

"No," she replied, a little ashamed of herself. "I'm that sorry; I'm a little on edge, just now. I should be thankin' you fastin'."

He looked at her a little blankly and she could sense he was confused, so she made an effort to control her accent and held out her hand. "I'm Kathleen Doyle."

He did not take her hand, but corrected her with a tilt of his head. "No; you are Kathleen Sinclair."

She processed the interesting fact that he was no chance stranger and he had not, as yet, offered up an explanation for his presence. "When I'm workin', I use Doyle."

He thought about this, his scrutiny never wavering. "What is a 'knocker'?"

Doyle considered, and countered with, "Who are you?"

There was a gleam of amusement, barely discernable in his pale eyes, even though his impassive expression did not change. "I think it best I not say."

She considered again. "Well then; I won't say anythin' about this if you won't. Do we have a bargain?"

"Yes." Not a gabbler, he was.

This was a huge relief, and she teased, "You should say, 'Done,' and then we should shake hands to seal it."

"Done." He took her hand formally for a moment. "We must leave."

"I'll be needin' my gun back, first." There'd be no explaining this away if she came home without it.

Her companion obligingly pulled both weapons from his jacket pockets. "Which?"

"This one." She took it, and bent to return it to her ankle holster, hoping he didn't realize it was illegal and she shouldn't have it in the first place—since he was a foreigner, he probably didn't know any better.

"That is a fine pistol," he observed. "You should be more careful with it."

"No argument, here." At his gesture, they began to walk in silence, he heading back to the clinic without needing direction. Interesting; she now knew why she felt as though she was being followed, earlier. And when they'd shaken hands, she noted he wore a very fine Breguet watch. She'd met only one other man with such a watch, and putting two and two together, thought she may know why her rescuer had been following her; it appeared there were forces other than Acton trying to keep her safe—although not necessarily for the same reasons. If what she'd guessed was true, then she had nothing to fear from this one, and so accompanied him back to the clinic without another qualm.

CHAPTER 3

As SHE WAS BEING DRIVEN HOME IN THE DRIVING SERVICE'S town car, Doyle texted Acton that she was on her way and tried to decide what to confess—ironic that this dilemma was hard on the heels of her resolution to have no secrets from him. Yet again, she had acted recklessly—although she never seemed to realize it until afterwards—and had done something dangerously foolish. This tendency of hers was one of the reasons he wanted her to find another line of work, and if she confessed that she was equally adept at inciting a ruckus whilst doing volunteer work, no doubt he'd forbid that, too. Faith, if Acton had his way, she'd be locked in a flippin' tower like a flippin' princess. That she'd been an idiot was inarguable, and she went cold at the thought of what the consequences might have been if her rescuer hadn't shown up. She had no one to blame but herself, and she'd be ridiculously careful from here on out; best not to let Acton know how close she'd come to complete disaster, and instead make yet another effort to mend her headstrong ways. On the other hand, her fair skin bruised easily, and she would surely have to explain the marks on her arms and her knees—there was no chance at all that he wouldn't notice them; he noticed every detail.

She still hadn't made up her mind when she put her key card in the slot and entered their flat. When they'd married, she moved into Acton's expensive flat in an exclusive building overlooking the park, and she was just now becoming accustomed to living in the lap of luxury—she was indeed a stranger in a strange land. If her mother were still alive, she'd laugh and call Doyle a thistle dwelling amongst the lilies, and she'd be exactly right.

Her impatient husband came to meet her at the door, and she obligingly walked into his arms—he'd showered, and no longer smelt of scotch but instead she breathed in the faint scent of expensive soap, which must be some kind of aphrodisiac because it always inspired the kind of thoughts the nuns at St. Brigid's School would deplore. She met his kiss with equal fervor, grateful for a reprieve and aware that he was in need of the kind of comfort only she could offer him, and that her own need was just as pressing, after her scare. The urgency of the situation was such—apparently—that retreat to the distant bedroom was not an option, and so Doyle soon found herself situated on the rug in front of the fire and divested of her clothing by an eager husband. While Acton was giving the length of her body his full and undivided attention, he must have noticed her scrapes because he made his way northward again to kiss her neck and whisper, "What happened to you?"

"Michael," she stalled, raking her fingernails lightly along his back, "If you are goin' to call a halt to the proceedin's, I will not be answerable."

But he was Acton and would not be diverted, despite her best efforts. "Give me the short version, then."

Doyle lifted her head to meet his mouth with her own, and murmured against it, "A donnybrook; I had to fight off a man who wanted drugs." This, she decided, was an accurate though grossly redacted version of events.

This gave him pause, and she could see he was winding up to ask some very pertinent questions, so she chided in annoyance, "I thought you didn't like to talk durin' sex."

"Does it hurt?"

"I'm goin' to hurt you one if you don't finish up, Michael."

"You don't dare; I still outrank you."

She started to laugh—there was no help for it, and she could feel him chuckle in his chest as he rested his mouth on the side of her neck. "Now look what you've done; you've broken the mood, Michael."

"Allow me to mend it, then." The conversation thus concluded.

Later, she lay cradled with her back against his chest, drowsily watching the fire and listening to the rain against the windows. "When we were first solvin' cases together, I used to try to make you laugh. It was my sacred goal, it was—you were such a sobersides."

"I had an entirely different goal." He ran a meaningful hand along her hip.

She smiled in appreciation. "Then we were successful, the both of us."

"I more than you," he admitted.

"Don't go to therapy anymore," she said suddenly. "We're runnin' out of scotch."

"No," he agreed.

Faith, she thought with surprise—that was easy.

He ran his hand down her arm and stroked the back of her hand, then laced her fingers with his as she could feel his breath on the nape of her neck. "You don't want to tell me, do you?"

"No," she admitted. "I was a monumental knocker and I am thoroughly ashamed."

She waited, to see if he would leave it at that. He was silent, and so she decided to add, "A man came to help—a Good Samaritan—and it all turned out all right. I learned my lesson, and I'll find some other way to help."

"Good," he said. "I worried."

She had to smile. Of course he did, poor man. "And I had another idea; if I concentrate on these vigilante murders, there's little fieldwork involved—the leads will be in the cold case files." Shifting to her back, she turned to look at his face, illuminated in relief by the firelight. "Less worry."

"Thank you." He leaned to kiss her, then lay down on his back, whilst she twisted to prop herself on her elbows and look down at him—such a handsome man, he was. She lifted his hand and kissed his wedding ring. "I'm sorry I'm such a crackin' trial."

"Worth every moment." He pulled a tendril of her hair from her temple and fingered it. "I would like to tell you something, but I'm not certain I should—you are such a Puritan."

With a shake of her head—it tickled where he pulled at her hair—she regarded him with amused surprise; Acton was not one to gossip. "You must, now, Michael; I promise I will try not to be righteously shocked."

"Nanda is so grateful that Timothy has employed her at the clinic that she is offering him the only commodity she has available."

There was a moment of astonished silence. "Michael," she breathed, thoroughly shocked despite her promise. "He did not take advantage of her in such a way, surely."

"Didn't hesitate."

"But Aiki's not dead three months."

He pulled the tendril through his fingers. "It sounds to me as though both parties are well-satisfied with the situation."

She thought about this in wonderment. "He tells you?"

"Indeed. He asks for advice."

This was too much for Doyle, and she couldn't help laughing at the thought. Acton tugged at the tendril, pretending to be offended. "And what is so funny about that, if I may ask?"

"Nothin' at all," she assured him. "You are the grand master, my friend."

With gentle pressure, he pulled her head to rest on his chest. "It is good to see him so happy."

She made no comment, and squeezed him fondly as she stared thoughtfully at the fire. Timothy's recent unhappiness had been due to what he thought was his sister Caroline's unexpected suicide, but she had actually been killed by Acton. Not that Caroline was an innocent victim; Caroline had unsuccessfully tried to murder Doyle, and had successfully murdered Nanda's husband, Aiki. "All very symmetrical, it is," she observed in wonderment. "The irony is thick on the ground."

"Yes," he agreed soberly. Doyle knew he was thinking about that terrible scene when Caroline had died with Doyle as a witness to it—she was made very unhappy when Acton dispensed his own version of justice, and in turn, Acton didn't do well when Doyle was unhappy.

Trying to regain their previous tone, she observed lightly, "Promise me you'll never tell Nanda that you're payin' her salary at the clinic; you'll not be cashin' in on that particular commodity."

He closed his eyes. "She could ply her wiles all she might; you've knackered me out, and I've nothing to draw from."

"It's self-preservation, it is—it's the best defense to keep you from strayin'."

He smiled to himself, and made no rejoinder. Doyle truly did not get jealous—she was absolutely certain of him, after all—but she knew it pleased him when she teased. After a minute, she realized he'd fallen asleep, which meant he must be more tired than his usual; normally he was good for another session, at least. Smiling, she closed her eyes and followed his lead, listening sleepily to the rain and thanking all available saints and holy angels that she'd averted yet another disaster. Acton was going to quit therapy, and for the first time in a long while there were no clouds looming on the horizon; this marriage business wasn't so hard, after all.

CHAPTER 4

*T*HE NEXT MORNING, DOYLE AND ACTON WERE PREPARING TO leave for work when Reynolds arrived. Reynolds was their domestic, and despite the fact that the presence of a servant made Doyle feel as though she were in an episode of *The Thin Man,* she was fond of him—although it may have been only because their last domestic had tried to poison her, and so by contrast this one seemed exceptional. Doyle had the feeling that Reynolds was aware of a great deal more than he let on; he was very discreet, however, and Doyle knew he was well-pleased to work for them, being as Acton was a renowned figure and it probably gave him boasting rights at the butlers' pub, if there was such a thing.

"How cold is it, Reynolds?" she asked. "Heavy coat or light coat?"

Reynolds considered this question, giving it the weight it deserved, then suggested, "Light coat and scarf," and went to fetch them out of the hall closet. As he held her coat for her, Doyle could sense a flare of alarm from the servant, and turned to regard him with surprise. "What is it?"

He said only, "Will you be in for dinner tonight, madam?"

"I will, but Acton won't." The illustrious chief inspector was going to give a lecture at the Crime Academy, much against his inclination. However, he was brilliant at his job, and Doyle reminded him that he should make a push to improve the corps that served him; he had given her some very useful instruction when she had first worked with him—although in retrospect, she realized that mainly he'd wanted to keep her eyes on his. Nevertheless, the criminal justice system would be best served if he shared his knowledge, even though Acton was not by nature a teacher.

I wouldn't mind teaching—if I knew anything, she thought as she arranged her scarf around her neck. However, her perceptive ability couldn't be taught to another, and she was not very proficient at the scientific part of her job. Once a month, the charity clinic gave classes on first aid and immunizations, and she was thinking that perhaps she could assist with these, although they may want volunteers who knew more than one language. She didn't—unless you counted Gaelic, of course. She would ask.

Acton shrugged into the coat offered by Reynolds and reminded her, "It will be cold in the basement, so bring your gloves, Kathleen. And make certain your mobile is working, if you please." Doyle was slated to spend a tedious day looking through cold case files in the basement—which was the next thing to a dungeon—and mobile service was spotty at best. Her thankless task would be to sift through the files in search of old, unsolved cases that had an apparent link to the murders by this vigilante, who—unlike your ordinary serial killer—was trying very hard to hide the fact that he was one. Usually serial killers were remarkably vain, having a narcissistic complex that was almost frightening to behold. The fact that this one was different only strengthened the working theory that he was a vigilante, and was murdering people solely to right past wrongs, rather than to serve some weird power-ego complex, like they taught you at the Crime Academy.

She and Acton had brainstormed at breakfast, trying to come up with some new search criteria in an attempt to narrow the broad database, much of which was unfortunately in hard paper format. Their old search criteria hadn't been very helpful; they had first decided she should try to see if there was a pattern to the law enforcement personnel in the cold cases, the theory being that someone assigned to the old cases got tired of seeing the villains get off, and after reaching a had-it-up-to-here flash point, started dispensing Wild West justice. It was a good working theory, but the personnel involved in the cold cases had not been so consistent that there was an obvious lead. This morning, Acton had suggested she check to see if there was a pattern in the case-workers from social services—hard to imagine a case-worker type as a vengeful murderer—but they were in need of a common theme, and it was elusive at this point.

"Good-bye, Reynolds; I'll be seein' you later." The servant bowed his head, and she eyed him narrowly. Something was up, and she'd winkle it out of him this evening—he would be more forthcoming when Acton wasn't present.

Once at work, she parted from Acton in the lobby, and then tried to pin a smile on her lips—truly, it was a gauntlet every morning just to make it to her desk.

"Good morning, Officer Doyle." The desk sergeant's voice rang out respectfully from across the room.

She entered the lift and mingled amongst other well-wishers who radiated good will and affection. "DS Doyle; good morning." "Good morning." "Good morning, ma'am."

I hate this, she thought; I wish everyone would just go 'way.

After emerging from the lift, she made her way through the cubicle forest to her new station—a slighter larger cubicle to reflect her new rank—nodding at those who immediately halted whatever conversation they were having to smile and greet her. Finally, she made it to the safe haven of her desk, feeling miserably guilty about her bad attitude, and harboring a lingering conviction that she should have just left stupid Munoz to drown.

Ever since she'd leapt off Greyfriars Bridge into the Thames, she'd been afforded a strange new respect; instead of every-one's wondering how Acton could have made such a monu-mental mismatch, now they all thought him very discerning in recognizing her obvious merit beforehand. Doyle was now—and forever would be—the bridge-jumper and a hero; will-she or nil-she. There was little question it was this and this alone that had prompted the powers-that-be to promote her forthwith—even though her scores on the test weren't very good—and little question this was the reason Munoz was pro-moted right along with her. The two of them were yoked, now, and according to the storyline, had to play the part of de-voted friends, even though this was not the case at all. Ironic, is what it is, thought Doyle, as she grimly sought refuge in her tall latte; in all things give thanks.

Almost immediately, she pulled up the computer files from the now-closed turf war case, and reviewed her notes about a walk-in witness named Gerry Lestrade, a driver working for the racecourse who hadn't been very helpful, considering he had put himself forward as a witness. At the time, Doyle had the impression that he was wary, and more intent in trying to find out what she knew than in telling her anything of inter-est. There was nothing in the file to indicate he was French, but blue-collar Gerry had been wearing a Breguet watch, which should have rightfully set him back several years' salary. She pulled up his photo, and felt her scalp prickle as it did when she was making an intuitive connection. Her mysteri-ous rescuer must be French, then, and was no doubt affiliated with Savoie's group. Savoie was a shadowy French kingpin in the arms-selling business, and the turf wars had exposed a plot by a Russian national named Solonik to muscle in on his territory. At the time, none of the villains involved were aware that Acton himself had instigated the turf war, decimating their ranks so that the London underworld was still reeling.

Doyle leaned back in her chair and sipped the latte thought-fully. It seemed a logical conclusion that the mysterious and powerful Savoie had deemed it in his best interests to send some foot soldiers to keep tabs on the fair Doyle—no doubt the man had twigged Acton's role in the turf wars, and was trying to ensure that business would not be disrupted again by a vengeful DCI. This theory seemed sound, and also explained why she was certain her rescuer meant no harm to her—her intuition was rarely wrong, and indeed, he'd intervened to save her even though by all indications he should have kept a very low profile.

Her thoughts were interrupted by Inspector Habib, who approached with his measured stride to pause before her cubicle entryway. He was her supervisor, and any qualms he may have entertained about Acton's having married outside of his caste were now set aside in light of Doyle's actions in saving DS Munoz, who was the object of Habib's rather awkward affections.

"Good morning, DS Doyle."

Don't throw your coffee at him, she cautioned herself. "Good mornin', sir. DCI Acton has requested that I work on the park murder cases today, with your permission." Habib would never countermand Acton, but she always offered him a fig leaf of authority, being as he was her supervisor.

"Any leads?" Habib was aware of her theory, although it necessarily had to be kept quiet in the event the vigilante killer was currently working in the justice system.

She shook her head. "None as yet, sir. DCI Acton and I were trying to come up with search criteria this mornin'; he wondered if I should have a look at social case-workers, although this seems a little unlikely."

But Habib was not going to disagree with Acton, and crossed his arms thoughtfully. "If the obvious is not helpful, then we must pursue the less obvious." He thought about it. "Are any of the personnel the same, in the cold cases?"

"Some—but not with any consistency, and no one who seems at all likely as a suspect."

"Could any of the victims instead be an ABC murder?"

The reference was to an Agatha Christie story, in which it appeared that a serial killer was at work when, in fact, the killer had a single, intended victim and hoped to obscure the crime amongst the many. Doyle had already rejected such a theory, and again shook her head. "Unlikely, sir; all the victims are almost certainly killers who—for one reason or another—escaped justice in an earlier cold case. There are four fairly solid cold case connections, thus far; and perhaps two more. I just need to find the common thread."

He nodded, the gesture quick and bird-like. "It may be helpful to discover what led the vigilante to realize, in hindsight, that justice had been denied."

This was a different way of looking at it, and Doyle knit her brow. "I was thinkin' that it was someone who just snapped, after too many killers went free."

"Perhaps. Although there may also have been an external trigger; the vigilante came into knowledge, in some manner—knowledge that no other would have."

This theory was discouraging, as it could mean she was looking for a needle in a haystack; if the vigilante was not a frustrated justice system worker, he could be anyone.

"Keep looking," Habib offered, reading her aright. "If you can find another murder connected to a cold case, the commonality may become more apparent."

"What commonality is that?" Munoz asked as she passed by, sporting a scowl that was nevertheless attractive in a smoldering-gypsy sort of way. Doyle could no more smolder than she could stay out in the sun without a heavy coating of SPF 50.

"DS Munoz; come, we are in need of your insights." Habib came as close as he could come to sounding hearty. "DS Doyle is looking for a commonality in the park murders."

Munoz paused to offer with heavy irony, "Everyone died in a park."

"Excellent insight," Doyle responded crossly.

"It may be important, that they were in a park." Habib was willing to go to any lengths to humor his crush, which did not seem very professional to Doyle. She then remembered that Habib was a pale shadow compared to what Acton would do to humor his crush, and bit back a skeptical retort. She truly needed to improve her attitude; theoretically, Habib could get her fired—although with her newly-celebrated status, it was more likely Doyle could get him fired. With an effort, she moderated her tone and pointed out the obvious: "It doesn't make much sense to me; there's the risk of witnesses, out in the open."

"But he is not on CCTV, correct?"

"Correct," Doyle conceded. The killer was careful to avoid having the crime caught on the cameras that recorded most public areas in London.

Habib continued, "He must believe there is more of a risk indoors."

This was actually rather a good point, and one that Doyle hadn't considered, which was all the more annoying. "I suppose that points back to law enforcement—he can't meet the victims where he works or lives."

Munoz propped an elbow on the cubicle wall, thinking it over. "Do the victims know he's there, or is it an ambush?"

"Forensics thinks they walked abreast, so presumably he's not someone who would be incitin' alarm."

"A woman?"

"Perhaps," Doyle conceded. "If she wore track shoes and weighed about one-seventy."

"Unlikely." Habib disagreed with a little shake of his head. "Women do not shoot at heads."

Although this seemed a sexist remark, Doyle knew better than to question him because he knew a thing or two, did Inspector Habib. Munoz, however, was not so certain, and flipped her hair back. "I don't know; some women could do it, I think—if they wanted to get the job done with only one shot."

"There are always exceptions," Habib willingly agreed.

Honestly, Doyle thought, eyeing him in disgust; love is a shameful, shameful thing.

This tenet was to be proven true with Munoz's next remark. "Doyle, I need you to come with me to the bookstore at lunch; I'm trying to get one of the clerks there to ask me out."

And poor Habib's heart lies bleeding on the ground, thought Doyle; Munoz had no tact. Or didn't care. "No. I am *not* goin' to tell the story yet again."

"You won't. And I'll pay for lunch, I promise."

Doyle rose and hoisted her rucksack with resignation. "Right, then; I'm headin' for the cold case basement. Text me when you're ready." She was under no illusions; Munoz *never* paid for lunch.

CHAPTER 5

*D*OYLE MADE HER WAY ACROSS THE ELEVATED WALKWAY BE-
tween the two Scotland Yard buildings, and then down to the
adjacent building's basement, where the cold case files were
stored. The more recent files were electronic, with only the
preserved physical evidence needing storage space, but the
older cases were stored in dusty cardboard boxes; row upon
row behind a security fence in the chilly and poorly-lit cold
case basement. Doyle signed herself in and began making a
preliminary check-through of the cases on her list. If any appeared to be of interest, she would have them delivered to
her cubicle for further review.

It was tedious work, although it wasn't as cold as it had
been in the past. As she thumbed through the old files, she
gradually removed her gloves, her coat, and eventually her
sweater, and even then felt a little warm. Acton must have
told them to turn up the heat, she decided—over-protective
knocker; a shower would be needful when she emerged from
this swamp. After she'd compiled a list of fifty files—the max-
imum she could bear to handle at one time—she could hear
someone approaching from the distant entry door, and
Williams called out a greeting so as not to startle her. Clam-
bering down from the wheeled stepladder, she was only too

happy for an excuse to take a break. Noting that Williams held a cup, she asked, "Is that coffee?"

"Have some." He handed it to her. "It's not very hot anymore, though."

"Just as well—it's warm work, here in the dungeon. Did Acton send you?"

"No—Munoz couldn't get through, so she texted me since I am in this building. She says you're supposed to meet her."

Doyle sipped the coffee and checked her mobile—she and Acton had been exchanging occasional texts during the morning, but Munoz must have a different provider. "Thanks; I lost track of the time, being as this is fascinatin' legwork."

He seemed a bit preoccupied. "Anything?"

"A spider. And a quiverful of possibilities; it's a sad testament, the number of career criminals who wind up gettin' themselves murdered. Not a healthy line o' work."

"I can't muster up much sympathy, I'm afraid. How are you—are you all right?"

"I am right as rain, my friend." She said it lightly because he was emanating some muddled emotion and she didn't want to venture into the personal—Williams had been romantically interested in her, and even though she was now married to his commanding officer, she caught the sense that, on occasion, he continued to yearn.

"That's good." He studied the floor for a moment.

Men; honestly, she thought with an inward sigh. "I am learnin' a few things amongst the cobwebs; I found a cause of death I don't recognize." She checked her notes. "Cerebral ischemia."

He lifted his head. "That means death by strangulation—pressure on the carotid artery."

Setting down the coffee for a moment, she blew a wayward tendril off her forehead as she re-did her ponytail. "Faith, Williams; do you know *everythin'*, or is it somethin' you've studied for the DI exam?"

This remark coaxed a half-smile from him, and he shrugged. "I was going to medical school when I changed course."

Surprised, she reached again for the coffee cup—he was making no attempt to reclaim it, after all. "Truly? You were supposed to be a doctor?"

"No, I was supposed to be a detective, but it took an externship with the coroner for me to realize it."

Nursing the coffee, she considered this in silence for a moment, as there was definitely more to this story than he was letting on. He did not elaborate, though, and so she confessed, "I always wanted to be a detective—and a nun, too. A detective-nun, I suppose."

"That's a rather small demographic."

"And just as well—I wouldn't have been a good nun; I lose my temper too much." That, and as it turned out, she very much enjoyed being ravished on a daily basis by her husband, but best not mention this before the very buttoned-up DS Williams. As she gathered up her things, she indicated a file in her stack. "Here's one who lost his temper in spades; the CID suspicioned that the suspect murdered the neighbor because the neighbor had poisoned the suspect's cat—a vengeance killing, it was, like a Greek play."

"I could see that."

She glanced up in surprise as he lifted her rucksack from her hand. "Whist, Williams; never say *you* have a cat?"

He gave her a look. "I'm *kidding*, Kath."

Making no comment, she bundled up her discarded coat and wondered why his comment had come across as true. Perhaps he meant he could understand a vengeance killing, and indeed, this was a subject that should best be changed— she was aware that Williams had been Acton's henchman in a vengeance killing and *truly*, she should think before she spoke; it was her besetting sin. As they made their way down the aisle, she asked brightly, "What are you about, today?"

"I have to go testify this afternoon; we have a suspect dead to rights but he won't enter into a plea deal."

"You're to testify in court?" Doyle wasn't certain whether she was envious; she tended to gabble under pressure, and would probably say something she oughtn't. Usually the lead officer testified at the trials—although Acton probably didn't like to testify either, come to think of it; he was not one who liked being challenged.

"Yes; Acton said he'll be away, so I'm to run the show."

"Good luck to you, then." Acton must be preparing for his class at the Academy—although he hadn't mentioned that he was going home for the afternoon. "D'you think the trial is just the suspect wantin' a show, then?" Oftentimes, repeat criminals knew they were headed back to the nick, but gloried in the attention of a formal trial and the stories it would give them to tell their mates in prison. It was a waste of time and resources, but there was that whole presumption-of-innocence thing that required the Crown to put on a case, if the suspect would not cooperate.

"We'll see; are you headed out to lunch?"

"You can't come," Doyle advised him bluntly. "Munoz is trying to enslave some hapless man, and she'll be the one who's murderin' me if I show up with the likes of you and queer the pitch."

"I only wanted to suggest you pull on your sweater before you go."

Hearing the constraint in his tone, she looked at her knit top in embarrassment, thinking she must have smudged it, leaning into the dust.

"There are marks on your arms," he explained, his voice carefully neutral.

Glancing down in confusion, Doyle could see bruises, above her elbows and on her forearm; fingerprint bruises that clearly indicated where a man had handled her roughly. She could feel the color flood her face at Williams's unspoken assumption—he had been protective of her once before, when he feared Acton would abuse her, and they had quarreled over it; he couldn't know that Acton would never harm her.

"I—I was in an altercation," she stammered as she realized that she couldn't tell him the truth. "Not at work," she added hastily; Williams would already know she had not been involved in such a struggle on duty. She concluded a bit lamely, "It wasn't Acton."

"Right, then."

He stood in silence whilst she donned her sweater, mortified because she hadn't disclaimed very credibly. They called for the lift, and because she couldn't leave it at that, she continued stiffly, "I was in a tussle at the charity medical clinic— the one where I'm volunteerin'. I bruise easily, and it was truly nothin'. I appreciate the warnin', though; I'd rather not have to keep explainin'."

"Just have a care, Kath; you're a bit reckless, you know."

As the bridge-jumping incident had proved this beyond a reasonable doubt, she could make no rejoinder, and they parted as he stepped out onto his floor.

CHAPTER 6

MUNOZ WAS WAITING WITH BARELY-CONCEALED IMPATIENCE, and Doyle apologized for the delay as they headed out the front door, the desk sergeant leaping up to hold the door for them with a respectful greeting.

"What is the strategy?" quizzed Doyle as she shrugged into her coat and pulled on her gloves—it was brisk outside. "Should I start loudly extollin' your many virtues so that he can hear? Or are you just goin' to faint at his feet?"

Munoz gave her a sullen look. "I've already spoken to him; I'm just giving him an opportunity to ask me out. You have enlisted me to come along while you buy a book."

Doyle considered her assignment. "Any particular book?"

"Nothing embarrassing," directed Munoz; "I don't want him to think I am hanging around with someone stupid."

Doyle stifled an urge to purchase a stack of pornography and inquired, "And are you goin' to be payin' me back after we perform this little morality play?"

"Shut up, Doyle; you can afford it." Munoz had been interested in Acton, and was annoyed that Doyle had made such a spectacular match under the radar, so to speak.

"If I may be sayin' so, you are in a foul mood, for a temptress."

Munoz's full red lips thinned. "I went to a community outreach last night, and all everyone wanted to ask about was the *incident.*" She said the last word as though it were an epithet.

Doyle shrugged in resignation. "I imagine the PR department is thinkin' they may as well make some hay." Munoz was trying to raise her profile with the PR department, and they were nothing loath as she was a telegenic minority female, and thus a good face to put forward.

"I don't like being cast as the victim." The beauty ground out the words, and her scowl deepened. "It's demeaning, and no one sees *me* anymore."

Biting back a retort—honestly; it never paid to save someone's life, nowadays—Doyle suggested, "Saints, Munoz; then use your wits and turn it around. After all, you took a knife with my name on it."

They walked in silence down the street for a few moments. "I did, didn't I? Why doesn't anyone remember that?"

"You need to remind them. And if you are recruitin' the kids, explain how important it is to exercise and stay strong, because that is why you survived."

"I'm a lot stronger than *you.*"

"No argument here, DS Munoz." Mother a' mercy, thought Doyle; how many more months of this? As they were almost to the bookstore, Doyle took the opportunity to change the subject. "What's this favored fellow like, if I may be askin'?"

"Nice," Munoz replied with a touch of defiance. "Smart—he's a graduate student."

It was intriguing that Munoz was interested in a bookstore clerk, graduate student or no. She tended to pursue high-profile men with money—as well she could; she was beautiful and tempestuous, a combination that was very attractive to men for reasons that escaped Doyle. Ever since Doyle's abrupt and unheralded marriage, however, the girl had expressed an interest in finding someone marriageable, and perhaps the graduate student was the result of this new search criteria.

They walked into the store, chatting casually so that the target would not realize that he was, in fact, a target. This subterfuge, however, was completely unnecessary; a young man spotted Munoz immediately, lit up like a candle, and hurried over to greet her.

"Isabel—I'm off for lunch in a minute; can you join me?"

The offer courteously included Doyle, who was well-aware of her expendability and demurred, explaining she had a limited time to make an important purchase. With a convincing show of deigning to make a concession, Munoz agreed to accompany him, and Doyle was thus left alone to examine some of the books displayed on the tables—in truth, she wasn't much of a reader, and it seemed clear that Munoz's offer of a meal was nothing more than a bait-and-switch. She was thinking about ringing up Acton to see if he could take a break from his class preparation, when she realized that the man next to her was intensely interested in her, and standing a little too close—he may be a pervert, best move aside. Without looking up, she moved away, but he moved right along with her, his acute interest unabated. Thinking to render a quelling stare, she glanced up and met the level gaze of her rescuer from the night before. "You will meet me at the religion section, if you please." He turned and was gone almost before she registered that it was indeed he.

Her first reaction was dismay; she'd put that little episode behind her, and did not like to think that shadowy kingpins had assigned people to monitor her movements—which was foolish; she shouldn't put her head in the sand, and may as well discover what was afoot. Besides, she owed him a debt of gratitude and her instinct told her he was no danger to her. If anything, he was puzzled, or bemused, or—or something; she was not what he'd expected. Feeling as though she was in a spy movie, she wandered through the aisles, reading the display signs until she located the religion section, which was regrettably unpopulated, although this was probably why it was chosen. She saw the man, thumbing through a Wesleyan tract, and approached to stand beside him. "Are you a Methodist, then? I wouldn't have pegged it; you are far too handy with your fives."

He glanced up at her with a grave expression. "Yes? What does this mean?"

"It means you pack a decent punch, my friend, and I'm that grateful. What can I do for you?"

"You are Roman Catholic?"

Hard to imagine he was here to discuss comparative religions, but she tried gamely to keep up. "Indeed I am."

"Yet you are leaving your husband?"

She raised her brows in surprise. "No. Is that the rumor? Have you been speakin' to Munoz, by any chance?"

He shut the book softly. "Who is Munoz?"

"You ask a lot of questions, for someone who took an oath of silence."

This remark indeed silenced him for a moment, and the pale eyes regarded her thoughtfully. I think I am so flippant with him because he is so serious, she thought, and resolved to tread a bit more warily; there was something a bit—cold, was perhaps the right word—about him. Not a gregarious soul, was this fellow.

"Last night, you were not wearing a wedding ring."

"Oh—no, I didn't want to wear it in that buildin'; it belongs to his family." Apparently while she was noticing his watch, he was noticing her rings, or lack thereof. "I'm wearin' it now." She wiggled a gloved finger.

For some reason, she sensed that this was good news to him, which seemed a little strange—although he didn't seem intent on flirtation. But although he gave no outward sign, he was definitely relieved to confirm she wasn't leaving her husband.

"Acton." His accent placed the emphasis on the second syl-
lable.

"Yes; Acton."

The man frowned slightly, remembering. "He is a knocker."

"Indeed he is," she replied gravely. "But do not say that I
said."

He regarded her in silence, and she wondered what he
wanted—it was his secret meeting, after all. Perhaps she should
help him get to the point, as she was hungry. "You are related
to Gerry Lestrade, I believe."

Bull's-eye; she intercepted a flash of surprise, quickly suppressed. "Who is that?" he asked, and it was a lie.

She was unsurprised, and a bit philosophical; small blame
to him for his wary confusion, if what she suspected was
true—that Savoie's people were worried they'd be treated to
another helping of Acton's misplaced vengeance if anything
happened to her. Meeting her rescuer's eyes, she said with all
sincerity, "There is no need to follow me about anymore; all
problems have been resolved." Solonik was in prison, Acton
was now aware that he'd been runnin' amok for no good reason, and so things had settled down. Please God; amen.

Her companion tilted his head slightly. "What problem has
been resolved?"

Hesitating, she decided she may as well spell it out. "Solonik's
in prison, and the dispute over the smugglin' rig has—well, has
settled." Best be careful, she didn't want to make him nervous.

But apparently she'd guessed wrong, as he tilted his head
again in a very European gesture. "You mistake; it was Solonik
who asked me to find you."

She stared at him in shock for a long moment, completely
surprised. "*Solonik* sent you?" This did not bode well, but after
a moment, she realized what must be afoot. "I see—he must
love his little boy very much." Doyle had sat in when Acton in-
terrogated Solonik, and the suspect—not knowing the constable who accompanied him was Acton's wife—had tried to

blackmail Acton by threatening to harm his wife. In return, Acton had threatened to harm Solonik's child, and Solonik had immediately conceded the stand-off, and plea-bargained to a long prison term. So; Doyle revised her theory to surmise that her rescuer was now assigned to make certain no harm came to Acton's wife so that no mistaken revenge would then be taken against Solonik's son—Acton being a revenge-taker of the first order.

In this, however, she was again mistaken, as the pale eyes were suddenly intent on hers. "Solonik has a little boy?"

"Never you mind," retorted Doyle a bit crossly. "And I am grateful for what you did, my friend, but it is like pullin' teeth to carry on a conversation with you."

He ducked his chin, considering this, then concluded, "Very painful."

"Like licorice at Christmas," she confirmed. "And I thought we agreed we weren't to speak of all this again."

"Solonik asks that you meet with him."

Doyle stared at him, yet again completely astonished. "In *prison?*"

He gave her a look. "Of course—where else?"

After a moment, Doyle smiled, almost relieved, now that she had hit upon the final and correct theory for these strange events. "No."

But he was not to accept her bald rejection without demur. "He asks me to tell you he wishes to apologize, and say prayers with you for the forgiveness of his soul."

"No." Doyle explained kindly, "Mr. Solonik is only tryin' to get Acton's goat."

Her rescuer stared at her blankly.

She sighed; honestly, it was like being one of those foreign language translators at the Crown Court on docketing day. "It means he's tryin' to find a way to annoy Acton, and I can assure you, that would do it nicely. I won't be aidin' and abettin' him."

He thought about this for a moment, studying her, and his

next comment seemed off-topic. "You did not want to tell Acton of last night; why is this?"

She decided this was none of his business, and replied in a mild tone, "I won't be visitin' Solonik, and I'm sorry to disappoint you if that was your errand, because I am ever so grateful to you. You can tell Solonik that I'll accept his apology from afar, and that I'll be prayin' for his poor, misguided soul." Put that in your pipe, Solonik; you're in dire need of prayers, you are. She concluded, "Thank you again, but I should be gettin' back to work."

He nodded, but as she turned to leave, he said, "Wait."

She turned to him and raised her brows.

"Why does Solonik wish to apologize?"

There seemed no harm in telling him. "He threatened to kill me, but he didn't know I knew of it." She paused. "It's rather a long and complicated story." He made no response, and she turned and left, walking back to work with a steely resolve not to glance behind to see if he followed. Turning over their strange and disjointed conversation in her mind, she tried to decide whether Acton had to be told. Her husband hadn't touched the scotch last night—too busy touching her, he was—and he was to stop therapy; the last flippin' thing he needed was to hear flippin' Solonik was having Savoie's people follow her about—Acton would probably blow up the flippin' prison. And strange as it sounded, she knew her rescuer meant her no harm, even though he was not sure what to make of her. With any luck, this would be an end to it.

Struck by a sudden thought, once back at the Met, she asked the desk sergeant if she could have a look at his laptop—Acton sometimes monitored her laptop and she didn't want to give him any clues about her misadventure in the projects. With quick fingers, she drew up the homicide docket for the Metro area in the past twenty-four hours. She found what she suspected she might; her assailant from the projects had been murdered late last night, shot twice in the head, execution-style. Staring at the photo on the screen, she decided she was not surprised—indeed, she'd half-suspected as much, considering who her rescuer worked for. He probably felt he'd done her a favor.

I married Acton, and now I meet the most interesting people, she thought. Lucky me.

CHAPTER 7

*D*OYLE WOUND UP EATING A CANTEEN SANDWICH AT HER DESK while she worked on the cold case files. She was cross-indexing the old crimes by creating a spreadsheet of pertinent facts about the victims, the type of crime, and the personnel who worked on the cases, including the judges and courtroom personnel. It was detailed and tedious work, which explained why she was all too willing to catch Munoz's attention when the girl passed down the aisle between their cubicles. "So— how did it go with the graduate student? I'm deservin' of a report, bein' as I was instrumental in the battle plan."

"Success," reported Munoz with a self-satisfied air. "We're going out tonight."

"He seemed smitten; it is surprisin' such tactics were needed or necessary."

"I think he was intimidated, at first." Munoz smoothed back her glossy hair. "A lot of men are."

"He's only dazzled," Doyle assured her. "In no time a'tall he'll be takin' gross advantage of you."

"No one takes advantage of me," the beauty declared with a brow that arched at the very idea. "My problem is that I get bored too quickly."

With acute regret, Doyle bit back a rejoinder about a certain Irishman pretending to be a Russian, and instead offered, "Patience is a virtue, DS Munoz."

The other girl drew up a corner of her mouth in derision. "That's a laugh, coming from you."

Nettled, Doyle returned, "Not everyone is as lucky as I was."

"Oh-ho, so you'll admit it was sheer luck? What—was Acton drunk at the time?"

This hit a bit too close to home, and Doyle retorted hotly, "Lucky he didn't fall for the likes o' you, he is."

But Munoz was aware she'd landed a punch, and pronounced with no small amount of satisfaction, "He'll wake up; it's only a matter of time, with a man like that."

Doyle rose to her feet and clenched her fists. "Take. That. Back."

Abruptly, Munoz subsided and exclaimed in exasperation, "You're right; I have to take it back—can't you see? You always have to win, now."

Although she still glowered, Doyle saw the justice of this remark and sank down into her chair again with a thud. "It's *ridiculous*, is what it is."

With a sound of extreme annoyance, the other girl agreed. "Yes, it's ridiculous. I'm lucky my date isn't even aware of the stupid *incident*."

But Doyle reminded her with heavy regret, "He will be; no one can let it go, the *stupid* knockers."

They contemplated this sad fact a bit glumly, Munoz's impressive breast rising and falling with a sigh. "No, they can't let it go. And you will have the upper hand for all eternity."

But Doyle suddenly raised her head and met Munoz's eyes. "No. No, I don't have the upper hand. You would have done the same for me; it was only luck that it was me instead of you." They paused for a moment, both of them considering this profundity in the silence it deserved. Doyle insisted, "It's true; you would have, Izzy."

Munoz nodded in reluctant acknowledgment, but still could not quite concede. "I know how to swim, though, so it wouldn't have been the same."

Now it was Doyle's turn to consider this, seriously and with a knit brow. "I don't think that matters; we're even."

The other girl slowly agreed, "Yes, you're right; it was only a matter of luck—that it was you instead of me."

"And you and I both know it, even if no one else does."

Munoz blew out a breath. "I can live with that."

"Cheers." Doyle went back to her spreadsheet as Munoz walked away.

In the late afternoon, Samuels came by and asked if anyone was interested in going to a local pub after work. Samuels worked with DCI Drake's team, and was nice enough. Plain vanilla, Doyle's mother would have described him.

"Can't," Munoz called out from across the aisle way. "I have a date."

"I was goin' to look in at Acton's lecture," Doyle demurred. "Is Williams done with his trial? Perhaps he's available."

"He's working late; got to stay atop the ladder, after all."

There was a rumor afoot that Williams was soon to be promoted to detective inspector, and Doyle hastily intervened before Munoz could reiterate her extreme vexation over such a potential turn of events. "What does Drake have you workin' on, Samuels?"

"If you'd like, I'll walk with you over to the Academy and tell you about it."

Doyle had spent little time with Samuels and so was a bit surprised by the offer, but agreed with good grace as she began to pack up her rucksack. She was not sociable by nature, but had to make an effort if she was to rise in the ranks, being as it was a time-honored truth that socializing at work stood one in better stead than the most glowing of reviews. And the Academy was but a few blocks away, so there was little fear of being stuck trying to make conversation—she'd had her fill of thorny conversations this fine day.

They exited the building; the evening-shift desk sergeant was not as big a fan as the day-shift one, but nevertheless he nodded to her respectfully. Samuels began to tell her of a field investigation he was working on; a weapons ring had been unearthed, and a cache had been discovered in a garden shed. "You should have seen it; guns hanging on pegs along the wall like so many gardening tools."

Doyle had a twinge of conscience; she was aware that Acton smuggled illegal weapons himself—although he didn't know that she knew—and she surmised there was a similar cache in the safe at home. She hoped Samuels wasn't investigating Acton all unknowing, which would be a dodgy little development for the illustrious chief inspector. However, this seemed unlikely, as Acton no doubt kept his finger on the pulse of all such investigations. "Were you in on the arrests?" Her assailant at the projects was the first time Doyle herself had ever tried to arrest anyone, as Acton tended to keep her away from any situation that was remotely dangerous.

"No—they'd cleared out. But we're close; we've been getting a lot of good tips." He paused. "Have you ever been in a shoot-out?"

"No. You?"

He turned his head to watch her for a moment. "No? I thought you'd been wounded."

A bit startled, Doyle kept her voice neutral and said truthfully, "No, no one's ever shot at me." She did have a bullet wound in her calf where she had accidentally shot herself whilst shooting the trainee who wanted to kill her, but this was a well-kept secret. How Samuels came across the idea that she'd been wounded was a mystery—although he'd been present when her soggy self had been pulled from the Thames; perhaps he'd seen her scar. In any event, it seemed he'd lost interest.

"So—Holmes is giving a lecture."

"Indeed he is, and a good thing. He knows so much; it's to the betterment of us all if he gives us a glimpse."

With a smile, her companion could only agree. "Of course—he's a legend. What's he like? I mean, when he's not at work; what does he do?"

She thought, I suppose I could tell him that Acton suffers from an obsessive mental condition that leads him to kill anyone who proves to be a threat to me, makes him insatiable when it comes to sex, and drink too much on occasion, but instead I'd better behave myself. "He's very private, Samuels."

"Sorry," the other apologized with a small smile. "Nosy by nature, I'm afraid."

To show she wasn't offended, she teased, "Are you? I wondered a little that you took this job." Samuels did not show to advantage next to his colleagues; he seemed to lack any real passion for detective work.

"I'm not as mad about it as the rest of you, but I do enjoy it," he protested. "It certainly pays well."

Doyle had the strong impression he felt he'd said something very amusing. Hoping she hadn't embarrassed him, she changed the subject. "Have you identified the suspects in the garden shed case?"

"Not as yet."

Interestingly enough, this was not true. He's a confusing one, she thought; he doesn't match himself, or something.

"Here we are."

They had arrived at the Crime Academy, and as they passed through the door, Doyle grimaced in remembrance. "Faith, I'm glad I'm quit of this place."

He laughed, "Surely it wasn't that bad."

But she could not agree. "I'm not much of a student, my friend; I'd still be here if Williams hadn't helped me pass ballistics."

Samuels laughed again, but slanted her a knowing look

that annoyed her, as it seemed to imply there was something going on betwixt herself and Williams. She shrugged it off; she couldn't let it bother her—gossip always ran rampant in any workplace, and she and Williams were thick as thieves.

They walked to the main lecture hall, but it was locked. Doyle peered through the window in the door, but it was dark inside. "We must have missed it—I might have mixed up the time."

"Or it was cancelled," Samuels suggested.

This seemed unlikely; certainly Acton would have let her know. "Maybe."

Samuels called to two trainees who were passing by in the hallway. "Did DCI Acton give his lecture?"

"Oh yes, it was three to four o' clock," answered one. "Very interesting."

"How annoyin'," said Doyle with a smile. "I got my times crossed." It was puzzling; she was certain Acton had said the lecture would make him miss dinner.

But her thoughts were interrupted by one of the trainees, who ventured, "You are Officer Doyle, aren't you ma'am?" The woman emanated waves of respect and goodwill.

With her pinned-on smile, Doyle admitted, "Indeed I am."

The young man added reverently, "The instructor spoke of you at class today; about—about how important it was for us to have each other's backs, no matter what. It is an honor to meet you." They all shook hands, whilst Doyle tried to think of something profound to say and came up short.

"Carry on," said Samuels easily, and they walked away. "Look at you; you're a rock star."

"Just lucky to be there when I was," she demurred, thinking about her discussion with Munoz. Doyle's belief system didn't really recognize luck as such, but it was an easier, shorthand way to discuss weighty issues like providence and grace.

"Want to share a cab?" asked Samuels as they approached the street.

"No thanks, I'll take the tube." She was reluctant to take a cab, since to do so always made her miss Aiki, and although she was supposed to call the concierge's driving service, Doyle found she wanted to walk for a bit so as to clear her head. It had been a strange day, between Williams, and her rescuer, and Samuels, and Acton not being where he said he'd be; an overabundance of men putting her through her paces—although Munoz was in there, too, so it hadn't been only the men. Hunching her shoulders against the chilly wind, she walked for a block toward the tube station, thinking about the park murders. She was making headway on the case—even though nothing leapt out off the page as yet. It would; she was certain. She had a feeling, she did, and her feelings were usually reliable. There was a common denominator and she would find it—she knew she was close.

On the other hand, Acton would not be happy when she did solve it, because this case kept her out of the field, and he was a first-class fretter. Reminded, she pulled out her mobile and noted that he hadn't texted her for over an hour—perhaps the short-lived therapy had done some good, after all. Perhaps they could even think about starting a family again; her pregnancy earlier this year had been a surprise, and before her miscarriage she'd had mixed emotions about her impending motherhood. The loss had been painful, and now she found she was rather eager to try again.

With an inward sigh, she abandoned her idea to take the tube at rush hour, and instead rang up the driving service; she needed a few more minutes of peace and quiet because there was a hovering uneasiness that she could not shake, and the last thing she needed was for someone to recognize her on the tube.

Once home, she noted that Acton had not yet arrived. She greeted Reynolds, who had made something that smelt delicious for dinner, and informed him, "Reynolds, I believe you saw my bruises this mornin'. I was attacked by an assailant, and I promise you it wasn't Acton."

"No, madam," he agreed. "I could not imagine Lord Acton would do such a thing." He exchanged a look with her, and much was unspoken. "Do you need medical care?"

"No; I've weathered many a bruise, my friend. But in the meantime, I'll have to cover them up, or the Domestic Violence Unit will be arrestin' my poor husband. If we have to break him out of gaol, Reynolds, can I count on you to cover the flank?"

"Certainly, madam," the servant agreed, and took her coat.

CHAPTER 8

Acton returned just as Reynolds was preparing to leave, so the servant paused to take his briefcase and coat. Doyle was seated at the table, the files spread out around her as she continued to compile her spreadsheet. Acton told Reynolds there was a list of items to be purchased in his coat pocket, and then absently ran a hand over Doyle's head as he passed by on his way to the fridge. Interesting, she thought. When he was compelled to stroke her head, it was usually a sign that he was worried—although he had headed to the fridge, and not the liquor cabinet. "How went your lecture?"

"As well as can be expected. There were some intelligent questions, which is a good sign."

"I went to have a look-in," she offered, watching him.

He met her eyes as he pulled out the orange juice bottle. "At the wrong time?"

"Yes, they said it was earlier."

"My fault; I should have let you know—I didn't realize you'd stop in."

"And I so wanted to heckle you," she teased. In truth, she thought her presence might have been helpful; he was famously reclusive and did not suffer fools—it was not beyond the realm of possibility that he would dress down some poor trainee for asking the wrong question.

"I'm sorry, Kathleen." He passed behind her on his way to the main room, and as he did, he gently placed a hand on her head.

Although he was on his way out, Reynolds offered, "May I prepare you a plate, sir?"

"I'm not very hungry, but thank you."

Reynolds departed, and Doyle kept typing as Acton stood by the windows, drinking orange juice straight from the bottle as he looked out over the city. She was not paying attention to her work, though, instead thinking about how he could not stop touching her head and how he had given her a string of equivocal answers so that she could not spot a lie. He was a wily one, was Acton, and he'd also been drinking, although he was doing a masterful job of trying to obscure this fact. She wondered if he was caught up in something having to do with the illegal guns-running—now, there would be a crisis to top all the other ones, if he were to be caught and prosecuted. It didn't bear thinking about, so she didn't think about it anymore—it was only on her mind after her conversation with Samuels.

"Anything of interest in the cold cases?"

She paused in her pretend-typing. "I found one new commonality—and it's a wrinkle. Drake was the DS on one of the underlying cases, and the DI on one."

He crossed his arms and bowed his head, thinking. "I don't see it," he said finally.

"No, me neither." DCI Drake was Acton's equivalent in rank, but nothing like Acton—no one was, after all. Drake was rather full of himself and something of a Jack-the-lad; he'd been reprimanded more than once for having sexual liaisons with female staff. It was hard to imagine Drake bestirring himself enough to be a vigilante.

"How about someone under Drake's command?" Acton asked thoughtfully.

"Good idea, I'll get to that next; right now I'm finishing up court personnel."

"Judges?"

"A variety," she reported. "Colcombe was the one who turned up the most, but he's dead, so if we think it's the same vigilante for all of these murders, it can't be him."

Acton set down the juice container and walked closer to the windows, thinking aloud as he reviewed the street below. "Here's a working theory: this vigilante was not certain, at the time, that these murderers had escaped justice. He waited until—with hindsight—it was irrefutable."

"I suppose that would explain the lapse of time," she agreed, although she wasn't certain what "irrefutable" meant—Acton was going all House-of-Lords on her again. She held out a hand to him. "Come sit next to me, Michael; I don't care if you've taken a tipple after havin' to do your wretched class. It's only me, remember?"

He bowed his head for a moment before taking her proffered hand. "Sorry. I didn't want you to know."

"Knocker." To smooth out any awkwardness, she reviewed her notes and continued the discussion as though there hadn't been any interruption as he seated himself next to her at the table. "So, if that is our workin' theory, who is our vigilante? What type of person would wait so long to serve up justice?"

Acton leaned back in his chair and gazed out the windows again. "Ethnicity of the victims?"

"Mixed. Three black, two white, one Middle Eastern."

He considered this in silence. "Is there a pattern as to the timing?"

"If there is, it's not obvious. And he's been changin' the caliber of the weapon and the site of the entry wound to cover the fact it's the same killer, but it's always to the back of the head."

He crossed his arms and lowered his chin to his chest. "So we have a vigilante who wishes to remain anonymous, meets them in an innocuous setting, and then takes them by surprise, with no confrontation."

She paused, as this was an excellent point, particularly as she now knew what "innocuous" meant. Trust Acton to cut to the nub of it, and point out this rather odd aspect of the case. "Yes—he's not someone who wants to let them know they are payin' for their sins. He just kills them—no accusations or drama." A very strange vigilante, then. Much struck, she added, "And I suppose Munoz is right yet again; the fact that the murders are all in a park is important—because the settin' is non-threatenin'."

"Or he is comfortable in such a setting. The logistics are difficult, with the CCTV cameras, but he makes it work." Nearly every public area in London was under the scrutiny of a security camera; the vigilante was careful to do the crimes at night and in an area where there was a seam in the coverage. The ERU video-reviewers had found nothing about the various people who'd been filmed walking to and from the kill sites to incite any interest; nothing stood out.

Thinking of all this, Doyle typed a summation note and recited aloud, "So he's the type of person who's done his homework; he's somehow become certain of the victim's guilt in an earlier, unsolved murder, and he arranges to dispense justice off-camera, with little evidence to show for it, and enough people in the area so that we cannot focus on anyone in particular." She frowned. "It's soundin' more and more like he's someone from law enforcement, isn't it?"

Acton tilted his head in polite disagreement. "But the victims were not alarmed; the footprints show they walked abreast, and the posture of the bodies does not indicate a defensive struggle, or an attempt to escape."

Doyle blew out a breath, stymied yet again. "Right you are; these victims would not have been comfortable and unsuspectin' if they were walkin' along with a law enforcement type."

Acton offered, "It was not a bad idea, though; it does seem the killer knows his forensics."

"Don't humor me when I have a dumb idea," she reminded him dryly.

"You never have a dumb idea," he protested, and leaned to kiss her, which was very much appreciated and inspired her to take a break and close her laptop—sometimes it was best to stew about it for a bit, when she was coming up empty.

"It's a crackin' shame there are so many variables. Habib thinks if I can find another vigilante murder, the commonality may become more obvious."

"The abundance of variables is what makes it all the more interesting." Acton leaned back in his chair to review the city lights. "And consequently more satisfying when it is resolved."

She hid a smile at the high-flying language. "Easy for you to say; you're not the one sloggin' through the dusty files." Feeling stiff, she stretched her arms up over her head, holding one wrist with the other hand and then flinching at the contact with her bruises.

Immediately, he reached to take hold of one of her hands, sliding back the sleeve. Oh-oh, she thought; here we go.

He firmly pulled her chair around to face him, and began unbuttoning her shirt. "Stand up, if you please."

"I'll be warnin' you, it's not pretty." She stood, and allowed him to peel off her shirt.

He lifted an arm and examined it. "Christ."

"You mustn't blaspheme, Michael," she scolded gently.

He lifted the other arm. "*Christ.*"

"It looks worse than it is; you of all people know that I bruise easily." She smiled down at him, teasing. When they'd first married, he often bruised her during sex and was wracked with guilt afterward. Sometimes he still did, when he got carried away.

But he was not to be distracted. "Who did this?"

As this was not an avenue she wished to pursue, she said

with finality, "A man who wanted drugs, I told you; I was helped by a passerby and we subdued him—it's water under the bridge, it is." He was furious—she could feel it—and it didn't help matters that he was bosky, to boot. "Michael," she said quietly. "Please."

He met her eyes. "Why don't you want me to know?"

"You already know the answer to that, my friend," she replied softly. Let him think that she was worried he would run amok—which indeed he would, if he caught the slightest hint of what had happened. She bent down to kiss him gently, and he withstood this assault for a long moment—which only showed how upset he was—then pulled her onto his lap, albeit very carefully. "Let's go to bed," she whispered. "I want to show you some areas that remained unbruised; at least for the time bein'."

Sometime later, she sat once again at the table, rosy of face and dressed in her robe, considering new ideas for search criteria based on their earlier conversation. Acton was on the sofa, supposedly reading a file, but she could feel him watching her. It didn't bother her; he would watch her for hours, sometimes.

"I have a question," he finally said.

"Ask away."

"When are you going to wear the dress in your drawer?"

She raised her head, amused. She hadn't worn a dress in many years, but on impulse had purchased a very chic black one, some months ago. It remained hidden in her drawer, awaiting an appropriate occasion. "It is impossible to surprise you, Michael. You are an incurable Section Seven." The reference was to the anti-stalking law.

"The dress has been there for quite some time," he offered in his own defense.

She admitted, "I bought it for Brighton."

There was a poignant pause. While Doyle was recovering from poisoning and her miscarriage, Acton had planned a weekend trip to Brighton to cheer them both up. The pleasure trip was cancelled because Acton had killed Caroline, and then stayed in town to help Timothy with his sister's apparent suicide.

"Shall we reschedule?" he offered.

She thought about it. Neither one of them was much for going out nor traveling; they were very content to live quietly with each other and away from other people—not that it had been very quiet, thus far. "Perhaps when it is warmer; then we can swim." He had promised to teach her to swim, after the bridge-jumping incident.

"Will you put the dress on now, so that I can see?"

"You'll just take it off," she responded with a smile. "At least wait until the bruises fade."

He relapsed into silence. Something is afoot, she thought, and wished she knew what it was.

"I must travel to Trestles," he said.

This was out of the clear blue, and she stared at him in surprise. Trestles was his estate somewhere to the north of London; he held an ancient barony. His mother, the dowager Lady Acton, was a very unpleasant woman whom Doyle had met on one memorable occasion when she'd been forced to throw the old harridan out of the flat. Doyle had never been to Trestles and, truth to tell, was reluctant to go—Acton had married well beneath him, and a visit to his ancestral estate would only drive home this undeniable fact. However, as he could not spend the night away from her, this meant she was to accompany him.

"You may stay here, if you like."

Immediately, her instinct went on red alert. "I don't know, Michael; wither thou goest, I will go. It's past time I took a look at the place, I think."

She caught a glimpse of dismay, quickly extinguished. Whatever was afoot, he wanted her well-away from it, which only meant she'd best hang on to his coat tails like grim death. "Right then; I'm not certain when we will go, as yet."

Trying to hedge, he was. "Are there horses at Trestles?" She had been put in the presence of horses during the investigation of the racecourse murders, and—to her profound surprise—had discovered that the idea of riding a horse was very appealing. "You can teach me to ride, instead of swim."

He had recovered his equilibrium, and replied, "Fair enough." Rising, he walked over to look out the windows again, and she watched him out of the corner of her eye. She could ask what was distressing him, but it would only force him to give an equivocal answer so she wouldn't know he was lying. As it was a stalemate, she would await events.

"Anything happening tomorrow?" he asked.

Tomorrow is the worst day of the year, she thought. "I was goin' to go over to the church after work, and spend some time with Nellie, if that's all right."

He turned to her. "Will you be home for dinner?"

"Yes," she said, looking up and smiling at him. "Indeed I will."

CHAPTER 9

*T*HE NEXT DAY, DOYLE ASKED HABIB IF SHE COULD LEAVE WORK early. "Personal reasons," she explained. Terrified that he would intrude on House of Acton family matters, Habib readily agreed, which was exactly what Doyle had expected.

"Where are you going?" called Munoz from across the way.

"Church," answered Doyle. Then, changing the subject, "How goes it with the lamb to the slaughter?"

"Good," Munoz airily replied. "He is very nice to me." This was said in the tone of someone trying to convince herself that this was a good thing.

"Not a lot of chemistry?" asked Doyle sympathetically, who knew how important this was, post-Acton.

"We'll see. It's early days."

Doyle was beginning to pack up when she received a text from Williams. "Just checking in," it said. Doyle surmised this was code for "Is Acton still beating you?"

"I'm good; how R U?" she answered. She would make it clear there were no problems that DS Williams need worry about; it was actually a very dicey situation for him—he was Acton's man and, she surmised, more loyal to her husband than to the CID.

"I have nu coffee."

She smiled at her mobile screen. "Can't, leaving early. To-morrow, promise."

"OK."

Gathering up her rucksack, she headed out.

Doyle attended St. Michael's church near Chelsea, which is where she'd lived prior to the Acton invasion. She still at-tended, out of loyalty and friendship, even though it was tech-nically no longer her parish. The small church had been in dire financial straits until Acton had requested instruction in Roman Catholicism; now he was a regular contributor, and the church had a brand-new roof to show for it.

Doyle entered the nave, which was nearly empty at this time of day, and met her friend Nellie, an older Filipino woman who capably helped Father John manage the parish. The two women walked together to the Mary chapel and lit a candle, then knelt together and recited a rosary. Father John walked by at one point and briefly rested a hand on Doyle's shoulder; she went silent for a few beads, until she could control her voice again.

Afterward, Doyle readied to leave. She asked Nellie if she could leave her electronic devices in the office, and come by to pick them up later.

"Shall I come?" asked Nellie gently.

"No, thank you. I will be fine."

Doyle rode the tube to Holy Redeemer Cemetery, and walked the path until she came to her mother's grave marker. She hadn't much money when her mother died two years ago today, and the small stone plaque simply read: "Mary Doyle." Doyle took a small brush out of her rucksack and carefully brushed off the marker. She then sat cross-legged next to it, and wept for half-an-hour.

She knew that her mother would not want to see her so upset, and knew that it wouldn't matter a pin to her if Doyle never came to this sad, sad place. But she did. She and her mother had only each other, and so she felt compelled to come to the last place on earth she'd been, on the last day she'd been here.

Her grief was not as sharp this time; her loss not as unbearable. Time does heal, she thought, and so much had happened since last year. She spoke aloud to her mother, knowing it was merely therapeutic, and that her mother did not reside in this grim, crowded cemetery. It was cathartic for Doyle to say aloud what she'd accomplished in the past year, and how much she missed her. She spoke of Acton and her extraordinary marriage; she didn't mention he was a peer, as she wasn't sure her mother would approve. Each to each, her mother used to say; no point in marrying chalk to cheese.

She spoke of her miscarriage, and dissolved into a fresh bout of tears at the guilt she felt for not being enthusiastic about the baby. Her mother, abandoned and alone, had managed to raise Doyle whilst scraping together a living for them both, and had never, ever complained. Just when it seemed that Doyle would be able to return the favor, her mother had been gathered up. She bequeathed to Doyle her undaunted determination and her sense of humor, and Doyle missed her every single day. In all things give thanks, thought Doyle; there's no point in having faith unless you put it to use.

The light was fading, and so Doyle readied to leave. She placed a hand on the marker in a gesture similar to Father John's, and then rose to make her way back down the path.

Outside the gates, Acton was waiting, leaning on the Range Rover with his hands in his coat pockets as he watched her approach. She quickly wiped her cheeks with the palm of her hand—Acton didn't do well when she cried. He stood upright, and pulled her into his arms, resting his cheek on the top of her head. Trust him to know what day it was, and where she would be; she didn't know why she had even attempted the subterfuge with her electronics.

"Want to talk?" he asked quietly, his voice resonating against her head.

"No," she replied into his shoulder.

"Want me to go?"

"No."

They stood together and night fell quickly, as it tended to do this time of year. He finally said, "It's cold; button your coat and we'll go fetch your mobile."

"I'm glad you came, Michael."

"Next time may I accompany you?"

She sighed into his lapel. "Oh, I don't know; there's a lot of weepin' and wailin' involved."

"I can handle it," he said firmly as he opened the door for her. "I love you."

Granting him a wan smile for this accolade, she slid into the car. She was emotionally drained and just wanted to go to bed, but she was indeed glad he'd come; she hadn't told him about her plans because he overreacted when she was upset about anything, and this visit was always the queen of all upsets.

They returned to the church to fetch her things, and Acton visited with Father John for a few moments, making plans for his next class of instruction. Whilst waiting, Doyle turned to observe the faithful who were beginning to file in for the evening service, and then she saw him. He was seated near the back, watching her. Doyle met his eyes for an astonished moment, and watched as he deliberately raised a hand to display a small paper wedged between his fingers; then lowered it. For one confused moment, she thought her rescuer attended her church, but then he rose and left without looking back.

CHAPTER 10

*I*N A CASUAL MANNER, DOYLE STROLLED TO THE BACK OF THE church and retrieved the wedge of paper, left on the pew. It said: "Tomorrow. Same time and place."

After tucking it in the missal box, she dithered, trying to decide what was best to do. She'd already made it clear she wasn't going to fall in with whatever plan Solonik was cooking up, and she definitely didn't want her rescuer to believe she was now at his beck and call—although he'd had some questions of his own at their last meeting, so perhaps he wanted to meet again because he was seeking more answers about Solonik. It didn't matter, she should put an end to it; nothing good could come from another meeting, and her rescuer was definitely wearing out his welcome. Trying to come to a decision, she looked toward the sanctuary to see if Acton was coming, but he was still in conversation with the good father. Perhaps she should confess it all to Acton; it was Solonik, after all, and she was far out of her element. On the other hand, Acton himself was edgy for undisclosed reasons, and he was still recovering from the stupid therapy sessions that seemed to have done no good at all. She could go tomorrow and see what her wretched rescuer had to say; it was not as though she could be duped into doing something she didn't want to do—she was wise to them. If it turned out to be anything remotely alarming, then she would confess the whole to Acton.

Her husband came up the aisle to take her arm as they left the church. "Hungry? Shall we pick up Chinese?"

"No need for such a sacrifice," she teased. She was fond of Chinese food; he was not. "Is Reynolds in?" She would rather just go home and collapse; Reynolds could prepare something.

"No, he's left. I'll make you something."

This was a sweet offer; Acton was no cook, having had various lackeys to do for him his entire life. "Soup does sound good." Hopefully, he couldn't ruin soup.

"Should I pick up some fruit pies? You can wait in the car."

"Faith, Michael—you're to be killin' me with kindness; have done, please." She had developed a taste for prepackaged fruit pies, and he feigned horror whenever she ate one; it was a sure sign of the depth of his affection that he was willing to do such a shameful thing.

As they drove home, he brushed his thumb across the back of her hand; back and forth, back and forth. She caught his hand and lifted it to kiss it. "Thank you for comin' to get me today."

"I wish I had met her."

"She would have liked you," Doyle lied. Her mother would have been twice as intimidated as Doyle had been on meeting Acton, and that bar was set pretty high. No need to say it aloud, though, it was sweet of him to pretend that he and her mother would have anything in common other than her fair self—although perhaps that would have been enough. Her mother would have very much approved of how much Acton loved her and wanted to take care of her, and all tiaras and hereditary estates would have been of secondary importance. Thinking of it, she asked, "Will you be buried at Trestles when you die?"

There was a slight pause. "Yes, along with everyone else who has ever held the title."

"Then I will be buried there, too." She hadn't really thought about it before—about how his history was now her history.

"I know it's been that kind of day, but do you think we can speak of something else?"

"Sorry. I was just thinkin' about it."

Once home, Acton managed the soup, and then asked if she would mind if he worked on his case for an hour—he was working on some high-profile investigation, and was very tight-lipped about it; she thought it might be a corruption scandal because she knew he'd met with the Home Secretary and the detective chief superintendent, which would seem to indicate there was a delicate political component. She'd assured him that she was in no need of tending, and so he'd retreated to the bedroom whilst she addressed her thankless spreadsheet yet again.

I need a good idea, she thought, and was frustrated because she knew there was *something* here; she needed only to make one of her intuitive leaps. Unfortunately, she had no control over her perceptive ability, and so was left to entering data into the database and waiting for whatever it was to jump out at her. She thought of the case-worker angle, and how Habib had said that when the obvious was not working, it must be something less obvious. A solicitor, perhaps? But she hadn't focused on the defense attorneys for the same reason she hadn't focused on the case-workers; a criminal defense attorney would be the last person who would decide he was tired of seeing the villains go free, one would think. On the other hand, that would explain the rather timid killings; it was someone who had to steel himself—or herself—to do it.

Her thoughts were interrupted when Nellie rang to see how she did, and also to enlist her help at the Christmas masses. Doyle agreed to read at midnight, then paused. "I'm not sure if we have plans, so put me down in pencil until I check in with Acton." It would be their first Christmas together, and she did not know what he usually did—perhaps he went to Trestles and drank wassail, or roasted a boar in the fireplace, or something.

Nellie indicated her approval of such a wifely considera-tion, then she and Doyle spoke of Nellie's family, which took some time as Nellie had quite an extensive family. They rang off, and Doyle felt better; she had been neglecting her old friend in favor of her new husband, which was to be expected, but was regrettable.

She opened up the daily homicide report as she did every day to see if any of the fresh set of victims was on record as a suspect in a previous murder, but nothing stood out. Acton continued busy, on his mobile and speaking to someone in low tones, so she texted Williams, who in Doyle's opinion was almost as smart as Acton. "RU working?"

"Yes. 'Sup?"

"Busy? Need ideas."

"On the cold cases?"

"Yes. Need commonality ideas, other than personnel."

"Race? Gang affiliation?"

"Already done."

"Kind of crime? Child predator?"

"Already done." It made her feel better that he had the same ideas that she had. There was a pause. "Come on, DSW."

"Thinking. Where R U?"

"Home. Don't ask what I M wearing." She probably shouldn't tease him, poor man.

"Guilt?"

"?" She didn't follow.

"Juror let him off, felt guilty?"

She thought about this idea. "Wouldn't b same juror on all."

"Right. Sorry."

Doyle paused, struck—perhaps guilt was indeed the emo-tion they were looking for. She'd presumed this vigilante was frustrated with the justice system in general; perhaps it was more personal than that.

"RU there?"

"Thinking," she answered.

"Acton there?"

"Yes."

There was a pause while Doyle thought about this new idea, turning it over in her mind. "Guilt is good idea," she typed.

"?"

"Someone felt responsible."

"Defense team?"

She stared at the screen. Now, that was why Williams was on the fast track to DI; it had taken her days to have the same idea. "Haven't really checked," she admitted.

"Parole?"

This was a decent suggestion, as a parole-worker was not as likely as a case-worker to be a hand-wringer, and would also see firsthand the perils of letting a murderer off the hook. "Good one."

"Lunch? (friends)"

She smiled; he had promised they could just be friends and thus far, he'd kept up his end of the bargain. Still and all, she was reluctant to spend a lot of time alone with him and besides, she was already meeting with her rescuer tomorrow at lunchtime—not that she was looking forward to it. Lifting her head, she realized she could assuage her conscience by enlisting the eager-to-help DS Williams. "Can U make early lunch? Need small favor."

"Done."

"Deli OK?" The deli was next to headquarters and near the bookstore.

"OK. Text."

"Thanks." She signed off, and then jotted down the ideas she and Williams had come up with before she forgot them.

She'd enlist Williams to cover the flank when she went to meet with Solonik's man—that way she'd be perfectly safe, just in case things went south for some reason. I'm turning into Acton, with my frettin', she thought. I have to get used to the fact there are no crises looming and relax—it's jumping at shadows, I am.

She looked at the clock and debated evicting Acton from the bedroom; she was tired and it had been a long and wretched day—tomorrow could only be better.

CHAPTER 1 1

DOYLE WAS AWAKENED EARLY THE NEXT MORNING BY ACTON, who pulled her against him and left no doubt as to his intention.

"I see how it is," she teased sleepily. "Abusin' my helpless self."

"You fell asleep, last night," he murmured into her mouth.

"And whose fault is that, if I may be askin'?"

"Hush," he said, and she did.

Afterward, she lay with him and he seemed disinclined to rise, which was a wrinkle—usually he was up with the birds. He held her cradled against his chest, stroking her arms and hands while she closed her eyes, supremely content. "How is your mysterious case comin' along?"

"Very slowly." His hands paused. "I believe those who gave me the assignment may have not been forthcoming with me."

"Oh. That *is* a handicap."

"It is indeed," he replied absently, and began his stroking circuit again.

"So they want your help, but they're hopin' you don't find out the sordid details?"

"Something like that."

"And you're willin' to be duped? That doesn't sound very much in keepin', Michael."

He let out a breath that stirred the hair on the top of her head. "It keeps me interested."

She giggled. "Like me."

He ran a caressing hand down the front of her, north to south, lingering on the south. "Like you."

She sighed. "It's lucky we are—that we found each other."

"It was I who found you," he corrected, his hand gently emphasizing the point.

"Faith, I'm forgettin'. Then you put me in a headlock, and dragged me to the altar."

"My finest hour."

She giggled again, and wondered at his willingness to lounge this morning; he wasn't a lounger, was Acton.

Absently, he lifted his hand to pull loose a tendril of hair from her temple. "Any progress on the working theory?"

"No one of interest was murdered yesterday—leastways, as far as I can tell. Williams and I brainstormed for ideas, and he came up with guilt, which is an interestin' theory; someone feels responsible for some reason—a guilty vigilante, rather than a vengeful one."

He thought about it. "Perhaps; but nevertheless there was a trigger. Something prompted him to go after them all at once, all these years later."

This made sense, she supposed, and Acton was Acton, so attention should be paid. "What sort of trigger, d'ye think?"

He played with the tendril of hair. "Something cataclysmic, that sickened him. It was no small thing for this vigilante to purchase a variety of guns and then to kill so many. He couldn't live with himself."

"Or *she* couldn't," she reminded him.

"I would be surprised if it was a woman."

"Habib said women don't shoot at heads."

"In general," he agreed.

"Are we so predictable, then?"

"Not you."

She lifted his hand to kiss it in appreciation, then let it go back to its stroking circuit. "Speakin' of which, what would you like to do for Christmas?"

The question amused him. "I have no idea. What are my options?"

Turning over to prop herself up on her elbows, she stared at him through her tousled hair. "Michael; you don't celebrate *Christmas?*"

He continued amused. "Now I do, apparently."

Frowning at him, she said with all earnestness, "You were in sorry straits, my friend. I came along just in the nick of time, if I may be sayin' so."

"So it seems." This with a gleam of amusement as he spread his fingers and pulled them through the fall of her hair.

"Are you teasin' me?" she asked suspiciously.

"Never. I was indeed a sorry fellow until you wandered by."

This was of interest, and she ran a fingertip along one of his dark brows. "Did I wander by? I don't remember ever bein' within three floors of you."

"I saw you out my window."

Inordinately pleased by this glimpse, she smiled—he was not one to wax sentimental, and he rarely made any reference to his condition. Nevertheless, she'd always wondered how this whole Section Seven thing had started. "Did you? And that was that?"

"Yes; that was that."

Very pleased with him, she nestled up against his side, and dropped a kiss on his chest as his arms came around her. "Good one."

He made no response, and they lay content for a few moments until she remembered the original topic of conversation. "We could have Timothy over—for Christmas, I mean—unless he goes somewhere else. And we could go to Midnight Mass, if you like."

"Right then; I'll ask him. Shall we include Nanda?"

"As long as they're not goin' to be havin' sex everywhere."

"No, that's our prerogative."

She laughed and raised herself up again. "Not on a High Holy Day, Michael; is Father John teachin' you *nothin'*?"

"Haven't touched on that one yet."

"I'll touch you one, I will." She suited action to word, and naturally, this gesture initiated another heated session that left the bedcovers on the floor and two of London's finest destined to be late for work. Doyle's mobile pinged, and she stirred herself to check the screen. "Munoz wonders where I am."

"Let her wonder. Shall we stay home this morning?"

With a hand, she smoothed her damp hair away from her face. "Can't; it's meetin' Williams for lunch behind your back, I am."

"How is that going?"

This was an interesting little wrinkle; Acton, by all accounts, should not be happy that Williams was so fond of her, but he seemed unalarmed. Of course, as he'd pointed out, it meant that Williams would never put his own interests above hers. "Well enough—he's behavin' himself." Best not mention he'd kissed her; that was a one-off because she'd nearly drowned, and it seemed appropriate to throw caution to the wind at the time.

Acton sat up, reached for his mobile, and began to listen to the messages left for him as she slid out of bed and went to shower, feeling his gaze follow her—a shame he was willing to lounge about the one day she had multiple assignations lined up. And Munoz wanted something, too—she wouldn't be contacting Doyle, else.

As she showered, she realized that her husband had not mentioned the visit to Trestles again—perhaps she'd spooked him, with her talk of ancestral boneyards. That, or he was planning to go without telling her. Frowning, she spread her fingers and let the warm water flow between them—this was an odd thought to pop into her mind; Acton didn't like to go

any distance away from her. But perhaps he planned to confront his horrid mother about something, and didn't want
her as a witness—he may be planning a day trip with Doyle
none the wiser, and was hoping she'd forgotten the conversation. She should let him know she truly didn't mind; they should
have no secrets from each other, it wasn't healthy. Feeling a
twinge of guilt about the Williams kiss, she amended—or at least
no secrets that mattered.

CHAPTER 1 2

MUNOZ WAS LYING IN WAIT AT DOYLE'S CUBICLE, HOVERING with an aura of impatience mixed with unhappiness.

Just grand, thought Doyle with foreboding. Now what?

"Why are you so late?"

Doyle set down her rucksack. "Acton wanted to inspect my notes."

The other girl made a sound of derision. "You need to think of a better euphemism; that one's stupid."

"I'm sorry; I don't have your experience," Doyle shot back, blushing. "What is it you're wantin'?"

Munoz took a look 'round and lowered her voice. "Can you go for coffee?"

"For the love o' Mike, Munoz; I just got here and I'm late already."

"I need to speak with you."

Doyle paused, because whatever it was, it was worrying the usually unflappable Munoz and she had a quick flash of deep uneasiness from the girl; best she discover what was frettin' her. "All right, then. Canteen?"

Munoz made a face, and Doyle couldn't blame her; they avoided going to the building's canteen together because everyone in the room would think they were *precious*, and begin whispering about them. "Conference room?"

"I don't want to be overheard." It was a poorly-kept secret that the conference rooms were subject to monitoring.

Doyle blew out a breath. "I'm runnin' out of options, Munoz—want to walk outside? I have to head over to the deli to meet Williams soon, anyway."

"Why are you meeting Williams?" Munoz was immediately suspicious.

"Because he's my secret boyfriend."

The other girl grimaced in distaste. "It's tacky to have sex with two different men on the same day."

"Wise words, and I will keep them to mind. Give me a mo' to warm up my latte." Doyle's daily latte had grown cold, sitting on her desk, so she warmed it up in the kitchen microwave as she shrugged back into her coat. "How is the new beau?"

"Nice."

Doomed, thought Doyle; but at least it gives her something to do until a better option presents itself.

They walked outside in silence, and Doyle realized, after a moment, that Munoz was embarrassed, so she softened her tone and asked, "What's botherin' you, Izzy? I promise I won't bite."

Munoz looked up ahead and stuck her hands in her pockets. "I was contacted by a tabloid to give an interview about the rescue."

Doyle smiled in amusement at the picture thus presented. "Faith, Munoz; did you strangle 'em on the spot?"

"They were going to pay me five hundred pounds, and they told me it would not say the information came from me."

Doyle blinked. It was a princely sum; she could see why Munoz was tempted, although it seemed strange the reporter didn't want to reveal that the source of the story was the damsel in distress. "What did you say?" Obviously there was a problem of some sort, as the other girl was uneasy—perhaps she'd told them Doyle was drunk at the time, or something.

Munoz studied the pavement. "That's just it; the reporter asked a couple of questions about the rescue, but seemed much more interested in anything I could say about you and Holmes."

The light dawned. "Ah—was the reporter a man named Maguire?" A few months ago, Doyle had a small kerfuffle with Maguire, who had wanted to run a page-seven story about Doyle's unexpected marriage to Acton. Perhaps he was still intent on following through, despite his earlier decision to show her some mercy.

"No," said Munoz. "It was a woman; I have her card." She fished it out of her coat pocket, and handed it to Doyle. It displayed the logo of a popular tabloid that featured sensational, anonymous stories about celebrities, and was imprinted with the name "Jennifer Smith."

"What did you tell her?" Doyle asked with some misgiving—although Munoz wouldn't know much, if the subject was Doyle's marriage to Acton. Doyle didn't know that much, herself.

"Nothing," Munoz admitted. "I didn't like where it was going."

"Good one, Munoz." Doyle touched the other girl's elbow with relief. "Acton would not have been happy."

"I know—I didn't want to get the sack over something stupid like this. But the reporter was not happy with me, and ended up not paying me anything."

"But you did the right thing, Izzy, and I appreciate it—truly I do."

"I thought you should know." The other girl paused, frowning. "She also asked me some questions about TDC Owens."

Doyle stared in surprise, a sinking feeling in her midsection. "Owens?" Owens was the trainee that Doyle had killed, and why anyone would be asking about his disappearance was a mystery—and not one of those nice mysteries with cats; more like a dark and ominous mystery.

Munoz exclaimed in annoyance, "Why is everyone so interested in Owens? Remember—Rourke was asking about him, too."

Rourke was an Irish villain in the turf wars who'd met a bad end; he'd been posing as a banker to date Munoz, apparently with the sole aim of winkling information from her. Doyle paused with that thought—was it only a coincidence that two different and apparently unrelated persons were laying siege to Munoz for information about Owens? Acton famously said that he didn't believe in coincidences, and so Doyle's uneasiness grew. "Did this reporter mention Rourke, too?"

"No—thank God for small favors." The story was not a pretty tale; Munoz had not shown to advantage, having been hoodwinked by the charming Mr. Rourke.

Knitting her brow, Doyle digested these rather alarming revelations. "I'll tell Acton—maybe he can bring some pressure to bear on the paper."

"Don't," urged Munoz, her gaze meeting Doyle's in alarm. "He'll think I'm an idiot."

This was a fair point, and besides, Doyle should not discourage Munoz from making any future confessions she may need to make. "I won't, then—I'll just tell him I discovered this reporter was sniffin' about, lookin' for a story."

"Don't tell Williams, either." Munoz was interested in Williams, as was nearly every female on staff at the Met. Except for Doyle, ironically.

"I won't—I won't say anythin' about it, I promise."

They parted, Munoz heading back into headquarters while Doyle made for the deli, texting Williams that she was en route. It was starting to drizzle and she'd forgotten her umbrella, but there was a table available inside, as it was too early for the lunch crowd. She settled in to wait, thinking about what Munoz had revealed. She'd little doubt that the reporter was looking to put up a story about her marriage to Acton, in the same way that Maguire had tried—it was an intriguing story, and even more so now, after the bridge-jumping incident. Acton was a well-known figure—the titled, brilliant-but-reclusive detective who solved high-profile murders, and the fact that he'd married a first-year DC out of the blue only added to his mystique. But why would anyone couple their story with TDC Owens's mysterious disappearance? No matter what angle she studied this from, the answer made her very uneasy, as it appeared that someone was aware that the trainee's disappearance was somehow connected to the House of Acton. Owens had been a detective trainee, but in truth he'd been infiltrating the racecourse—another foot soldier working for one of the underworld players who were trying to muscle in on the racecourse smuggling ring. He'd gotten sidetracked from his dark doings by his attraction to Acton, and his unfortunate fantasy had led him to believe that he only had to murder Doyle to have Acton for himself.

Plenty of villains had died in the ensuing turf war, so it would be logical for his employers to simply presume that Owens was just another casualty; it was strange that the man's disappearance was being traced to Acton and her fair self.

"Hey." Williams pulled up a chair.

She shook herself out of her abstraction. "Hey, yourself."

"Anything new to report?"

Being as she didn't want to confess that she was too busy having sex to work on the case since last they spoke, she shook her head. "I like the guilt angle, though; I was gettin' nowhere with a straight vigilante, there were too many variables. This may start a new string."

"Do you need help? My caseload is not very heavy, just now."

"I do," she admitted, grateful for the offer. "Most of the information on the cold cases is in hard copy, and it's time-consumin'. I have a feelin' I'm just on the brink, and it's frustratin' as all get out."

"Happy to help." He paused for a moment, studying his hands on the table. "I wanted to tell you something."

Of course he does, thought Doyle, resigned. He's flippin' Williams.

He met her eyes with a small smile. "We're friends, right?"

"Right," she agreed easily, having a very good guess where this was going.

He chose his words carefully. "I hope you will not hesitate to let me help you, if you should ever need help—no questions asked, and no matter who is involved."

Doyle replied with all sincerity, "I appreciate the offer. Thank you." She decided she wasn't going to argue again with his premise, that Acton could ill-treat her. He'd seen Acton in one of his black moods, and it was indeed a fearsome sight. Everyone wants to rescue me, she thought; it's ironic, is what it is—*I'm* the one who's the rescuer. With a suddenness that almost made her jump with surprise, her scalp started prickling, as it did when she was making an intuitive connection. What? She thought, perplexed; what is it about Williams's offer—

He continued carefully, "There is sometimes a—an unwillingness to face a difficult fact—"

"What happened, Thomas?" She asked him softly, every nerve attuned. "Did someone else have bruises, once?"

The blue eyes met hers in surprise, and there was a frozen moment whilst she could tell he was trying to decide whether to go forward or to withdraw. Her intuition prompted her to ask gently, "Can't you tell me?"

Slowly, he replied, "My cousin. I had a cousin who was about ten years younger." He bent his head for a moment. "She'd have fingerprint bruises—where she shouldn't have. She died when she was twelve; a drowning accident." He raised his head. "A couple of years later, when I was doing my externship at the coroner's office, I saw a girl with the same sort of bruises and learned what it meant—she'd been molested. I also learned about cerebral ischemia and what a broken hyoid meant." He raised a finger to his throat, and Doyle nodded; a broken hyoid usually indicated death by strangulation.

"My cousin—my cousin had the same indicators; I just didn't recognize it for what it was at the time."

Doyle nodded sadly. "Yes—you realized that her death was a murder, in hindsight. Who did it? D'you know?"

"Her father—my uncle. I had nothing concrete, but I just *knew*. I think she'd gotten old enough to threaten him with exposure, so he killed her."

"Yes; I imagine so." This was, unfortunately, not an unusual sequence of events, as they had discovered in this business. "Faith, Thomas; I am so sorry." And at that moment, the world lost a very fine doctor but gained a very fine detective, instead. "You canno' be so hard on yourself, Thomas Williams; you canno' rescue everyone."

The steady gaze met hers. "I can try."

But her own gaze did not waiver. "Not this time—I swear to you on my mother's soul that it wasn't Acton; my bruises were hard-earned, they were, and my attacker paid a very steep price for them."

He searched her eyes, then nodded. "Right then; I'll say no more."

They sat in silence for a few moments. "How on earth do you face him—your uncle, I mean?"

Her companion examined his hands again. "No longer necessary; he died last year—fell and drowned while crossing a stream on his property."

This was not true, but she observed in a mild tone, "Now, there's justice and irony shakin' hands."

"Sometimes it all works out."

Another lie; but she already knew this—already knew why her scalp had been prickling and her intuition was practically beating her over the head to pay attention. Williams's situation was similar to their working theory on the vigilante murders; there had been a trigger, just as Acton had speculated. A trigger made Williams recognize a murder in hindsight, and then he became a vigilante in his own way—probably with Acton's help; two men who felt the justice system needed an occasional helping hand. She wondered whether Acton had experienced a similar trigger, one that had started him down his own path.

Suddenly certain, she told him, "I think we're lookin' for a vigilante who's consumed with guilt instead of vengeance, just as you suggested. Might well be a case-worker, or someone on the defense team—someone who helped the murderers get off and then realized, somehow, that he'd truly mucked it up."

He nodded. "All right; where do you want me to start?"

"Let me think about how to divide up the task; in the meantime, I need a favor."

"You need only ask."

She glanced at the time on her mobile. "I'm goin' to meet a reluctant witness in the bookstore shortly, and I'd like you to cover the flank."

This did not set well, and he was suddenly on high alert. "Is he dangerous? I'll come in with you."

"No—if you're there he won't speak, but I'd like an excuse to leave if it's goin' nowhere. Could you ping my mobile about twenty minutes after I go in? If I don't answer, come and extricate me with some excuse." She paused. "And please do not mention this to Acton."

This remark caused no end of alarm, and he raised his brows. "Kath—"

She raised her own brows in response. "Oh—is this a problem? And here I thought you sincerely meant your fine speech of five minutes ago." It was masterful, truly; she had him caught by his own promise.

"What is this about?" he asked heavily.

"Not sayin'. Are you in?"

"Of course." He wasn't happy about it, though.

She wasn't afraid of her rescuer; she truly didn't think he was a danger to her. But one never knew, and she couldn't quite like the way he'd followed her around, yesterday. "That's grand of you, Williams, and much appreciated," she said cheerfully, and gathered up her things to go.

CHAPTER 13

ONCE IN THE BOOKSTORE, DOYLE MADE HER WAY TO THE RELIgion section, which was as deserted as the last time. Her rescuer held a Bible, thumbing through it as he waited for her. "Anythin' in there about the wages o' sin?" she asked.

He looked up, and replaced the book. "Who is in the cemetery?"

There seemed no harm in saying. "My mother."

He tilted his head in sympathy. "My mother, also. And now my brother."

"Gerry?" she asked in surprise.

He regarded her with his unreadable pale eyes. "I did not say that Gerry was my brother."

"I think he is. Or a cousin, or somethin'."

His eyes narrowed in suspicion. "Why do you think this?"

She shrugged. "I don't know; I met him, you know, and you rather remind me of him." And her perceptive ability told her this—although it was true that sometimes it led her astray.

Apparently, he was willing to concede the issue. "A different brother is dead. You knew him—he was a policeman here, in London."

With dawning realization, she struggled to control her reaction. Holy Mother of God; the chickens were coming home to roost with a vengeance, and suddenly all the coincidences were no longer coincidences. Her mouth dry, she managed to offer, "I am that sorry for it; who was he?"

"He used the name Owens."

She feigned surprise, no small feat, as she wasn't very good at subterfuge. "TDC Owens is dead? Are you sure? No one knows whatever happened to him."

Her companion fixed his pale, cold gaze upon hers. "Solonik, he says he knows."

Thinking to throw a wrench, she ventured, "Maybe Solonik had him killed, and that's how he knows. Solonik is not a good man." This last said with some emphasis.

"Perhaps. I will find out." He watched her for a moment. "You think Solonik is taking Acton's goat."

"Yes, I do." She met his eyes candidly. "What do you think—has he told you what he plans?" Perhaps her rescuer would turn coat on Solonik; she had the very strong impression he was a bit beguiled by her fair self, despite his hard-as-nails appearance.

He shook his head. "No, he has not told me what he plans."

This was not true, and they stood together for a moment, at an apparent impasse. She wasn't quite clear on the purpose of this meeting—although it may just have been that he wanted to speak with her again. She should be nice; hopefully he'd never find out what happened to his wretched brother, but if he did, any measure of goodwill she could establish would be needful—she had no doubt that this man was a very tough customer. To this end, she said lightly, "Did you inform Mr. Solonik that I'm wise to his wily ways?"

He paused, and replied, "He says it would be best if you come to see him; he must warn you."

Suddenly wary, Doyle was silent. This sounded more like the Solonik she knew, and her rescuer was now a bit grim—or grimmer than his usual. "Warn me of what?"

Her rescuer lowered his gaze for a moment. Oh-oh, she thought in alarm; this is serious.

"There is information about Acton that is being gathered up by Solonik. Weapons, killings."

Doyle stared at him, trying to hide her horror.

"He wishes you to meet him to speak of it—of what is to be done."

Blackmail. Controlling her first flare of panic, Doyle brought herself under control and thought about it carefully. So—this was a fine incentive to bring her before him; Solonik was bound and determined, he was. It could be a ruse—Solonik was already aware of Acton's unlawful propensities; falsified evidence had put the man in prison, after all. He was trying to manipulate her so as to wreak some kind of revenge on her husband, and she should play along, perhaps—at least until she knew what-was-what. On the other hand, perhaps the only goal was to get her to visit the prison for some reason, and it would be best to stoutly refuse, no matter the incentive.

Whilst she tried to decide the best strategy, her mobile vibrated. "Excuse me," she said, and texted "OK" to Williams.

"You must come to see him, to discuss this problem. But you must not tell Acton."

She mustered up a confident expression. "He's bluffin', my friend; he doesn't know anythin' that could hurt Acton." She'd see if her rescuer was willing to give her any proof, so as to gauge the seriousness of this ploy.

Her companion shrugged. "Your husband does not act wisely, sometimes. He drinks too much, and tells secrets."

This seemed a little ominous—that they would know about the drinking—but she raised a skeptical eyebrow. "It's clear you've never met him; no one would call Acton a gabbler."

With a measured movement, he pulled two photographs from his inner jacket pocket, and handed them to her.

Doyle stared at the photographs; almost unable to process what they portrayed. They were of Acton and the woman reporter from the *London World News* who had spoken to him at the crime scene. Both were seated at a small round table—as though at a nightclub—and the light was dim. They were leaning with their heads together, speaking intimately. In one photo Acton's head was bent and his mouth was next to her ear while she listened, smiling knowingly. Both were smoking, and Acton held a tendril of hair from her temple between his fingers.

Doyle wasn't aware that she swayed until her rescuer put his hands at her elbows to steady her. "Ah-ah; do you need to sit?"

Lifting her gaze, she met his a little blankly. "This makes no sense."

He lifted a shoulder, in a gesture that seemed very French. "The men—sometimes they cannot resist; it is the way of it."

"No." She reviewed the photos again, trying to find two thoughts to put together. "That is not the way of it."

"It is painful—like the teeth in the licorice," he observed with a trace of sympathy. "You are upset, but we will talk of what is to be done, and you will feel better."

She raised her head again, and with a mighty effort, pulled herself together. "I'll not be makin' any decisions, just now."

He put a finger under her chin so as to hold it steady and looked into her eyes, speaking seriously. "I think you should speak to Solonik—you must be very careful."

She had the strong impression he was trying to decide whether to kiss her—which was symmetrical in a strange way, but nevertheless not appreciated—and so she pulled her head back.

"Kath?" It was Williams, standing in the aisle beside them and looking like murder.

The rescuer released her immediately and faced Williams, assessing him. Williams's hands curled into fists at his sides.

"Williams, please wait outside, I'll be out in a moment," Doyle said as calmly as she was able.

"Go outside, Doyle," he replied, never taking his eyes off the other man.

Williams was a head taller and at least a stone heavier, but

Doyle had absolutely no doubt as to who would prevail in a donnybrook, although she wasn't sure why she was so certain. "Thomas," she pleaded, "I am *beggin'* you."

He hesitated and met her eyes. "Who is he?"

"Believe it or not, he is a friend. Please wait outside, I will be right there, I promise."

"Call if you need me." Giving the other man a last, long look, Williams turned and walked away.

Doyle's rescuer turned to her in surprise. "He is your lover?"

"No," she said crossly. "Of course not."

He eyed her. "He wants to be."

But Doyle was in no mood, and snapped, "You're to mind your tongue; you've caused enough trouble already."

But he only shook his head. "It is not me, with the trouble-causing."

She took a breath, trying to quell the sick panic that threatened to overwhelm her, and remembering that she should try to stay on his good side. "No; I suppose you're right. I'm just wantin' to shoot the messenger."

"So; what should I tell Solonik?"

"I don't know." She was trying to suppress the images in the photographs so that she could think clearly, and held her palms against her eyes for a moment. "I have to think. Can I ring you?"

"Yes." He reached for the mobile at her belt, then programmed a number into it. "Soon; I will need an answer."

"Aye, then." She took her mobile from his hand, turned, and blindly walked out.

CHAPTER 14

WILLIAMS WAS WAITING BY THE DOOR, ON EDGE. SHE DIDN'T look up at him, and walked past as though he wasn't there, but she wasn't the only one who was angry. "What the hell was that?" he demanded furiously, keeping pace with her.

"Why didn't you follow the protocol?"

"I did—you didn't answer the second time."

She unbent enough to glance up at him. "Oh. I'm sorry—I didn't realize you'd checked in a second time." She was having trouble controlling her voice, so she lowered her head and stopped talking. The female reporter had been all dressed up at the crime scene, and Acton had been drinking; they'd been together when he got the call, and the brasser couldn't resist coming to the cordon, probably to take a gloating assessment of his stupid little wife. It was beyond all bearing, and although she'd never been able to fathom the unholy urge to murder before, it didn't seem so completely unfathomable at present.

It was raining, and as they strode past a pharmacy, Williams took her elbow and pulled her into the doorway. "Wait; let's talk about this for a minute—I think you owe it to me."

"I want to go home," she replied through stiff lips, and then wondered if that was a good plan; she may walk in on them—on Acton and the reporter. Bowing her head, she fought an almost overwhelming urge to cry.

"All right," he soothed, his tone less angry as he assessed her. "Let's put your things away—do you have an umbrella?" He gently pulled her mobile from her nerveless hand. "Let me help you."

Instinctively, she resisted, and as a result her mobile fell to the floor, along with the two photographs. She watched in frozen horror as they floated down, the images revealed. In a rush of fury, she scrambled to gather up the mobile and the photographs. "No," she hissed through her teeth, "I dinna' need your help." She sprang up, clutching the items with her right hand so that she could pound his chest with her left fist, emphasizing each word: "I—don't—need—your—*help*." Behind her, she could hear the shopkeeper's chair scrape back in alarm. She was past caring.

"All right—all right, Kath." Williams pulled her to him and she did not resist, but stood still in the circle of his arms for a moment. Pressing her forehead against the same chest she had just been abusing, she took a ragged breath and then offered in a small voice, "I am so sorry, Thomas. Please, *please* forgive me."

"Let's wait a minute," he suggested. "Until you feel more the thing."

She took some breaths and didn't move. He said nothing, but moved his hands gently on her upper arms in a soothing motion. There is something inherently comforting, she thought, about a broad-shouldered man—women must be genetically programmed to appreciate it.

Doyle's mobile vibrated and she ignored it. "How is your health, Thomas?"

He didn't miss a beat. "Better; I am trying to be more careful with my diet." Williams was a diabetic, and had a recent brush with insulin shock.

"That's grand." She lifted her head and stepped back, smoothing down her hair self-consciously. She turned to the shopkeeper, who was staring at her in alarm. "I'm so sorry." Her mobile vibrated again, and she carefully tucked the photographs into her rucksack and then reviewed the text message. "Acton thinks there's another park murder. I should go."

"Want me to come?"

"Best not." It was clear he was not offering his aid just to process the scene; he had her back, did DS Williams, and suddenly she was reminded of what the anonymous instructor at the Crime Academy had said—that it was important for them to have each other's backs, no matter what. Acton is in trouble, she thought, briefly closing her eyes; and I do have his back—no matter what. There must be a method to his madness, but oh—how I'd like to brain him with a joint stool for putting me through this.

"At least let me drop you off." With a decisive movement, Williams lifted her rucksack. "Here's a fiver—buy an umbrella while I get a cab."

"All right," she agreed, and purchased an umbrella from the shopkeeper—who continued to eye her askance—before going out to meet him and the waiting cab at the curb. "It's at the Heath—I'm not sure exactly where, though."

"I imagine it will be obvious." He instructed the driver, and they drove off.

After a few minutes, she said in a stiff voice, "Please do not mention any of this to anyone." She was certain he'd seen the photographs, although he hadn't betrayed any reaction.

Williams glanced over at her, but made no reply, so she said to him with careful emphasis, "If you say anythin' to Acton, Thomas, I swear by all the saints I will *never* speak to you again."

"That wouldn't matter—if I thought you were in trouble."

She was angry again, and tried to rein in her temper. "So when you gave me your fine speech about unconditional help, you really meant you will help by runnin' my life for me."

Williams said nothing for a moment. "How did you meet your bookstore friend?"

With a sigh, she answered dryly, "Not at church."

"No, that's pretty obvious."

She debated for a moment what to tell him, then decided that the truth was most expedient. "He saved my life."

He glanced at her in surprise. "How was this?"

She shook her head. "I'd rather not say. It's complicated."

"I'll bet," he agreed, and Doyle knew they were both thinking about the photographs. "If you need me you will ring me?"

"Yes. I'm sorry I hit you—I don't think I've ever hit anyone in my life."

"Makes me feel special, then." The cab pulled up to the curb where various police vehicles were parked, lights flashing, and a cordon had been marked off, with PCs stationed along the perimeter. Without another word, she left the cab and walked toward the yellow tape, concentrating on putting one foot in front of the other.

The crime scene was up the hill, and she pulled her coat close around her as she trudged in the soft, wet turf. The rain had paused, but it was threatening again, which meant the SOCOs would have to hurry if they were to recover anything of interest. This time, the body was left in a forested area of the heath, perhaps another attempt to mix up the m.o., as the others had been left in city parks within a two-mile radius.

Coming to the top of the rise, she walked toward the small canopy that had been erected to shelter the victim from the incipient rain. The body was not very far from the road, she noted, and thought it was in keeping with the vigilante's methods; forensics had concluded the other victims had been killed where they were found. The vigilante must have lured them somehow, as it seemed unlikely these particular victims would be the park-visiting types. The wives or girlfriends had not been helpful; the victims had received no strange visitors or unknown calls in the days before the attacks. It was unclear how they were contacted, and unclear how they were lured to their deaths in peaceful surroundings.

Acton's tall figure could be seen, studying the scene, and he walked to meet her once he spotted her. "Here you are; I couldn't reach you." Although the words were mild, he was emanating waves of concern.

She'd wondered how she would react upon seeing him again, but she found that her main reaction was to be honestly perplexed; he was genuinely fretting because he couldn't get hold of her for an hour, but was willing to run a risk that might make her leave him forever. Her initial reaction still held true; it all didn't make any sense.

"Sorry; I was in the bookstore, and I had the ringer off."

His gaze sharp upon hers, he leaned in to ask, "What's happened?" His antennae were very fine-tuned when it came to her, and the fact that she was in a bookstore probably gave him pause, too, as it was not her natural habitat.

"I've had a crackin' foul day, my friend." He waited, but she offered nothing further, instead indicating the scene with a nod of her head. "What's the report?"

They turned and walked together toward the canopy. "A woman, this time. Bludgeoned a live-in boyfriend years ago, but got off with a battered woman syndrome defense."

Doyle crouched beside him and reviewed the body, face-down with an entry wound in the base of the skull, her limbs close to her torso. "She didn't know it was comin'—no attempt to struggle or flee."

"No; shot from behind while walking. Unlikely we'll find trace evidence, and with the cold it will be difficult to establish exact time of death."

"Sir; it's looking to rain again." The SOCO photographer lingered near Acton, and Doyle, in her current mood, suppressed an urge to pick up a shovel and deck her with it.

"Right, then; let's have a look." They stood, and he accompanied the photographer as they walked through the scene, scrutinizing the ground and occasionally asking for a photo, although it didn't appear he was very enthused about what he saw. He gave permission to bag the body, and the crew leapt to comply, as it was cold and miserable.

Doyle watched them and thought about this odd sort of vigilante, carefully trying to hide his purpose, even though there were many who'd think him a hero—no one would mourn these victims, and he was no doubt banking on the fact that no one would be fervently pursuing justice for them. It must be as Acton surmised; he was only doing it because he could no longer live with himself, and was trying to atone on some personal level.

Drawing a ragged breath, Doyle decided it was past time that her wayward husband did some atoning himself; there was nothin' for it. Therefore, when he returned to stand by her side, she observed in a quiet tone, "I didn't know you smoked, Michael."

He paused, and kept his eyes on the ground for a long moment before he raised them to hers. She returned his gaze calmly, and said nothing. He was wary. Good.

"I smoked at university," he admitted.

There was a long pause. "Is there anythin' else I should know?"

A member of the SOCO team approached, but Acton held him off, signaling to wait as he bent his head to Doyle. "What have you learned?"

"Now, that's not a proper answer, is it?"

Acton allowed the SOCO to speak to him, and gave instructions for the clean-up phase and a thorough search of the area between the street and the kill site. He then took Doyle's arm and led her a small distance away, where they could stand under her umbrella and not be overheard. Meeting her eyes, he repeated something she had once said to him. "You know that I love you, and I will love you until the day I die."

"That day may be fast approachin', my friend. Are you goin' to be tiresome about this?" It drove her mad when he was up to something and refused to tell her.

He thought about it carefully. "For the time being, yes."

She made a sound of extreme impatience and refused to look at him.

"Remember your promise." He'd made her promise that if there was a chance she would leave him, he would be given a warning.

"We're not there yet," she conceded, "but we're circlin' the airport." She didn't want him to think he had carte blanche to drive her mad, which, unfortunately, he did.

"Let's go home," he said quietly.

"Can't. I haven't accomplished a thimbleful of work as yet."

"Bring it home; I will help you."

She glanced at him, scornful. "Are you sure that you don't have other plans?"

"Don't." He drew her to him, and kissed her forehead, much to the embarrassment of the PC who was posted at the hilltop.

"All right; I suppose if I'm with you, Habib won't sack me."

They descended the hill to his car, and Doyle stayed quiet as he checked in with his assistant on his mobile, informing her that he could be reached at home, but only if it was important. She looked out the window and reflected how interesting it was that—once she was beside him—she was reassured; whatever was going on, his single-minded focus on her fair self was unshaken. This did not change the fact that she had multiple crises piling up, but at least her husband's fidelity was not one of them.

Acton said quietly into the silence, "I had to get into her flat."

She continued to gaze out the window, and shook her head. "That won't wash, my friend—as if you ever needed anyone's permission." Acton was a first-class picklock.

He corrected himself. "I had to get into her flat, and watch her once she was there."

"Why?"

He paused. "I'm afraid I'd rather not say."

She thought about this, and drew the obvious conclusion; whatever scheme Solonik had cooked up, Acton already knew and was working to counter it. She felt immeasurably better— she'd bet on Acton over Solonik any day of the week. She needed to know, however, what sort of sacrifices his counter-plot called for. "Did you—" She was having trouble saying it.

"No," he replied immediately.

She wanted to make sure he wasn't being wily, so she made herself say it. "Did you have sex with her?"

"No." It was the pure truth. She was surprised at her relief; she'd already assumed the worst.

"I pretended that I had drunk too much."

"Good one." Acton could always perform, drunk or not, and usually more than once. "But I'll have your promise—on your honor, Michael—that there'll not be a second attempt made."

"No," he agreed immediately, then hesitated. "I may have to see her again, and lead her to think otherwise."

She turned to stare at him in disbelief. "You're a step above a prostitute, then?"

He replied a bit grimly, "It is important, or I wouldn't spend another moment with her."

This was the truth, and she decided she wouldn't press him; he didn't want to tell her, but it was clearly all wound up in the Solonik plot, somehow. Her rescuer had implied that Acton was telling this brasser his dark secrets, which was ludicrous—Acton didn't even tell Doyle his dark secrets. So the logical conclusion was Acton was turning the tables, somehow. She would hold out hope he wasn't to be arrested at any moment, and meanwhile do what she could to put a spanner in Solonik's wheel at her end—there were certain things that only she could do; certain truths that only she could hear, and if she disclosed what she knew to Acton, there was little doubt he'd lock her up somewhere and never let her see the light of day again.

When they returned to their flat, they spent the last part of the afternoon cross-indexing this latest murder. It was encouraging; this victim could indeed provide some fresh insights. She was female, so commonalities might stand out more. Doyle could see from the report that the victim had a mother, living in Brockley, which was a respectable middle-class neighborhood—not someone indoctrinated from birth to distrust the police. The woman had been informed of her daughter's death, and was willing to speak to the detectives, to offer whatever help she could.

As for how to behave with her maddening husband, Doyle decided she would not sulk, but that she would make it clear he had run a huge risk, so that in the future he would think twice if a similar situation arose—there had to be a heavy price to pay. To this end, she was subdued and didn't tease him, or speak more than was necessary. He helped her, and they brainstormed, but she could sense his underlying concern, and when he began to absently roll a strand of her hair between his fingers, she decided to have pity on the wretched man. She gently disengaged his hand and kissed the palm, and his arms were around her immediately; his cheek pressed against hers. "Kathleen. Forgive me."

"It's all right, Michael." They went to the bedroom and he was tender and careful and said sweet things to her, which told her that he had been very worried, indeed.

As they lay together afterward, he asked quietly, "Are you going to tell me how you knew?"

"No." It was a time for secrets, apparently; and it would be up to the fair Doyle to perform yet another rescue.

CHAPTER 15

*T*HE NEXT MORNING, DOYLE AWOKE WITH THE FEELING THAT she had a great deal to accomplish in a short amount of time. Acton was still abed as a result of his contrition tour—he'd insisted the night before on dressing and taking a walk down to the corner coffeehouse to purchase her an extravagant concoction. She was tired from the emotional day and their lovemaking, but she went anyway; she knew he wanted to make it clear that he'd repented of his transgressions and besides, they hadn't been out together publicly in a while, and maybe his stupid reporter would hear of it. One silver lining from her rescuer's revelation—Acton was going to be very careful from here on out.

She slid out of the bed even though Acton's hand was resting on her hip, and leaned to kiss him to show there were no hard feelings. "Too much to do. And besides, Reynolds is due any minute."

"Can we meet for lunch?"

"I'm to interview the latest victim's mother; I'm not sure what my schedule is goin' to be, dependin' on how it goes." She was not going to go out of her way to make him suffer, but on the other hand, she was equally determined not to go out of her way to accommodate his guilt. She was RC, after all; guilt had its uses.

They prepared to go to work and Reynolds arrived, disclosing almost immediately that he had been contacted by a tabloid, hoping to acquire personal information about them.

"Did they offer you five hundred pounds?" This inquiry earned Doyle a sharp look from Acton.

"I do not know, madam; I'd hung up before terms could be discussed."

Doyle turned to Acton. "I forgot to tell you that a reporter was fishin' for information from Munoz." Rummaging through her rucksack, she found the card and showed it to Acton. "It's a false name; I checked with the tabloid yesterday."

He made no response, but nodded and pocketed the card—nothing could be said before Reynolds, but little doubt it was his reporter, digging up dirt for her nefarious purposes—or Solonik's nefarious purposes, more accurately. For a brief moment, she considered telling Acton what had happened, and that Solonik was trying to blackmail her into taking some as-yet-undisclosed action, but she rejected the idea almost immediately. Acton would put paid to any attempt by his better half to render aid, and she had the very strong feeling that her aid was essential, for some reason. I'm to be spending my time with villains and brassers, she thought with resignation—it'll be like the old days in Dublin, it will.

She and Acton drove into work together, and parted at the lifts in the lobby. He kissed her, even though there were many interested onlookers, which was unusual for him; he was not openly affectionate in public. The contrition tour continues, she thought.

"Are we all right?"

"Please, Michael; have done. I'm tryin' to get past it." She could feel his anxiety and softened. "I'll ring you up later and let you know; maybe we can meet up after work—some place that has a smokin' section." This sally earned her a relieved half-smile, and they parted on amicable terms.

Once on her floor, Doyle looked both ways down the aisle-way to be certain the coast was clear, then slunk over to Munoz's cubicle to use her desk phone, as the other girl was not yet in. Pulling out her mobile, she scrolled to find her rescuer's number, then dialed it on the desk phone. He did not answer, but when Doyle began to leave a message at the beep, he picked up. "Whose telephone is this?"

Not a man for preliminaries, thought Doyle. "I would rather not use my mobile to be callin' you." He could draw his own conclusions.

"It does not matter; mine is a disposable. What should I tell Solonik?"

"Tell him I will meet with him, tomorrow or the next day if he wants."

"Very good."

"Are you to be comin' along?"

This surprised him. "No."

"Oh; do you think I'll be safe?" She was hoping to convince him to accompany her when she spoke to Solonik—if she could get them to converse with each other, she could see what there was to see. At present, she had several unformed theories, but was not certain how to go about testing them.

But he was not to be so beguiled, and instead temporized, "I will drive you, but I will not go inside."

This was better than nothing, and much appreciated; she was not used to driving, and taking a side trip to Wexton Prison on public transportation would have been complicated. "That would be grand—thank you. Text, and let me know when and where to meet you."

She recited her mobile number, and as she did saw an incoming text from Williams: "Need to talk ASAP."

She rang off, and was preparing to respond to Williams when Munoz spoke from behind her, making her jump. "Making a secret date? I didn't know you had it in you."

As Doyle had no ready explanation for using the other girl's phone, she took refuge in bristling. "None of your business, Munoz."

Munoz only laughed and deposited her rucksack on the desk. "I'm only kidding, you idiot; lightning wouldn't strike twice."

Doyle found this comment unfair; it wasn't as though she was not attractive to men. There was Williams, certainly, and Solonik's henchman, who also seemed fascinated to some extent—but not enough to escort her into the prison, more's the pity. A shame she could never boast of them to Munoz, although the other girl would probably rattle off three of her own and trump her without even breaking a sweat.

One such candidate appeared, as Habib made his measured way toward them. "Good morning, DS Doyle; DS Munoz."

"Give me more homicides," Munoz complained. "I need to raise my profile." The rumors about Williams's promotion were biting at her, apparently. "All I've got now is unsolvable burglaries and larceny-by-trick." Belatedly, she added, "Sir."

Habib's serene brow furrowed, as Munoz's worries were his worries. "I can recommend you to the Women's Issues Task Force."

But Munoz made a face. "Immigrants forced into prostitution—no, thanks, I already did a round with Drake."

"It's what the papers like—women's issues.'" Doyle reminded her. "And it's nothin' short of slavery, truly. You'd be fightin' the good fight."

"I'm not good with wailing women," Munoz confessed bluntly. "I'd rather be dealing with dead people."

Much struck, Doyle could only applaud this shrewd self-truth; Munoz would have little tolerance for oppressed and exploited women—she'd be more likely to give them the back of her hand. Doyle had the same handicap, but for different reasons; there was too much emotion involved, and she'd be exhausted all the time.

"Do you need assistance in your park cases, DS Doyle?" Habib had apparently latched upon an easy avenue to appease the disgruntled beauty.

"No," protested both girls at the same time.

Habib nodded in concession. "No; it would be best if you did not work together until the press's interest has died down—there would be a danger of compromising the cases." Reminded, he asked Doyle, "Is there any information to be learned from the new case?"

"What new case?" Munoz made no effort to conceal her annoyance at another corpse having made its way into Doyle's caseload.

"Another victim, we think—although we're keepin' it quiet. A woman, this time."

This was of interest, and Munoz paused in her sulking. "Really? What's her history?"

"Killed a boyfriend, she did."

Munoz lifted a well-groomed brow. "And got off? I wish I had known it was so easy."

Habib shook a playful finger. "Now, DS Munoz; I will not believe some young man could make you so angry."

"And this woman did get murdered, for her sins," Doyle reminded her. "Crime does not pay."

But the other girl was lost in thought. "I think I could murder someone, if the need arose."

Been there, thought Doyle, but she warned Munoz, "Best say nothing incriminating—you don't want DI Habib to be a witness for the prosecution."

"I wouldn't get caught, Doyle." Munoz regarded her with a full measure of scorn.

You're no Acton, my girl, thought Doyle, and then cautioned herself, lest she accidentally say the wrong thing aloud.

Hastily, Habib changed the subject. "Any leads?"

"Yes, sir; this one's got a cooperative mother, and I'm due to interview her soon." Doyle glanced at her mobile to check the time, and was reminded she should respond to Williams, who had texted again.

"What does Williams want?" Munoz was a sharp-eyed shrew, she was.

"He wants to make sure you aren't assigned to any of his cases."

"Very funny, Doyle. I'll work on his cases, and he'll like it."

Before it could be determined if this was, in fact, an off-color remark by his subordinate, Habib quickly intervened to suggest they come to his office to review the team's assignments.

"Can't," said Doyle, quickly backing away. "I have my interview, I do." With a last, triumphant glance at the other girl, she escaped.

CHAPTER 16

*D*OYLE'S MOBILE PINGED AS SHE TRAVELED ON THE TUBE TO the mother's house in Brockley. Williams again; she'd forgotten to get back to him. "NEED.2.TALK," the message said, and she regarded the screen for a moment. Very demanding, he was, with his capital letters and all. If it was anything important, he'd just spell it out, which meant he wanted to check in with her after the many and varied traumatic events of yesterday. She should be grateful, he'd been nice and—more important—he'd been circumspect, but she didn't want to think about the Acton-and-the-reporter crisis just now; she'd a grieving mother to interview.

"Busy—soon," she replied, and mentally girded her loins as she approached the listed address. This was the worst part of the job—meeting with the bereft relatives. Doyle didn't mind examining the victim's grisly remains or confronting the unrepentant killers, but it was a hard, hard thing for someone like her to come face-to-face with those who—through no fault of their own—were forced to pick up the shattered pieces of their lives and carry on. Raw grief, shock, and anger were a miserable combination to pick up like a tuning fork. Squaring her shoulders, Doyle knocked on the door.

In response, the door opened a crack, a chain suspended

across the gap. A small woman of perhaps fifty years peered out. "Mrs. Bennet?" Doyle asked. "I'm Detective Sergeant Doyle from the CID—we spoke on the phone." She showed her identification.

"Yes," the woman said, closing the door slightly to release the chain. "Please come in."

Doyle was ushered to the sofa where a tea was laid out—faith, strawberry jam, too. The woman asked if she would partake and Doyle accepted, noting that the woman seemed composed and resigned. Sad, but not bitter or hysterical, which was a blessing. "I am sorry about your daughter," Doyle began gently as she was seated. "Please accept my condolences."

The woman met her eyes. "It's just as well," she said calmly. "Will you take sugar, dear?"

After a startled moment, Doyle accepted—she wasn't much of a tea drinker, but coffee did not seem to be in the offing. "You are not surprised, then?"

The woman handed her the steaming cup. "Oh, I'm surprised all right. But it is just as well; better she's in the ground than another one dead."

Her own grief fresh in her mind, Doyle tried to make sense of it, and came up short. "I'm not certain what you mean, Mrs. Bennet."

The woman looked a little surprised. "You're with the police; you know that she killed those two—and the first one still a boy, really." Shaking her head with resignation, she dipped her little finger in her cup to test the temperature. "There would have been more."

"Your daughter was acquitted the first time," Doyle noted carefully, "—and I'm not aware of any other suspicious deaths."

"Oh." Mrs. Bennet knit her brow. "Her husband died also—killed in a robbery, they said. But I knew she was behind it; that she'd arranged for it. They were not getting on."

"I see." This information was definitely not in the case file, and so Doyle took a stern tone with the woman. "Did you withhold your suspicions from the police?"

"Oh, no," the other woman disclaimed, startled. "But nothing could be proven."

They stared at each other in silence for a moment, the mantel clock ticking in the background. "Tell me about her," said Doyle finally.

Absently, her companion stirred her tea without drinking it. "She had a terrible temper—from her father; he was killed in a football brawl. She was wild. I had a time, trying to rear her up, but—she was wild. And pretty, which meant men would pay attention to her. But then—" She stared into space for a moment, remembering something unpleasant.

"Yes?" prompted Doyle.

"She would follow them, and become jealous for no reason. The fighting and throwing things—it was terrible to see." With a world-weary sigh, the woman grimaced as she remembered. "She would convince herself they were cheating on her, you see."

Know how that feels, thought Doyle. "So you believe she killed them both?"

Mrs. Bennet met her eyes. "Oh, yes," she said simply. "I know; I am her mother."

Doyle sipped her tea and was thoughtful. Apparently there were more hazards to motherhood than the wretched morning sickness; mental note.

"It was the newspapers, the first time," the woman added sadly. "The newspapers made her up to be a victim, and didn't rest until she was acquitted. She loved it, and played it up— had her snap in all the papers."

Yes, thought Doyle, thinking of Acton and his flippin' reporter. The newspapers have a lot to answer for, they do. "Do you have any idea who would have killed her?"

The woman knit her brow. "She'd taken up with a married man—his wife, perhaps?"

"D'you know his name?" Doyle set down the cup and saucer and dutifully wrote down the boyfriend's name, knowing it would be a dead end. A cuckolded spouse would not be inspired to become a vigilante. "Did she have any unusual visitors, d'you know? Or mention who she was to meet when she went to the Heath?"

"She didn't share her doings with me," the woman confessed. "She knew I wouldn't approve."

Someone else didn't approve, thought Doyle. A vigilante, who took the imperfect justice system into his own hands, years later, so that it wouldn't be obvious that this was indeed his motivation. A private wrong that needed to be made right, done by someone who could no longer live with the terrible guilt.

"She was so brassy; thought she couldn't be touched—thought she could get away with anything."

Like Acton, thought Doyle, unbidden. Suddenly she froze, her scalp prickling; there was something here—something just out of reach—

"It was the papers, they could tell any story they wished, whether it was true or not."

Mother a' mercy, thought Doyle, staring at her in horror; that's it—they're framing Acton. That's what Solonik is about, he's framing Acton for these murders.

"What is it, dear?" Mrs. Bennet leaned forward, gently concerned.

"Oh—nothin'," Doyle replied through stiff lips, and forced herself to calm down. That theory was flawed six ways to Sunday; there was no planted evidence—or any evidence at all, come to think of it. There was no indication that Acton was the object of some Solonik-backed frame-up—and it wouldn't be much of a frame-up unless there was some planted evidence. Use your head, lass.

"You look like you've seen a ghost, and I can't blame you—a young thing like you, having this kind of job. More tea, will that help?"

"No, it's all right; I'm the bridge-jumper." Doyle was surprised that she'd admitted such a thing, her scalp prickling yet again. Now, why was *that* important?

"I'm afraid I don't understand—do you need to lie down? You're a little wan, I think."

Doyle smiled. "I only meant that I was in the papers, myself, because I jumped off Greyfriars Bridge to save someone. So I may be small, but I am mighty."

Mrs. Bennet was suitably impressed. "*Did* you, dear? Well, I never." She shook her head in apology. "I'm afraid I don't read the papers anymore—they've caused me no end of trouble."

"It's a two-edged sword," Doyle responded absently, still trying to understand whatever it was she was trying to understand. "Sometimes they cause trouble, but sometimes they're the watchdogs, savin' the day." And I need to find out their role in this little drama, she thought—there's something here; something I'm missing. Perhaps the vigilante is a woman, after all—a nasty brasser with a fine coat. Such a shame if I have to put her in the nick; she would have to pass the time playing cards with Solonik.

"If you say so," her companion agreed with little enthusiasm. "I don't think they much care about the truth, anymore."

Reining in her wayward thoughts, Doyle packed away her occurrence book and rose. "I won't take up any more of your time, Mrs. Bennet, but I will let you know when we find out who killed your daughter."

"Do you think you will?" the woman asked with little enthusiasm, smoothing her skirt.

"We will," Doyle replied, and knew that this was true. "Murder is murder."

"If you say," the other offered doubtfully. "Not everyone thinks so."

"I do." After thanking the woman for the tea, Doyle took her leave. Once outside, she pulled out her mobile, checked in with Acton, closed out the latest message from Williams, and searched for the address of the *London World News*.

CHAPTER 17

*D*OYLE TOOK THE TUBE BACK INTO THE CITY, AND, FOR ONCE, wasn't buffeted by the emotions of the people around her because she was too busy mulling over her next move. Acton would no doubt be very unhappy with her brazen self, but he was currently residing in the doghouse, and therefore had no standing to complain. Besides, she knew he was meeting with the DCS mid-morning on his high-profile case; hopefully he'd be too busy to check her movements through the GPS unit in her mobile. Coward, she scolded herself; you have nothing to be ashamed of, and shouldn't be made to feel as though you are skulkin' about—you need to face this brasser down and find out whether she's murdering people, left and right.

After exiting the tube, she walked two crowded blocks to the offices of the *London World News* and entered through the revolving door. Once inside, she was surprised how familiar it felt, and paused for a moment. It reminded her of the Met in a strange way—the ionized atmosphere of busy people, engrossed in their work. They think what they do is every bit as important as what we do, she realized. It's a counter—counter-something; Acton would know the right word.

After reminding herself not to think about Acton, just now, she approached the reception desk to show her identification and ask if Mr. Maguire was in. The woman directed her down the hallway to his office, and Doyle made her way to the open doorway and stood, waiting to be noticed.

Maguire sat at his desk, a pencil in his mouth as he typed on a laptop, his gaze upon a sheaf of papers beside him. Her interest sharpened; he seemed better put-together than when last they met. He was slimmer, and less rumply—perhaps he had a new source of income, did Mr. Maguire. As he hadn't looked up when she paused in the entry, she ventured, "Mr. Maguire, do you remember me? Detective Sergeant Doyle."

Maguire looked up in surprise, the pencil clenched in his mouth.

"I thought I'd stop by and offer my thanks again—you saved me from myself, if you'll recall."

The pencil dropped into his hand as he smiled broadly. "Well, come in, then." He indicated a chair. "Nice to see you again, Detective."

"I'm here on business, but I thought I'd come in to give my regards. You were very kind not to take advantage of my foolishness."

"Don't tell anyone I've been kind—it will ruin me." He leaned back in his chair. "Rescued anyone lately?"

"No," she admitted. "I'm tryin' to lay off; it's too hard on my husband."

"How is that husband of yours?"

She smiled. "Still very private."

"Touché," he said, and laughed.

With a rueful duck of her head that was very unlike her, she continued, "You'd be surprised how hard the tabloids are diggin' to find information on him; you'd think he was royalty, or somethin'."

"The tabloids?" He was genuinely surprised, which she duly noted. "Which one?"

Doyle named the one identified on the false card given to

Munoz, and he shook his head. "You'd think they had bigger fish to fry."

"Exactly," she agreed. "It's annoyin', is what it is." So; Maguire was not behind the attempts to discover information, which didn't surprise her—he was not the type to go back on his word.

With a gleam, the reporter cocked his head. "If you'd give me an exclusive, it would put an end to it."

"Good one," she replied with a smile. "But not a chance, my friend."

He leaned forward with an intent expression, trying to persuade her. "The public would love the human interest angle; confirmed bachelor, tragic past, he up and marries his pretty young partner, working-class Irish is now a baroness. They solve crimes together, etc., etc." He leaned back in his chair, imagining it. "It's tailor-made for page seven."

Doyle had been given pause by the reference to tragedy. What tragedy? Did Maguire know about Fiona, who had been murdered? Watching him thoughtfully, she shook her head. "You missed your chance—now it's all old news."

"I let you off the hook, is more like it." His chest heaved with an exaggerated sigh. "I must be getting soft."

"And I've thanked God fastin' ever since."

"Don't know as God had anything to do with it," he corrected her with amusement. "You haven't been on the job long enough—someday you'll be as cynical as I am."

Not a believer, she concluded, and was not surprised; he was a bit hardened at the core, was Mr. Maguire. "Well, I do owe you. If there's anythin' I can help you with—other than singin' like a canary—please let me know."

"I'll remember that. What brings you here today?"

"I'm looking for a reporter I met last week, only I've forgotten her name. She was doing a story on the murder in Tilden Park."

Although his manner was casual, she could feel his attention sharpen. "That would be Cassie Masterson. Do you want to speak to her? I think she's in the office."

They looked at each other for a long moment, and Doyle knew that Maguire knew about Masterson and Acton—perhaps everyone did; everyone in greater London. Concentrate, she commanded herself. "Yes; we've hit a stickin' point, I'm afraid, and I thought I'd compare notes with her." She said the words evenly, but knew that her blush betrayed her—no doubt he thought she was here trying to spy on her rival, like a schoolgirl. Faith, what a miserable, *miserable* mess.

Maguire rose to see her out, and she could feel his sympathy, which only made her blush harder as he took her hand. "It was a pleasure to see you again, Detective—you are one of the bravest people I've met, and I've met more than a few."

With this not-so-subtle offer of encouragement echoing in her ears, Doyle proceeded down the hall to Cassie Masterson's office, and found the woman leaning against her desk, talking on her mobile. She looked up as Doyle stood in the doorway and then hastily rang off, radiating extreme satisfaction at Doyle's unexpected appearance. Thinks it's her birthday and Christmas, rolled into one—the brasser, thought Doyle; and considered arresting her just for the sport of it. A shame she hadn't brought along the heavy handcuffs.

"Officer Doyle, good to see you again." They shook hands, and Doyle waited while the woman removed some files that were piled up on a chair. "Sorry about the mess."

"I'm sorry to be interruptin' your work," Doyle replied as she sat down, "but I am followin' up on the Tilden Park murder, and I wondered if you would mind sharin' some information."

"Not at all," Masterson replied with a slow smile, only barely suppressing her glee at this unlooked-for turn of events. "Do you mind if I smoke?"

"No," said Doyle, suddenly miserable. "Not at all." She was forcibly reminded that, although Acton may not have had sex with this woman, the preliminaries had certainly been explored. She thought of Acton's long, gentle fingers and felt a little sick—it was not a good idea to come here; she must be mad. While Masterson lit a cigarette, Doyle pulled herself together with a monumental effort. Courage, she exhorted herself; you can do this, and no one else can hear whether she's telling the truth. Focusing like a laser beam, she began, "I am investigatin' a series of murders which may be connected."

"Serial killer?" Masterson asked with interest as she exhaled. Paradoxically, the press loved a serial killer.

"Perhaps—we've had a series of victims with some similarities."

"Really? What sort of similarities?"

Annoyed that her companion was asking questions as opposed to answering them, Doyle tried to decide what could be disclosed without jeopardizing the cases. "The victims seem to be criminal types."

Masterson drew on the cigarette and eyed her. Thinks I'm an idiot, Doyle deduced.

Tapping her ash, the woman offered, "Wouldn't that be a pretty generalized correlation?"

Mother a' mercy, Doyle thought in dismay; she talks just like Acton.

"Are you hoping to garner some press coverage to help you out?"

Thus prompted, Doyle tried to look guileless, which was not by any means a stretch. "I was hopin' that you'd discovered somethin' about the Tilden Park victim. Do you know anythin' of him?"

Tapping her ash, Masterson bowed her head to hide a smile. "Very little, I'm afraid; I've been distracted by other matters."

Stay focused, Doyle reminded herself, resisting an urge to bristle and hurl insults; you have the upper hand in this, after all. "Did you research the victim at all?"

"Only what I've heard from others."

Doyle stared at her in frustrated disbelief. What was wrong with the *stupid* brasser that she couldn't answer a straight-forward question with a straightforward answer? It was not as though Doyle could ask her outright if she'd killed the flip-pin' victim.

The woman leaned back her head to blow a stream of smoke. "Does Acton have a theory?"

Resenting the implied familiarity, Doyle replied stiffly, "DCI Acton has other priorities, just now."

"Of course he does," the other agreed with a half-smile, and Doyle chided herself for giving her the opening—truly, this interview was not going at all how she'd planned it, al-though to be fair, the plan had involved a fantasy about a nightstick that was probably doomed from the start.

Masterson crossed her arms, the smoke from the cigarette drifting upward as she looked out the window for a moment. "I understand he has a commitment that will take him out of town over the weekend."

Outraged, Doyle immediately concluded that her wretched husband was going to take this wretched brasser to Trestles for some mysterious reason, and fought an urge to dump the ashtray over her head. She reconsidered, however, as it seemed unlikely this was to be a lover's tryst—not with the fearsome dowager in residence. Perhaps Acton meant to murder Mas-terson, which was not beyond the realm of possibility; if this were the case, however, Doyle reluctantly conceded she would have to work to prevent such an occurrence. "Yes; DCI Acton has some pressin' interests at present."

Lowering her gaze, the woman bit her lip and Doyle chided herself yet again. No more openings for double entendres, she vowed; think before you speak, for the *love* o' Mike.

After a moment of silence, Doyle decided she should try a different tack; she'd try to find out whether Masterson had researched the murder victims—or for that matter, if anyone had. "I would like to look at some of the records of older crimes—before everythin' was put online. Do you know who it is I speak to? Is there microfiche, somewhere?" Microfiche was a now-obsolete process to store documents on film.

"I'll be glad to take you to the archives," Masterson offered with every appearance of willingness. She stubbed out her cigarette in the ashtray and rose to lead the way, and Doyle had no other recourse but to follow along in her faintly per-fumed wake.

CHAPTER 18

*D*OYLE AND MASTERSON DESCENDED THE WORN WOODEN steps into the newspaper's archives. Another dungeon, thought Doyle—only this time there's a dragon, to boot. Masterson approached a microfiche machine and indicated Doyle should sit. "Let me show you how it works—should we start with the Tilden Park case?"

Doyle nodded, wracking her brain to think of a way to bring up the next necessary topic of conversation. "Do you sign in to use this?"

"No—since you can't check anything out, there's no need."

Naturally, thought Doyle with resignation; no record of who may have been researching old cases—faith, but I'm getting nowhere. "I'd like to search for the victim's name; he was involved in a prior."

Masterson walked her through the old technology until Doyle was presented with a dim copy of an article from eight years ago. Masterson leaned to look it over. "Foster child, it looks like."

"Arson," said Doyle, who already was familiar with the cold case. "He was fourteen, and suspected of burnin' the house down while his foster parents slept."

"Nasty brute."

Doyle paused, trying to decide if the comment meant any-thing. "It was never proved, the arson; he was young and it was played off as an accident."

"Does Acton ever talk about his own experience?"

"No, he's very private." And Doyle had no idea to what the woman referred; there was that, too. Best find out, mental note; hopefully he hadn't tried to burn down the manor house.

"A very intriguing man."

That's why she's sticking by my side, Doyle realized. She's digging for information—and enjoying the irony of the situ-ation, which is mean-spirited of her. But then again, so am I, on both counts, so I suppose we're even. "He is indeed. His technique is a wonder to behold—he studies patterns and forensics, and the next thing you know he's solved the case."

"You must be very proud of him." There was a subtle under-tone that was recognizable even though Doyle had never heard it before; the condescension the knowing girlfriend feels for the unknowing wife.

Gritting her teeth, Doyle held on to her temper with both hands and continued, "I wish I had his talent. Mainly I search and slog for patterns, and just when I am nearly mad with frustration, the case-breaker walks through the door with the crucial evidence, through no effort of my own."

Masterson smiled indulgently. "Happens that way in this business, too. A lead will fly in out of the blue."

Doyle turned to her, suddenly chatty. "Once I was inter-viewin' a witness—seemed to be a dead end—and toward the end of the interview he casually mentioned he had taken an incriminatin' photo with his mobile. It broke the case; nearly knocked me over."

"Really?" asked Masterson politely. "How extraordinary."

"It was the Solonik arrest. Did you cover the story?"

"No," she replied, knitting her brow. "Was it recently?"

"A few months ago. He was an underworld player."

The other woman offered vaguely, "I think I remember the case—quite a catch for Acton."

"It was," agreed Doyle. "Did you know the history?"

"I'm afraid not; not my beat." Masterson made sure to give Doyle the impression that such cases were ten-a-penny to a seasoned reporter, although a young DS with little experience might think otherwise.

The other woman's mobile rang, and as she read the screen, Doyle felt the leap of excitement. Grand; it must be the illustrious chief inspector, checking in to bill and coo. Her ears on the stretch, Doyle turned back to the microfiche machine and pretended to read whatever the article said.

The reporter spoke in a low voice, sounding very much like a cat at the cream pot. "Yes—I'm all set to go."

Not on my watch, thought Doyle grimly.

But apparently the thought of toying with his poor deluded wife was even more appealing than exchanging sweet nothings with Acton, because she murmured, "Do you mind if I ring you right back?"

Doyle wondered what the general reaction would be if she chimed in from the background and said hallo to him. Best not.

The woman rang off and leaned in to read over Doyle's shoulder, very pleased with herself. "I can see if any of the reporters on the byline remember anything; shall I ring them up?"

Before Doyle could respond, however, she looked up in surprise to see Williams, approaching from the base of the stairway. Faith, she thought crossly; it wants only this.

"Hallo," smiled Masterson, straightening up. "May I help you?"

"I'm here to gather up DS Doyle," he explained, and shot a glance at the aforesaid Doyle that conveyed his conviction that she'd lost her mind. "I'm sorry to interrupt."

"I'm Cassie Masterson." The other woman held out her hand and tilted her head coyly.

Two-timing poor Acton, thought Doyle in outrage. A brasser, through and through.

"Of course; I know of your work," said Williams with his rare, lopsided smile. "Thomas Williams; a pleasure to meet you, Miss Masterson."

She laughed and reluctantly relinquished his hand. "Please— Cassie. Are you in major crimes, also?"

"Don't spread it around, they haven't caught me yet."

Masterson threw back her head and laughed as though he'd said something witty, whilst Doyle shot him a disgusted look from behind the floozy's back.

He turned to Doyle, chiding. "Did you forget our interview?"

"I did," she admitted, mainly because it was mythical. She gathered up her rucksack, wondering what was afoot that Williams felt he had to come and drag her out of here. "I'd best be goin'—thank you so much for all your help, Miss Masterson." She hadn't been invited to call the other woman Cassie—probably because she didn't have an XY chromosome. Not that she'd want to use it, anyway—such a stupid name and fit only for a twelve year old, it was. Poor Acton, having to make up to a woman named Cassie; it was well-beneath his dignity.

After the reporter bestowed upon Williams a last, lingering smile, they parted at the top of the stairs and made their way out of the building. Williams was fulminating about something, but she was annoyed in her own right, and said in a hostile tone, "Don't mind me, go back and chat her up, if you'd like."

But DS Williams was not going to hear it. "What were you *doing*? You're smarter than this."

So, Williams remembered who Masterson was from the photographs—he was a sharp-eyed one, mental note—and must also think she was here trying to case her rival. This was humiliating, and since she couldn't very well tell him she was trying to discover whether the woman was a likely suspect, she took refuge in being put-upon. "This is none of your business, Thomas."

"It's my business if I had to spend the last hour tracking you down—why didn't you answer me?"

They emerged onto the busy street and Doyle retorted, much upon her dignity, "I've been busy detectin'. If it's so important, why didn't you just ring me?"

"Are you *mad*? I can't call about this and take the chance it would be intercepted."

This seemed over-dramatic, and she eyed him sidelong. "What is it we're talkin' about, then?"

With his jaw set in a resolute line, he indicated they should retreat down a quieter side street. "Don't pretend you don't know, Kath."

This remark was alarming, as there were many and sundry secrets she was currently keeping—best be cautious. "Take hold of your wrathful self, Thomas; I can't say that I care for your tone."

But he only glanced over his shoulder, and replied in a terse tone, "And I can't say I care for the company you keep."

This seemed unfair, and she replied with much scorn, "And here I thought you fancied her—although if you take up with a reporter, you'll run the risk of being called up by Professional Standards."

"That's not who I meant, and Professional Standards would be the least of your worries." He glanced down at her, very grim. "I know who he is."

She halted in surprise. "You know who the killer is?"

He stopped also, and took a careful canvass of the immediate area. "No, idiot. Your friend at the bookstore."

This seemed anti-climactic, and somewhat off-topic. "You do? Who is he?"

"You can see my dilemma—Kath, what *on earth* are you thinking?"

Perhaps it wasn't anti-climactic, as Williams was emanating equal parts distress and concern. She stared at him. "Who is he?"

He stared back. "You don't know?"

"No."

He bent his head and ran a distracted hand though his blond hair. "Holy Christ, you will be the death of me."

"Don't blaspheme, and tell me, Thomas; for heaven's sake."

He raised his head. "He's Philippe Savoie."

"*Savoie?*" She thought about it for a perplexed moment, then shook her head. "No, I don't think so, Thomas."

"You can think whatever you want, but it's him. He's on the Interpol List, the Watch List, and any other list you care to name. He's recently come over from Eastern Europe, and the Home Secretary's people are all on end trying to figure out why he is here."

But this was too far-fetched for Doyle, who was aware, as Williams was not, that her rescuer was working for Solonik. One would think Savoie would not stoop to such a thing, being as he was apparently atop the pecking order in the criminal mastermind world. "I don't think so, Thomas; why are you thinkin' so?"

"I lifted his prints off the photographs you had."

She stared at him, astonished. "When?"

"When you were buying an umbrella and I was hailing the cab. The driver had some cellophane tape."

She was all admiration. "*Good* one, DS Williams—I had no idea."

He shrugged his shoulders. "You were distracted."

"You are truly an *excellent* detective—you'll be a DCI in *no* time."

"Can we get back," he said heavily, "to the topic at hand?"

This, of course, was fraught with problems, because she didn't know how much Williams knew of Acton's doings, and she couldn't very well tell him that Solonik was hip-deep in some retribution plot—a retribution plot that apparently involved the notorious Savoie. With all honesty, she confessed, "I'm afraid I can't tell you. But I am certain that Savoie's not a danger to me."

Williams took another careful look around the area, thinking. "How can you know that?"

"We are friends. And he did save my life—truly."

"What if he goes after Acton?"

So; Williams apparently remembered that Savoie had been inclined to kiss her—and truth to tell, there was no reason for any of these arch-criminals to pay the slightest attention to her, save the fact that she was Acton's wife, and therefore his vulnerability. With a start, she suddenly remembered what Savoie had revealed; Owens was his brother, and he was trying to find out what had happened to him. Holy Mother of God, the fair Doyle had killed the dreaded Savoie's baby brother.

"What is it?" Williams was watching her like a hawk.

"Nothin'," she replied, and wished it were true. "Look, Thomas; I can't tell Acton about all this, not yet."

But Williams was firm. "I think you must tell him."

She thought of Acton, and his certain reaction when he learned that she was consorting with the likes of Solonik and Savoie without his knowledge. But I do have his back, she reminded herself; and no one else can do what I can do to help him. "Not yet," she replied, just as firmly. "But I will need your assistance tomorrow, or the day after. No questions asked," she reminded him ruthlessly.

He nodded, and she could sense he was relieved because at least he'd been enlisted to help. He is a good man, she thought with a pang of conscience. "I'm that sorry I'm such a crackin' trial, Thomas."

"Don't take any chances, is all."

She had to smile. "Have you forgotten who it is you're speakin' to, DS Williams?"

CHAPTER 19

ON THE WAY BACK TO THE MET, DOYLE TOOK A CALL FROM
Munoz. "Samuels is dying for bangers and mash and wants to
go to the pub on the corner."

"Done," said Doyle. She was ready to eat something fortify-
ing, after her many trials this fine day. "Williams will come, too."

"Come where?" Williams asked as she rang off. "I can't
spare any more time today."

"All work and no play," Doyle chided him. "I owe you lunch
and *please* offer Munoz a homicide project; she is drivin' me
and Habib crazy."

"She needs a new boyfriend."

"Not you," Doyle cautioned.

He made a grimace of distaste. "Christ, Kath, do you think
so little of me?"

"You mustn't blaspheme," she reminded him. "I think you
are pickin' up bad habits from Acton."

"You are full of strictures, aren't you?" he offered mildly as
they descended the stairs to the tube.

There was a slight pause. "I'm afraid I don't know what that
means."

"It means you certainly like to tell me what I can and cannot do."

Stricken, she looked back at him as she passed through the

turnstile. "Faith, Thomas; I do beg your pardon. I don't have the orderin' of you, and I shouldn't behave as though I do. I'm that sorry that I'm soundin' like an archwife."

"Just so we're clear."

They waited on the platform, Doyle filled with remorse because it was true; she took gross advantage of Williams due to the fact he had a soft spot for her. She should be a better friend, else he'd not come to her rescue as he did with alarming regularity. To this end, she thought she should show an interest in his personal life, as a good friend would. "Are you seein' anyone, yourself?"

Although his expression didn't change, he was suddenly amused—saw right through her, he did. "I'm thinking about Cassie; she seems ready for a go, and I wouldn't have to spend a lot of money on dinners to get there."

She turned to look toward the coming train. "You are *horrid*, is what you are."

"I'd be helping you out."

This was the first he'd hinted at what the photographs depicted, and she hesitated, wondering whether she should discuss it at all with him—he was too shrewd by half, was DS Williams. "More like you'd get busted back to DC again."

Despite her attempt at lightness, he must have heard something in her voice because he put a hand around her shoulder, squeezing her to him briefly. "Sorry. I shouldn't have said."

His sympathy was almost her undoing, and she struggled with her emotions as they boarded the train. It would only be to his benefit, one would think, if Acton were indeed cheating on her, since Williams would presumably be the leading candidate to fill the vacancy as husband number two. Instead, he was solidly in her corner, despite the fact that her latest brush with retribution-minded kingpins may wind up costing him his job. The train was crowded, as it was lunch hour, and she looked up at him as they swayed, hanging on to a pole.

"The whole thing is not at all what you think, Thomas. I'd like to tell you more, but I don't think I can."

He nodded, unsurprised—they had already discussed the fact that divided loyalties may work to prevent complete honesty between them—he was loyal to Acton, too. "I'm a little worried that you are in over your head."

This was indisputably true, as Williams was aware that Savoie—of all people—had handed her the wretched photographs. "I have a handle on it, I promise. And if I need backup, I'll call you in two shakes, my hand on my heart."

"Excuse me," said a woman in a tweed coat, standing beside them in the aisleway. "Aren't you the police officer from the papers—the one who jumped off the bridge?"

"I am," Doyle confessed, pinning on her smile and cursing her hair color. "I am pleased to meet you."

"Officer Doyle," a businessman affirmed, sticking his newspaper under his arm to awkwardly shake her hand in the crowded space. "I thought it was you. Well done."

"It was nothin'," Doyle protested, blushing. "Truly."

"Makes ya think t'police ain't all rotten," a dubious man in a knit cap chimed in. "Restores yer faith. Mind effen I takes a snap wi' me mobile?" He then muscled his way over to lean in with Doyle, raising his mobile to take a photograph of them. A palpable ripple of interest flowed through the train car.

"Our stop," announced Williams, even though it wasn't, and he extricated them out the door and out onto the platform, Doyle bidding good-bye to her well-wishers, who exuded copious amounts of good will and a strange sort of shared pride.

They walked quickly in silence for a few minutes, navigating their way up the escalators and onto the street. "Thanks," she finally said.

"It didn't seem like you were enjoying yourself."

"No—I hate the attention. And it's hardly fair, Thomas; you were a rescuer as much as I was."

"Not true—you deserve every ounce of it."

"It's the papers," she conceded with sad resignation. "They've made me the bridge-jumper, and so I ever shall be; amen." Her scalp prickled, suddenly. What? she asked herself, exasperated. Why is that so important, for the love o' Mike? Again, it eluded her and she was left with a faint feeling of frustration—it happened this way, sometimes, and it made her feel that her perceptive ability was standing beside her, tapping its foot with impatience.

Her thoughts were interrupted by her companion, who remained unsettled even though his outward appearance was benign. "Do you have an end goal?" They were taught at the Academy that there should always be an end goal—one way or another, so that the public's money would not be wasted on a detective's whims.

"I do." Best not mention the end goal was to save Acton from having to share a cell with Solonik—Williams needn't be in on that little secret. Besides, while she was aware that Williams acted as Acton's henchman in the occasional administration of rough justice, she didn't know if he knew of Acton's gun smuggling, which was a whole other kettle of blackmail-worthy fish. Mother a' mercy, it was hard to keep track.

As if on cue, her mobile pinged. It was Acton. "Lunch?"

She smiled a bit grimly, aware—in the way she was aware of things—that he knew she'd been speaking to Masterson. She decided to let him stew. "Sorry, lunching with W and M." She paused, then decided to add, "Will drop by after." Sometimes when Acton stewed, things got rapidly out of hand—best be careful.

"I wish you would think again about consulting with him about this."

Teasing, she glanced up at Williams as she sheathed her mobile. "What makes you think that was Acton? Maybe it was Savoie."

"Was it?"

She shook her head. "I wouldn't tell you—you'd lift his mobile number with cellophane tape while I wasn't lookin', or somethin'."

But Williams, having determined that dark forces were at play, was in no mood. "Not a laughing matter, Kath."

And that's why I'm married to Acton, she thought as they strode along in silence. Acton always thinks I'm funny. Well—maybe not always; but most times.

They came to the pub—one of the posh kind that was mainly pretending to be the real thing—and once through the door, she was met with the welcome and ubiquitous scent of bacon and ale. Munoz and Samuels had secured a booth in the corner and waved them over. "You've been busy this morning," said Samuels, moving over for her.

"I've been visitin' like a county nurse, I have. What are you havin'?"

"We've already ordered; you're having bangers and mash whether you like it or not."

She noted that Samuels's gaze drifted between herself and Williams with a gleam of speculation that she did not appreciate, but there was no point in getting nettled; she was well-used to being the object of gossip, after all. "Like it," she replied easily. "What's news?"

Samuels shrugged in his negligent manner. "Still hunting contraband. We had a tip, and made a raid on a suspected cache, but they must have been warned because it was cleared out by the time we got there."

"Bad luck," said Munoz, who was well-pleased to be situated cheek-by-jowl between the two men. "The trouble with tips is the informants; they take whatever the police will give them, and then happily grass to the suspects that the police are on their tail—a double recovery."

But Doyle was doubtful. "I wouldn't want to be playin' a double game with the smugglers. Too easy to wind up floatin' amongst the reeds at the bottom of the river."

"We had one two days ago—a dead informant," Williams offered. "Now we have to start all over, cultivating someone else."

"He was in the river?" Munoz knew all there was to know about being fished out of the Thames.

"His head was."

While Munoz took this opportunity to express her feminine horror at such a grisly turn of events, Doyle wondered at the nuances she sensed. Yet again, Williams appeared unruffled, but inwardly he was unsettled about something; wary, and grave—or graver than his usual. She wondered what the newly-dead informant had been informing about; she should follow up with Acton, mental note.

Samuels changed the subject. "Acton has been butting heads with the deputy commissioner about the contraband protocol. Have you heard who prevailed?" This was directed at Doyle.

Doyle said honestly, "Haven't a clue what you are talkin' about, Samuels." She reflected that this was the second time in a few days that Samuels was fishing for information about Acton, and, in light of certain recent events, decided this was yet another mental note, as she couldn't very well start jotting reminders on a napkin. Faith, she thought crossly; I only wanted some flippin' lunch, not another stack of flippin' problems.

The harried waitress served the plates out, and as Doyle reached to assist, Munoz observed, "Will you look at the bruise on your arm, Doyle? How did you manage that?"

"Acton beats me," she replied easily, and they all laughed except Williams. "It's fadin', now. You should have seen it at first—as black as the third horseman."

"I imagine you bruise easily," offered Williams.

"My curse," agreed Doyle. "And I sunburn like you wouldn't believe."

"Then it's just as well you don't swim," said Samuels, and they all laughed again. He continued, "Speaking of such, how is your wound, Munoz? I wish I had a knife wound; it would make me more interesting to the ladies."

"I'll show you." Munoz was nothing loath as she shifted in the narrow booth to pull at the back of her sweater. "Can you see it?"

Samuels willingly helped pull the sweater down to expose the wound, although Doyle imagined that Munoz was hoping Williams would do the honors. The others duly admired the small red scar, not yet faded.

"Impressive," said Williams. "They should give you the George."

"I don't know," Doyle teased. "I admit I'm a bit disappointed—it looks more like a chicken pox scar."

"Not at all," chided Samuels, running a finger across it. "Don't listen to her, Munoz; it makes you look piratical, and dangerous."

"Sometimes it itches." Munoz confessed as she shrugged her sweater back in place.

"Have you told your beau the tale?" Doyle knew Munoz would appreciate any reference to her admirer, as Williams hadn't chosen to pursue that role.

"He has not yet seen my scar; I'm not certain he deserves to."

This remark was followed by some good-natured raillery from the men about the injustice of women who played hard-to-get, and Munoz was very much in her element.

"I'll warn you; he'll look for a girl who's not so coy." Samuels grinned at her. "Can't hold out forever, or you'll lose him."

"He'll wait, and be grateful for the opportunity."

Doyle was thoughtful, remembering her interview with Mrs. Bennet. "Has a man ever cheated on you, Munoz?"

"Is Acton cheating on you? Wait; let me go put on some lipstick."

The men found this sally exceedingly humorous, although Doyle could not quite appreciate it as she would have a week ago. Merciful God, she offered up; don't let any rumor of

Acton and Cassie Masterson reach Munoz's ears, I am *begging* you. "No, idiot; I had an interview this mornin' about a girl who bludgeoned her boyfriend to death because she thought he cheated on her."

But Munoz was unimpressed. "I can't imagine any man is worth bludgeoning to death; too much effort."

"That's the spirit," Williams smiled. "After all, you'd get blood spatter on your shoes."

"I'd know enough to wear my wellies," Munoz chided him with a look. "But it would still be too much effort. Poison is much tidier."

"Yes—it's such a strange and brutal reaction, no matter how upset you are." Even in those first terrible moments in the bookstore, Doyle had never contemplated violence against Acton.

"It's not about love," Munoz explained patiently, a forkful of mashed potatoes poised. "It's about control. The person is nicked—obsessive, and can't stand the thought of losing control. When they kill the other, they regain control again."

Doyle decided she'd rather not delve into a discussion about persons who were nicked and obsessive, and hurriedly turned the subject toward local sporting events, which was a tedious topic, but did not hit quite so close to home.

CHAPTER 20

AFTER AN HOUR, WILLIAMS REMINDED THEM THAT HE HAD TO get back to work, and Samuels bowed his head in mock-obedience. "Yes, sir; by the way, when's the announcement to be made?"

"What announcement?" asked Munoz, like a hound to the point.

With a gesture of his head toward Williams, Samuels continued, "Youngest DI since Wensley. And well-deserved." He lifted his glass in a mock-salute.

"Congratulations, Williams—you deserve it." Doyle was aware that Williams was not best-pleased by this rather heavy-handed revelation, not to mention it was a crackin' shame that the news was dropped on Munoz unawares. For a moment, Doyle considered taking cover under the table.

Munoz, however, was not so foolish as to allow her chagrin to get the better of this opportunity to sweeten up Williams, and offered polite and seemingly heartfelt congratulations. I should watch and learn, thought Doyle; I let my temper get the better of me time after time—it's the hair, it has a lot to answer for, it does. Although Acton can't keep his hands from it, so there's that.

Samuels inquired of Williams, "Will they move you to an office?" This was a continual point of much jealousy and complaint, and although the question was asked in a mild tone, it was a potential mine-field.

Rather than answer, Williams said to Munoz, "I'm working on the Wexton Prison corruption case, and I think a female detective might help break the code of silence, considering the type of men involved. Do you suppose Habib could spare you for a morning or two?"

Munoz's dark brows drew together, not fooled by this proffered olive branch. "Are you trying to buy me off?"

Williams flashed his rare smile. "Yes."

"Buy *me* off, instead," suggested Samuels with a smile. "Corruption is right up my alley."

But Williams only shook his head. "Sorry—you don't look like her."

Naturally, it was this comment that won Munoz's grudging acceptance, and Doyle was all admiration—beneath that buttoned-up façade, Williams was very adept at subtle manipulation, another talent she lacked. Doyle had forgotten her wallet, so instead of paying for his lunch as promised, he wound up paying for hers. "Sorry," she said in an aside as they rose to leave. "I owe you on all fronts."

"No one owes anyone for anything." He met her eyes briefly and she was reminded that DI Williams carried a torch for her, and she'd best keep it to mind so that she didn't encourage any foolishness—not that she'd do it purposefully, it was only that sometimes she forgot how complicated this relationship business was. She hadn't much training or experience in it because before she met Acton, she'd neatly avoided everyone.

As though she'd summoned him by the very thought, Acton himself met her at the door as they were leaving. "Detectives," he greeted them brusquely, and the others hastily and deferentially took their leave. Having routed them, he stood before her on the sidewalk for a silent moment, his enigmatic gaze resting on hers. "I thought I'd buy you a cup of coffee."

"I'd rather have a cup of cap-in-hand, husband."

"Then you shall have it, but first you'll have to explain to me what it is." He tucked her hand in his arm and began to lead her away, toward the Abbey.

"I'll give you a hint; if you are takin' her to Trestles to have sex with her, I am goin' to tear down the flippin' building, stone by stone."

"No," he disclaimed immediately. "I am taking her there to allow her to examine the archives."

Suspicious, she knit her brow and eyed him sidelong. "Is that a euphemism?"

She caught a flash of amusement. "No."

"Well, then; I'm that relieved. But you are goin' to fill me in on the whole, or I'll know the reason why."

He squeezed her hand against his side with his arm. "Shall we buy some coffee and walk along the embankment?"

This was a bit alarming and an indication of his concern—Acton was not much of a stroller-about. Or it may be an indication that he was taking no chance at being overheard. "Please—although if anyone recognizes me, glare them away, as you did Munoz and Samuels."

They bought coffee from the corner franchise, and walked toward the broad pathway beside the Thames, the breeze blowing steadily now that they were on the river. He seemed disinclined to start his confession—probably because he wasn't certain how much she knew. Not the type to share his innermost thoughts with the wife of his bosom, was Acton. With this in mind, she decided it was probably best to fire off a warning round. "She's workin' with Solonik, isn't she?"

The question surprised him, and he responded with extreme caution. "Why do you think this?"

Impatient, she hunched her shoulders against the cool air.

"I figured it was somethin' like that, so I asked her some questions about the Solonik arrest. She lied and said she didn't know anythin' about it—or him." She glanced up at his profile and gently shook his arm. "And it doesn't take much of a leap, Michael; *someone* is tryin' to do you over, and he's the prime suspect."

"I would not be surprised," he admitted.

"What does she know?" This was a dicey question, as Acton did not know how much Doyle knew—or guessed—about his own underworld connections.

"I am not certain."

Although this was an equivocal answer, it nonetheless was true, which made sense to her; Solonik must only know bits and pieces; otherwise, there'd be no need to apply pressure to the fair Doyle, hoping she'd grass up information. We shall see, Mr. Solonik, she thought grimly; I've a few arrows in my own quiver, I do.

They were quiet for a few minutes as they walked past the Westminster Pier, where small groups of tourists waited for the next ferry. When they were clear again, he asked, "What else did you discuss with her?"

"The Tilden Park murder—I was lookin' through the microfiche, hopin' there'd be a record of who was looking at the old news coverage of the arson case, but no luck. Miss Masterson was kind enough to assist me." She glanced up at him, quirking her mouth. "She *is* attractive, Michael—at least you have good taste."

"Don't," he said abruptly. "I would much rather just kill her."

This was true, and Doyle was not at all surprised—Acton being who he was. "All my moralizin' is having an impact, then?" Talk about mixed emotions.

But he avoided a direct answer and instead explained, "It would pose no solution because another would be sent to take her place. Instead, the solution must thwart any such further attempts."

Considering who they were dealing with—and Acton's own dark doings—this seemed a tall order. "And have you such a plan? It must be a corker."

He raised his head to survey the area, as was his habit. "I do. I doubt that I can win a bidding war, so I will offer something no one else can."

The penny dropped, and Doyle turned to stare at him. "She's thinkin' she'll be the next Lady Acton."

He nodded, as though the topic were nothing unusual. "Yes. I haven't broached the subject in so many words, but the idea has been planted."

She knit her brow, much struck. "You are like Timothy's Nanda, then—offerin' up the only commodity you have available."

He glanced at her in amusement. "Not quite; here we're talking about the title—and all that goes with it."

"You're a handsome thing, Michael," she assured him. "Don't sell yourself short." She walked along and considered what she'd learned in the silence it deserved. It wasn't a bad plan; Masterson might be willing to spike whatever plot Solonik was hatching in exchange for the heady possibility she could succeed Doyle as the next baroness, and therefore the keeper of the secrets of the House of Acton. It would be tempting to any woman—small wonder she treated Doyle with such poorly-concealed triumph. "And you're takin' her to Trestles to dangle the bait."

He was amused again. "So to speak, I suppose."

"I think I should come along, Michael."

It was his turn to be surprised. "You have nothing to fear, Kathleen, I promise. I plan to hold her at arm's length, and tell her that I must be very circumspect; I cannot allow a scandal just now, if divorce is on the horizon."

"I'm not worried about that, Michael." This was not exactly true; if their future hinged upon it, she imagined Acton would make whatever sacrifices necessary—and men were men, after all. "It's just that I think it would appeal to her if I was there—the competitive aspect of it. She very much enjoyed toyin' with me today, and would positively relish more of the same." Fumbling for words, she tried to explain what she knew instinctively. "She loves the intrigue—the secretiveness—of knowin' something no one else does." Thinking about it, she raised her gaze to his. "I imagine you've already twigged that about her, which is why she's ripe for your counter-plot. She'll love the thought that she's goin' to carry off the palm, with me all unknowin'."

Gazing into the distance, he thought about this. "You may be right."

"I am right, my friend. And it will have the added bonus of giving you a ready excuse to be keepin' your unfaithful self chaste. Tell her that I found out about the trip, and I've invited myself along; be regretful, and ask if she'd like to reschedule—I bet she'll be cock a' hoop about it, instead."

"All right," he agreed. "But only as long as it's clear she's cock a' hoop."

"She'll be merry as a grig," Doyle assured him. "Mark me."

They paused to stand at the railing for a moment, looking out across the brown and churning river. Reminded, Doyle asked, "Whose head was fished out of the river?"

"I beg your pardon?"

"Williams said an informant's head was pulled from the river, and that now you'll have to cultivate a new one."

"Did he indeed?"

She eyed him, surprised. "A fish tale, was it? What—to frighten Munoz? Good luck to him, if that's the object." Reminded of something else, she asked, "Is he to be promoted? Williams, I mean; Samuels said as much." Thus prompted, she turned to him intently and continued, "Samuels—I keep meanin' to tell you that Samuels is fishin' about for information." Staring at her husband, her scalp prickled and she made the intuitive leap. "Samuels is some sort of informant for the wrong side, isn't he? Williams was givin' him a warnin', speakin' of heads in the river."

"Good God," said Acton mildly.

"It's exhaustin', sometimes," Doyle admitted, thinking over this new wrinkle. "What is goin' to happen to Samuels?"

"That is not your concern, I'm afraid."

She looked to the river again, trying to piece it all together. "Do you want me to ask Samuels about Solonik, like I did Masterson?"

"I'd rather you didn't. I'm afraid I'm not at liberty to say anything more."

"All right," she replied a bit crossly. "But I'm catchin' on like a house afire, here."

"It is impressive," he acknowledged. "But I still cannot say."

Teasing, she added, "I twigged you and this Masterson brasser in a pig's whisper, if you will recall. It's exactly what you deserve, for strayin' off the straight-and-narrow."

"How did you manage it?" he asked in the same mild tone.

"Nice try, Michael."

He accepted defeat with good grace, and bent his head to hers. "With that in mind, I'll have to meet her for a drink after work." He pulled out his mobile and scrolled. "To implement the cock a' hoop protocol."

Laughing, she leaned her head fondly against him. "Well then; have a nice date, but keep the present baroness to mind, if you please."

"I'll be home by dinner," he assured her with his half-smile.

CHAPTER 21

*I*T WASN'T UNTIL DOYLE WAS AT HOME, SETTLED IN BEFORE HER laptop and entering notes on her spreadsheet, that it occurred to her that Acton hadn't revealed his supposed solution to the Masterson problem. Outfoxed me again, she thought in chagrin; he lets me gabble on until I get distracted—which happens more often than not—and then he holds his cards very close to the vest. She leaned back in her chair, gazing out the windows and thinking about it with her fingers laced behind her head. He was trying to make Masterson turn coat by pretending they could have a future together, but—presumably—at some point she would realize that Acton was not about to divorce his misfit of a wife. Then what? Acton said he needed a solution that would ensure another wouldn't be sent in Masterson's place, but there was also the tricky business of Masterson herself; if she had the goods on Acton, and then felt she'd been spurned or duped, presumably she'd be all too happy to help Solonik bring Acton down. It was hard to imagine how her husband expected to carry the day—not without following through and marrying the stupid brasser. Perhaps he could do it quietly, and then lock her in the attic at Trestles, like the brooding hero in that book about the governess. She frowned at nothing in particular, thinking this over. Wouldn't work as a long-term solution, she decided with regret.

Her unhappy thoughts were interrupted when Acton texted her with his symbol. This was much appreciated—she'd been trying not to imagine where they were or what was going on. He is working, she told herself firmly, brushing a wistful thumb across the mobile screen; and he has a plan, even though he doesn't want to share the particulars with you—remember that whole tendency to gabble.

The pretext for the visit to Trestles was to allow Masterson to view the archives, which sounded very dull and stuffy, but provided an excellent excuse to invite a journalist to stay for a few days and at the same time, drive home the point that the storied history could be hers, along with the handsome man who held the title. Doyle had no doubt that Acton planned to spend long hours closeted with Masterson, and wondered what his mother would think of such a thing—the dowager despised Doyle, but a journalist would be just as unwelcome, one would think. All in all, the weekend was shaping up to be a rare crack, and Doyle was rather surprised that she was so willing to participate in this miserable morality play. However, she knew, in the way that she knew things, that it was important that she attend, for some reason, and so attend she would.

With a mental sigh, she returned to her spreadsheet on the park murders, organizing her notes from Mrs. Bennet's visit and the microfiche at the *World News*. She'd tentatively eliminated Masterson as the murderer—although for a journalist, she certainly couldn't seem to answer a direct question with a direct answer—and so she went back to Williams's guilt theory, which seemed more and more valid, based on what she'd learned about Mrs. Bennet's daughter and the Tilden Park victim. Both were let off from earlier murders with the aid of public opinion, and both had gone on to murder again. It made sense that someone felt responsible, and wanted to right all past wrongs. It was odd that the vigilante had waited so long in both instances, but perhaps he was biding his time so as to obscure the commonalities between the murders. And Acton thought there might have been a recent triggering event, but it seemed a very tall order, to try to determine what it could have been.

She looked up the defense team personnel who had worked these two cases originally, and found a small but encouraging lead; they had been handled by the same barristers' chambers at the Inns of Court, although different barristers were involved in each trial. This was not much of a coincidence, actually; there were only four Inns of Court, and therefore a limited number of barristers who appeared in the Crown Court. But the solicitors for each case—the attorneys who handled all but the court appearances—were completely different, and so any glimpse of a commonality was welcome. Doyle decided she would pay a visit to the chambers and debated when to do so; she hadn't yet heard from Savoie about her proposed visit to Solonik, and that should take priority over everything else. There was no time like the present, though, and she could always cancel if the need arose. She texted Williams: "RU there?"

As always, he answered promptly. "Hey."

"Can U go on a lead in AM? Talk to barrister at Inns of C."

"OK. What M I 2 do?"

She realized he thought this was the favor she needed with no questions asked, and so explained, "I will go 2. Need to check out defense on cold cases."

"OK. Pick U up?"

"Please. How's 9?"

"Field kit?"

"No need."

There was a pause. "French translator?"

Ah—he was wondering if this had to do with Savoie, and she gazed at the screen, feeling a pang of guilt. Mainly, she seemed to excel at making the men folk fret. "No need."

"C U then."

"Thanks."

She rang off, and noted it was still early, although it seemed later to her. Come home, Acton, she pleaded mentally. I'll start thinking about what you're doing, else. As she stared at it, her mobile pinged, surprising her so that she nearly dropped it. The ID said "unknown," and so she stifled her disappointment and answered, "Doyle."

"Tomorrow," said Savoie in his brusque manner. "One hour, from one to two."

This was workable, but it also meant that tomorrow she was going to be as busy as a fishwife at Lent. "Right, then. What time do we leave?"

"Twelve." He then named an intersection a few blocks from the Met in a quieter area. She pictured it and asked, "Northbound or southbound?"

"Northbound," he said, and rang off.

She rang off also, and stared out the window at the view again, thinking. She would create a protocol and stick to it; Acton would have no cause to accuse her of being reckless. Her conscience stirred, but she firmly quashed it down; she needed to do this and no one else could—once she had her answers, she could always tell Acton. In the meantime, she'd best prepare.

A half-hour later, she heard Acton's card in the slot and looked up with relief as he came in through the door. "Hallo, husband; how was your date?"

He came over to run a distracted hand over her head. "Reynolds has left?"

"There's somethin' in the oven, if you're hungry. Are you needin' a shower, first?"

He gave her a look as he headed over to the fridge. "Now, there's gallows humor."

"Don't give me any ideas, my friend. How did it go?"

He paused with the door open, in the process of drinking orange juice straight from the bottle. "You were right."

She offered with all modesty, "I know my brassers, I do."

He paused, swirling the juice in the bottle for a moment before lifting it to drink again. "You and I will leave Friday morning, and she'll be there by the afternoon."

"Can't wait. Did you work up a thirst, chattin' her up?" She was trying to gauge him, but he was buttoned-up, was Acton, and giving her no glimpses.

He grimaced. "I was compelled to drink some rum concoction."

"Oh—oh, Michael." She couldn't help laughing. "How *dare* someone force you to drink rum—quick, where's the trusty scotch?"

"God, no—I can't mix the two." He closed the fridge, and briefly opened the oven door to look inside.

"Did the rum concoction have a paper umbrella?" Abruptly, she turned back to her laptop. "No—no, don't tell me; I don't think I could ever look upon you in the same light."

There was a long pause. "You are extraordinary. I am so sorry, Kathleen."

She looked up at him, standing quietly in the kitchen—he probably didn't want her to catch the scent of cigarette smoke, which was a forlorn hope—and took pity on him. "I am jokin' so I won't start throwin' things, is all. Bring your rum-soaked self over here, and we will speak of somethin' else."

"How does your research go?" She could feel his relief as he came to stand behind her, leaning in to review her screen.

"Williams is takin' me to one of the Inns tomorrow—one of the chambers was involved in two of the original non-convictions, so I thought I'd flash my warrant card and rattle the cage a bit."

"Doubtful they will rattle," he remarked, reading her notes. "They have an excellent reputation."

"There's no attorney-client privilege, anymore, since the client is dead," Doyle insisted. "Mainly I just want to get them talkin'." Acton would know why this was, and he leaned in with his hands on the table on either side of her, reading thoughtfully. Doyle caught the faint scent of the brasser's perfume and resisted an urge to pull him over to the sink by his tie and thoroughly douse his head under the spigot.

He remained doubtful, and straightened up. "They won't want to speak of the old case, you know—even if they were not involved in these killings. The fact that a killer got off doesn't make them look good."

"I think there's somethin' there," she persevered, her brow knit. "It's one of those feelin's."

"Then by all means."

She leaned her head back so as to look up at him. "How goes your case-that-must-not-be-spoken-of?"

"I believe the people who have given me the assignment may not wish me to succeed."

As was his usual, he delivered this rather shocking assessment in a matter-of-fact tone, and she turned in the chair to face him, thoroughly alarmed. She was aware that "the people" who had given him this assignment were high up in the government. "Then what's the purpose, for heaven's sake? Why send you on a sleeveless errand?"

But he continued buttoned-up, and would not elaborate. "It may be an attempt to contain a scandal. I'm afraid I can say no more."

"Do you need me to listen to someone?"

He crossed his arms, and she had the impression that he'd already considered this idea. "It is a delicate political situation. It would be helpful to have you listen in, but I am not certain how I can bring it about."

"I could be disguised as a maid," she suggested. "I could wear one of those very short skirts, and have a feather duster."

With a smile, he leaned to kiss her brow. "I would pay good money."

She pulled on his tie, hand over hand, and brought his mouth to hers. "Come to the shower and I'll give you an eyeful, then."

"Done," he said, and gathered her up.

CHAPTER 22

*T*HE NEXT MORNING DOYLE OVERSLEPT. ACTON'S CONTRITION tour had included several extremely satisfying lovemaking sessions, along with a visit to the kitchen after midnight to fetch some ice cream for sustenance. After a groggy look at the time, she reached for her mobile and texted Williams. "B there in a few."

Acton was preparing to leave and speaking to his assistant on his mobile as he packed up. Teasing, she sat up and dropped the covers to flash him, which inspired a smile and a warning glance toward the kitchen, where Reynolds presumably lurked. He rang off, and came over to rest his hands on the bed to kiss her. "We'll pack for Trestles tonight—it will be chilly."

"Of course it will. Are there gargoyles?"

There was a pause. "It is quite a nice place, actually."

Her wretched, wretched tongue. "I'm sorry, Michael—I truly look forward to seein' it."

But he met her eyes in understanding as he straightened up. "We'll make the best of it; I do have some fond memories."

This was true, and made her smile, to think of him wandering around his ancestral estate, doing whatever it was the aristocracy did—pheasant hunts, or some such. "I'll manage, never fear."

He leaned to kiss her on the top of her tousled head with a great deal of feeling. "There's my girl; call me if you find anything of interest."

Fondly, she watched him go, and wondered if Masterson was busily packing as they spoke—packing and gleefully calculating Acton's net worth; Doyle herself had no idea.

She dressed, and thanked Reynolds when he handed her a coffee in the kitchen. "Wish me luck, Reynolds; we travel to Trestles tomorrow."

The servant stilled. "Is that so, madam?"

Faith, she'd blundered again, but she'd best break the bad news. "I don't think you're to come—not this time." Definitely not; the fewer witnesses to this little psychodrama, the better.

But the servant had already regained his composure and said evenly, "No, no—certainly not; the staff might be put out."

Doyle hadn't considered this aspect, and it was her turn to be still. "Saints, Reynolds; do you suppose there are 'staff'?" Perhaps her hope for few witnesses was a forlorn one.

Diffidently, Reynolds wiped the counter with a tail of the kitchen towel. "Oh yes—an estate that size would have a full regimen. It is said to be very well-run."

His desire to take a gander at the storied pile was almost palpable, and so she cautioned, "I can't imagine how they manage to keep anyone; his mother is a crackin' harridan."

"Has the dowager Lady Acton visited here?" He seemed surprised and small blame to him; the woman's name was never mentioned within these less-storied walls.

Doyle quirked her mouth. "You'd be horrified, Reynolds. I fought with her tooth and nail like the low-country guttersnipe I am."

"I will be at hand, next time," he assured her. "I know just how to handle such a lady."

"You are a prize, Reynolds." As she packed up her electronics, she was cautiously optimistic that there would, in fact, be a next time, and that she would still hold sway here after the coming weekend. Last night it certainly seemed that Acton still considered Doyle the best of all potential baronesses, and hopefully she'd come out of today's prison visit with a whole skin.

Her mobile pinged; it was Williams, and so she hurriedly bade Reynolds good-bye and made her way downstairs, where Williams was waiting at the curb. As the doorman shut the door behind her, she explained, "Sorry—I overslept." Best not attempt a euphemism with Williams, he was sensitive on the subject of sex and she'd learned that lesson the hard way. So with no smart remarks of any stripe, she gave him the address and explained her reasons for wanting to visit.

Williams, however, expressed the same skepticism as Acton had. "Unlikely they'll be impressed by the warrant card, Kath. And they'll not be interested in speaking of their failures."

"Their successes, you mean; they got them off, after all."

But he shook his head as they wound their way through the traffic. "I can't imagine a barrister takes any pleasure in getting someone off who goes on to kill again."

"That's why I couldn't do it—defend someone I know is guilty."

"No—me neither, but that's who we are and what we do. Their point of view is that no one really knows for certain about guilt, and they work to keep the system honest."

Diplomatically, Doyle made no response, as she was uniquely situated to know a defendant's guilt for certain, and Williams had already demonstrated that he was willing to skirt the supposedly honest system. In fact, that was why a justice system that was generally perceived as too lenient was dangerous; vigilantes tended to spring up, and no matter how imperfect the system, it was miles better than allowing everyone to dispense their own brand of Wild West justice. Much struck, it suddenly occurred to her that—because of her abilities—she was the perfect vigilante; she could have no qualms about dispatching a killer who had escaped justice, because she'd know for certain that he had, in fact, escaped justice. But she would never do such a thing because of her faith; she believed in an ultimate justice, and—as she repeatedly cautioned Acton—you can't just go about killing people. Aside from its being a mortal sin, it showed that, in the end, you didn't trust God to sort it all out. Perhaps the freed killer was slated to perform some unknown task that was important in the grand scheme of things; it was best not to take the chance you were muckin' it all up. Hard on the heels of this thought, her scalp tingled. Frowning, she tried to catch hold of the elusive thread—what was it? Thinking aloud, she said, "He—or she—feels utterly wretched and hates it, but believes there would be no justice, otherwise."

Williams glanced at her. "What was that?"

Thoughtfully gazing out her window, she explained, "I was thinkin' about this vigilante's motivation."

Williams shrugged. "I doubt he hates it, Kath. He wouldn't do it if he hated it; no doubt it assuages his guilt."

She guessed at what "assuages" meant, and disagreed in a thoughtful tone. "I think he does hate it." No doubt Williams had felt nothing but satisfaction when he dispatched his uncle, or when he helped Acton usher other villains from this mortal coil; unlikely he could relate to this particular killer. "I think he's miserable. Or she—it may be a woman, if she's so repulsed by it all." Her scalped tingled again, and she knew she was on the right track. Or perhaps not; her intuition acted like a bucket boy to the fire bell whenever she thought about how she was forever to be known as the bridge-jumper, but why this was important completely escaped her. It all made little sense.

Williams, apparently, had avoided the more pressing topic as long as he was able, and asked in an even tone, "Have you discussed the French problem with Acton?"

"No," she teased, "Have you?"

He replied a bit grimly, "Not as yet; I don't fancy having my skin flayed off."

She shouldn't tease him; she knew he was worried and was practicing a restraint that was much appreciated. "Look, Thomas; I know it's a bit alarmin',"—her companion made a strangled, derisive sound that she ignored—"but I *promise*, he's bein' helpful." She paused, debating what to say, but decided she'd have to tell him something. "It's to Acton's benefit, but I cannot say more."

Williams was silent for a few moments, no doubt thinking of the photographs that Savoie had given her. "Why do you think he is a friend?"

"I told you; he saved my life."

He glanced at her. "Literally?"

"Literally."

He suggested carefully, "Is it possible—think, Kath; is it possible the situation was contrived to obtain your trust?"

"Not a chance."

He subsided, aware she wasn't going to offer anything more. "Will you at least not meet him again unless I am with you?"

"No; he doesn't like you."

Williams looked over to her, equal parts shocked and outraged.

She shrugged a shoulder. "It's probably just as well; you don't want someone like him tryin' to lure you away from the CID. You'd have to go live in Eastern Europe and wear flashy clothes."

Heavily, he replied, "Kath, it's not a joking matter; he's a very dangerous player. I wish you'd tell Acton."

She sobered, thinking of Savoie and the impression she'd gained—that he was quite cold at the core. "Yes, I am aware he is dangerous, and I'm bein' very careful." Reaching over, she placed a hand on his on the steering wheel and said sincerely, "I think he is very soon to scuttle back to his lair, and you won't have to worry about it another minute." She withdrew her hand and smiled. "And your guilt will be assuenged."

"Assuaged," he corrected, distracted.

There's another reason I'm married to Acton, she thought; he wouldn't correct me, and would probably misuse the word the rest of his life so as not to hurt my feelings. As Williams showed his ID to the gate man, she smiled out her window. Love that man, I do; hopefully I can save him from whatever Solonik's got cooked up.

CHAPTER 23

T HEY ASCENDED THE ANCIENT STONE STAIRS TO THE PRESTI-
gious chambers devoted to the representation of criminal defendants since medieval times. In keeping with police officers
everywhere, Doyle was more scornful than impressed. "A bunch
o' blacklegs," she pronounced as they crossed the threshold.

"Behave yourself," Williams cautioned in an aside. "Remember, you want a favor."

"Right you are; I'll be as subtle as a serpent." She couldn't
very well tell Williams that mainly, she wanted to ask a few
questions of those involved in the early cases, and see what
there was to see—if someone on the premises was a walking
mass of guilt and misery, perhaps she'd be able to spot it.

They approached the receptionist and identified themselves, Doyle explaining that they were investigating the murder of a former client. The receptionist seemed unimpressed
by her warrant card, but advised them she'd see if Mr. Moran
could give them a few minutes. Moran was a senior barrister
with a storied career, and had handled the trial for Mrs. Bennet's daughter, when the boyfriend had been killed. While
they waited, Doyle looked around the sumptuous offices and
remarked, "How come we're the good guys, yet we work in cubicles under fluorescent lights?"

But Williams seemed unaffected by this gross injustice.

"Because we serve the public, that's why. These people can charge as much as they like, and—given their clientele— money is probably no object. I imagine you've noticed that crime pays."

Doyle decided she should turn the conversation, as she had a very good suspicion that crime was paying off for Acton in spades, but before she could think of a safer topic, they were interrupted by the receptionist's return. "I'm afraid Mr. Moran is occupied at present, and unable to entertain visitors, but his junior will meet with you." With a nod, she led them down the hall and opened the door to a wood-paneled office, ushering them in.

The barrister's junior was a very self-possessed young woman dressed in a dark, tailored suit that nevertheless showed her figure to advantage. She introduced herself as Morgan Percy and her eyes lingered on Williams for a moment longer than necessary, despite her businesslike attitude.

Doyle shook hands and began, "We are investigatin' the homicide of one of your former clients—well, two of the chambers' former clients, actually; we are tryin' to determine if the murders are related."

As Doyle named the victims, the woman pulled her gaze away from Williams, a hint of skepticism contained therein. "And you think we will be able to cast some light on who killed a former client?"

"We're trying to pursue all leads," offered Williams. "We were hoping you would allow us to review your old files to look for any connections to the recent homicides."

Percy raised a brow at him. "I'm surprised the CID is concerned enough to turn over this particular stone. Aren't there other crimes with more appealing victims to consider?"

Faith, she's a little defensive for this early in the day, thought Doyle, but Williams fired right back.

"Are you conceding your former clients deserved to be killed, then?"

"Of course not," Percy protested, crossing her arms and leaning against the desk. "But you must admit this is unusual—wouldn't it be more efficient to follow up with known associates?"

Doyle explained carefully, "There is a—a concern—that this killer may be lookin' for similar victims."

This came as a surprise, and the other girl stared. "Similar victims? Other clients, do you mean?"

"Something like that, I'm afraid I'm not at liberty to say." Couldn't very well tell her that all the chambers' employees and the renowned barrister himself were potential suspects; they'd be ushered out the door with no further ado.

It may have been this somber revelation, or it may have been that Williams was a fine specimen, but for whatever reason, Percy decided to cooperate. "Very well. What is it you'd like to know?"

"Could we have a look at the two files?" asked Williams.

Doyle put in, "Or—is there anyone here who would remember workin' the cases? I'd like to ask a few questions, if I may."

Percy consulted her laptop and entered the names. "The Bennet file has been shredded as part of the routine purging, but we still have the other one." Lifting her phone, she asked a file clerk to pull it from storage. As they waited, she glanced over at Williams. "How long have you been doing homicides, Detective Sergeant?"

"He'll be a detective inspector soon," Doyle offered, thinking to boost his stock. "The youngest since Wensley." Doyle was not certain who Wensley was, but it sounded impressive.

Percy smiled at him. "You must be good at it."

"I do my best. It is interesting work."

"Indeed it is." They regarded each other for a long moment and Doyle was careful to hold her tongue—one needn't be over-perceptive to feel the chemistry in the room.

The clerk came in with a two-volume file, and Percy removed the ribbon tied around it and began to read the log. "Oh yes—I remember Mr. Moran talking about this one; the client was charged with killing his tutor." She looked up to explain. "He was enrolled in a social program to help disadvantaged youth, and a tutor was provided free of charge to help him pass the trade exam." Flipping through the pages, she displayed the mug shot. "Client was poor and black, victim was white, newspapers found it impossible to believe that the accused would compromise such an opportunity; a witness came forward with a shaky alibi, and a plea deal for probation was the end result." She paused and added honestly, "The prosecutors were nervous about black on white crime; at the time there was a lot of unrest in the black community."

"Public sympathy was with the accused," said Doyle aloud, unsurprised; it was the common theme in all the cases.

"Right or wrong, it was," Percy agreed. "When that's the case, it makes our job much easier; either to cut a deal or obtain an acquittal. The public reaction can govern how a case will be prosecuted."

But Doyle's sensibilities were offended by the unfair picture thus painted. "It doesn't seem right, when the jury pool is tainted like this. Justice should be blind."

"Our job is to represent our client," Percy explained, almost kindly. "Your job is to put him away. We each take whatever advantage we can."

Doyle decided she didn't want to start an argument about ideals, since everyone always seemed to think she was quaint, or something. So instead she asked a related question. "How can the defendants afford a firm like this? Who pays for it?"

Again, the girl looked upon her with the sympathy one reserves for someone as thick as a plank. "Where the case is high-profile, we often take the matter pro bono—free of charge. The publicity more than makes up for the cost."

"It doesn't seem fair," Doyle reiterated stubbornly, although she knew it was hopeless. "One suspect gets a first-class defense because he's caught the fancy of the press, while someone without such a cause goes to prison."

"The vagrancies of popular opinion," the girl agreed. "Often it doesn't seem fair."

As Doyle wasn't certain what "vagrancies" meant, she cut to the nub. "Would it be possible to give us a copy of the file, d'you think?" Mainly, she wanted to identify the other personnel who had worked on the case, since it didn't seem she'd be allowed to wander the halls, here.

"I don't see why not, but I have to check with Mr. Moran first. I don't have that kind of authority."

Williams rose and handed her his card. "If you wouldn't mind, please ask Mr. Moran if he would be available to discuss the old case with us—there shouldn't be any problem, now that the client is dead. We could come back whenever it is convenient."

Percy readily gave him her card in return. "I will ask him—again, I'm afraid I can't commit."

At this point, however, the interior door to the inner hallway opened and a distinguished older man poked his head in. After resting his unfocused gaze on Doyle and Williams for a long moment, he said to Percy, "Visitors, Morgan?" His words were slurred and he swayed slightly on his feet as he grasped the doorjamb for support. It was evident to Doyle that this was the renowned Mr. Moran, and it was just as evident that he was quite drunk at half-past ten.

Her color high, Percy rose and went to him, "Just a word, Mr. Moran."

"Mr. Moran," Doyle interrupted, rising to him and extending her hand. "How nice to meet you; I am investigatin' the murder of one of your former clients—could I have a moment?"

Her brazen attempt to get a read on the man was to be frustrated by Percy, who gave her an annoyed look as she gently pushed the man out through the door again. "Some other time, please." But the barrister resisted for a moment, his gaze fixed on Doyle. "Why, you—you're the police officer who jumped off the bridge."

"That I am, sir—"

"We must go," Percy insisted, and then firmly pulled the inner door closed behind them. Frustrated, Doyle was left to exchange a significant glance with Williams, and settle in to wait.

After several minutes, Percy returned and said smoothly, "I'm afraid Mr. Moran has no time to spare this morning, but please call, and I'll see if I can arrange another meeting." Her gaze rested on Williams.

As though nothing unusual had gone forward, he shook her hand. "Thank you, Ms. Percy; you've been very helpful. And please let me know when I can return to pick up the file."

"As soon as I get approval," she reminded him. The girl might be smitten, but she hadn't completely lost her bearings.

As they exited out the door and down the stairs, Doyle looked sidelong at Williams. "Well then, DI Williams; I believe you've made a conquest."

He quoted Percy, "We each take whatever advantage we can."

Yes; the same way that Acton was taking advantage of Masterson, Doyle thought as they crossed the courtyard. Using the elemental attraction between the sexes to further your purposes; I suppose it's been this way since there were sexes to begin with. She thought this might be important, but before she could consider why this would be, Williams said, "It's not yet eleven and Mr. Moran was quite drunk."

"Swilkin'," Doyle agreed. "Which is puzzlin'; he's had a long and distinguished career. Perhaps he has demons, or a guilty conscience." She wished she'd had a chance to ask some questions, she'd been *so* close.

Williams was skeptical as they approached the car park. "He doesn't seem like someone who would condescend to murder criminals in parks."

"You never know, in this business. And Percy was very eager to protect him; didn't want him talkin' to the likes of us whilst he was in his cups."

"Loyalty is a virtue."

As Williams was the grand master of loyalty, she couldn't very well argue with him on the subject. Still, she persisted, "Even if it's not Moran himself, I think there's somethin' here; public sympathy played a part in gettin' the victims off the first time, and that same sympathy got them these fine defense barristers, which in turn made the prosecution leery and more apt to back down in the face of the public pressure." She paused, warming to her theme. "And remember, our vigilante is someone the victims are willin' to meet—they're not the types who'd meet with just anyone who rang them up."

"Good point," he conceded. "Do you want me to do a background check on all personnel at the chambers?"

"Allow me," she teased. "You outrank me yet again, wretched man."

"Not yet, I don't. You probably shouldn't have said."

This was delivered with the faintest hint of a rebuke as they came to the unmarked, and hearing it, she swiftly apologized. "I'm that sorry, Thomas—you're right. I shouldn't be showin' you off like a prize pig."

He accepted the apology with a small smile as they slid into the unmarked. "After all, I don't show you off; instead, I help you escape from your adoring fans."

"We are both too famous for our own good."

"Like these victims," he added as he turned around in the seat to back the car out.

Much struck, she stared at him, her scalp prickling to beat the band. "Do you know, Thomas; sometimes you hit the nail right on the head."

"That's because I'm the youngest DI since Wensley," he replied mildly.

CHAPTER 24

AS THEY DROVE BACK TOWARD THE MET, DOYLE HAD THE GRACE
to realize that she was about to take advantage of Williams's
affection for her within the next ten minutes, and that she
was no better than Acton with Masterson or Williams with
Percy, to use him in such a way. I'm doing it to Savoie, too, she
thought with another twinge of guilt; I'm something of a
tease, I suppose—Munoz would be that proud.

She looked at her watch and assessed the street ahead of
them. "Thomas, I'm goin' to ask a horrendous favor of you,
and I'm miserably ashamed, but there's no one else I can ask
and it is *truly* important, or I wouldn't even think of it."

He glanced at her in surprise, but replied in a light tone,
"Kath, you aren't the first and you certainly won't be the last.
I am at your service."

Nothin' for it, she thought. "I was wonderin' if you would
carry my mobile for about three hours; if anyone notices, you
could say that I left it behind this mornin' at the Inn and you
are going to return it to me." He was no fool; he would realize
she was referring to Acton, and his tendency to track her
through her mobile phone.

He considered this request for a moment in the silence it
deserved, and then glanced over at her thoughtfully. "Do I
answer it?"

She was relieved, she half-expected him to refuse outright. "It's up to you, but please don't turn it off."

They pulled to a stop light. "And where will you be that I won't be?"

The words were said in an even tone, but he was a bundle of concern, no doubt thinking of Savoie, and how she'd refused to allow him to accompany her to the next meeting.

She pulled a knit cap from her rucksack and pulled it over her head, tucking in her tell-tale hair. "I'd rather not say, but if you don't hear word from me in three hours, you are no longer bound and may do whatever you will."

He was quiet and she worried that he was going to balk, or start asking questions that she was unwilling to answer. Instead, he mused, "When I imagine Acton as wanting to kill me, this is not the reason I would choose."

With a mental sigh of relief, she handed over her mobile as the light turned green and they started up again. "I am usin' you *shamelessly*, and I'm that sorry."

They continued a block until they stopped at the next light. "At least tell me where I should drop you."

She reached over to lift his hand from the steering wheel and kiss the back. "Thank you." She then opened her door to exit onto the busy street.

"Kath!" he called out angrily, but she kept walking, threading her way through the stopped cars until she reached the sidewalk, where she disappeared down into the tube station. She knew DI Williams like the back of her hand, and he would be given no chance to follow her.

She rode the tube the several stops to her destination, then walked the few blocks to the intersection Savoie had indicated. She was a few minutes early, and kept back from the curb, waiting with her face averted—it was a quiet, residential area and hopefully no one would remark a girl in a knit cap, hanging about.

A new-model black sedan with tinted windows pulled up to

the curb before her. There were no plates—naturally, she thought with resignation; I hope I am not being more foolish than my usual. Stepping down to open the door, she slid in next to Savoie, who said nothing, but pulled away and began to drive. The prison was about an hour away with no traffic, Doyle figured—although she was no expert at calculating such things, not being much of a driver. She looked out the window and went over the protocol in her mind. She thought about what she wanted to accomplish, and hoped she'd guessed right about Savoie's role in these matters—sometimes she was not the best guesser.

Her companion spoke first. "The big blond man."

She turned to him. "Yes?" She was not going to give him Williams's name.

"You trust him?"

"I do," she answered, a bit surprised. She waited, but he said nothing further. "Why?" she finally asked, unable to help herself.

He glanced at her, then returned his eyes to the road and cocked his head slightly. "Me, I am not so sure."

She didn't answer. Presumably he was prejudiced against Williams, which shouldn't surprise her.

"Did you show Acton the photographs?"

"I am not goin' to talk to you about Acton and the photographs," she said firmly. "Choose another subject."

He smiled, amused.

"What?" she asked.

He shrugged his shoulders. "You are not afraid of me."

"I should be," she admitted. "It's a wolf in sheep's clothin', you are."

"No, no," he protested with his thin smile, "I am the—" he gestured with a hand, trying to find the word. "I am the dog who rescues."

"Yes—the one that saves the people in the snow, with brandy." She frowned, unable to think of the right word, either. "But you never mentioned that you were Savoie, which truly puts the cat among the pigeons."

But he only gave her a chiding look. "You never asked for my name."

Stricken, she realized he was right, and was immediately ashamed of herself. "Oh—I am sorry; I should have done. Why on earth are you tanglin' with the likes of Solonik? I would think it beneath you."

She could see that he debated what to tell her—if anything—and so she prompted, "He doesn't know anythin' about your brother, you know. So don't believe him if he says he does."

This remark earned her another glance. "What do you know of this?"

"I know Acton didn't kill your brother. Instead, Acton was mentorin' him."

He thought about this. "You mean Acton was helping him."

"Yes—and it was quite an honor, because Acton is not one to be helpin' the young detectives. Owens was puttin' together a manual on bloodstains for him; he was that pleased to have such an assignment." Best not mention that Acton was keeping Owens close whilst he decided whether to kill him, it would only confuse the issue. "Solonik may be tryin' to get you to think Acton killed him." This was guesswork on her part, but made sense. She could think of no other reason the notorious Savoie would stoop to aid in Solonik's paltry revenge plot.

"You are worried I will come after Acton."

"Yes," she admitted readily. "That I am, and it would be *horrendously* unfair."

He tilted his head in mild disagreement. "He is not the good husband."

"We are not going to speak of that," she reminded him.

"We will," he replied in his brusque manner. "But not yet."

Doyle tried a different tack, mainly because she couldn't

figure out whether she was making any headway. "You did me a favor, so I do you a favor, by letting you know that Solonik is dupin' you."

"You give the cat a pigeon." He seemed very pleased with this attempt at the idiom.

"Well—yes; yes, I suppose I do." She now knew exactly how Acton felt when he didn't correct her. "D'you see? You shouldn't fall in with whatever the scheme is. Perhaps it would be best if you just returned home."

But this suggestion was roundly rejected with a definitive shake of his head. "First, I will find out what happened to my brother."

Mother a' mercy, thought Doyle in dismay, and lapsed into silence. Hopefully she'd made a dent, at least; he was very hard to read.

But apparently her companion had indeed decided to un-bend, and after a few minutes he offered, "I will do you the favor, also, and tell you to be very careful of Monsieur Solonik. You are *ingénue*, I think."

"I haven't a *clue* what that means."

"You are, ah"—he waved his hand again, searching for the words—"too trusting of the men."

"Never say so," she teased in mock-astonishment.

He smiled a bit grimly as he drove. "Yes. There is Acton, there is the blond man, there is me . . ." He paused, and con-cluded, "*ingénue.*"

"I will keep your advice to mind, then." It was all very ironic, of course, since she knew exactly who to trust and who not to trust. Most times, anyway; it was a little odd that he kept referring to Williams as being in the latter category.

There was a small pause in the conversation and then he spoke again—he was rather talkative, for a shadowy kingpin. "You will tell me what he says to you, yes?"

She did not need to feign surprise. "Don't you already

know what he will say? I thought you were in cahoots—and I'm that ashamed for you, I might add."

"He does not tell the truth about my brother, you said." He glanced over to give her another chiding look for forgetting this. "And me, I watch and I see." He paused, as though deciding what to say. "I do what I wish."

"I wish I could," Doyle retorted a bit crossly. "It's crackin' annoyin' to have all these dire plots and counter-plots to contend with."

"We will be cahoots," he said in a soothing tone. "You will tell me what he says."

"I will watch and see," she countered, and saw him smile.

They settled into silence, and nothing more was said for the remainder of the drive. Perhaps she had an ally in Savoie, and perhaps she didn't. Her instinct told her he was not a threat to her, but that didn't mean he wasn't a threat to Acton—or Williams, apparently, and she'd best be very careful; he tended to kill people, thinking he was doing her a favor.

She contemplated the passing scenery as they traveled through the shabby industrial area that surrounded Wexton Prison. It was obvious there was some sort of revenge plot against Acton at play—and Acton had his dazzle-the-brasser counter-plot to thwart it—but it was unclear what Doyle's role in these affairs was, other than to be intimidated. Best discover it, she concluded, mentally squaring her shoulders. Forearm is forewarned, Acton would say. She paused for a moment, because that didn't seem to be quite right, but her thoughts were interrupted when the car pulled to a stop at a tattered bus stop down the road from the prison gates.

"I do not want to be seen by the cameras," Savoie explained. "When you come out, telephone me."

Having taken her cue from him, Doyle had purchased a disposable phone for the occasion, and she handed it to him so that he could enter his number. It was different from the last one, she noted, and decided he must change it often. He was no doubt very good at covering his tracks, what with the Home Office having the vapors about his being here.

"Would you mind keepin' my gun?" she asked.

He nodded, and watched in silence as she released the Velcro fastenings and took off the ankle holster, leaving it bundled on the floor of his car.

"It is a fine weapon. Have you used it?"

"Once." Best change the subject. "If I'm not out in an hour, feel free to storm the place and break me out."

"*Bien sûr,*" he agreed with his thin smile.

After checking in the rear-view mirror to see that her cap was in place, she exited the vehicle, slinging her rucksack over her shoulder and walking toward the prison. Behind her, she heard Savoie turn the car around and drive away.

CHAPTER 25

*D*OYLE HAD BEEN REQUIRED TO MAKE PRISON VISITS ON A FEW occasions in the past, as often prisoners would be interviewed in connection with other crimes. As she entered through the doors and felt the oppressive atmosphere, she fought an almost overwhelming urge to turn on her heel and abandon ship. Not a good place, she concluded; no one here is content, and a good many are utterly despairing. Hopefully, she would not be joining the ranks of the utterly despairing anytime soon.

In this subdued state of mind she checked in at the visitor's desk as "Kathleen Sinclair" and showed her government-issued ID as opposed to her CID-issued one. She had little doubt if she revealed her professional identity, bridge-jumper fans would line up in short order and her better half would probably hear of this little excursion within the hour. There was always the chance Acton would hear of it anyway—he was another one who watched and saw—but she had little choice and could only hope to evade detection as best she was able. And only for the time being, she assured herself; I will make a clean breast as soon as I discover what I can, and then Acton and I will have no secrets from each other—or at least no secrets involving this latest crisis. She paused for a moment, and then decided that Savoie's participation needn't ever be revealed; his was only a minor role, after all.

After she passed through a metal detector, her rucksack was searched, and then she was escorted by a guard who eyed her in a way that was probably against regulations as he showed her into a visiting room that had the look of a place that no one ever bothered to clean very thoroughly. She was instructed to have a seat at a station that faced a reinforced glass panel through which she and the prisoner could speak, and noted that a security camera was mounted on the wall to monitor all conversations. The guard then withdrew to the door and she waited, the silence stretching out. She was acutely uncomfortable, and closed her eyes briefly in an attempt to regain her equilibrium. Impossible to imagine having to reside in such a place for an extended period of time; the atmosphere was oppressive, hopeless, and made her very anxious. Don't be committing a felony, she thought; mental note.

A gate clanged in the near distance, and she jumped slightly. Enough, she scolded herself; pull yourself together, for the love o' Mike—you're the flippin' bridge-jumper. And the aim here is to stop this evil plot to expose Acton, else he'll be having to serve out a sentence, with you sitting here in this miserable visiting room on a regular basis. Such a thought couldn't be borne; she honestly didn't know if Acton would survive such an experience, being as he was. Not to mention he would be a target for every vengeful inmate who was here, courtesy of him. Better that he married Masterson to scotch her plan—if it came down to that—than wind up here. Faith, she thought with no small surprise; I suppose I must truly love him.

Her thoughts were interrupted when Solonik appeared on the other side of the glass, dressed in prison garb. He smiled when he saw her, and seated himself so that they were face-to-face.

"*Rizhaya*," he began, his amused gaze resting for a moment on the cap that covered her hair. "We meet again."

"You look well," she replied politely. It was true; he did. He'd lost weight, and appeared much healthier—nothing like a prison diet, she thought. Although the last time they'd met, his throat had been sliced, so there was that. "I brought you somethin'." She pulled a well-worn Russian icon card out of her rucksack and displayed it to him; it was of St. Joseph, and had been taken from the body of his dead brother-in-law. It went without saying that the aforesaid brother-in-law was dead by Acton's hand.

They regarded each other for a long moment. She wanted to make it clear, without saying anything aloud for the surveillance camera, that she was wise to his scheming, and not one to be blackmailed or intimidated into doing whatever it was he was trying to accomplish by sending Savoie to plague her with his stupid photographs. No doubt Solonik assumed Acton's young and foolish wife could be easily manipulated, and she would disabuse him of this notion immediately. He saw her as Acton's vulnerability—which indeed she was; he must have been astonished to discover Acton had married—and so she would make it very clear that she had her husband's back, come what may.

Solonik broke the silence. "I thank you, *Rizhaya;* he is the patron saint of my hometown."

With a nod, she placed the icon card on the counter before her. "I'm thinkin' that you need all the help you can get—there may not be enough saints in heaven."

He bowed his head in acknowledgment. "I will treasure it, and think of our friendship."

This seemed a rather strange thing to say, being as this was the first time she'd spoken to him. Reminded, she set about to do a bit of truth-detecting. "I understand you have somethin' to discuss with me." She waited, wondering how he would broach the subjects he wished, what with the camera monitoring them overhead.

"You have met my associate?"

She blinked, as this seemed off-topic, but assumed he referred to Savoie, as she was aware of no other associates—unless he referred to Masterson. "A gentleman?"

He nodded solemnly. "My associate can help you solve your problem."

"Which problem is that?" she asked cautiously. She had more than a few, after all.

There was a flash of irritation, quickly suppressed, but his expression remained benign. "The newspaper reporter," he reminded her gently.

Confused, she knit her brow. "And here I thought she was your doin'."

"No," he said sincerely, shaking his head. It was a lie.

Ah—now we are getting somewhere, Doyle thought in satisfaction, and feigned confusion, which was not very hard to do, given the circumstances. "I don't believe you."

He leaned forward and lowered his voice. "No, she is not mine—and it would be in both our interests to resolve that problem."

Aside from being untrue, this seemed another strange thing for him to say, and so she asked suspiciously, "Why would you wish to help me?" She noted that he'd been careful not to mention Acton, or even refer to a husband, so she did the same.

He lowered his gaze for a few moments, studying his hands. He finally said carefully, "I am concerned that if too much information is discovered, it will not serve my interests. I have interests which are aligned with—someone who is close to you."

She thought about this for a moment, knitting her brow. "I don't understand," she finally admitted. It was true; she was at sea. I'm not cut out for cryptic conversations, she thought; I have enough trouble keeping up with the not-so-cryptic ones.

Again, there was a swift flash of irritation—and perhaps contempt—that belied his calm appearance. With a show of patience, he explained, "If the newspaper woman succeeds, then certain information will be made public. I do not wish this because I have my own interests." He gave her a meaningful look.

He referred, it seemed, to the illegal guns-running. Apparently he was intimating that if Acton's dark doings were exposed, this would throw a spanner in his own wheel of dark doings. She responded with cautious incredulity, "Surely you can have no further interests, bein' as you are locked up in this fine place."

He looked upon her indulgently. "*Rizhaya,* you are such an innocent; it refreshes me."

While she stared at him, trying to decide what he was about, he pressed his advantage, glancing quickly at the monitor and lowering his voice. "There is information about killings, and corruption. At the highest levels."

This rang true, and Doyle digested this unfortunate news, allowing her dismay to show. Unbidden, she had a sudden memory of the Home Office official who'd been the murder victim in the first case she'd worked with Acton, and her scalp prickled.

To her surprise, Solonik suddenly brought the meeting to a close, and rose. "I will say no more; you have only to contact my associate." He smiled. "Thank you for St. Joseph; I will pray for you in this most difficult time."

The guard indicated she should rise. "This way, Ms. Sinclair." She had the immediate impression the guard was pleased, and also contemptuous of her as he exchanged a glance with the departing Solonik.

Horrified realization dawned, and Doyle allowed the guard to escort her away, willing her feet to move only with an immense effort. Holy Mother of God, she thought; I've been roundly outfoxed.

CHAPTER 26

DOYLE WALKED UP THE ROAD TO THE BUS STOP, QUASHING down her panic and concentrating on putting one foot in front of the other. He doesn't know you know what he intends, she rallied herself; you can thwart it, now. And our Mr. Savoie will not be best-pleased to hear of this, either. Unless, of course, he was in on it from the start. She halted for a moment in the dusty gravel, utterly dismayed by this thought. Do not panic, she directed herself, and started walking again. You have the advantage, thanks to the guard who could not control his glee. I thank You for the warning, she offered up; now let's hope I can do a little manipulating of my own.

After reaching the bus stop, she turned on her mobile and texted Savoie. She then texted Williams to tell him her errand had gone well, and she would meet him back at the Met in an hour or so to retrieve her mobile, hoping there was no way for Williams to triangulate her location. Small matter if he could; she had bigger problems to worry about. She sat at the bus stop for a few minutes until the black sedan pulled up, and she opened the door and settled into the passenger seat.

"Saint Bernard," Savoie said immediately, very pleased with himself.

"Yes—oh, yes, that's it. And it's a wretched shame I don't drink, because I could sorely use some brandy."

"I do not drink, also," Savoie revealed.

"No, I suppose you need to stay sharp."

"I am the wolf wearing the clothes from the lambs," he agreed as they drove away. "I trust no one."

He was emanating good will—fond of her, he was—and she decided there was no time like the present. "I'm wonderin' if you'd mind bein' a Saint Bernard, just once more. I have a favor to ask."

He eyed her, not liking this talk of favors. "Why? What did he say?"

Doyle found that she was hungry, and couldn't face potential ruination on an empty stomach. "Can I buy you somethin' to eat?"

He shrugged his apology. "Me, I am not easy in strange places."

Of course not, she thought, I suppose that goes with the territory. "We can talk in the car, then, but would you mind if I buy a fruit pie somewhere? I am starvin'."

After a stretch of empty roadway, they came across a light commercial area and he stopped at a small market that served the local work force. Doyle went in to make her purchase, and returned to the car. After turning into a side street, Savoie parked the sedan along a nearly deserted road that fronted an abandoned industrial building. She'd bought a fruit pie for him—it seemed rude, otherwise—and he folded the waxed paper back and ate it without comment. Doyle passed him a napkin and reflected that she was alone and eating pie with a renowned killer in a deserted area. Nothin' for it.

"Whatever Solonik has told you, this is not about anythin' other than takin' Acton's goat. It is about revenge, pure and simple."

Her companion chewed on the pie and watched her, his expression unreadable.

"Acton put him in prison, and Solonik wants revenge, but Acton has the upper hand."

Savoie paused for a moment, puzzled by the reference.

"Acton has a way to make him do what he wants."

The Frenchman indicated he understood, and took another bite. "Solonik has a son."

She'd hoped he wouldn't remember; she didn't want an innocent child to be a pawn in all this. "Do you think we can leave him out of it?"

But she was to be given no such assurance. "Continue, if you please."

"Solonik wants revenge against Acton, but it cannot appear to come from him. The woman in the photo with Acton—she works for Solonik." She scrutinized his reaction carefully, but could not decide if he already knew this. Here goes, she thought, and took a breath. "But I think she is slated to be murdered, and Solonik will make it look like I paid someone to have her killed."

It went without saying that Savoie was to perform Masterson's murder, and truly, it was a well thought-out scheme. The police would be shown the photos, and Doyle would be seen as the jealous and vengeful wife. And now there was a roll of spanking-fresh prison surveillance tape, lending support to this story. She'd wanted to show Solonik that she couldn't be manipulated, unaware that this was not his intent; he sought only to bring her to him so as to frame her, and she'd fallen for it. Stupid knocker, she chastised herself; a bigger idiot never put her arm through a coat.

She pulled her attention back to Savoie, who was regarding her steadily as he silently finished up the pie. "The newspaper story Masterson is puttin' together about Acton would be published, and even if nothin' could be proved, he would be ruined. I would be in prison and Masterson—who is the only one who knows of Solonik's connection to all this—would be dead." She thought about it. "He's had a lot of time and nothin' else to think about; it is a crackin' good plan."

After pausing for a moment to fortify herself, she met his eyes. "I'm worried that you saved me that day—from the man who attacked me—not because you were a Saint Bernard, but because if I were killed, it would put paid to this wretched plan."

"No, no," he assured her immediately. "I was to have sex with you—with drugs, if needed—and take more photographs."

She stared at him in acute horror. "Mother of God," she breathed. Solonik would then use said photos to blackmail her—or torture Acton. Or both.

There was a small silence. "How much of this do you know?" she asked in a small voice. If he knew the whole already, matters were a bit bleak, and about to get bleaker.

He brushed the crumbs from his lap with the napkin. "I have the business interests here, but lately there have been some problems with the business interests. Solonik says to me that such problems would be no more if I would arrange this meeting, and arrange"—he shrugged a shoulder in her direction—"other matters also."

"In exchange for your cooperation, he'll give up any plan to muscle in on the contraband in the horse trailers," she guessed.

Her companion's cold eyes were suddenly intent on hers, and she realized that perhaps she was gabbling a bit too much. Hastily, she added, "And he'd tell you what happened to your brother." Solonik would no doubt finger Acton—whether he had any evidence or not—and a vengeful Savoie would then dispatch Acton without a second thought. For Solonik, all debts would then be well and properly settled.

She leaned toward him, intent. "D'you see? There is no guarantee that he'll not turn on you, too—like he will turn on Masterson. He's safe and protected in prison, after all; if he implicates you in Masterson's and Acton's murders, he'd then have the contraband operation all to himself."

She paused, trying to decide if he was buying what she was selling, but he was gazing into the distance and giving no clue as to what he was thinking. "You can't trust him, Philippe; perhaps you can help me stop him and we can take Solonik's goat, instead of Acton's."

He tilted his head and met her eyes. "I am a businessman. Will I be paid?"

She gazed at him in dismay. "Oh. Oh—I don't have much money of my own." She thought about asking Acton for whatever large sum such things must cost, and could feel herself turn pale at the idea. Perhaps she could get hold of the fungible assets, instead, but she discarded that thought immediately; Layton was first and foremost loyal to Acton, and he would regretfully turn her in without hesitation.

Her companion's voice cut into her thoughts. "Perhaps it is not money I wish from you."

Her eyes flew to his and his meaning was unmistakable as he slid an arm across the top of her car seat. "*Truly?*" she asked in abject astonishment.

"Come, come," he said reasonably. "Do not be *ingénue*."

With a mighty effort, she pulled her scattered wits together. "I'm afraid that is not an option, my friend."

He cocked his head and drew a finger along her shoulder. "Acton has this option. Such arrangements are not unusual—I will take a place in the city, nearby to where you live."

Frowning at him, she accused, "You are lookin' to take your photos."

"No, my promise—I would not do such a thing to you."

He didn't need to promise because it was true, and she stared at him in bemusement. He spoke casually, as though they were discussing the weather, and she was reminded of Acton, who also spoke casually about cataclysmic topics. She suddenly remembered Nanda, thanking Timothy with the only commodity she had available. She also remembered her musings in the prison waiting room; how she would be willing to give up Acton to Masterson if that was what it took to save him. As a result, she actually considered Savoie's offer for a long moment.

She finally shook her head. "I'm that sorry," she admitted. "I can't do it."

He said nothing, but bent his head and contemplated the steering wheel.

"You are a very handsome man," she offered sincerely, hoping she hadn't hurt his feelings; men were sensitive about such things.

He gave a quick bark of laughter—the first she'd heard from him—and it startled her. He withdrew his arm and started the car. "*Eh bien*; we will go back."

"What will you do?" she asked tentatively. Hopefully it did not include framing her for murder.

But again, he reminded her of Acton when he made no response. Instead, he turned to look at her with some severity as they turned onto the main highway. "You must tell no one what we have spoken of. No one. This is understood?"

"Yes, I promise." This was no problem at all for her.

He turned back to contemplate the road. "Done," he corrected her.

"Done," she amended.

"Be careful who you trust," he added.

She wondered if he was referring to Williams again. "All right," she agreed, and then tentatively teased, "Do I trust you?"

He smiled again. "*De vrai*; I am the Saint Bernard."

They drove the way back in silence, and as was his custom, he said nothing when she alighted at the drop-off place. The black sedan then drove away.

CHAPTER 27

*D*OYLE BEGAN THE WALK BACK TO THE MET. I AM IN WAY OVER my head, she thought with some anxiety. I should turn the whole over to Acton and spend the next few months learning how to cook. She remembered they were going to Trestles tomorrow and nearly groaned aloud. What to do?

She'd promised Savoie she would say nothing, and, like a coward, she was willing to honor her promise. Hopefully he was not going to help frame her for murder anytime soon, although he'd made no promises on that front. He *had* sworn off kidnap and rape, which was surely a step in the right direction. She'd blundered, though, when she'd revealed her knowledge of the contraband rig; she was married to a DCI and Savoie may decide he had no choice but to assure her silence—he was not the type to trust anyone, by his own admission. Except that he had a thing for her, apparently, and was disappointed she wasn't willing to jump into an affair, like her wayward husband. Annoyed, she hunched her shoulders. Between Williams and Percy and Savoie and Masterson, everyone seemed to think her notions of morality were a bit out-of-date. Honestly; it was time to start building an ark, or something.

Back at the Met, she shook the rain off her jacket as she walked down the hallway to her desk. Munoz materialized to stride along beside her, even though there really wasn't room enough for two abreast. "And just where have you been? I've had to cover for your worthless Irish behind again, and I am *not* your secretary."

"Who was lookin' for me?" Not Acton, Doyle pleaded mentally.

"Holmes, Williams, Samuels," said Munoz, ticking them off and very much put-upon. "And Habib."

Saints and angels; worse and worse. "I left my mobile at an interview this mornin', and I was out in the field before I realized it—could you text Williams and ask him to bring it?" This was an attempt at diversion, and it worked well; Munoz forgot her pique, and paused to raise Williams on her mobile.

Doyle collapsed in a heap at her desk as Munoz tailed along behind her, her fingers working the screen. "He's finishing up an interview—he'll be right over." Thoughtfully, the girl checked the time. "Maybe he's available for dinner."

"Ask him," Doyle encouraged, hoping to put off her inevitable reckoning with DI Williams. Reminded, she decided she'd best ring up Acton and take her medicine—Williams would be angry, whereas Acton would be worried, and she didn't know which was worse.

Using her land line, she rang him up and he answered immediately. "Kathleen."

"I'm back," she said cheerily. "I'm sorry about the mix-up."

"Are you all right?"

She was reminded that her husband was no fool. "Of course, Michael; I'll explain when I see you. Shall we go home together?"

"I'm home already; my four o' clock cancelled."

He'd gone home to fret about her; she was a sad trial to her poor husband. Although to be fair, he was an occasional trial himself, when he was off smoking in dim joints with conniving brassers. "I'll be there soon, then. First I have to see what Habib wants."

"I asked him to look out for you."

"Oh," she said, feeling wretchedly guilty. There was no explanation she could give as to why she hadn't contacted him; leastwise, not one that Munoz could hear. "I'm sorry—I'll make it up to you, I promise." Let him start thinking about sex; maybe he would forget about her many transgressions.

"Shall I come get you?"

Her attempt at diversion hadn't worked, and she'd need time to get her story straight, so she stalled. "I'll let you know; Williams is bringin' my mobile and perhaps I can get a ride. I'll finish up as quickly as I can." After bidding him good-bye, she rang off.

"You're in trouble," pronounced Munoz, eavesdropping without a shred of shame. "Poor planning; next time give me some story to feed to him."

"I'm not needin' your help with my husband, Munoz."

"I beg to differ; if you're going to make it up to him with sex, you can't be so subtle. Tell him you were out buying lingerie."

As this was a sore subject, Doyle glowered up at her. "I don't think sex should be a tradin' chip."

Munoz seemed to find this pronouncement very amusing, and laughed aloud. "Do you need to stay at my flat again?"

"No," Doyle said crossly. "It's none of your business, Munoz; I've had a crackin' foul day."

"No worse than mine," retorted Munoz. "At least Acton is stuck with you."

This hinted at a shocking turn of events, and in her surprise Doyle forgot her own shocking turn of events. "Never say the bookstore clerk broke up with you?"

Munoz's brows drew down ominously. "He said he needed to concentrate on his studies. He didn't give me a chance to break up with him, first."

"I'm that sorry, Munoz. Go out tonight and enslave some other poor man."

"I don't suppose you can come with me? We make a good contrast."

This seemed a dubious compliment, but in any event, flight wasn't an option. "I've got plans this weekend, although I'd honestly rather I didn't. Sorry."

Munoz sulked for a moment. "I'll call Lizzie from the lab; if Holmes is busy, she may be free to go." She shot an arch glance at Doyle under her lashes.

Faith, thought Doyle; now what? "Have I met Lizzie?"

"I doubt it," said Munoz with a great deal of meaning. "She's been given a lot of responsibility in the lab and I'll bet she's not subtle about the trading chip."

Doyle bristled at the implication. "Acton is not having an affair with a girl in the lab, Munoz; have done."

"Of course not," said Munoz, very much shocked. "As if I would suggest such a thing."

Doyle was well-aware that Munoz was taking her goat, so to speak, but found she was completely out of patience on this day of all days. "Not everyone is tryin' to steal Acton from me, present company excepted."

"Oh-ho, apparently I struck a nerve. I wondered why you were so touchy—has he finally come to his senses?"

Doyle seethed and said through her teeth, "If you *dare* spread such a rumor, I promise you will be made to answer for it."

Munoz resented the implied threat and took a step toward Doyle, only to have her arms restrained by Williams, who had appeared behind her.

Doyle felt herself color to the roots of her hair, and wondered how much he'd overheard. Munoz, having ascertained who held her, made no attempt to free herself, so Williams released her and said only, "No bloodshed 'til after hours."

"Can't take a joke," pronounced Munoz in disgust, tossing back her hair. Doyle held her head in her hands and counted to ten.

"Go to a neutral corner, Munoz," said Williams. "I need to give Doyle her mobile."

With a casual air, Munoz made her way over to her cubicle, making it clear she was in no way retreating.

Intercepting Williams's simmering emotions, Doyle decided she desperately wanted to go home even though she still hadn't decided what she should say to Acton; the morning's interview with Morgan Percy seemed like it was ages ago. "I was just leavin'; do you have my mobile?" Williams handed it to her, and watched her pack it away in her rucksack without moving. Here we go, she thought; I would give ten pounds to be left alone. Rising, she exited past him but he turned to follow her. She strode down the hallway but she couldn't out-walk him; his legs were too long. "Do we have to do this now?"

"Yes," he replied tersely.

"At least wait until we get outside, then."

They walked together in grim silence and exited the building. "I'm sorry I ditched you, Thomas, but I knew you would follow me."

"Where did you go?"

"I can't tell you."

"You are insane."

But she was in no mood and whirled on him. "Leave it, Thomas. It is not your concern."

He was angry, and bent so that his face was close to hers. "Of course it is—you can't do this to me, Kath. It's *me*."

"I don't need you to help me."

"Yes, you do." Distracted, he ran a hand through his blond hair. "Things have changed."

Oh-oh, she thought, surprise interrupting her fit of temper. This is big.

Williams glanced up to be certain no one was near, and lowered his voice. "Acton's filed for divorce."

Doyle felt as though the air had been sucked out of her lungs. She stared at him. "What?"

He hesitated for a moment, and even in the fading light, she could see that he was pale. "Acton is getting a divorce. He has already started the proceedings."

Unwilling to believe what this portended, she asked through stiff lips, "Where did you hear that—from Acton?"

He set his jaw. "I'd rather not say." Meeting her eyes, he continued in a grim tone, "You can't count on him to help you with all this, and you're going to need some help."

There was only one person on earth who would believe Acton was getting a divorce—Williams must have been meeting with Masterson. She remembered their friendly flirtation in the microfiche room, and closed her eyes for a moment, trying to remember if she'd had the impression they'd met before.

"Kath? Are you all right?"

Masterson was gathering information about Acton to ruin him—Doyle had assumed it was investigative work, but that seemed unlikely; Acton was an expert at covering his tracks. So perhaps she had a source—a very knowledgeable source—

"Christ, Kath; here—"

Williams supported her in his arms as she swayed on her feet, having trouble with her eyesight. Steering her to a bench, he pushed her head down between her knees and she breathed deeply for a moment, coming to grips with it, and vividly reminded of Savoie's comments about not trusting Williams. Williams, she thought with sick misery—he knows where all the bodies are buried; literally. Williams. Think, Doyle—don't let him know you know. Slowly she sat up, staring blankly ahead while he sat beside her, emanating anxiety.

"I'm sorry," he said gently. "I shouldn't have dropped it on you like that."

"I'm goin' to go home now." She brushed her palms against her cheeks; she was crying.

"I will drive you," he offered.

"No, you won't." She hoisted her rucksack on her shoulder and stood, feeling as though her chest was numb. She began to walk, head down, whilst she brushed at her cheeks—she could not stop crying.

He walked beside her, and bent to say quietly, "Do you want me to try to speak to him?"

"No," she said immediately. Faith, no; Acton would reach the same conclusion she had, and the repercussions would be swift and terrible. She needed to think. "Leave me alone, Thomas."

He dropped back, and she never looked at him again but she knew that he followed, watching, all the way to her door.

CHAPTER 28

WHEN DOYLE ENTERED THEIR FLAT, ACTON WAS WAITING ON the other side of the door. She walked into his arms and felt miserably guilty; he was all on end, and trying to hide it. She wrapped her arms around his waist, and wished she could think of something to say.

"Your hair is wet," he said softly. It was no doubt soaking through his shirt, but she was disinclined to move.

"I need to get another umbrella; I lost the one from the Heath somewhere."

"May I take your coat, madam?" Reynolds discreetly appeared, and Acton reluctantly released her. The servant threw Doyle an admonishing glance as he hung up her coat, and she grimaced at him in apology—no doubt Acton had been pacing like a caged animal.

She rose up on tiptoe to kiss her husband. "I hear the shower callin' my name; come and watch."

But these unsubtle divertive tactics—taking Munoz's advice, she was—were unsuccessful as he took a sharp, assessing look at her face. It was no doubt evident that she'd been crying; she was still on the verge of tears, and only fought them by refusing to think about that-which-must-not-be-thought-of. "In a moment," he said quietly. "Let me see to Reynolds."

"Oh—he was going to help me decide what to pack," she stalled. If Reynolds was dismissed, she'd have no choice but to face the music.

"I will help you pack," he said firmly. "Go shower."

She half-expected her husband to join her in the shower, but he left her to herself, which was nevertheless appreciated because she still hadn't come up with a plausible tale to explain her misspent day. After she emerged into the steam-filled room, she began to feel a bit less buffeted, and wiped off a spot on the mirror to scrutinize her face. Ragged, she was; and she hadn't the will or the energy to dry her hair. Acton had laid her robe out on the bed for her, and she gratefully draped herself in the luxurious folds before heading to the kitchen, where he was checking on whatever was in the oven.

"Hungry?" he asked.

"I suppose." She wasn't; not really—she was too miserable.

He straightened up and considered her for a moment. "I know where the fruit pies are hidden."

Of course he did. She started to laugh and then started to cry, ashamed and hiding her face in her hands. Acton was beside her in an instant, gathering her up in his arms and lifting her onto his lap as he settled onto a kitchen chair. The pent-up emotions of the day could no longer be contained, and she cried into his shoulder and clung. "I am *so* sorry, Michael—I am not a good wife, to make you worry so."

His voice resonated near her ear. "Can you tell me about it?"

She sniffled, and fiddled with a button on his cuff. "I fought with Munoz, and then I fought with Williams, and there are parts of it I truly cannot tell you; not yet."

"Right, then." He kissed her temple, gently. "Let me turn off the oven."

"You should eat," she insisted, brushing her eyes with the back of her hand. "I'll watch."

She did, and it looked so good that she began eating off his plate and then he began kissing her throat and in no time they were abed and she felt much, much better.

Afterward, she lay burrowed in the pillows, watching the flames in the bedroom fireplace. Acton held her nestled in his arm, his mouth against her hair. "You didn't want me to know where you were," he said quietly.

"I had a good reason," she offered in a small voice.

"Were you in trouble? Or under duress?"

"No." For emphasis, she propped up on her elbow and looked into his dark, unreadable eyes. "I wasn't. I was tryin' to help."

He laid a hand against the side of her face. "I trust you. I do. But if anything were to happen to you, nothing else would matter at all."

"I know, Michael—I am bein' very careful." *Never* let Acton know about Savoie; mental note.

"You shouldn't play such a trick on Williams."

Acton must think she'd duped Williams by leaving her mobile behind, but she didn't want to think about Williams; not yet. Instead, she kissed Acton's chest, wondering if he would let her change the subject. "What's the plan for Trestles?"

"Endure." He shifted so that she was lying tucked under his arm again. "We should pack for two nights, although we may only stay for one."

She nodded her understanding. Apparently, events were dependent on Ms. Masterson and her home-wrecking plans.

Acton lifted her hand and kissed it. "How are you at sulking because you are neglected?"

Here was a hint of his plan for the weekend, and she leapt upon it. "Faith, Michael; I can sulk with the best of them. I've lived cheek-to-jowl with Munoz for over a year."

"Good. Because someone from the staff at Trestles has been feeding Masterson information."

"Oh—I see." The penny dropped, and she realized why Acton wanted her to come along on this illicit archives-searching junket. "So I should hang about and see if anyone tries to cultivate poor, resentful me."

"If you would."

Saints, she thought distractedly; was *no one* loyal anymore? She suddenly remembered that Percy was—Morgan Percy had loyally protected her boss, unlike DI Williams, who was a back-stabber of the worst stripe. She frowned, forcefully struck by the *wrongness* of this thought. Impossible to imagine that Williams wasn't loyal to Acton—even if he fancied himself as the fair Doyle's husband-in-waiting. It was unthinkable; loyalty was his middle name, and besides, Acton had the goods on Williams, too—what with the whole shuffling the evil uncle off this mortal coil. She need only test it out; find a way to ask him some pertinent questions when she was with him again—no need to assume the worst, like a hysterical Nell. What ailed her?

"What are you thinking?"

She offered up a more generalized version. "I suppose I'm wonderin' whatever happened to loyalty."

"Sometimes other considerations get in the way—money, or power. It's the way of it."

Just because it was the way of it didn't make it excusable, and so she protested, "You are way too forgivin', Michael."

Absently, he began to stroke her upper arm where his hand rested. "It is not as much a matter of forgiving, as it is a matter of recognizing where loyalty is lacking, and using that lack to advantage."

No doubt he referred to Masterson, and his plan to dangle a better offer than Solonik's. Acton obviously knew of what he spoke—he was a wily one, and a prodigious planner. She wished she had a wily plan to address her many and sundry troubles, but unfortunately, she was fresh out. So instead, she pulled herself up to his ear and whispered into it, "Let's not go. Let's go to Brighton instead, and hide out." For emphasis, she gently bit his lobe.

With a small smile, he tightened his arms around her and closed his eyes. "Don't tempt me."

"We've no choice?"

"Unfortunately not."

She lay back down with a sigh. "It'll be a rare crack, what with your girlfriend there, countin' the silver."

He squeezed her against his side in mock-punishment. "Don't say it."

"Ach, husband," she pointed out fairly. "You're the one with the girlfriend, after all. How vulgar can I be? Can I throw the crested crockery at you?"

His response was delayed because he was feeling amorous again—faith, the man was on a hair-trigger—and he moved atop her, braced on his elbows so as not to crush her; although sometimes when he got carried away she did wind up a bit crushed. He murmured into her neck. "We may have to appear strained."

"No problem *a'tall* for me."

"Stop." His mouth moved southward.

Sighing with pleasure, she contemplated the ceiling. "I suppose I can pretend to be neglected, so long as you make it up to me at a later date."

"Done," he said, although his voice was muffled.

"Am I allowed to know the protocol?"

The question was met with silence. "Michael—I don't think you're payin' attention."

"Oh, I'm paying attention; believe me."

She giggled.

He pulled himself up and rested his forehead against hers, smiling. "There. That's much better."

She wound her arms around him before relaxing back into the pillows, closing her eyes. He lay atop her, and she could feel his scrutiny as he gently stroked back the hair at her temples. "Why were you so sad, Kathleen?"

She kept her eyes closed. "I can't be talkin' about it; I'll be sad again, and all your hard work for naught."

"Right, then."

He rested his cheek against hers—he hadn't shaved recently, but there was something very comforting about the brush of masculine whiskers against her delicate skin. I will wait and think about everything over the weekend, she decided, breathing in his scent. It can all wait a day or two; I'll decide what I will tell him then. Hopefully, my assorted friends and admirers won't run amok in the meantime. And Masterson will be out of harm's way at Trestles—although it didn't seem that Savoie truly planned to kill her—not yet, leastways. "Well then; let's get up and pack. Since Reynolds was given the boot, you are charged with choosin' the proper outfit for a wronged wife."

"I like this one," he said, running his hands down her body and kissing her neck.

"No—this is the mistress's outfit, Michael. You are mixed-up."

"There is no mixing the two of you."

"Then keep it to mind that I'm a Puritan—she just may suggest somethin' along those lines and I'm *not* goin' to share."

"Good God, no."

As he kissed her, she giggled again.

CHAPTER 29

*D*OYLE LEANED FORWARD TO PEER AT TRESTLES THROUGH THE Range Rover's windscreen as they came up the long, graveled drive. She'd seen a picture on the Internet, and the reality was every bit as imposing; the massive oak trees that lined the drive revealed glimpses of an ancient edifice of soft-hued stone—expanded and remodeled during the Georgian era, the Web site had said—set in acres and acres of well-tended pastures and woodland. It could have been a generic illustration under "ancestral estate" in the dictionary, and Doyle was a stranger in a strange land. "It's beautiful, Michael," she said sincerely.

"Yes." She caught a glimpse of emotion from him—a deep satisfaction mixed with something else—exultation? It surprised her into silence for a moment; he feels as though it is a prize, she realized—as though he'd won it after a battle of some sort. Which seemed a little strange, as he had inherited it—he was the latest Lord Acton in a lengthy string of them.

She wasn't given time to ponder, because he was briskly back to business as their destination loomed before them. "If you would, try to stay quiet and follow my lead."

"Oh—Michael." She turned to him in acute dismay. "Your plan is *doomed* if it's countin' on that."

He turned to give her his rare smile. "I have every confidence in you."

"Lead on, then." She wished she had every confidence; best button her lip so as not to overturn all of Acton's well-laid plans, whatever they were.

"I'd like to agree on a signal if I'd prefer that you left the room."

She gave him a look. "You could take a turn at brushin' your hair back, I suppose."

"Better that I appear annoyed. I will rub my chin, like this."

He demonstrated, and she nodded, hoping she'd remember. "Will it be safe to ring you up on my mobile, d'you think?"

"Only use it to answer me, if you don't mind."

This was not a problem; like a coward, she'd turned off her mobile that morning because there was a text from Williams. One crisis at a time.

They came to a halt before the worn stone steps that led up to the massive carved-oak front door. The door opened just as Acton came around to help her out of the car, and a dignified silver-haired gentleman in a black suit stood in the entryway, directing a younger man to fetch the luggage from the boot. As they mounted the steps, the silver-haired gentleman bowed his head just enough to preserve his dignity. "Very good to see you, sir; madam."

"Kathleen, allow me to present our steward, Hudson. He will oversee our stay."

As Hudson acknowledged the introduction, Doyle admitted, "I believe we have spoken on the telephone, Hudson."

"Yes, madam; I remember the occasion."

Of course he did; she'd had a largely incoherent conversation with him because she was trying to track Acton down, but had been too intimidated to mention to him that she was Acton's wife. Still and all, he did not seem aghast at having to condescend to meet her lowly self, and indeed, she had a quick flash of well-bred sympathy. So, she thought; even Hudson is aware I'm on Acton's least-favored list.

"The dowager Lady Acton is awaiting you in the drawing room; if you will follow me, please." With a dignified step, the steward escorted them down the marble-floored entryway.

Doyle almost stopped in her tracks at the sudden impression of curious watchfulness; she'd never been in a building that had housed so many generations, and she could feel a strong, fleeting sense of them, then it was gone. Surprised, she raised her gaze to the timbers in the high ceilings and so nearly ran into Hudson, who'd opened a wood-paneled door for her. "Lord and Lady Acton," he announced, and stepped back.

Doyle had a quick impression of wood walls and tasteful upholstery before she focused on the woman sitting ramrod straight on the settee. "Lady Acton," she said, and thought her voice sounded overly-loud in the hushed room. She had forgotten to ask Acton if she was supposed to dip a curtsey or bow her head, so she walked forward and offered her hand, because it seemed the best compromise.

The woman took it and said formally, "How pleasant to see you again, my dear."

This was, of course, not true, but came as no particular surprise; the only other time they'd met had resulted in an all-out donnybrook and Doyle had thrown the woman out of the flat. "Yes—thank you, ma'am," she replied, and wondered what she was thanking her for.

Acton came forward to kiss his mother on the cheek. "Mother."

"Please be seated; Hudson will arrange for refreshments and if you are not too fatigued from your journey, the staff would like to be presented."

Initially there was a small, strained silence whilst Hudson directed the footman to lay out the tea things, and so Doyle did what she did best when she was nervous, and started to talk. She extolled the virtues of the house and the beauty of the surrounding countryside. She recited the pertinent high-lights of their journey and expressed her gratitude that the weather had cooperated. Acton sat silently, looking slightly bored. Lady Acton's cold gaze moved from Doyle to Acton with no hint of what she was thinking. I sound like a complete knocker, thought Doyle, but she could not seem to help her-self; she was desperately trying to resist the urge to leap out the window and flee the scene. She felt a glimpse of approval from her silent husband, but her floundering performance was unfortunately no pretense.

Finally, there was a discreet knock at the door and they turned to face Hudson, who ushered in the other members of the staff as the dowager introduced them. "Our housekeeper, Greta; Greta, this is Acton's new wife, Lady Acton." Doyle nodded from her seat as the woman dipped a curtsey, and the dowager added, "Greta is our dear Marta's sister."

Doyle almost gasped aloud. Marta had been Acton's house-keeper in London, and she had been a willing accomplice in the failed poisoning attempt on the fair Doyle. But Marta had wound up murdered—although it was staged as a suicide—and unfortunately, her death meant they were never to find out whether the dowager was a co-conspirator in the plot. "It is nice to meet you, Greta," Doyle offered, trying not to think of the baby she'd lost. "I am sorry about your sister." Sorry she was paying for her sins, that was; unlikely that a poisoner would find herself clasped to the bosom of Abraham.

Greta nodded in sad acknowledgment. "Thank you, madam."

Doyle was then introduced to the cook, Mrs. Wright, who was plump and rosy-cheeked in the best tradition, and Mathis, the dark-haired upstairs maid who was assigned to as-sist Doyle. They said all that was proper, but Doyle was aware that both were making a covert assessment, the cook looking a little doubtful while the maid kept her thoughts to herself.

After Doyle made the acquaintance of the valet and the footmen, Acton checked his watch and rose. "If you would like to get settled, Kathleen, I will be in my office." He addressed Hudson, "I am expecting a visitor or two; please inform me of any new arrivals."

Doyle glanced at him with some foreboding. More than one visitor? Masterson and who else? Her better half, however, was already moving out the door, giving instruction to Hudson in a low voice. The dowager raised a thin hand toward the maidservant. "Mathis will show you to your rooms, my dear. I hope you find them to your satisfaction." She rose. "We shall reconvene for tea at four."

"Yes, ma'am." Doyle was left to trail along behind Mathis, feeling as though she were a teenager who'd been sent to her room. As they mounted the stairway, she decided to put a few questions to the maid who—truth to tell—seemed much more self-possessed than the new Lady Acton. "Are you related to Greta and Marta, Mathis?"

"No, madam. I am Mr. Hudson's grand-niece."

"Oh—I see. Did you know Marta at all?"

"Some, but she was mainly before my time; she went to live in London a few years ago."

Doyle feigned regret. "I feel so badly that I didn't know how unhappy she was—did you have any idea why she killed herself?"

"No, madam," said Mathis, and it was the truth.

"Did you hear anyone speak of it, here?"

The girl turned to face Doyle for a moment from the stair above. "It saddened all of us; a terrible tragedy."

Girl's a brick wall, thought Doyle a bit crossly. There's little point in having a ladies' maid unless she's gossipy, for the love o' Mike.

"Here we are, madam." The girl opened the entry door into a suite of rooms. "Please allow me to unpack your bag."

As the maid efficiently hung her clothes in a large armoire,

Doyle admired the sumptuous suite, and tried not to feel as though she'd gone through the looking-glass. The furnishings were elegant, the rug thick and luxurious, and the four-poster bed so high she wondered if she'd have to take a running leap to land atop the feather bed. Mathis offered no further comment, and so Doyle, feeling self-conscious, wandered over to the many-paned windows and found herself looking out over beautifully laid-out formal gardens. Resisting the urge to press her face to the glass, she gazed in wonder at the precisely-trimmed hedges and the geometric flower beds, arranged in alternating, vibrant colors. It was breathtaking, and she couldn't help but admire Acton's strategy; no reward promised by a Russian mobster could match this view alone. There wasn't an Englishwoman alive who hadn't fantasized about being mistress of such an estate, and it suddenly occurred to Doyle that *she* was the mistress of this estate—down to every flower in the flowerbeds. It was a far cry from walking with her mother to buy a soup bone because it was the week the rent was due. How strange life was.

She turned to the maid. "Such a pretty room, Mathis—but I don't see my husband's bag. Where will Lord Acton be stayin'?"

"In the master's chamber, madam."

"I see," said Doyle, and she did.

CHAPTER 30

*A*FTER MATHIS LEFT, DOYLE WAITED IN HER ROOMS FOR A TIME, feeling out-of-place and half-hoping that Acton would come to find her, even though she knew it wouldn't fit the protocol, which seemed to feature avoiding his neglected wife. As for her own protocol, she should probably shake her stumps and go do a little listening, since Acton thought someone here was leaking information to Masterson. At first she'd thought Greta a likely candidate, but on reflection, Greta's sister, Marta, met her end because she was overly-loyal to the House of Acton, and willing to poison the red-headed usurper because of it. Based on the family history, then, it seemed unlikely that Greta had turned traitor. On the other hand, with her sister dead, Greta may be thinking of a warm retirement in the Bahamas, and thirty pieces of silver would certainly come in handy. One thing was certain; if this manor house was anything like St. Brigid's School for Girls, the cook would have her finger squarely on the pulse of the place. With this in mind, Doyle made her way to the kitchens.

Mrs. Wright was in the process of preparing the tea, and seemed genuinely pleased to behold Doyle, looking over the offerings. "I'm empty as a pocket," Doyle confessed. "Don't tell the dowager that I was here, scrimblin' like a tinker."

With a conspiratorial chuckle, the cook served up a hot

scone. "If I may say so, you don't look like you're one for cu-
cumber sandwiches, my lady."

Doyle contemplated this remark as she pinched at the scone
and then quickly withdrew her fingers from the hot steam that
emerged. "Are the sandwiches truly made from cucumbers, or
is it cucumbers between bread?"

"Cucumbers between bread." The cook indicated the silver
tray on the far counter with a nod of her head.

"Oh," Doyle offered doubtfully. "Any chance that a slice of
fried ham can be thrown atop?"

The other woman smiled as she bent to check her breads.
"Well, we'll be having Cornish hens for dinner, as the master
is very fond of them."

Mental note, thought Doyle. I'll tell Reynolds about the
Cornish hens—that is, if I am still married by the time this
flippin' weekend is over.

The woman gave her a sidelong glance. "We're to have
guests for dinner."

This was said with an ominous undertone, and Doyle gladly
took the bait. "Relatives, I suppose." She sighed, and tried to
look very put-upon. "What are they like?"

But the conversation took an unexpected turn, as Mrs.
Wright paused to clasp her hands beneath her apron and be-
stow a measuring gaze upon her guest. "I understand that
your mother has passed on, so there's none to offer a bit of
advice, with you so young, and not knowing how to go on."

Very much surprised at being thus addressed, Doyle confessed, "It is true that I'm not very good at the goin' on."

"Well, here's a word to the wise, then. You'd best watch
your husband."

Doyle met her eyes, genuinely startled by the woman's can-
dor, but the cook was unrepentant, and nodded. "Best take
this chance to warn you, since I may not get another. Can't
beat about the bush—there's a woman coming who's got her
eye on him."

Cautiously, Doyle pretended to consider this. "He's always been somethin' of a flirt."

"I don't like the looks of this one," the other declared bluntly. "She'll have him, if she can, and it's up to you to put a stop to it."

"I think," ventured Doyle, "that you are over-estimatin' my abilities, here."

"Nonsense," the cook countered briskly. "You're young and pretty; remember, he wanted to marry you—not another."

"That's true." And the story was a good one; it was almost a shame neither this cook nor anyone else would ever hear it.

After assessing her for a moment, Mrs. Wright turned to address the tea, brewing in a large canister on the stovetop. "The master being who he is, there'll always be women after him—like this one; or Mathis. You'd better find a way to keep his mind on you, if I may be saying so. But no sulking," she added, and tapped the counter with a spoon to emphasize this last point. "There's nothing that will drive a man away faster. Better to provide good food and plenty of sex; men are simple creatures."

As Acton was the farthest thing imaginable from a simple creature, Doyle made no comment, but nodded thoughtfully in response to this pragmatic advice, noting with interest that Mathis the maid had been included in the list of hazards. Saints, she thought; apparently the place is riddled with brassers, and as Munoz was wont to point out, everything is always about sex. Or perhaps Mathis is in league with Masterson, and is trying to seduce Acton's secrets from him. But that theory made little sense; if that were the case, the maid could not be best-pleased to see Acton seducing Masterson, so to speak, and causing the reporter to stray from their stated goal. It was un-likely that the plan involved multiple seductions by all co-conspirators.

Doyle's train of thought was interrupted by the cook, who apparently felt it was necessary to steel Doyle's spine. "Make a push for him, and don't back down." The woman eyed her a bit doubtfully. "Everyone says you're very brave."

Doyle disclaimed, "It's been made up to be more than it is," and then wondered, yet again, why her scalp prickled whenever the bridge-jumping incident came up in conversation.

Before the other woman could make a reply, Mathis herself appeared in the kitchen doorway. "My lady is asking for you, madam. She is in the drawing room and would like the tea to be brought in."

Doyle rose immediately, looking self-conscious. "I must go—thank you, Mrs. Wright." The cook allowed an eyelid to close in a slow wink, and then went to assemble the tea.

Upon her entrance to the drawing room, Doyle was met with the sight of Acton, the dowager, and Cassie Masterson, all seated around the low table whilst Masterson laughed vivaciously at something Acton had said. He was smiling, with one hand casually holding on to the back of Masterson's chair, but looked up upon her arrival. "Hallo, Kathleen; allow me to introduce . . ."

"Oh—we've met. How are you, Ms. Masterson?"

Masterson stood and offered her hand in a friendly fashion. "Cassie—please. I am well, thank you. Have you had any luck with your microfiche search?"

"Some promisin' leads," Doyle replied, and was surprised to realize this was true. What leads? she thought, a bit bewildered. Mr. Moran and Morgan Percy? With an effort, she refocused. "I understand you are researchin' the archives, here. Are you followin' a story, then?"

"Cassie has an interest in historical estates," offered Acton, a hint of warm pride in his voice. "She has agreed to archive the estate documents for the past hundred years, as the recent history has been neglected." He bestowed his half-smile upon their visitor. "My fault, I'm afraid—I never seem to find the time."

Whilst Doyle processed the daunting fact that the last hundred years would be considered "recent," the dowager turned to ask her, "Did you find your rooms to your liking, my dear?"

"I did indeed—everythin' is lovely."

With friendly curiosity, Masterson asked, "Are you in the Georgian wing, or the Elizabethan?"

"The Georgian, I think," said Doyle, who hadn't a clue. "It overlooks the gardens."

"Capability Brown," pronounced Masterson.

"What's that?" asked Doyle.

"Capability Brown redesigned the gardens. They were Tudor, originally," Acton explained.

"Well then; that is excellent." Doyle feared that she hadn't completely erased the sarcasm from her voice; the brasser had studied up, apparently.

To cover the awkward moment, Acton suggested, "Shall we have our tea in the archives room? I can show Cassie how the documents are organized." He looked up at Doyle and absently brought his hand to his chin. "Come, Kathleen; you should become familiar, also."

Taking her cue from his signal, Doyle demurred. "Would you be mindin' very much if I take a nap, instead? I promise I'll catch up tomorrow." Doyle did her best to appear guileless and unaware that she was making a major conjugal error, but noted that the dowager regarded her narrowly with her hooded gaze.

"I will see you again at dinner, then," said Masterson, radiating glee mixed with anticipation.

She's taken her measure of me and thinks this is going to be like shooting fish in a barrel, thought Doyle as she said her good-byes. Here's hoping Acton knows what he's about, and here's hoping he can keep her at arm's length in the dusty archives—I'd send Mathis to chaperone if I wasn't worried Mathis would try to jump him herself.

As if on cue, the maid met her at the foot of the stairs. "Might I be of assistance, madam?"

"I'm going to my room for a rest, Mathis, but thank you."

"May I bring you coffee? Lord Acton tells me you are quite fond."

Unbidden, Doyle had a flashing memory of what it felt like to be poisoned, and barely managed to remain civil. "No. No, thank you."

In an unhappy frame of mind, Doyle returned to her room and climbed up to sit on the bed, looking out at the fading light and wishing she could seek some comfort from Acton. He is working out some clever plan, she reminded herself firmly; stop being such a baby and try to help him, for heaven's sake. Unfortunately, she hadn't gleaned much, thus far. The dowager despised her, but this was to be expected, and it boggled the mind to think that she could be working hand-in-glove with Solonik—it would be beneath her dignity to fraternize with a foreigner. Mathis was annoying, but didn't seem to be harboring any particular animosity toward her, and although Mrs. Wright had hinted that the maid was after Acton, Doyle did not garner that impression. Hudson, one would think, would sacrifice himself on the Acton family altar rather than betray them, and besides, Doyle had the impression that Acton trusted the steward, and Acton was not one to trust anyone. There weren't many more on the list of potential suspects; the cook seemed inclined to prop her up, rather than invite her to betray Acton—oh, she thought suddenly, her scalp prickling—I've missed something. Closing her eyes, Doyle tried to concentrate; there was something Mrs. Wright said that was significant—now, what was it?

There was a soft knock on the door, and Doyle's eyes flew open in hopeful anticipation—perhaps it was Acton. She opened the door to Hudson, however, who bowed his head gravely. "Lord Acton requests that you turn on your mobile, madam."

"Oh—I forgot it was off. Thank you, Hudson." The steward retreated, making no further comment, so Doyle shut the door after him and turned on her mobile. There were several text messages from Acton—the symbol he used to check in with her—and she smiled at the screen. Don't fret, you knocker, she thought; I know it's all a sham. She texted her symbol back, and added "Cereal?" Cereal was their code word for sex.

The reply came promptly: "No. Sorry."

She texted her symbol again to show she understood. If he crept into her room tonight, all their playacting would be for naught. Fair enough; it would be harder on him than on her.

There was another text from Williams, and Doyle reluctantly opened it. "RU OK?" it said.

Wary, Doyle decided she'd best answer. "Yes. Need 2 talk." She wondered if he knew that Masterson was here. She opened his first message—the one she'd ignored—and it said: "Call me?" Williams, she thought, feeling a pang of misery; if any of this is your doing I *promise* I will strangle you with my bare hands.

Whilst she held the mobile in her hands, Williams replied, "Now is OK—meet 4 coffee?" She stared at it thoughtfully. Apparently he didn't know she was away. Or—he did and was pretending not to know. Couldn't trust him until she found out. "Monday," she texted.

She waited a few minutes and the reply came, "OK."

You'd better hope it's OK, she thought grimly. Or you'll be left to Acton's tender mercies and believe me, my friend; he's neither tender nor merciful.

CHAPTER 31

*D*OYLE DESCENDED THE STAIRWAY JUST AT SEVEN, BECAUSE SHE imagined the dowager expected her dinner guests to be prompt. She was aware that as the current Lady Acton, she was not exactly a guest, but it was inconceivable that she would attempt to countermand the dowager, and so she was content to recede into the background and follow whatever lead Acton was willing to give her. She hoped she looked the part of the neglected bride; she wore the black cashmere sweater that Acton had selected, and she'd pulled back her hair with a black ribbon headband. The headband made her appear younger than her already-tender years, and so she applied some lip gloss as a counterbalance. Mathis had offered her assistance, but Doyle had declined, being as she really didn't need any help putting on lip gloss and the last thing she needed was a misguided attempt to make her more presentable. Nevertheless, she duly noted that the maid lurked outside in the hallway, pretending to arrange flowers but with her ears on the stretch. Search my room, if you like, thought Doyle with some spite as she closed the door; nothing worth seeing, my friend.

She entered the drawing room to behold Acton, the dowager, and Masterson, as well as another gentleman, all in quiet conversation whilst a footman served cocktails. Acton approached, kissed her cheek perfunctorily, and then brought her over to the gentleman. "Allow me to introduce my cousin, Kathleen; Sir Stephen Waite."

So; here was the cousin and heir who Acton so disliked, and Doyle looked him over with interest. Sir Stephen was a head shorter than Acton and had light brown hair and eyes; not Acton's dark eyes and coloring that he shared with his mother. A relative on his father's side, presumably—which made sense if he was Acton's current heir. Sir Stephen was scrutinizing her narrowly behind a benign expression, and Doyle had a brief impression of relief as he took her hand. "Lady Acton; your fame precedes you. I am honored to make your acquaintance."

"Why, what 'fame' is this?" The dowager raised her thin brows.

"You do not know of it? Lady Acton jumped off Greyfriars Bridge to rescue someone in the line of duty."

The dowager looked as though she had never heard of anything so vulgar, and so Doyle was moved to demur, "It was nothin', truly."

"Oh, it was a brilliant story," Masterson disagreed with a slight lift of her wine glass. "Three days coverage and an extra print run."

"A nine days' wonder," the gentleman agreed with just a touch of condescension.

Doyle could feel the color flooding her face as Acton interjected smoothly, "Cassie has volunteered to update the archives, Stephen."

Sir Stephen flicked Acton a speculative look, and then turned to Masterson. "Have you indeed? I commend you for taking on the task."

The other woman smiled her confident smile. "It is no hardship, I assure you. I did a series a few years ago about the history of the great houses, and I find the subject fascinating."

Doyle found this of great interest, as it indicated Acton had done his homework with this potential home-wrecker; Doyle would bet her teeth that this archives-sorting gambit was no chance assignment.

Very pleased to hold the floor, Masterson continued, "So far, I've sorted the documents into decades, but tomorrow I'll go through them more thoroughly to separate the wheat from the chaff, so to speak. It is completely fascinating; the details bring the storied past to life." She cast a respectful glance at the dowager, who only pursed her mouth and made no return.

Trying to charm the old guard, thought Doyle. Good luck to her; Masterson would be just as unwelcome a daughter-in-law as the vulgar bridge-jumper. She briefly met Acton's eye and noted that her husband was not happy that Sir Stephen had been patronizing to her—she knew the signs. Hopefully, they would refrain from fisticuffs in front of the newspaper reporter.

Sir Stephen could not share Masterson's enthusiasm. "Perhaps not as fascinating as you might hope; Trestles managed the two world wars without incident. On the other hand, the seventeenth century was one long crisis."

"Indeed," agreed the dowager. "It took a great deal of courage and political maneuvering to see that Trestles was preserved."

Masterson saw another opening to impress the dowager, and added, "It *is* extraordinary that it has prospered to such an extent—so many famous estates have fallen to the National Trust because the families were unable to keep them up."

There was a small silence, and Doyle was surprised to feel crosscurrents of strong emotion between the others, but before she could sort it out, the front bell echoed.

"That will be dear Melinda," announced the dowager to the room in general, and Doyle could sense Acton's flare of irritation. Saints, she thought. Now what?

Melinda proved to be a slender, languid, and quintessentially aristocratic woman approximately Acton's age who glided into the room in a negligent fashion. She immediately approached Acton, lifted on tiptoe to kiss him, then wiped her lipstick from his cheek with a thumb. "Acton, you *devil.* You, married! Which one is she?" She looked at Masterson and Doyle, then decided on Masterson as the more likely candidate, so that Acton was required to inform the newcomer that his bride was, in fact, the unlikely Doyle. Undaunted, Melinda embraced her and whispered loud enough for the others to hear, "We have *a lot* to talk about."

Ah, thought Doyle; here is someone with carnal knowledge of Acton, no doubt invited by his mother to cause trouble before she was made aware that Masterson was already primed for the role. Just *crackin'* grand.

Melinda deftly lifted a vodka tonic from the proffered tray, and revealed to Doyle and Masterson that she had been a neighbor until she married and moved away. "I traded my husband for a great deal of alimony," she confided. "Better luck to you." This was directed at Doyle, who wasn't certain how to respond.

Melinda then turned to Masterson. "Are you here with Stephen?"

"No." Masterson offered no further explanation, but had the look of someone relishing a delightful secret, which made Doyle long to draw her weapon and shoot her dead.

"Cassie is a newspaper reporter," Sir Stephen offered. "She writes about the great houses."

"As a sideline," Masterson corrected with a smile. "Mainly, I cover major crimes in the Metropolitan area—that's how I met Acton."

"You must be busy, then." Melinda waved a vague hand of disinterest.

"Yes—unfortunately London has no shortage of major crimes."

"Deplorable; it is the foreign element, no doubt." The dowager's gaze rested briefly upon Doyle.

"Cassie does commendable work," Acton offered. "The press is a necessary component of law enforcement."

That this was an out-and-out falsehood came as no surprise to Doyle; Acton had no use for newspapers except for those rare occasions when he needed the public's help with a crime.

"It is rewarding work," agreed Masterson, her gaze resting thoughtfully on her wine glass. "But like most career women, I have sacrificed the personal for the professional. I would very much like to have a family, some day." She carefully did not look at Acton, nor he at her, and Doyle would have rolled her eyes if she had not been so surprised—Masterson was lying. About what? Wanting a family? Having a family?

Doyle decided to test it out. "You've never married?" She realized it sounded as though she was trying to appear superior, but decided that it would fit the protocol if she were petty, and awaited an answer.

"No," said Masterson, smiling sweetly. "I'd never met the right man."

She used the past tense, of course, the brasser. Doyle could feel Acton's gaze on her and knew he wanted her to drop it. Doyle complied, but not before she processed the interesting fact that Masterson was indeed lying.

The dowager took this opportunity to pronounce, "Marriage is the foundation of civilization; it must be the ultimate object of every woman."

Doyle duly noted that she was lying, too.

Melinda tossed her head at Sir Stephen as she lifted another drink from the tray. "Listen to your aunt, Stephen; you must take your cue from Acton, and marry someone young and fecund."

Doyle was not sure what "fecund" meant, but noted Stephen's flare of carefully suppressed fury at Melinda's baiting. I am going to be wrung out like a dishrag by the end of this evening, she thought with resignation, and then felt her mobile vibrate. "Excuse me." She stepped aside to read the screen, which contained a message from Habib. "A murder," it said. "Perhaps related."

"My son may not have mentioned that mobile phones are not permitted at dinner." The dowager's tone was icy.

Doyle looked up. "I beg your pardon, ma'am. Michael, may I speak to you for a moment?"

With palpable reluctance, Acton excused himself and stepped aside to confer with her.

"D'you have any ammo on you?" Doyle whispered. "Bein' as I may not have enough to shoot them all with one clip."

"Wait for my signal," came his unruffled reply. "What was the call?"

"Habib. He thinks there's another park murder."

He met her eyes with regret. "We can't leave, I'm afraid. Not until tomorrow evening at the earliest."

"You're killin' me, here, my friend. Munoz is dyin' to jump on this case."

"Call Williams and have him supervise the SOCOs. He'll not miss anything."

Doyle noted that to any observers, Acton's attitude was one of suppressed annoyance, at odds with his words to her. "Would you mind callin' Williams yourself? We're quarrelin'."

"I dare not leave you alone," was the surprising reply, and he was dead serious.

"I'll text him, then; although your mother may throw my mobile against the wall."

"My mother," he replied in a mild tone, "is no longer the mistress of Trestles."

"I'll mistress you one, I will," she retorted crossly, scrolling for Williams's number. "I've half a mind to throw myself into the nearest moat."

Hudson bowed from the doorway. "Dinner is served."

CHAPTER 32

*T*HE GRAND DINING ROOM WAS DOMINATED BY A HUGE MA-
hogany table, centered between walls lined with red silk fab-
ric and positioned beneath an impressive crystal chandelier.
A painting with some mythological scene involving a bull—
Doyle was not well-versed in things mythological—was promi-
nently displayed on the wall across from her, and a confusing
array of plates, glasses, and silverware glittered on the table.
Acton was seated at the head with Doyle to his left, and Sir
Stephen on her other side. Melinda and Masterson sat across
from them, the dowager at the foot. Conversation was going
to be difficult, as Doyle was naturally soft-voiced and the table
could seat twenty. It seemed, however, that the now-tipsy
Melinda was willing to take up the mantle as the footman la-
dled out the soup.

"Tell me about yourself, Kathleen; I know absolutely *nothing* about you."

"I'm from Dublin, originally." This seemed self-evident, but
there wasn't much else to recite. She couldn't very well de-
scribe St. Brigid's, or her first paying job at the fish market.
Nothing like a job at the fish market to encourage one to en-
roll in the local police academy.

"Our stable hand is from Ireland," offered the dowager.
"You must meet him."

"Do you still have family in Ireland?" asked Masterson. She was no doubt thinking it would be nice to have Doyle out of the country, once she'd usurped the throne.

"No—both my parents have been gathered up." Best not to mention she left her father's murder scene to go off and marry Acton; that would probably be considered more vulgar than the bridge-jumping incident. "I came to London to be a police constable, and then I enrolled in the Crime Academy to be a detective."

"And then you met Acton and *none* of us were invited to your wedding; *shame* on the both of you."

The last thing either of them would have wanted was extraneous people at their wedding, so Doyle offered diplomatically, "It was a bit spur-o'-the-moment, I'm afraid." Understatement of the century.

Melinda addressed Acton archly, leaning forward with her elbows on the table. "Is that so? I never fancied you for a romantic."

"I have hidden depths," was his reply, and Doyle was careful not to meet his eye.

But Masterson was unhappy with this topic, and switched it back to one that would feature herself. "Is there any chance I can enlist your hidden depths to help with the archives tomorrow?"

He smiled at her, sorry to disappoint. "I'm to ride in the morning with a friend."

This was true, and before Doyle could process this unexpected announcement, he added, "and I promised Kathleen I'd give her a riding lesson."

Doyle glanced up at him, a bit surprised, as this was news to the aforesaid Kathleen.

"You haven't ridden?" The dowager allowed her features to register well-bred dismay. "Ever?"

"No, ma'am," Doyle affirmed. And then, because she was

unable to stop herself, "Although I *have* been hangin' about the racecourse of late."

The dowager drew her brows together in disapproval. "Have you riding dress?"

"No, ma'am," said Doyle again. "I have not."

"There's a pair of Fiona's old boots in the stable," offered Acton. "They should fit."

"A sad business," said the dowager with a small shake of her head, and Doyle belatedly realized she was referring to the late Fiona, and not her own failings. "A ridiculous and dangerous job for a woman; small wonder she was murdered."

As Doyle also worked at the CID, and did not feel that Fiona in any way deserved to be murdered, she made no comment. She noted, however, that Masterson had perked up. "I remember that story—did the Yard ever solve her murder, Acton?"

He admitted with regret, "The trail went very cold." That the trail went cold by his own contrivance remained unmentioned.

Masterson shrugged slightly in an expression of understanding. "You can't solve them all, of course. But there is hope; Lady Acton is currently trying to put some cold cases to bed." She emphasized the title slightly; testing out the way it sounded when spoken aloud.

"That I am," acknowledged Doyle. "And it's a tough row to hoe because the evidence is a bit sketchy. If the victim is not sympathetic—or if there are no relatives cryin' out for justice—sometimes the detectives workin' the case are not as thorough as they should be."

"It is fortunate there was press coverage, then," offered Masterson with some complacency. "The microfiche records should help."

"There is a big difference between publicity and evidence, though." Doyle brought to mind her conversation with Williams and Percy. "The publicity sometimes manipulates the evidence."

Masterson, however, did not care for this remark, and bristled a bit. "There is nothing more important to an investigative reporter than journalistic integrity, I assure you."

"You must admit," Sir Stephen observed with a cynical twist of his mouth, "that oftentimes it appears the reporter is supporting an agenda." Doyle noted that Sir Stephen had been awaiting an opportunity to needle Masterson—a first-class needler, he was.

"I suppose that's true," Masterson conceded. "But then the reporter runs the risk of losing credibility. Above all, you can't jeopardize your credibility—that's the only thing you have, in this business."

"The same is true in our business." Acton bestowed upon Masterson a half-smile of approval, and Doyle noted that one of his hands was out of sight beneath the table. With a mighty effort, she resisted an urge to pin it to the table with her fork to keep it within sight.

The interminable dinner party continued through yet another course, this time fish in a white sauce. Doyle did not care for fish as a result of her stint at the fish market, and pushed it around with her fork, longing to fly away to London so as to take a gander at the latest corpse.

"How does McGonigal, Acton?" The dowager shook her head in dignified sorrow. "A sad business about Caroline—I was quite fond of her."

Acton replied, "He does well, despite his loss. In fact, he has met a very nice woman."

"I will dine with him and meet her, the next time I am in town," the dowager pronounced generously, and Doyle could not resist meeting Acton's eye for a millisecond. She could only imagine the dowager's reaction upon meeting Nanda, impoverished and fresh from Rwanda with a baby in tow.

For Masterson's benefit, the dowager explained, "Caroline

and Timothy McGonigal are old friends of Acton's from school. Regretfully, Caroline took her own life recently."

"Oh—I am sorry to hear it. Was it unexpected?"

"Indeed," said the dowager. "Wouldn't you say so, Acton?"

"Baffling," agreed Acton, who'd shot Caroline dead.

Melinda spoke up a little too loudly. "At the risk of speaking ill of the dead, I'll admit I always found her *annoying*. And she didn't like me at all." Thinking about it, she then added fairly, "Timothy's a good sort. Glad he's happy; probably feels liberated, without the sister hanging about."

"Indeed," said the dowager hastily, steering the conversation away from Melinda's too-honest observations; "Timothy was always such a nice boy—Acton's father was very fond of him. They shared an interest in music."

Doyle's ears pricked up. She realized she'd never heard anyone speak of Acton's father, including Acton. As she had been fatherless herself, she hadn't really noticed but now, on reflection, it seemed a little odd; she had no idea how long Acton had held the title. Knowing instinctively that Acton would continue to avoid the subject, she debated whether or not to pursue it here, whilst she had a chance. Instead, Masterson did it for her.

"Was your father a musician, then, Acton?"

"Yes," Acton said briefly, and Doyle's antennae quivered.

"He was *renowned*; wrote scores and won medals and such," explained Melinda, making expansive gestures as people did when they drank too much. She leaned forward to conclude dramatically, "And then he *disappeared*." She saw that this revelation was met with surprised silence by Doyle and Masterson, and so she lifted her glass to them and smiled. "No secrets among family, what?"

Doyle wasn't sure which was more startling; discovering that Acton's father had disappeared, or having Melinda casually placing Masterson at the same familial level as herself.

"Disappeared?" asked Masterson, like a hound to the scent.

She realizes Acton doesn't want to discuss it, but can't help herself, thought Doyle; all that journalistic integrity and all. The atmosphere was strained, and as neither Acton nor the dowager made a response, Sir Stephen stepped into the awkward silence and replied briefly, "Yes, many years ago. He was eventually declared dead."

Doyle could sense Masterson's avid interest, but it would be impossible to pursue the subject further, in light of the resounding silence coming from Acton and his mother. She dropped her gaze to her plate to hide her uneasiness; Masterson was absorbing disturbing information that could further Solonik's schemes, if she were ever diverted from her current pursuit of Acton's honors. For the hundredth time, Doyle hoped that Acton knew what he was about; all it needed was for the drunk Melinda to start talking about what it was like to have sex with Acton, and her evening would be complete. While she worried, Acton touched her leg gently, and she was immediately comforted. He was more than a match for all of them, and she shouldn't panic like a green recruit.

Thankfully, Melinda had turned her languid attention to Masterson. "Do you cover the Royals?"

"Heavens, no," laughed Masterson. "I leave that to the tabloids; instead I serve the public."

Hearing the phrase that Kevin Maguire had once used, Doyle asked, "Have you worked with Kevin Maguire?"

"I have," Masterson said to her kindly, as if pleased a child had asked an intelligent question. "Maguire is an institution at the paper—larger-than-life."

"A very nice man," remembered Doyle.

"And very knowledgeable," agreed Masterson. "He makes it his business to know everything about everyone."

Saints, thought Doyle in distress, sensing the woman's smug satisfaction. Maguire has told Masterson everything he knows about Acton, which was probably quite a bit, since he'd been working on an exposé when Doyle had convinced him to drop it. Doyle didn't like to think that Maguire would allow Masterson to use his information for blackmail, or revenge, or whatever Solonik's purpose was; Maguire didn't seem that sort.

"Shall we play bridge after dinner?" The dowager turned to Doyle with a lifted brow. "You do play bridge, my dear?"

Doyle felt Acton's gaze upon her as he fingered his chin, and so she demurred, "Not very well, I'm afraid."

"Yes; it may be too confusing for you. Instead, Acton will help you keep score."

Hatchet-faced *gargoyle*, thought Doyle, feeling her color rise as she fixed her eyes on her plate and pressed her lips together. Your poor husband probably fled in horror, and it's a wonder your son didn't shoot you long, long ago. He's not one to hesitate.

Acton turned to Masterson and suggested he partner her, and she happily agreed, giving him a glance that indicated she would be very happy to partner him in other ways, as well. The dowager and Sir Stephen made up the table, with Melinda content to freshen up her drink and join Doyle as an observer. "A shame about her," Melinda offered in a sympathetic aside, her words slightly slurred. "I quite like you."

"No you don't," said Doyle, and it was true.

CHAPTER 33

*A*FTER A FEW HANDS OF BRIDGE, ACTON RESTED HIS CHIN ON his hand and so Doyle stood and announced with poor grace, "Well, I'm for bed."

As though reminded of his obligations, Acton solicitously escorted her to Mathis at the foot of the stairs, and asked the maid to see that she was ready for her ride in the morning. He then kissed Doyle's forehead distractedly and headed back to Masterson. For Mathis's benefit, Doyle watched him go and pretended to silently fume as she ascended the stairs.

The maid offered no comment, and saw her to her room. "If you need anything, madam, please ring me—you have my cell programmed? I will knock in the morning to be certain that you are up."

Doyle clambered onto the feathery bed to lie awake and think about what she'd learned. She didn't sleep well in a strange place, and on top of that, she hadn't slept without Acton's arms around her since the day after they were married, so she was reconciled to a restless night—hopefully it would be the only one, and they could leave for home tomorrow. She was very sensitive to atmosphere and it was thick as soup in this place, between the miserable assortment downstairs and the vague feeling of watchful generations, hovering about. Hurry Acton, she pleaded mentally; solve the problem. I need to get back and sort out a serial killer and a French kingpin, and not necessarily in that order.

As for Acton's problems, they didn't seem any closer to a resolution, either. Doyle had duly noted that Mathis the maid was a bundle of suppressed wariness, despite her demure manner—but small wonder, with such a monumental scandal brewing for all to see. Doyle just couldn't see the maid conniving with someone like Solonik, though; the slyness wasn't there, although it was there in spades with Cousin Stephen—a likely villain if there ever was one. Doyle had also begun to wonder if the person leaking information from Trestles was even aware of Masterson's role; Doyle hadn't caught the feeling that any of them shared a secret with the reporter, which seemed strange. Acton was probably doing the same thing—watching for any significant interaction between Masterson and one of the others. She tried not to imagine what else Acton was willing to do for the cause, but it was best not to dwell on it; she could only hope that he would not run the risk of making the fair Doyle so unhappy again.

Hard on this thought, the key turned in the lock and Acton himself came in, holding a cup between his hands as Mathis closed the door behind him. "If anyone asks, you sent a text asking me to bring up warm milk."

"Mother a' *mercy*, I'm a pill." She lifted her face for his kiss. "How goes your schemin'?"

"I wanted to assure you that all is in train." He leaned against the bed and lifted a palm to her cheek, still warm from the cup. "I am sorry it is so uncomfortable for you, Kathleen. If I could spare you this, I would."

Doyle thought it an opportune time to mention, "Mrs. Wright implied that you were diddlin' the maid."

He bent his head for a moment to smile. "No, although I've been closeted with Mathis once or twice because she is working for me, assigned to keep an eye on you."

"Oh—oh, I see. Well, it's irritatin', is what it is. Why didn't you tell me?"

"Sometimes," he explained in a diplomatic tone, "your thoughts are a little transparent."

This was unfortunately true, but didn't mean that Doyle appreciated having it pointed out. "I'm that sorry—but I can't hold a candle to your girlfriend, who acts like she owns the place already. That's a dinner party I won't be forgettin' for a good while."

"A necessary evil," he said only, and fingered her hands in his. "What else did Mrs. Wright have to say?"

"Mainly, she was exhortin' me to do battle with the pretender, and tryin' to make me believe I had a fightin' chance. She cooks up an excellent scone, by the by."

He was silent for a moment, and then shifted the subject. "You didn't eat much, tonight."

"Can you be blamin' me, husband? It's a rare wonder I didn't upend the table."

"Melinda—" he paused. "Melinda was a long time ago."

"Clearly. Your taste has improved by leaps and bounds, my friend."

He smiled at her tone. "My mother would be very content to drive you away."

"She can't do it," declared Doyle with some spirit. "And I doubt she'd be happier with nasty Cassie, anyway."

"No," he agreed.

He seemed lost in thought, and she respected his mood for a few moments, then steeled herself to say what needed to be said, remembering her visit with wretched Solonik in the wretched, wretched prison. "I want you to know, Michael, that if it came down to brass tacks and you had to do somethin' desperate—like marry the brasser to keep her in check—I would understand."

Acton paused in fingering her hands, and lifted his head to stare at her. "What nonsense is this?"

Calmly, she reiterated, "I just want you to know that if I had the choice of savin' you by lettin' you go, I'd rather do that."

"Not an option."

He was annoyed, and she tried to tease him. "I could be your mistress, for a switch; only think how it would horrify your mother."

"Kathleen, have done."

She subsided into silence. Touchy, he was.

After a moment, he lifted her hand to kiss it. "I am sorry I snapped at you."

"It was not a good idea, perhaps."

"You should have more faith in me," he said, gently chiding.

"Then I'm sorry, too." She hoped he wouldn't forget what she'd said, just in case.

He took a breath and reluctantly relinquished her hands. "I should go; I will see you tomorrow morning."

"Don't let her climb onto your lap; that's my territory." This was a reference to a very satisfying session of lovemaking that had begun spontaneously the other day; best to remind her husband what-was-what.

"Don't worry; I will tell her that it is important not to jump the gun."

"Just as long as no one is jumpin' your gun, my friend."

With a wry mouth, he gave her a look as he shut the door behind him.

She sat for a moment with her gaze on the closed door, thinking. He'd not mentioned the horse-riding tomorrow, but it seemed unlikely it was a chance ride with a friend, as he'd said. And another thing; he hadn't explained why he'd appointed Mathis as watchdog. He was a world-class fretter, of course, but perhaps the jury was still out with respect to the dowager-as-poisoner. Sir Stephen was a dirty dish, and there was no love lost between he and Acton—but it seemed unlikely he was a danger to her; she was a trained police officer, after all, and theoretically able to handle herself. Lying back into the soft pillows, she propped her arms behind her head. And tied up in this tangle was the strange fact that Acton's father had disappeared, long ago. There was something there that made everyone uneasy—she wished the conversation at the table had continued for a few more minutes. Although the subject shouldn't have been raised in the first place—nothing like airing the dirty linen before a news reporter; Melinda was a crackin' idiot.

She hadn't realized that she drifted off to sleep until she dreamed a strange and uncomfortable dream; a figure stood before her—that of a middle-aged man, dressed in some sort of war gear. He had bad teeth, and his hand rested on the hilt of a sword.

"Go 'way," she said, annoyed. "I've nothin' to do with any of this."

He made no reply, but she thought she heard a dog, howling mournfully in the distance.

She tried again. "I'm naught but a shant, and a mackerel snapper, to boot. You have me confused wi' the bridge-jumper."

With a start, she was suddenly wide-awake, sitting up in bed and listening to the silence. The moonlight filtered through the curtains, and the house was still. She lay back down, her heart beating in her throat, longing to go and find Acton.

CHAPTER 34

*D*OYLE WAS AWAKENED THE NEXT MORNING BY MATHIS'S SOFT knock. "Are you up, madam? It's eight o' clock."

"Yes, Mathis. Thank you." Trying to pull herself together, Doyle checked her mobile to find text messages from both Williams and Acton.

She was ashamed to admit she was more interested in what Williams had to say about the latest murder. "Secured the scene, SOCOs on it," it said. "It's a twist. Talk soon?"

"I hope," she texted back. "Will let U know." A twist—leave it to Williams to say nothing further; although he was probably being tentative because he was worried there was still some constraint between them. With exquisite frustration, she rubbed her face in her hands, yearning to be back in the thick of it. On some level, she was aware that she should have already solved these murders, but it was tantalizingly out of reach—she was being dense, for some reason, and her instinct needed a bit of a push. Perhaps this latest case—the one with the twist—would offer the final clue. It was confusing because it was all tied up in everything else.

She paused in surprise, her fingers poised before opening Acton's text message. It was all tied up in everything else? What did *that* mean? Unbidden, she remembered her dream, and Acton's missing father, and Sir Stephen's patronizing attitude. I am stark, raving mad, she thought in disgust, and opened up Acton's message.

"Breakfast room. Coffee w/lots of cream."

She smiled at the screen and scrambled into her jeans and jacket, braiding her hair in the back because there was no time to tame it. If the brasser wasn't up yet, hopefully she'd have a few blessed minutes alone with her husband.

Mathis showed her to the breakfast room—which wasn't half as cheerful as its name implied—and Acton greeted her with a chaste kiss that did not fool her for a second; there were lustful thoughts behind that indifferent façade. "Did you sleep well?"

"Very well," she lied. "And you?" She gave him a look.

"Bring your coffee, and I'll walk you over to the stables."

Ah—he must want to speak where there was no chance they could be overheard, which was a welcome sign. They walked together out the back door and into the gardens, the gravel crunching beneath their feet as they made their way away from the main building. Acton wasn't one to make idle conversation, and so in the silence that ensued, Doyle looked around her as she breathed in the cold, crisp air, trying to ignore the vague, unsettled feeling brought about by her dream. They passed through the back garden; the hedges and fountains laid out in neat geometric patterns, and continued toward the outer buildings that bordered the fields behind the manor house.

"What was the garden planner's name? Captain Black?"

He smiled. "Not quite—Capability Brown."

She raised her cup in homage. "Well, whatever his name was, it's so very beautiful, Michael. Are there any dogs, here?"

"No—no dogs. Why?"

"Just wonderin'. D'you think we will live here, someday?"

"I hadn't really considered it."

This, interestingly enough, was not true. She was fast coming to the rather dismayed realization that he loved this place, even though he never spoke of it. I will love it also, then, she assured herself stoutly. One only has to become accustomed, is all.

They walked in companionable silence for a few minutes while she sipped her coffee and the birds called from the spreading elms that lined the utility road. Deciding that it was past time he made a report, she inquired in a mild tone, "You didn't tell me of your night, husband; did you finally push the brasser out the door?"

"She definitely didn't want to leave."

"Answer my question, Michael."

"Yes, I pushed Ms. Masterson out the door and sent her upstairs and I did not have sex with her."

"Thank you," she said, and took another sip.

He looked up at the sky for a moment—it was a bit overcast, but not threatening rain. "In fact, I impressed upon her the importance of staying low-key and out of sight today, so she will spend the duration locked within the archives."

She glanced up at him, suddenly alert. "What is it?"

He met her gaze, his own benign. "What is what?"

Crossly, she looked away. "I hate it when you don't tell me what's goin' on."

But he deftly changed the subject. "Speaking of which, do you know what Williams wants to tell me that he can't say over the phone?"

Doyle could feel her color rise. "Williams is a tiresome *knocker.*"

"I see. Should I be forewarned?"

She debated what to say, wishing she was as fast on her feet as he was. "It is important that I speak with him first, Michael. Promise me."

He regarded her thoughtfully. "You alarm me."

She realized she'd have to tell him something, and so disclosed with unfeigned exasperation, "He has taken it into his wooden head that you are—are not doin' right by me." This was close enough to the truth, and hopefully no more need be said.

"He saw the photographs?"

Now it was Doyle's turn to stare. "*You* saw the photographs?"

"They were in your rucksack. I wondered how you knew."

This was fair enough; she should have burnt them if she didn't want him to find them—he was Acton, after all. "Well, it was a terrible shock, and Williams did see them by accident. But that is water under the bridge," she added hastily, hoping he wasn't going to ask who took them. Hopefully, he would believe they were sent to her anonymously; she'd carefully cleaned the incriminating prints.

Acton thought about it, his chin on his chest. "So Williams wants to take me to task?"

Doyle had to smile at the picture thus presented. "It would seem so." They looked at each other, Acton with a gleam of humor and Doyle starting to laugh—it truly was funny. "Let me fix it."

Acton tilted his head in acquiescence. "I had no idea he was that brave."

Or that stupid, she added silently; we shall see if DI Williams is also that deceitful.

He unlatched the stable yard gate and gestured her through. "I have time to give you a riding lesson before my visitor arrives."

She eyed him. "The mystery man."

"Yes," he admitted without shame. "The mystery man."

As they entered the wooden building, the stableman promptly came forward. When she'd been investigating the racecourse, Doyle noted that stable folk all tended to look alike and this one was no different; wiry and lean, with sandy hair and a face that did not register his hidden resentment as Acton made the introductions. "This is Grady, who has handled the stables very ably for many years."

"I'm that pleased to meet you, my lady," the man said perfunctorily, and it was not true.

"The pleasure is mine," Doyle replied with a polite smile, and a small silence ensued. No, not at all pleased to meet me, thought Doyle. He was from Ulster—a proddy, as her mother used to say—and it was never meant as a compliment. Unhappy, he was, having to make nice to the enemy.

"Have you saddled Buckle?" asked Acton.

"Yes, sir; she's ready to go."

Acton turned to Doyle. "Let me find your boots, first."

She followed him into the tack room, where several pairs of spare boots were stacked in a tack box. After pulling a pair, he dusted them off with a rag and glanced over toward Grady, who was lingering outside the door. In a quiet tone, Acton asked, "Is this going to be a problem for you? He's been here so long I'd forgotten about his origins."

"Not a'tall; it's a peaceful colleen, I am, and I've no interest in The Troubles. The boyo will just have to be gettin' over it."

With a nod, he held out the boots for her inspection. "These belonged to Fiona; I think you're about the same size."

She sat on the tack box to pull them on, resisting the urge to make a flippant remark about stepping into the dead woman's shoes. Grady came to stand within the doorway, and it was evident he was aware he hadn't shown to advantage in his first encounter with the new Lady Acton. "How are the boots, my lady? I have a lead rope ready, here."

"Good," said Acton as he checked his watch. "Allow me to take you around the yard for a few turns."

Her husband led her to a stall where a grey mare was tied to an iron loop, flicking her ears forward in idle interest at their approach. "This is Buckle. She's very gentle."

Doyle reached up and timidly patted Buckle's neck, mainly because she felt it was expected of her, and the two men were watching. She was a bit nervous, having been fascinated by horses, but never having been within calling distance of one. Acton led the mare into the stable yard, then came around to stand beside her at the stirrup. "Ready?"

"As ready as I'll ever be, I suppose."

He hoisted her up, and whilst he adjusted the stirrups, Doyle studied the ground, which now seemed rather a long way down.

"All right?" asked Acton, with a final tug on the strap.

"Yes," she replied firmly.

After he demonstrated how to hold the reins, he began to lead the horse outside and toward the yard. Doyle held on like grim death, but once she began to entertain a cautious hope that the animal was not going to break free and run wildly away, she could not suppress a delighted smile.

Her husband noticed. "Good?"

"Oh, it's grand. Look at me, Michael; I'm horseback ridin' like a nob."

He was very pleased, she could tell. "You are a sight, Lady Acton."

"Don't say it too loud," she cautioned, "your girlfriend may be lurkin' about."

But he met her eyes, suddenly serious. "You must let me know if she is being untruthful—about anything at all."

"I will, then." Thus prompted, she told him, "She was lyin' yesterday about not havin' a family."

Surprised, he glanced back over his shoulder as the horse stepped placidly along. "Is that so? She is married?"

"I don't remember what it was, but she was not tellin' the truth."

He glanced toward the stable, thinking about this. "If you would, pay careful attention, henceforth."

"I will," she agreed in a solemn tone. "Henceforth." She wondered if he'd been drinking; hopefully he would keep his wits about him, what with all the plots and counter-plots and keeping one's wife in the dark so that she wouldn't say the wrong thing at the wrong time.

"The same for my visitor, please."

Ah—the penny dropped, and she realized there was a method to this outing, and he must want her to listen in; she wouldn't be needing a French maid's outfit, after all. "I see how it is," she teased. "Workin' me like a rented mule."

But apparently this touched a nerve, and he looked up in apology. "I must beg your pardon, Kathleen. But the stakes are quite high."

"I'm teasin' you, Michael, is all. I take it the visitor is connected to your mysterious Home Office case?"

"I'm afraid I cannot say," he said, and it was true, which was his way of telling her that indeed he was.

"I hope I don't muck it up," she warned. She was nervous, thinking of his important case—the one where he thought he was being misled, somehow.

He glanced back at her with interest. "How would you know whether you'd mucked it up, one way or the other?"

This seemed a fair point, and she thought about it for a moment as he led the horse along. "I suppose I don't know; not always. But usually I do." Come to think of it, she hadn't had a misfire in a while—perhaps because as she got older, she grew more accustomed to sorting things out. It was a burden, sometimes, sorting out the important lies from the unimportant ones.

"Can you tell me anything about it?" His voice was gently curious as he interrupted her thoughts. "When did it start?"

He knew she didn't like speaking of her perceptive abilities, and she never had spoken of it with anyone, except him—and on the first day she'd met him, no less. Still and all, already he had a very shrewd understanding of it, and so she forced herself to answer calmly. "As far back as I can remember. I'd get—impressions, I guess you'd say. I suppose the surprise was when I realized no one else . . ."—she paused in acute distress, unable to go on.

With a dismayed movement, he stopped the horse and came to her side to lay a hand on her leg. "Let's not speak of it, then; I am sorry I pressed you."

She pulled herself together. "No; I'm the one who's sorry, Michael. I just know I'm never supposed to say."

He met her eyes with his own, the expression therein very grave. "No; you must never tell anyone else, Kathleen."

This was self-evident; she could easily imagine the problems that would arise. She hated being the bridge-jumper; imagine if it were discovered that she was the truth-detector. "I won't, Michael. I hope I'm not that dense." As he turned to resume their walk, she added fairly, "Although I think Aiki knew."

"Aiki?" He threw her a surprised look. Aiki was the cab driver, murdered by Caroline.

"And your ancestors." This slipped out, almost without conscious volition, and as a result, he stopped in his tracks and turned to stare at her. A bit flustered, she explained, "I had a dream last night—they are unhappy about your cousin."

He stood quite still. "And what do they think of me?"

Embarrassed, and wishing she hadn't brought it up, she replied a bit crossly, "I've no idea, Michael. It doesn't work that way."

But he did not move, and she had the sudden impression he was very disturbed, for some reason. Before she could make an inquiry, however, voices could be heard from the stable, and he turned his head. "Stay close, if you would."

"I would," she agreed, and hoped she could sort it all out; between nasty Masterson, the mysterious visitor, and her equally mysterious husband.

CHAPTER 35

"*H*OWARD," SAID ACTON, SHAKING THE MAN'S HAND. "I WAS just giving my wife her first riding lesson."

The man nodded to Doyle in a remote, polite manner. "How do you do, Lady Acton; it is a pleasure."

Doyle smiled in acknowledgment, noting that Acton hadn't given out the man's last name. He looked very much the Home Office type, though—slender and rather furtive, a sleek member of the popped-collar crowd that haunted the posh restaurants in the West End. Doyle tended to pay little attention to government folk, because nearly everything they said was couched in a semi-lie, and it was too exhausting to try to listen to them. The semi-lies were more rife lately, as the Home Office had experienced more than its usual share of scandals over the past year. The Immigration Minister was forced to step down in disgrace over his connection to a prostitution ring that preyed on immigrant women—some very unsavory doings had been unearthed by the squad formerly known as Vice, but the extent of the goings-on had been kept largely quiet from the general populace. To no one's real surprise, the Minister had promptly killed himself, which further helped to keep the whole scandal contained. DCI Drake was involved somehow, too—Doyle hadn't been paying much attention at the time because she'd been busy trying to make

Acton believe she was a competent detective. She remembered that there'd been some problems with bribery and corruption, too—although that type of thing seemed par for the course, nowadays.

Acton was every bit his visitor's match in aloof, public-school politeness. "Thank you for coming, Howard; it would be best to stay clear of the house, as there is a newspaper reporter researching the archives."

The man moved his shoulders in a graceful semi-shrug. "I shouldn't stay for long, anyway. I've got to keep watching that pot, and hope it doesn't come to a boil."

"Grady will get you a mount, and then we'll be off. Would you mind my wife for a moment?"

"With pleasure."

After handing over the lead rope, Acton disappeared into the stable and could be overheard speaking to Grady whilst Doyle and the Home Office gentleman smiled politely at each other.

"I am honored to meet you, Lady Acton. I read of your courageous action in the paper."

"Thank you," said Doyle, and tried to think of something pertinent to ask so as to forward whatever her task was, here; subtlety was not her strong suit. It also didn't help that she wasn't certain what she was supposed to try to find out, although hopefully Acton would lead the conversation where he wished it to go.

"Too many would have stood by; I fear I would have been one of them."

With some surprise, she caught a glimpse of what lay beneath the man's polished, smooth veneer, and began paying very close attention. "Truth to tell, I wasn't thinkin' much at the time."

"Well, it was very inspiring; would there were more with your mettle. Acton is a lucky man."

"I'm remindin' him of this on a regular basis." The remark

was absently delivered, however, as she covertly contemplated Howard from the Home Office, her scalp prickling to beat the band.

He gave her an obligatory, polite chuckle, but was hiding his impatience as he looked to see whether the lucky Acton was to appear soon. "I'm sorry to take him from your side, but it won't be for long. A beautiful estate, you have here—I've missed horseback riding; too busy all the time."

Doyle considered him. "Do you have a dog?"

He glanced up at her quickly, trying to hide his bemusement at this non sequitur. "I do."

"I see." She didn't want him to think that Acton's wife was a bit nicked, and so she added lamely, "Acton doesn't, and I wondered if he would like to have one."

He smiled at her, and it was the first genuine smile he'd produced. "I recommend it; they're a bloody nuisance, sometimes, but it is nice to have someone around you can trust completely."

Before she could reply, Acton approached, leading a black horse, while Grady led another. "Here we go, Howard; a good excuse to clear our heads."

"Yes; an excellent excuse and I'm grateful indeed."

Grady came to take Doyle's lead rope while the other men mounted up. She was then treated to the impressive sight of her husband mounted on a restive black horse, and could not find two thoughts to rub together. Faith, she thought a bit breathlessly; this is exactly why women read those romance novels.

"We should return within the hour, Kathleen; I will see you after your lesson."

This directive apparently was given to ensure that she hung around the stables until they returned, but this would not be a hardship, as between the residents of the manor house and the bristling Grady, the stables seemed the lesser of the two evils. The two men rode away toward the expansive meadowlands whilst Doyle watched and attempted to tamp down the lustful feelings thus engendered.

"Would you like to try to take the reins, my lady?"

Doyle was in no mood to be forced-polite, and neither was the stable hand, so she spared them both. "No thank you, Grady; mainly, I'd like to make a few calls—I've a case I should be checkin' in on."

The Irishman was only too happy to help her down from the horse, and with no further ado, Doyle scrolled up Habib as Grady led the placid Buckle back to the stable.

"DS Doyle." Her supervisor's clipped voice could barely be heard as there was a lot of ambient noise in the background.

With a guilty start, Doyle remembered that it was the weekend; one tended to lose track of such mundane things as what day of the week it was, here in the elevated climes— maybe that was why Acton liked being here so much. "I'm sorry to be botherin' you, sir, but I haven't had a chance to check in on the latest park case, and I was wonderin' if you could bring me up to speed, so to speak. I'm visitin' my husband's estate." Hopefully, this would be considered a valid excuse for her dereliction of duty, and would also serve to remind him on which side his bread was buttered.

Apparently it did, as Habib's modulated voice registered his approval of this ceremonial milestone. "I see; I understand the estate is most impressive."

"Oh, it is, sir; they live like your maharajahs, and I'm a stranger in a strange land."

There was a pause. "You are confusing Pakistan with India, perhaps."

"Oh yes—sorry." Now, there was an epic misstep—never make an attempt to joke around with Habib; mental note. She sped on to business so as to cover her lapse. "The victim is in the morgue?"

"Indeed. A white male in his sixties who sustained a single gunshot wound to the back of the head while standing. He was formerly a member of the Health and Care Professions Council, supervising social workers."

"A do-gooder, then?" She was surprised enough to forget that she shouldn't interrupt her superior officer when he was giving a report. This was a wrinkle; the other victims had all been unsavory types. It didn't much sound as though this one was in keeping with the others.

She was about to point this out when Habib continued, "It would seem. But his record indicates he was charged with a Section Five about eight years ago, and the charges were dismissed."

Doyle considered this in surprised silence for a moment; a Section Five was a pedophile, but the other park victims had been former murder suspects—this must be the twist that Williams had referred to. "It doesn't quite fit the profile, then."

"No; but if it is the same killer, this difference may be significant."

"Yes; I suppose that's true." She chewed on her thumbnail and wished she was back in London, seeing to the follow-up for herself. "I'll try to return later today; or tomorrow at the latest."

"I understand the chief inspector has asked DI Williams to do the groundwork in your absence. You may wish to coordinate with him."

"I will, sir; thank you." Nothing for it; she'd have to speak with the traitorous Williams sooner or later, anyway. Mentally girding her loins, she rang him up and he answered immediately.

"Where are you?"

She cautiously decided there was no harm in telling him. "I'm at Trestles for the weekend."

"Christ, Kath; I was worried. I thought our French friend had coshed you, or something."

"He's not goin' to cosh me, and you mustn't blaspheme, DI Williams."

"Have you heard from him lately?"

"No." Trust Williams to remind her of yet another unre-solved crisis; Savoie was probably lurking around the next corner, after having figured out that the fair Doyle murdered his baby brother. "I told you, I'm at Trestles."

There was a pause. "Everything all right?"

But she needed to cross that bridge when she was face-to-face with him, so she firmly turned the subject. "Never mind about all that; I just rang off with Habib and I want to hear about this latest victim. Do you think it's the vigilante killer?"

He was Williams, so naturally he was not going to leap to conclusions. "I think it's a possibility, but it doesn't look like there's a cold case murder in the background, this time."

"There's a murder, somewhere," she replied, and was sur-prised to realize this was true. "Keep diggin', please. Hope-fully, I'll be back on the case first thing Monday."

"All right; let me know when you get in."

"And don't be talkin' to Acton until you've talked to me. It's very important."

But this request was met with resistance; she was coming to realize that Williams, despite his reserved nature, had a stub-born streak. "I think I can help, Kath. It's a man-to-man thing."

"No, it's not, and don't you *dare* speak to him before I talk to you. I mean it, Thomas Williams."

"All right," he agreed with reluctance. "It sounds like you are back to normal, at least."

She quirked her mouth at this equivocal compliment. "Meanin' that I'm a shrew, I suppose."

"Meaning you're back on your feet. It's good to hear."

"Right, then; I'll speak with you soon." Thoughtfully, she rang off. He certainly didn't sound like he was in the process of stabbing Acton in the back, but she needed to speak to him in person to be certain. In any event, he definitely had some explaining to do.

She wandered around the stables, avoiding Grady and idly looking over the horses until she could hear the rhythm of approaching hoofbeats. Leaning over the stable's Dutch door, she watched Acton and the Home Office gentleman sweep into the yard, their horses' coats gleaming with damp exertion. "Michael," she called out. "Might I have a word with you?"

CHAPTER 36

ACTON SLID OFF HIS HORSE AS GRADY MOVED IN TO TAKE HOLD of the bridles. "A moment, Howard."

"Of course." As the other man dismounted, Acton strode over to the stable.

Doyle was trying to decide how to explain to her husband that she was nearly *melting* with lust and was sick to death of celibacy, but Acton, bless him, needed no explanation, and took her arm to lead her into the tack room, where he shut the door and began mauling her about in the dim, dusty room.

"Quickly," he murmured against her mouth as he unfastened the button on her jeans, but she needed no encouragement as she ran her hands under his riding coat and across his back, which was slightly damp with perspiration. It was all a bit tricky, as her jeans were tight and he was impatient, but in a matter of moments she was being discreetly serviced against the bales of hay stacked against the wall, making soft sounds into her husband's neck and mindlessly aware that this may not be the wisest course of action in the midst of all the various crises, but that they were both in need of this particular brand of reassurance and wasn't he *something*, in his tall leather boots.

In an impressively short amount of time, they were untangling limbs so that she could wriggle back into her jeans, all lustful feelings momentarily sated and all order momentarily restored in the world. As he leaned in for one last kiss, she noted, "Miles better than the last time I was locked in a tack room, I must say."

But he was not in a teasing mood, and said only, "Let me check you for straw. Stay close, now."

They emerged into the stable yard, where Howard was quietly discussing his horse's finer points with Grady. Acton took her elbow and casually approached to join in the discussion, but Doyle could only listen without comment, blushing to the roots of her hair. Although he was hiding his amusement, their guest was clearly aware that his host had been rogering his wife in the tack room. "I've enjoyed this visit immensely," he said when there was a pause in the conversation. "But I must return to London."

"Stay for luncheon?" offered Acton politely. "I can show you the Gainsborough."

"You tempt me, but another time." He met Doyle's eyes briefly, the glint of amusement still contained in his own as he said gravely, "Lady Acton; it was a pleasure to speak with you. Your husband is indeed a lucky man."

Doyle didn't know where to look, but managed, "I count my own luck, sir."

Acton bent his head and ran a casual hand over his horse's rump as Grady led the sleek animals away. "You will consider what I suggested?"

"I will indeed. It is very sound advice."

Doyle brushed her hair from her forehead.

Acton turned to face him, and the men formally shook hands. "Will you be available to meet again Monday? I can arrange for privacy."

"I'll make myself available—pending events, of course."

They walked their guest to his car, and then stood on the gravel as he drove away and out of sight. Acton was preoccupied as he took her elbow to begin the walk back to the manor house, and so she remained silent, respecting his mood, until finally she could contain herself no longer, lifting an anxious face to his. "Howard is not what he seems, Michael."

"No," he agreed absently, deep in thought.

"No—no; it's not what you're thinkin'. He is not pampered, and—and spoiled. He's brave; and—and *true*, I guess you'd say. Truly brave; not pretend-brave, like me." She paused, struggling to put it into words so that he would understand and finding that she was having trouble controlling her emotions. "He's a patriot. If he were Irish, he would be someone like Michael Collins at the Easter Risin'." She drew a breath. "I think he's in danger—his dog—" she paused, and decided to skip that part. "I'm worried he may not be alive much longer."

Acton watched her with a shuttered expression, but she could sense he was surprised. "I was going to arrest him Monday."

"Oh." She was taken aback, and not certain what to say in response. "You mustn't, Michael."

He stopped, and faced her, his unreadable gaze searching her face. "Why did he lie, then?"

"I don't know, Michael. I don't think he trusts you much."

He lifted his head and contemplated the distance for a moment, thinking this over. "Is there any chance you are mistaken, Kathleen?"

Doyle had a swift, unbidden memory of her night visitor with the bad teeth, and shook her head. "No, I am not mistaken."

He seemed to come to a decision. "Right, then; I must make a call; if you will excuse me?"

He stepped away to scroll up his mobile, and she waited at a small distance, thinking over this latest development and wishing, for a moment, that she was back selling fish and not having to deal with ominous and shadowy events that had some unknown bearing on the fate of the kingdom. After he engaged in quiet conversation for a few minutes, he pocketed his mobile and fell into step beside her once again. He made no comment, and as they returned to the manor house through the formal gardens, she ventured, "Someone is runnin' a rig on you? To frame Howard?"

"I'm afraid I cannot discuss it." With a fond arm, he pulled her against his shoulder, briefly. "I appreciate your help—I hope you don't feel I am taking advantage of you."

"Advantage was taken, and mightily appreciated," she teased wickedly.

He smiled slightly, but warned, "You'll have to tone it down a bit, please. No one will believe we are on the brink."

She sighed and subsided; reminded of the original crisis that had brought them here in the first place. "Aye, then; fun's over."

"If you would, make it clear you are unhappy—the next few hours will be crucial."

"Should I stay in my room and sulk?" This said half-hopefully.

But he squeezed her elbow in apology. "No; you must be present. Remember that she thrives on the intrigue. And you must signal if she tells an untruth."

"How 'bout if I pop her with a baton across the chops? Would that be signal enough?"

But he had to reach for a responding smile as he opened the wrought-iron gates that led back to the main building, and it didn't take someone with her perceptive abilities to sense that he had a great deal on his mind. In her best supportive-spouse manner, she offered, "Whist; not to worry, my friend—you're a fine actor and Masterson is completely taken-in."

"Yes. Let us hope so."

There was something in his tone that made her eye him sidelong, but he gave nothing away, so she continued, "Speakin' of which, have you had a chance to do any sleuthin' amongst the staff? We should find out who's the snake in the chicken coop."

He glanced at her. "Solonik's source is Mrs. Wright."

She was so profoundly surprised that she stopped to stare at him. "*Mrs. Wright?* The cook? Are you certain, Michael?"

He nodded his head. "Yes. In fact, you are the one who tipped me off—she warned you not to let Masterson steal me away, remember? Why would she even know that this was in the offing, at the time she spoke to you?"

Thinking about it, Doyle could only concede what seemed like a very good point. "Oh. That never occurred to me, I'm afraid." Faith, she was an idiot; after all, Acton had warned her to be on the lookout for someone trying to cultivate her. "But—it doesn't make any sense, Michael; I *know* she was genuinely in my corner."

He explained patiently, "Indeed, she is. She doesn't want Masterson to be swayed by me so as to disrupt their plan."

The light dawned. "Oh. That's why she wanted me to fight for you—she was mad at her cohort for bein' susceptible to your counter-plan." Honestly; for a detective she was a dim bulb, sometimes.

The manor house rose before them and Acton cautioned, "You must not give it away; not yet. Perhaps you should try to avoid Mrs. Wright—I'm afraid there is a good reason you were never put on undercover detail."

This was true, and she couldn't even be offended; subterfuge was not her strong suit. "I suppose I can't argue; you read my mind back at the stable, when I was dyin' for a go."

"Only because I was thinking along the same lines, myself."

Playfully, she knocked his arm with her own. "You'd been thinkin' along the same lines since the breakfast room, husband."

"True."

His smile was less abstracted and more genuine, and thus

encouraged, she added, "Well, Howard found it all very amus-in'—I can't hide this blush under a barrel."

Acton made no further comment, but she could see that he was amused, himself, which was a good thing; he was on the verge of one of his black moods, and hopefully she could keep it at bay. His black moods tended to leave a lot of mayhem in their wake, with her fair self desperately trying to hold him back by the coat tails. "Any chance we can go home today?" With the Howard-who-was-not-what-he-seemed development, perhaps all plans had changed.

His voice was apologetic as they approached the back door. "Probably not, I'm afraid. I must await events."

"I do like it here," she lied diplomatically. "But I'm dyin' to have a look at this latest vigilante victim. There's a twist."

His interest sharpened, as it always did with the disclosure of a new crime. "What is it?"

"Well, so far it's a Section Five, but I imagine there's a murder lurkin' about somewhere."

He walked along in silence for a moment, and watching him, she ventured, "No? No murder, d'you think? Has the killer moved on to pedophiles?"

But Acton replied slowly, "No—instead I wonder if it is an ABC murder."

"Oh—that's what Habib thought, originally. You mean this was the intended target, all along, and he is trying to confuse the issue by killin' the others?"

They had come to the back door steps, and so he concluded by saying, "I will only suggest that you keep such a thought in mind."

"I will; I'll fill you in when I know more."

He opened the back door for her, and with a mental sigh, she accompanied him indoors. Not only was she not a proper candidate for subterfuge, she was also not cut out for this miserable situation—where everyone was wearing a polite mask to cover their hatefulness and Acton's flippin' ancestors were eyeing her every move. Hold on to your temper, she cautioned herself, and trust Acton—although sometimes she had to save him from himself; he tended to rack up an impressive body count when he was in one of his black moods. She'd best cling to him like a barnacle, and hope that religious instruction was making a dent.

"We'll be back in time for the five o'clock mass tomorrow, I promise," were his parting words to her, and she was yet again reminded that—to her husband, at least—she was as transparent as a pane of glass.

CHAPTER 37

DOYLE HID IN HER ROOMS LIKE A COWARD UNTIL MATHIS routed her out by knocking to announce that luncheon was being served. She then descended the stairs to discover that the other inhabitants were gathered together in the dining room, where the meal was arrayed informally, on a sideboard—which meant there was only one attentive servant instead of three. She looked around for Acton, but he wasn't yet in evidence; instead Sir Stephen listened with a cynical expression as Masterson chatted up the dowager about her stupid research in the stupid archives, the reporter doggedly cheerful in the face of the older woman's polite disinterest.

They greeted Doyle, Masterson overly-kind; no need to be uncivil to the poor wife, who was soon to be given the boot. Thinking of boots, Doyle was reminded of the torrid session in the tack room and managed to maintain her equilibrium— although she remembered to be sulky, which wasn't difficult when Masterson sat beside her at the table and began enthusing about the beauty that was Trestles.

Into this happy scene, Acton appeared to survey the lunch offerings. Doyle noted that the servant made some innocuous comment, to which Acton made an equally innocuous reply. Since this was very unlike the Acton she knew, she decided that this fellow must be, like Mathis, loyal to him and making some sort of report. She was reminded that they were not certain whether the dowager had been behind the poisoning episode, and wondered if the servant had been keeping a sharp eye on the bisque. Contemplating the contents of the porcelain soup bowl before her, Doyle decided that she was truly not very hungry.

"And how was your ride, Acton?" asked the dowager, and Doyle couldn't help but notice she hadn't been asked.

"Kathleen did very well for a first outing," offered Acton in a tactful tone. He had the choice of sitting beside Doyle or sitting beside Masterson, and he chose Masterson, smiling at her warmly. "Are you covered in ancient dust, Cassie?"

Delighted, the woman laughed and threw back her head. "I did have to shower." She glanced at him under her lashes and paused so that he could use his imagination. "I will say that I've gone through most of the twentieth century, and everything is now a bit more Bristol-shape."

Acton settled in to eat, apparently having no suspicions about the bisque, which made Doyle relent and take a few tentative spoonfuls, herself. He asked, "Did you come across anything startling?"

Masterson laid a casual hand on his arm. "Not at all—I positively *long* for the thrilling eighteenth century."

"Seventeenth century," corrected Sir Stephen in a sour tone. "That's when things were dicey."

But Doyle wasn't listening to him, as she was too busy brushing her hair off her forehead. Masterson was lying yet again; it seemed one couldn't find an honest home-wrecker, nowadays.

"I can help you finish it up this afternoon—perhaps we can unearth a scandal or two." Acton gave the other woman a meaningful glance and Doyle felt her color rise. Honestly; they might as well have at it right here on the mahogany table—no need to retreat to the drafty archives.

While Doyle struggled with holding on to her temper, Sir

Stephen stepped into the charged silence. "I believe the twentieth century was remarkably scandal-free. Trestles was too isolated to be bombed during the Second World War, and I don't believe any children were evacuated here from London."

"No," said Masterson, shaking her head so that her hair tumbled around her shoulders while Acton watched, fascinated. "Nothing of interest—Trestles remained largely unaffected, except for the rationing, of course."

Doyle brushed her hair off her forehead again, trying but failing to find a reason for these falsehoods, which seemed to have no particular point. Was Masterson trying to downplay the damage actually sustained during the wars?

"Will you create some sort of synopsis?" continued Sir Stephen, who was observing the open foreplay on display with a cynical twist to his mouth.

Masterson dragged her gaze away from Acton's. "Yes, I'll add a synopsis to the ones already written—going all the way back to the Conquest and the Domesday Book. Future generations will then add to mine; it's humbling, really." This said in a pious manner that actually hid a surge of exultation.

Doyle carefully unclenched her jaw and kept her gaze downcast. The reminder of the estate's storied past—and Acton's affection for it—served to suppress her natural inclination to say something she'd regret. All this misery was worth it, if Acton could divert Masterson from Solonik's revenge-wreaking plan. Not to mention Acton would not do well in prison, although she was fast coming to the conclusion he'd probably take it over from within, or mastermind some spectacular escape. Therefore, when Acton rested his chin on his hand, she willingly played her role, and stood rather abruptly. "I'll be needin' to go have a lie-down; if you'll excuse me."

As though reminded of his duties, Acton dragged his attention away from Masterson to display a touch of concern. "Are you unwell, Kathleen?"

"Just a bit of a headache," she explained with a mulish

mouth that made it clear this was naught but an excuse. "I'll be fine." She pronounced it "foine," just to show how upset she supposedly was.

The dowager rose also. "Allow me to call for Mathis, my dear."

"No need, ma'am." Abruptly, Doyle turned on her heel and stalked out of the room without another glance toward her wayward husband. As she ascended the staircase toward her rooms, she was congratulating herself on making a believable contribution to this stupid holy show when Mathis appeared before her in the hallway, meeting her eyes and then glancing with emphasis behind her.

Now what? thought Doyle with annoyance, and turned to discover that the dowager was making her stately way down the hallway in pursuit of her. With an inward sigh of resignation she waited, deciding that since she was supposed to be in a temper, there was no need to be conciliatory to the old battle-axe. "What is it you're wantin', ma'am?"

The other woman gazed at her for a long moment, her expression unreadable. "May I come in?"

Deciding she really had no choice, Doyle opened her door and replied in a less-than-welcoming tone, "If you wish."

The older woman followed, and then dismissed the servant with a nod. "That will be all, Mathis."

"Yes, madam." The girl shut the door behind them, her meek gaze downcast.

There was a small silence whilst Doyle stood her ground and fought the urge to start talking—she had a shrewd suspicion that the dowager was trying to intimidate her into saying something she oughtn't. Best to follow Acton's advice and say little—and anyway, by all appearances, she was soon to be cast out from this place, never to darken its doors again. Perhaps this little visit to the hated daughter-in-law was an attempt to buy her silence, or something. If this was the case, Doyle decided she'd pocket the old harridan's money without a qualm, and happily confess to Father John.

The older woman's words, however, were not at all what she'd expected. Instead, with icy precision, she was asked, "What is the meaning of this ridiculous charade?"

Doyle stared at her in confusion. "And which charade is that, ma'am?"

"Pretending you are at odds with my son."

Doyle hid her surprise; apparently the cold face masked a keen insight, and caution was advised so that Acton's well-laid plan—whatever it was—would not be disrupted. "My relationship with my husband is my own business, thank you very much."

If it was possible, the woman stiffened even more, and pronounced with thinly-veiled distaste, "Come; I will know what you are about—this is my home."

"Technically," Doyle pointed out, "it is mine."

Almost imperceptibly, the other woman flinched. Good one, Doyle.

But the blow did only momentary damage, as the dowager's thin brows rose in well-bred disbelief. "You *dare* speak to me in such a manner!"

Doyle found that she was warming to her theme. "Oh, you would be amazed at the extent of the brass, your ladyship. Now, if you have nothin' further to say, you may leave the premites."

"Premises," the other corrected her with full scorn. "And I will not be ordered about by an ignorant upstart like you."

A defiant retort was regretfully swallowed; Doyle could not lose her temper and start throwing her weight around, not with Acton in the process of throwing her over downstairs. Stymied, she offered stiffly, "If you'd prefer Miss Masterson, you are welcome to her."

But the other woman lifted a corner of her mouth in a

grim smile. "Nonsense; any fool can see that my son is besotted with you."

This was edging far too close to the truth, and Doyle decided that drastic measures were necessary as she tried to match the other Lady Acton in frosty scorn. "I am not goin' to discuss my husband with you. Will I be needin' to throw you out, yet again?"

The dowager gazed at her, her gaze incredulous. "He is *not* a normal man. Surely you are aware of this?"

If Doyle was in a temper before, now she was furious, and wished she had a sword at the ready, like the night visitor. Stepping forward in a menacing manner, she ground through her teeth, "Dinna ye *ever* be sayin' such a thing to me again or I willna be answerin' for meself."

"Kathleen?" asked Acton from the doorway.

With a mighty effort, Doyle reined in her temper and turned to face him, her chest heaving. "Oh—oh, hallo, Michael. I was just speakin' with your mother."

CHAPTER 38

"*I* SEE," SAID ACTON. "MOTHER, WOULD YOU MIND IF I SPOKE to Kathleen for a moment?"

"Of course. My dear, I will visit with you later." With just a trace of dignified condescension, the dowager drifted past them and out the door, where Mathis waited deferentially.

The door closed. "What was that about?" he murmured in a quiet tone, listening for a moment with his ear pressed against the panel.

Doyle watched him anxiously. "She knows it's a charade—the Masterson thing. I didn't give it away, Michael, I *promise*."

But he did not seem at all concerned, and indeed—if she was to gauge his mood—she would have to say he seemed very satisfied, which seemed a little strange. "No—you are doing very well. Can you quarrel with me? Loudly?"

"I suppose," she offered hesitantly. "About Masterson, d'you mean?"

"Pick any topic," he replied, and straightened up to approach her. Lifting the porcelain vase from the bedside table, he offered it. "Break this, if you would."

"Oh, Michael; I don't think I can—it's so very pretty."

With no further ado, he cocked an arm and threw the vase against the fireplace hearth, dashing it to pieces with a resounding crash.

Thus prompted, she marshaled her sense of ill-usage—not difficult at all, truly—and raised her voice. "Get *out*; go off wi' your rigmutton, and the divil take the both o' ye."

"Kathleen . . ." he cautioned, in the tone of a man trying to keep a quarrel private. He then leaned in to kiss her mouth, quickly, and strode over to exit out the door, indicating that she was to slam it behind him, which she did with great relish, the sound reverberating up into the rafters.

"My wife would like to rest," she could hear him say to Mathis. "Please see to it that she is not disturbed."

Doyle listened to his footsteps retreat down the hall and allowed her gaze to rest on the splintered vase for a moment. She was almost certain that he was heading to the archives to whisper sweet nothings into Masterson's vile ears, but there had definitely been a shift in his attitude; the black mood still hovered, but he was grimly satisfied, for some reason. It all had something to do with Masterson's lies about the history, but Doyle was at a loss as to what was the point of it all, and so knelt to begin carefully picking up the shards, just to feel useful.

Almost immediately, Mathis entered after a perfunctory knock, armed with a dustpan and whisk broom, which made Doyle wonder if there was a peephole somewhere. "Here, please let me get that, madam."

"Gladly," said Doyle, who nevertheless continued to pick up the shards and cradle them in her hand. "I have a terrible temper, I'm afraid—I blame the hair."

But this attempt at raillery fell short, as Mathis only smiled politely as she knelt down beside Doyle. "It's naught, my lady."

"My husband is a very patient man."

This attempt to provoke a reaction also fell short, but Doyle had a quick flash of something she'd grown accustomed to—swiftly suppressed incredulity that someone like her husband would willingly consort with the likes of her fair self. Doyle's hands stilled for a moment, as she was struck with a terrible, terrible thought. What if—what if Acton *wasn't* willingly consorting—

"May I take that, madam?"

Mathis held out the dustpan to collect the shards, and Doyle willingly relinquished them, all too happy to change her train of thought as she brushed off her hands. "I'm doin' a bunk, Mathis; I need a little walk-about to cool my head." She eyed the maid sidelong, as it wasn't at all clear that she would be allowed to wander about without a keeper.

But apparently she was not to be confined, because Mathis only smiled. "Of course, madam. Would you like an umbrella?"

"Does it look to rain?" This was all that was needed; a thunderstorm and flickering lights, in keeping with this flippin' gothic pile.

"Perhaps not; but one never knows."

"I'll take my chances, then."

Ten minutes later, Doyle was walking out under the massive oaks that lined the front drive, her hands in her pockets and her thoughts a bit bleak. She knew the signs; whatever scheme Acton had underway was about to come to fruition, and try as she might, she couldn't figure out how he was going to extricate them from this miserable situation, short of marrying Masterson to shut her up, or—even worse—cutting a bloody swath as only Acton could. And his mother had twigged him, which didn't bode well; hopefully she'd not upset his plans out of pure spite.

As if on cue, she was hailed and turned to behold Sir Stephen approaching across the broad lawn. It wants only this, she thought with resignation—I've got to be careful to give nothing away, although I probably wouldn't know if I did, come to think of it.

But being plumbed for secrets was apparently not to be a problem, because the man was too consumed by glee beneath his outwardly solemn and sympathetic manner. Why is it, she thought in annoyance, that everyone is so willing to accept Acton's betrayal of me without a moment's hesitation? She then remembered her Terrible Thought, and decided not to follow up on this particular rhetorical question.

Sir Stephen stood before her, slightly out of breath and trying to adopt the manner of a sympathetic friend without much success. "Would you mind company? Or would you rather walk it out alone?"

"I may walk out the gates and just keep on walkin'," she replied with what she hoped was the right touch of embarrassed ruefulness.

"I don't recommend it; Meryton is six miles away."

Doyle presumed this was a reference to the nearest town. "Is that where you live?"

He arched his brows, sardonically amused. "No, I live here."

This was unexpected, and so she stammered, "Oh—oh, I see."

His mouth twisted in a cynical smile. "Acton is too—too occupied to deal with the day-to-day estate matters, so I stay at hand to assist Lady Acton."

Doyle resisted the urge to remind him that she was the incumbent Lady Acton, as by all appearances she was soon to be given the boot, and besides, she wanted to find out what he was up to. Sir Stephen was the sort of person who was always up to something—she knew the type; his scheming made him feel superior.

As he fell into step beside her, he continued almost kindly, "It takes some getting used to, I know; but in no time—I am certain—you'll be over this rough patch and you'll take up the reins here, yourself."

This was such an out-and-out falsehood that she had to suppress a smile. His gleeful mood was probably because Masterson was on the far side of child-bearing, and the odds were better that he'd continue as the heir if she were to dethrone the fair Doyle. Or he was gleeful because Acton—to all appearances—was behaving badly, and there was no love lost between the two men. As they walked along in silence, it occurred to her that—although Sir Stephen would seem to be a prime suspect—Acton had never assumed that his cousin was the one feeding damaging information to Solonik. But the answer was simple, when she thought about it; Sir Stephen would not want to sully the glory that was Trestles by slandering the current baron, in the same way that Acton dangled that same glory before Masterson to dissuade her from bringing it down. I don't know about the supposed glory, Doyle thought with some skepticism, but I do know that this place is brimful of secrets. Her scalp prickled, but she ignored it.

"How did you enjoy Buckle?"

It took Doyle a moment to realize he referred to the morning ride, and then she replied, "Buckle seems an excellent horse, and I only wish I were an excellent rider."

He chuckled in a patronizing manner, and then said diffidently, "Grady tells me Acton had a visitor."

"He did, but I was not introduced."

She said it in a sulking tone that hopefully would put an end to this particular line of inquiry, but the other offered with false disapproval, "He didn't? Well, that wasn't very respectful of him, was it? Could you tell if it was someone he knew well?"

Doyle found she was beyond irritated with Acton's assorted relatives, and wished she knew what was best to say. "I think it was Miss Masterson's brother—or uncle, or somethin'." She scowled in disapproval whilst congratulating herself on thinking of something that furthered Acton's scheme and at the same time put an end to any more questions on the subject.

"Oh—then I will say no more." Again, he hid his glee behind a sympathetic guise. "Look, if it's any consolation, Acton has the occasional passing fancy; it means nothing." He shrugged. "Melinda is a perfect example."

This was said because he wanted to make certain the dim bride realized Melinda's true purpose as an irritant, but Doyle decided that two could play at this game. With a knit brow, she glanced at him in surprise. "Oh? And here I thought Melinda was *your* flight o' fancy." This, because it was true, and because he was probably sleeping with the tedious woman only to spite Acton. Not that Acton was spited, of course; he was too busy having his way with a certain red-headed baroness in the stables—the only bright moment in an otherwise thoroughly forgettable weekend.

Thus confronted, Sir Stephen hastily disclaimed, "Oh, no—no, not at all; Melinda and I are old friends, is all."

This was untrue, but more to the point, her comment threw him off so that he was blessedly silent for a few moments, and with the feeling that she had the upper hand for a change, Doyle took advantage. "How are you related to Acton? There's little resemblance, I think." As Acton was tall and darkly handsome, this could not be construed as a compliment.

Sir Stephen bowed his head in ironic acknowledgment. "We are second cousins; our grandfathers were brothers."

Interestingly enough, this was not true.

CHAPTER 39

"Madam," Mathis called out. "I thought I'd fetch you an umbrella." The maidservant smiled at Sir Stephen as she approached from across the lawn. "I am so sorry to interrupt, but I think the rain is coming on."

So—apparently she was not to remain alone in Sir Stephen's company as the mists began to creep in, but Doyle was unalarmed; she had no sense that her companion meant her any harm, because in his eyes, she was soon to become irrelevant. And despite his general loathsomeness, he was not the type to take action; at heart he was a coward. Not like Acton, she thought; no one could ever accuse Acton—or his ancestors, for that matter—of being cowardly. Suddenly she had to pause for a moment, almost overwhelmed by her instinct, beating her over the head to pay attention. What? She thought in bewilderment; what is it I'm missing here? Acton is brave, Sir Stephen is not; Howard is brave, I am not—and neither is the vigilante killer. He's a coward, and he needs my help.

"I should go back." She spoke the words aloud without thinking; saints and holy angels, she needed to get back to the Met, to find out why this cold-blooded killer—who was a coward— needed her help.

The other two understandably interpreted Doyle's remark

as a desire to return to the manor house. "Of course," Sir Stephen said, with a solicitous hand to her elbow. "It is growing quite cold." He then cast an appreciative glance at Mathis as they turned to head back, and the maidservant smiled coyly in response, despite harboring some very unchristian thoughts about the man. Apparently, Sir Stephen hoped to spite Acton by cutting in with Mathis, too, and was unaware that Mathis would just as soon give him a swift knee to the groin. I'd so much rather be back in London, Doyle thought irritably, where at least the villains are forthright. Hard on this thought, the maid's mobile pinged, and she entered a quick text without remark. My man's checking up on me, thought Doyle, unaccountably annoyed. Perhaps I should return the favor.

"The dowager Lady Acton would like to give you a tour of the orangery today," the maid offered. "Is this a convenient time?"

Doyle had no idea what an orangery was, but she knew for certain that she wasn't going to get buttonholed by the stupid dowager again—now, there was a lesson learned. Instead, she replied a bit grimly, "I'd rather visit the archives, if you don't mind."

With a quick flash of alarm, the maid nodded in acquiescence. "Certainly, madam."

"Best warn him," Doyle advised.

Although Sir Stephen put a hand to his mouth, Mathis didn't miss a beat, and pulled out her mobile to send a text. "As you say, madam."

They returned to the house, and Hudson—after a bare moment's hesitation—escorted her to the archives, which, he explained, were formerly the solarium. Doyle nodded in feigned interest, but was secretly rethinking her fit of temper after seeing the steward's reaction; she shouldn't be interrupting Acton at the risk of oversetting his plans. Although it wouldn't hurt to appear childish and stupid, certainly; and it had the added benefit of authenticity, too.

Therefore, she stood on the threshold of the former solarium—whatever *that* was—and beheld Acton standing decorously across the room from Masterson, who was seated at the massive desk in the middle of the room, looking up with a smile but clearly very intent on her work and not at all interested in the tall man who happened to share the room with her. Doyle wasn't fooled; the woman looked upon her visitor with equal parts pity and exultation.

"Kathleen," said Acton, stepping toward her. "How nice of you to check in; I hope this means you are feeling more the thing."

"Yes," Doyle replied stiffly. "I was wonderin' if I could have a word, Michael."

"Of course." With only the barest hint of reluctance, Acton accompanied her out into the hallway. "Careful what you say," he murmured, very softly.

As there was no one within earshot, Doyle interpreted this to mean that the walls had ears, and that Sir Stephen and/or the dowager probably had their own recruits amongst the staff. "I'm sorry, Michael—I shouldn't interrupt, but I was walkin' out front, and thinkin' about the vigilante killer. I think . . ."—she knit her brow, trying to put it into words—"I think he's afraid, and I think I need to be takin' a good hard look at this latest murder."

If Acton thought this an odd topic for this particular moment in time, he gave no indication. Instead, he crossed his arms and asked in a very public-school voice, "Of what is he afraid?"

Poor man's been drinking, she thought, and small blame to him. "'Of' I don't know yet, my friend. But I'm dyin' to find out if this is indeed an ABC murder." She also teetered on the edge of telling him that she was going to do something drastic if she was forced to face another meal as the slighted bride, but she didn't say it; she needed to drum up some patience from somewhere, and play her flippin' part.

Acton drew his brows together, thinking over what she'd said. "Check in with the coroner about this latest murder; look for any discrepancies, however slight. And don't overlook the usual motivations—money, or jealousy. The killer may be trying to appear a vigilante to distract from a motivation that is not so pure."

She nodded, even though she knew down to the soles of her feet that these were indeed vigilante murders; no point in trying to explain the inexplicable to her better half. "Williams said the victim is still at the morgue, so I'll be payin' a little visit, first thing Monday."

There was a small pause whilst they regarded each other, and much remained unspoken. He tilted his head toward the closed door. "Would you like to have a look 'round the archives?"

As his hand was nowhere near his chin, she agreed with a show of reluctance that was not feigned. "If I must."

They re-entered the stone circular room, and Doyle dutifully listened as Acton described the various stages of the estate's history, carefully shelved in fireproof cabinets, century by century. "Some of the earlier historical documents were lost to a fire, but Trestles has been fortunate in that most remain intact."

Masterson couldn't resist, and lifted her head to offer, "Yes, there was a fire in the original Norman section—a casualty of the Glorious Revolution in 1688."

"No," Doyle corrected her absently as she surveyed the rough-hewn walls that rose around her. "It was only a maidservant bein' careless with a candle, and it was 1683."

As the woman stared at her in surprise, Doyle decided it would probably be best to make an exit before she was tempted to explain that the room had actually started out life as a chapel, not a solarium, and so she took her leave of them, pleading a desire to have a lie-down.

Doyle returned to her rooms, berating herself for barging in the way she had, and relieved that Acton had not been unhappy about it. Hopefully, she looked the part of an unhappy wife on the cusp of having her dreams shattered, and just as hopefully, Acton would be done fawning over stupid Masterson sometime soon. With a sigh, she sank down on the edge of the bed and gazed out the diamond-paned windows to watch the rain fall on the gardens, trying not to think of the others throughout the centuries who'd sat here and done the same thing.

Mathis knocked softly, and entered to stand at respectful attention. "Lord Acton wonders if you'd rather have your dinner brought to your room, madam."

"I would indeed, Mathis. Thank you." This was welcome news, and meant that her husband knew she was dreading the prospect, or he was worried she'd give the game away, since she'd already demonstrated her impulsive tendencies. Either way, she'd gratefully hunker down and go to bed early—tomorrow couldn't come fast enough.

It was not to be a peaceable night's sleep, however. Once again, the knight stood before her, one hand on his sword whilst the other held a baby in the crook of his arm, which did not seem a very good idea, considering the rough hauberk he wore. And no one would think it very hygienic, as he was generally grimy.

"You again," she said crossly. "Go 'way. I didn't even know about Capability Brown and you've got Acton all worried up, you do. Why is that?"

There was no dog this time, only the muffled sound of voices in the background, speaking quietly, as though plotting in a church.

"I'm only pretend-brave," she insisted. "And I don't much like it here, but don't tell Acton—although I think that's the whole point, isn't it? That you can't tell Acton."

Suddenly her eyes were wide-open as she stared into the moonlit darkness of her chamber, listening to the rain on the window and trying to catch her breath.

Chapter 40

GLUMLY, DOYLE SAT AT THE BREAKFAST TABLE AND TRIED TO ignore the discreet speculation directed her way by the silent servants, as well as the more overt speculation directed her way by the dead persons in the rafters. I can see why Rochester's mad wife burned the place down, she thought as she picked at her poached eggs. The idea has a great deal of merit.

Her thoughts were interrupted by the entry of her husband, who leaned in to kiss her forehead and lift a triangle of toast from her plate. "Pack; we're leaving."

She stared at him, hardly bearing to hope. "Truly?"

"Truly," he confirmed, taking a bite. "The sooner, the better."

"Thank the saints. What do I say to your mother?"

"I will make a painfully transparent announcement that we are called away. You will make your apologies, but be subdued."

"Are we breakin' anythin' this time?" She rather regretted missing her chance.

"Only metaphorically. I'll meet you in the main hall in twenty minutes so that we can take our leave."

Although she didn't know what "metaphorically" meant, Doyle needed no further encouragement, and hurried up the stairway to her rooms, remembering to try to look upset as Mathis joined her to offer assistance. "Thank you for your help, Mathis; I hope I'll be seein' you again." This said with fatalistic sadness.

"Sooner rather than later, I imagine," was the enigmatic reply as the maid zipped the bag shut with an efficient movement. "Have a safe journey, madam."

The footman carried her bag down the stairs, and at its foot stood Sir Stephen, feigning concern. "What is this I hear? You are cutting your visit short?"

"I think somethin' has come up," Doyle replied vaguely. "Somethin' havin' to do with work."

"Is that so?" He attempted a jovial tone. "I hope it is nothing that requires another leap into the Thames."

Doyle's scalp prickled and she paused. "Perhaps it is. Nothin' would surprise me, anymore."

Apparently, he interpreted this remark as a desire to do away with herself, because he held out a hand in protest, vaguely alarmed, "Surely not; matters are not so bad, are they?"

He was half-hoping, but she assured him, "That's not what I meant—and in any event, I'd not be tryin' to trump God."

His lips twisted into a thin smile. "Oh yes—you're RC, how could I forget?"

But Doyle wasn't really listening, because it had occurred to her that God worked in mysterious ways, and perhaps she shouldn't be quite so short with the night visitor, however unwelcome his visits.

Any further conversation was cut short as Acton came into the great hall, flanked by his mother and Masterson, the latter trying to hide her disappointment at this unexpected turn of events behind a bright smile. "I should need only another weekend, I think, just to do some cross-indexing."

"Of course," said Acton in an offhand manner. "Only check in with mother, first."

The dowager held out a formal hand to Doyle, her composed features masking her displeasure. "So nice to see you again, my dear; have a safe journey."

"Thank you," said Doyle in an equally polite tone. "The pleasure was mine." Now *there*, that was a well-delivered line; not good at subterfuge, my eye.

The atmosphere was thick with undercurrents as Doyle followed the footman out the door to the waiting car while Masterson held Acton back for a moment, pleading with him in a low voice. She was probably trying to get him to stay—as if he would create such a scandal, even if he were truly at odds with his wife. No, my friend, thought Doyle with grim satisfaction, we are shaking the dust of this place from our sandals; I sincerely hope I never live to see you making up to my husband again.

Acton slid in behind the wheel, Hudson closed the door behind him, and they were away, the Range Rover's tires crunching on the gravel. Warily, Doyle turned to take one last look at the manor house as they exited the gates, the massive front door barely visible at the end of the tree-lined entrance road. I am going to have to come to terms with Trestles, she thought; I've got to stop being such a flippin' baby. Taking a breath, she recited, "I'm given to understand that you're trustin' someone you oughtn't, and that drastic action may be needed." She paused, thinking it over. "I think it has somethin' to do with blackmail."

He looked at her, profoundly surprised, and before she lost her nerve, she added, "And there's a woman who's not English, but no one seems to know this."

He took her hand in his. "Are you all right?"

She blew a tendril of hair off her face with a quick breath. "Well, this weekend was a rare crack, and no mistakin'. Although on the bright side, I think I'm pregnant again."

There was a small pause. Shouldn't have sprung it on him like that, she thought with remorse; sometimes she forgot that she shouldn't just speak her mind to him, willy-nilly.

After his initial surprise, she sensed a rush of immense satisfaction from her husband that he could not contain. "Is that so? Isn't it too early to know?"

"We'll see, then; I have it on good authority." Yet again, she tried to suppress the Terrible Thought that had occurred to her whilst picking up the broken vase; that she'd been purposely thrown in Acton's path for no other reason than to warn him of the plot against Howard—of the unknown national security threat—and that it hadn't been a case of Acton falling for her like a ton of bricks on seeing her fair self passing beneath his window. It would explain a lot, though, and actually made a lot more sense than the idea that the reclusive Lord Acton suddenly decided to cast in his lot with an Irish baggage fresh from the Crime Academy.

No; she argued with herself fiercely—he loves me; I can feel it down to my *bones*. And if there was ever any doubt, one need only look to our sex life; surely that's not a necessary part of the terrible you-were-only-needed-to-warn-Howard theory.

They drove for a few minutes in silence, Acton no doubt considering what she'd said, and trying to decide if she was certifiable. But instead, he asked, "Would you like to drive? This is a good place to practice."

Doyle turned to him with delight, all depressing theories abandoned for the moment. "Oh—may I?"

"I have some calls to make." He stopped the car, and they walked around to switch places. After he helped her adjust the seat, she began to drive; cautiously at first, and then with more confidence as it became clear there was little traffic and the road was fairly straight. Acton watched her for a few minutes and then—apparently satisfied that he wasn't about to perish in a fiery crash—pulled out his mobile and scrolled for a number, waiting for the answer on the other end.

"It's me."

There was a pause, while Doyle could faintly hear Masterson's voice, the words indistinguishable but the tone unmistakably relieved, now that Acton was shown to be still pursuing her despite his abrupt abandonment this morning.

He continued, "I've been thinking of what we discussed. You were amusing, but I've decided you are not worth the scandal. In any event, if I were to re-marry, I'd best find someone younger. So please do not contact me again." He then rang off.

The brutal words were so completely at odds with his open pursuit of the woman over the past two days that Doyle took her eyes from the road for a moment to gaze upon him with shock and dismay. "Oh; oh—Michael; do you think that was wise? She'll do her worst."

"I hope so," was his reply as he scrolled up a different number.

Doyle decided she'd best concentrate on driving, and turned her attention back to the road. She heard someone answer on the other end, and her husband said, "Is Previ in? This is Lord Acton." Doyle had already noted that Acton tended to use his title when he was trying to get through to someone; it worked every time.

"Previ, it is Michael—Michael Sinclair. I am so sorry to bother you on a Sunday, but I'm afraid something rather strange has come up."

He listened, and then said with a touch of embarrassed reluctance, "I met a reporter from one of your papers, the *London World News*. Her name is Cassie Masterson; she covers major crimes."

While he listened to the response, Doyle waited, her ears on the stretch.

"I know it sounds odd, but I believe she has become fixated on me; she keeps turning up." He laughed, self-consciously. "It's a bit embarrassing. You know I am newlywed, and my wife is very annoyed."

Doyle's mouth dropped open and Acton casually put a hand on the steering wheel to direct the car back into the correct lane.

"There may be a psychological condition, so I've handled her carefully, but I wonder if someone could—discreetly—look into it." He sounded embarrassed again. "She has some very strange fantasies; believes I am an arms dealer, or some such thing. Thinks I am going to leave my wife for her."

He listened, and while Doyle couldn't hear the words the other man said, she could hear the apologies and assurances in his tone.

"Thank you," Acton said. "I feel rather guilty, turning her in like this, but the problem seems to be escalating."

After listening a bit more, he apologized again and rang off.

"Michael," breathed Doyle. "That is *diabolical.*"

"Yes," he replied briefly.

She glanced at him, wary; he was staring straight ahead, and the black mood was fast approaching, which meant she had only a limited amount of time to prime him for information. "Are you tryin' to get her to shoot you dead, out of spite? I don't know if that's your best plan, my friend."

But he replied with perfect sincerity, "I confess I was tempted to shoot her; and on more than one occasion. But then another would be sent in her place—and the next one might not be so malleable."

"And you mustn't go about killin' people," she reminded him gently. He tended to forget.

"That, too." He reached to place an apologetic hand on her leg. "I must beg your forgiveness, Kathleen, but this seemed the best way out."

"Whist; it was a rare crack, it was. Never had a nicer time, I assure you." There was a small pause whilst she tried to make sense of this particular way out. If Masterson had been willing to double-cross Solonik by taking up with Acton, that plan was now in ruins. I am going to be very unhappy, she thought with a surge of annoyance, if all that playacting was for *nothing*.

"I confess I am tired," he said suddenly, his warm hand moving gently along her thigh.

She hid a smile. "And you can also confess you've been drinkin' like an alderman during the course of this wondrous weekend."

"Yes." He sighed, his chest rising and falling. "I couldn't sleep without you."

She glanced at him sidelong. "As long as you weren't sleeping with her."

He faced her and leaned in, intent. "I wasn't. I swear it."

This was true, and a relief. But before she could make an inquiry about what was to happen next, he began kissing her neck, his breath warm against the nape while his hands wandered over her breasts.

"Oh," she said, her hands gripping the wheel. "I don't know as I can multi-task, Michael."

"There is a small road coming up to the right," he murmured into her throat. "Perhaps we should stop for a bit."

"All right." She carefully turned the vehicle into the small lane off the highway, and drove on the unpaved road for a few seconds while his attentions escalated. All in all, she was willing; when the black mood was upon him he wanted either to have sex or get drunk—and neither one too gently. Therefore, when he reached to turn off the ignition, she did not hesitate to clamber onto his lap, kissing him something fierce even as the car started rolling and he had to reach around her to put the gear into park. While the windows steamed up, Doyle decided that the warnings the nuns always gave about avoiding intimacy in cars *surely* did not apply after one was married, and happily settled in to enjoy herself.

When the storm was spent, they lay on the lowered passenger seat, limbs entwined, damp and unmoving. Not enough room in these cars for this, she thought, although where there is a will, there is indeed a way.

His mobile pinged, but he ignored it, instead pulling his fingers slowly through her hair. "You will be re-bruised. Sorry."

She gently bit his ear. "I'll sorry you one, I will."

He chuckled deep in his chest and she thought, good; maybe she could stave off the worst of it so that his wits were about him when Masterson made her next move.

After they straightened up, he pulled out his mobile, entered some digits, then reached for hers and did the same. "I'm blocking her calls."

"I see," she said, although she didn't at all. "D'you want to stop and get a drink, or d'you want to get home?"

He kissed her mouth, lingeringly. "You are a commendable wife. I will wait for home."

"Aye then," she said, starting the car as though she knew what she was doing. "Home it is."

CHAPTER 41

WHEN THEY WALKED INTO THE FLAT, ACTON IMMEDIATELY poured himself a tall scotch and stood, gazing out the windows and lost in thought. Doyle was rather proud of herself; she drove all the way back to their parking garage without mishap, although Acton had to help her gauge the distances to park the car in the slot. He'd been quiet, saying little on the drive, and she respected his mood and made no comment, trying to hide her concern. Apparently, she had not been very successful.

"If I tell you what is planned, will you try to relax?"

"Yes," she replied, and sat down on the sofa, taut as a bowstring.

He began to pace, holding the glass by the rim in a casual hand. "The object is to make her angry—to humiliate her. To provoke her into attempting to run the story immediately, so as to take a revenge."

There was a pause. "D'you think that is the best plan, Michael?" she asked in a small voice.

"Yes. Her editor will be made aware that there is a situation. Anything she offers will be carefully scrutinized, and it will be unbelievable."

"What if she has evidence," asked Doyle carefully, "—evidence of the unbelievable?"

He paused to look at her. The scotch was half gone and she could see he was making an effort to focus. "If you discredit the source, the quality of the evidence has no relevance."

She thought about this; her scalp prickling. "So that even if you build a case on a hard-and-fast fact, if no one wants to believe you, no one will."

He turned back to the window. "Yes—something like that. You should know this better than most; perception is as powerful as empirical knowledge. It is what helps the species survive."

She was silent, not quite following, but hoping he knew what he was about.

"I planted some information in the archives that she will attempt to use; Previ and those who control the paper will know immediately that it is not true."

"Saints," said Doyle admiringly, feeling the tension drain from her body. "Somethin' about the war?" She remembered the discussion at the table, back when Masterson was lying about not finding anything of interest.

"Yes, the second war. She found information that indicated my grandfather was a Nazi sympathizer—that he had supported the Third Reich."

"But he hadn't?"

"No. The story is not well known, but he was very mechanically-minded, and was fascinated with airplanes. During the Battle of Britain, he volunteered to help piece together the damaged planes at great risk to himself."

Doyle was not clear on the historical reference, but she well understood that any accusation that the man was a Nazi would be disbelieved.

"There were also some documents suggesting my mother did away with my father and fought to recover insurance proceeds, which were disallowed due to the suspicious circumstances."

"Michael," she breathed in admiration. "They will think

Masterson is *ravin'* mad." Doyle realized this was perhaps not the most diplomatic thing to say to Acton, and hastily added, "She'll be sacked."

"More importantly, she'll be discredited." He set his glass down with a sharp click; it was almost empty. "I am going to bed; I would appreciate it if you would accompany me." He held out a hand to her.

"My pleasure," she teased, feeling immeasurably better as she took his hand. "You're makin' up for lost time with a vengeance, if I may be sayin' so."

He stopped suddenly, and faced her, running his hands down her arms. "Perhaps you should eat something first. You are in a delicate condition."

She smiled to herself, and gently placed her palms on his chest. "Right, then; go on, and I'll meet you in a few."

He covered one of her hands with his. "If it is a girl, we shall name her Mary."

After a moment's struggle with her emotions, she found her voice. "It's a very old-fashioned name, Michael."

"Nonetheless."

She stood for a moment, watching her husband make his slightly unsteady way toward the bedroom, and offered up her heartfelt thanks—God had given her another go, and she would relish every moment; every sick morning. And thanks to all available saints and angels that there was no question of paternity; she owed Savoie an enormous debt of gratitude for rescuing her that night. Hopefully she would not have to shoot him, like his stupid brother.

Reminded, she checked her mobile to see whether any unknown numbers were listed under recent contacts, but it appeared that Savoie hadn't made any attempt to contact her over the weekend. This was not necessarily good news; she felt it was important to keep in his good graces so that he wouldn't be distracted if Solonik dangled more riches before him. But it was unlikely someone like Savoie would be moved by riches; more like Solonik would promise him some lucrative rig, or damning information about his baby brother's last days.

With a sigh, she moved from crisis number two to crisis number three, and scrolled up Williams's number. "Hey."

"Hey, yourself."

"I'm back from the wars."

"How did it go?"

"It's a long and sordid story, and not worth repeatin'. I wanted to have a talk with the coroner tomorrow mornin' about our latest victim, and if you'd come along I'd appreciate it." She added belatedly, "Sir."

"I have an interview at nine—can we meet at ten?"

"Who's the interview with?" she asked, immediately suspicious.

"Morgan Percy, the junior we met at Moran's chambers."

She tried for a moment to imagine how Morgan Percy would fit in with any Solonik-connected scheme, but gave it up as unlikely. She then thought of suggesting that Williams should smile once in a while during the interview, so as to seem more approachable, but decided she shouldn't be giving him helpful advice about the opposite sex until she first found out if he was ruthlessly stabbing Acton in the back. And besides, Williams had a stubborn streak, and if she suggested he smile, he'd probably scowl the poor girl down, just to be contrary.

"It's about the Wexford Prison corruption case; you are welcome to come along."

She hid a smile, as this last was not exactly true. "No thanks; I'll take the opportunity to have a lie-in—it's an exhausted casualty I am, from the aforementioned wars. I'll see you tomorrow."

She rang off, and almost immediately had an incoming call, which she assumed was Williams, having forgotten to tell her something. "Hey," she answered, lifting a slice of hot toast to the plate with quick fingers.

"We must discuss your problem." It was Savoie.

Speak o' the devil, and up pops crisis number two again. Doyle paused, and slowly lowered the plate to the counter. "Yes; well—I may need a bit more time to hold a bake sale, or somethin'."

There was a silence. "It means you sell baked goods—like cakes—to raise money," she explained.

"You have no money? How can this be?"

"It's Acton who has the money," she explained in an apologetic tone. "I've always been as poor as a church mouse—believe me, if I could pay for all of this to go away, I would."

"I understand," he said generously. "I was a mouse in the church, also."

"There you go."

"But we must meet tomorrow; I think I can make the arrangements to solve all your cracking problems."

"If you could pull off such a trick, I'd be cock a' hoop, my friend." She was wary, though; he was not the type to be generous.

"In the evening—I will meet you at the same place. I may come late," he cautioned. "I have another meeting, first."

She swallowed. "Are you meeting with Solonik?" Hopefully she would not be going to her doom, although the bookstore seemed an unlikely place for bloody revenge-taking.

He did not deign to answer, but instead repeated, "Go after work and wait. I may be late, but I will come."

As she opened her mouth to agree, she realized he'd already rung off.

CHAPTER 42

"*S*EVRES," SAID REYNOLDS REVERENTLY AS HE LIFTED THE VASE from the gift packaging. "And worth a pretty penny, if I may say so." He glanced at her, a hint of alarm in his eye. "Am I unaware that it is your birthday, madam?"

"No—there is no particular reason, Reynolds. Acton is very thoughtful." The vase was identical to the one he'd smashed at Trestles, and in the future she'd best be careful about what she admired aloud, mental note.

The package had arrived whilst Doyle was explaining to Reynolds that the next time they went to Trestles, she would bring him along to knock some heads together, and the servant, as always, expressed his willingness to do her bidding.

She placed the vase carefully on the mantel. "The steward's the type that will be there till the crack o' doom, though. You'd have to challenge him to a duel, or somethin', to pry him loose."

"Oh, no—I'd be quite content to assist Lord Acton as his valet," the domestic demurred. "I have no ambition to steward a large estate." This was untrue, but forgivable, as everyone had a secret ambition. Her own, for example, was to survive the next three crises.

Acton had slept soundly the night through, and then in the morning had risen early to sit at his desk, addressing the workload that had been stacking up in his absence. Upon Reynolds's arrival, the servant had taken an assessing look at him, and then had taken pains to stay out of his way until he left for work. Doyle could hardly blame him; she imagined Acton would not be easy until he knew what had happened with Masterson and the newspaper.

On the way to the morgue, she thought over how she'd best handle Williams, and then decided that nothing she did *ever* went according to plan, so she may as well just see how it went and gauge the situation as it unfolded. He was waiting outside when she arrived, holding a coffee cup, which she eyed with longing; she'd decided to cut back on caffeine and it was already killing her.

"Have some," he offered, reading her aright.

"Just a sip, then." Taking the cup, she accompanied him down the stairs into the cold storage room, where the remains of those who'd died unattended deaths were stored until the coroner decided whether there was anything of interest to report to law enforcement. Dr. Hsu, the coroner, knew they were coming, and greeted them in his usual subdued manner as he pulled out a drawer that contained the body of a sixtyish white man, a member of the prestigious Health and Care Professions Council. They gazed upon the still, sunken face for a moment, and Doyle was struck—as she always was—by the enormous difference between a live person and a dead person, and how inexplicable it was that most just took it for granted. "Anythin' of interest to report?"

The coroner shrugged. "Not much, I fear. Dead as a result of a small caliber bullet, fired from close range to the back of his head. Victim was upright; had no defensive wounds and was probably unaware."

She looked to Williams. "Anythin' at the scene?"

"Nothing. No casings, no footprints."

Doyle nodded as she contemplated the decedent. They'd already established that this killer knew how homicides were investigated, and also knew the police wouldn't be too keen on evidence recovery in the first place—a bad one met a bad end, and a good riddance. She said to Williams, "Acton said to look carefully at any discrepancies, however small, but this one seems very similar to the others, at least in terms of evidence."

The coroner offered, "No signs of alcohol or drug abuse. Last meal was a beefsteak."

"So not a thug," Williams observed. "That's different."

"The female victim who beat up her boyfriend was not a thug, either," she reminded him. "Just an unlikely murderer, which is what helped her get off."

Williams indicated the corpse. "Well, I suppose you could say he was an unlikely Section Five, and that helped him get off."

This seemed of interest, and she lifted her head. "Tell me about that, then."

Obligingly, he pulled up a screen on his mobile, and recited, "He was involved in charities for at-risk youth; raised money for the safe house program run by the Council. He—along with some other civic-minded people—started an organized sports program at the city parks; the idea was to give disadvantaged boys positive team-building experience, and keep them out of trouble. From what I can glean, there had long been rumors of pedophilia, but then a formal complaint of molestation was actually filed by one of the boys about six years ago. The mother had already made an extortion attempt, however, so the authorities felt they didn't have much of a case—since it may have all been a frame-up—and the accused man was a civic leader." With a thumb, he closed the screen. "It won't be easy to research the cold case; the alleged victim died in a car crash, and the mother died in a drug deal gone bad about six months ago."

Doyle met his eyes. "Is there any evidence that might implicate this victim as the perpetrator for either of *those* deaths?"

He nodded, slowly. "Good catch, DS Doyle; I will put some-one on it."

She quirked her mouth. "If you wouldn't mind. And I appreciate the pretense that I outrank you; pigs will fly."

With a shrug, he opened his mobile again to make a note. "It's your theory—you figured out we had a vigilante in the first place. I'm happy to work as a team on this one."

The words hung in the air, and the moment was upon her—nothin' for it. "Let's go into the consultation room, Thomas. I need to ask you somethin'."

After indicating to the coroner that they were finished, they stepped across the hallway into the small chamber where grieving relatives gathered before viewing the remains of their loved ones. It held several chairs and a bouquet of fake flowers in a futile attempt to lighten the grim atmosphere, and Doyle shut the door behind them with a click. "I need you to give me an honest answer, if you please."

If he was surprised by this turn of events, he hid it well. "Right, then."

"How well do you know Cassie Masterson?"

He was caught off guard, and waited for a long moment before saying cautiously, "I had some drinks with her."

This was true, but not information enough. "And how did that come about?"

She could see that he didn't want to tell her, and her heart sank.

"Why do you ask?" he countered.

All thought of a careful and measured interrogation flew out the window. "Thomas," she whispered through stiff lips. "Are you *workin'* with her?"

His brows came together in puzzlement. "No; I work with you, remember?"

Doyle hesitated, trying to figure out how to get the information she needed. "How many times have you spoken with her?"

"Once. We had some drinks. What is this about?"

She swallowed. "I don't think that is exactly true."

He stared at her for a moment, then abruptly confessed, "I rang her up and pretended interest—we had a few drinks together, and"—he tilted his head—"and so on."

"You *slept* with her?" Men were a completely different breed, Doyle thought in amazement as she stared at him. Truly.

"I was trying to spare you the knowledge. You're rather strait-laced."

Bemused, she could only agree. "It's a proper Puritan, I am." Of course, there were the recent sessions in the stable and the Range Rover, but that was conjugal, and so a different sort of thing altogether. "Why on *earth* would you be doin' a line with the likes of her?"

"Aside from the obvious?"

She made a face. "Stop it, Thomas, you're givin' me the willies."

He took a breath, thinking about his answer. "I suppose I was trying to figure out what was going on. It seemed so—so unbelievable that Acton would throw you over for someone like her."

"Well, Masterson didn't find it so unbelievable, and a good thing. She was collectin' information against Acton—was plannin' an exposé about—about some of his recent activities." She gave him a significant look; no need to go into detail with Williams—he probably knew more about it than she did.

Williams stared at her. "*What?*"

"Yes—Solonik put her up to it. But she was gettin' information from someone on the inside."

He was suddenly angry. "And you thought it was *me?*"

"No—well, not truly, anyway; will you *listen?* Acton found out about the plan and began doin' a line with her, trying to make her think she could be the next Lady Acton so she'd break with Solonik."

The light dawned, and Williams lifted his brows. "Those photos."

"Yes," she agreed. "Those wretched photos."

He regarded her for a moment, thinking. "But you didn't know about Acton's plan at the time—you thought it was real."

"Indeed I did; and you have the bruises on your chest to show for it."

Smiling slightly in acknowledgment, he persisted, "So why this interrogation? Why did you think I was working with Masterson?"

"You spoke of Acton's filin' for divorce—remember? She was the only person who would know of such a thing; Acton was lyin' to her."

He thought about this. "So that night when you were so upset, you weren't going to faint about the divorce, you were going to faint because you thought I was helping her bring down Acton."

"Exactly."

"And as I am still alive, you did not tell Acton."

She shook her head. "I just couldn't believe it, despite what it seemed." She remembered what Acton had said about perception trumping evidence—right again, that man. "So please don't try to talk Acton out of filin' for a divorce."

He laughed. "No; that would be hazardous to my health."

She smiled in return, immensely relieved, but knowing that she'd never truly believed it in the first place. "I don't think Acton would have believed it either, Thomas, if that makes you feel any better—so not so hazardous, after all."

"So where do things stand? Do I need to attempt another— infiltration of the enemy?"

"Oh—that is *disgustin'*. You will stop it, Thomas Williams, or I will give you the back o' my hand. Acton has a very good plan to turn the tables, and you mustn't interfere."

He nodded, and opened the door for her. "So we are good?"

"We are," she assured him as they passed out into the linoleum hallway. "We always will be—I'm sorry that I doubted you, even for a moment. Although I must say I can't admire your taste."

"It was strictly in the line of duty. She's too old for me."

"Not to mention she is the anti-Christ," she reminded him with a look.

"That, too. Speaking of which, what has happened to your French friend?"

Seeking his own sexual favors, she thought as they approached the stairway. "Playin' least-in-sight. Hopefully he'll tire of this little sightseein' trip and go back to his lair."

"Remember that you are naïve, by your own admission," he cautioned.

"Not about him." This was true; she had no illusions.

He glanced at her sidelong. "Do I get to hear the story?"

"No," she said firmly, "you don't. And no detectin', either; it would give you grey hair."

"All right," he agreed, and it was not the truth.

To change the subject, she switched back to the task at hand as they climbed the stairs. "I think this victim was the one that was intended from the beginnin'; they're all ABC murders, with the difference that the other victims deserved to die, also—or at least in the vigilante's eyes. It is important that this one was a Section Five, and not a murderer. Or not originally, anyway; pendin' what we find out about the other deaths."

But Williams was Williams, and not a leaper-to-conclusions. "Do you really think it is that significant? Section Five is a despicable crime—right up there with murder."

"Yes," she agreed diplomatically, aware that Williams had meted out his own justice on the subject. "But I truly believe it's the key to this case, Thomas."

They paused on the landing, and he must have been thinking about his own experience also, because he offered, "Perhaps the vigilante is a relative of an unknown victim—another boy who'd been molested."

Doyle knit her brow. "I don't know, Thomas—that theory doesn't account for all the other murders of murderers. I think the killer is someone who felt he had to right all wrongs because *this* was the triggering event; he knew, in hindsight, that this man was not the civic leader that everyone thought he was—probably when the molested boy and the mother conveniently died. Suddenly our vigilante had it up to here, and set about killin' this one, along with all the others who'd gotten away with murder, due to misplaced public sympathy."

She paused, still frowning because there was something important here—she was tantalizingly close; so close that her scalp wasn't even bothering to prickle. Slowly, she said aloud, "Their subsequent crimes made it clear they were guilty in the first place, and should never have gotten off. They were not the sympathetic victims that the papers made them out to be." Much struck, she cleared her brow. "Faith, I can relate; I'm not who the papers make me out to be, either."

But Williams shook his head slightly. "I disagree, Kath—you are one of the few people who are exactly what you seem."

She couldn't help but smile in response to his tone. "Yes, DI Williams; I am aware there's a good reason that I'm not on undercover detail. But as for the bridge-jumpin' heroine, believe me; that's all puffery and sleight-of-hand."

Realization suddenly dawned with such clarity that she had to steady herself by grasping the stair rail. It was almost anticlimactic, and she mentally castigated herself as a complete knocker for not seeing it sooner. It *is* all tied up in everything else, she realized, and I suppose it was so obvious, I overlooked it completely.

"What is it?" He watched her narrowly. In a way, he was almost as adept as Acton in reading her—she should work on being less transparent; mental note.

"What is what?" she replied in all innocence, imitating Acton at his most infuriating.

"Don't hold out on me," he warned. "You tend to get into trouble."

This was true, and she was touched by his concern. "I have to follow up on somethin'; I'll let you know as soon as I have a grip on it." She pulled out her mobile, and began to trot up the stairs to the top while he watched her from the landing, unmoving. "Don't forget to follow up on the other murders."

"Yes, ma'am," he said heavily, as though she were his superior officer, and she laughed, the sound echoing down the stairwell.

CHAPTER 43

DOYLE SAT ON A PARK BENCH, WAITING, AND THINKING ABOUT the vigilante killer and the hindsight murders—murders that didn't seem like murders until the person killed again, and then the belated, horrified realization that a murderer had been set free to murder again. I've had my own fill of hindsight, she thought—what with the night visitor at Trestles. But apparently I'm tasked with the delivery of yet another warning, and this one just as important as the others.

It was a bit chilly, and she put her hands in her coat pockets, hoping she needn't wait too long.

"Ho there, my lady."

Kevin Maguire approached, looking less and less like a rumpled, out-of-shape newsman, and more like someone who was fighting a wasting disease. Unfortunately, Doyle was familiar with that look, having watched her mother waste away. "Mr. Maguire; thank you for comin'."

Maguire sank onto the bench beside her, smiling ironically. "I suppose you already know that as we speak, there is a huge row going on in the editorial offices, and Cassie is about to get sacked in journalistic disgrace."

While this was welcome news, she feigned puzzlement. "And why on earth would I be aware of such a thing?"

He smiled and shook his head, looking around him at the peaceful surroundings as he pulled out a cigarette. "I would never want to cross your husband."

"I find him very amiable, myself."

Maguire laughed aloud. "Someday you must tell me the story—I promise I won't publish it."

"You couldn't," she said frankly. "No one would believe it, and you'd wind up like Masterson."

"I don't know," he ventured, still smiling as he drew on the cigarette. "I have learned—after many years in this business—that people will believe anything."

She said a little sharply, "Particularly when a newspaper tells them to believe it."

Sobering, he turned to regard her thoughtfully. "I take it we are not here to discuss Cassie, or your redoubtable husband."

"You can't just go about killin' people, no matter how just the cause."

There was a long pause, and then he drew on the cigarette and offered diffidently, "I'm not sure what you mean."

Doyle placed a gentle hand on his arm. "You're comin' to the end, as we all will. Now is not the time to be blottin' your copybook."

He gazed at her in amusement. "There is no God. There is no one keeping track in a big, golden account book."

"I would hate to be in your shoes and find out otherwise."

He stared at her for a moment, and she wasn't sure what he was thinking. "Perhaps I am trying to redeem myself; to make up for past hubris."

Doyle wasn't sure what the word meant, but she understood the gist. "Leave retribution to God, Mr. Maguire."

He took a drag and scoffed, "There is no God."

"I can see," she said thoughtfully, "that we are not makin' any progress, here."

He gazed over at the ordered flowerbeds and blew out a breath of smoke. "I love places like this—love them. The parks are a breath of calm in the midst of all the evil; all the insanity. When you've been covering major crimes as long as I have, your view of the city gets a little warped."

"Yes; you led the campaign to convince the Council to start up the recreation program at the parks for at-risk youth. Only in hindsight, you realized—with proper horror—that you'd only helped to serve up innocent victims to a monster."

Tilting his head back, he rested his gaze on the spreading branches above them. "I thought I knew him. I thought I knew *people*. I was so certain of their inherent goodness."

"You were a bit naïve, perhaps." Ironic, that everyone thought *her* naïve, when she knew humankind better than most.

"I tried to shape opinion to fit my own views. And good people died—or worse."

She touched his arm in sympathy again, reacting to the underlying bitterness. "Surely these were the rare exceptions in your career."

With a chuckle, he tossed the cigarette stub onto the pavement before them. "You'll not give me comfort, although I appreciate the effort. It is such a seductive, heady feeling, you know. You are so sure of your own righteousness; your own power. If you are proved wrong, it only makes you all the more arrogant."

"It is the ultimate sin," she noted gently. "To believe that you are unanswerable."

"Stop trying," he said with a smile. "It's not going to work."

"I have no choice," she offered in apology. "I have to keep tryin'; it's a long journey through eternity—imagine bein' relieved of this burden of guilt."

"I am relieved of it," he assured her as he gazed out over their surroundings again. "Almost."

Her scalp prickled, and she ventured, "Is that so? How many more on the list?"

"Only one."

Doyle leaned forward to beg with all sincerity, "Please, please, reconsider. I know a good man to talk to, who would keep whatever you tell him private."

"A priest." This pronounced with mild contempt.

"A good man," she reiterated. "He will not judge, but he may help to take the guilt away."

"On the contrary, I'm putting the guilt to good use."

She sat still for a moment and contemplated him, feeling that she was at an impasse. Impossible to try to make an arrest—she'd no evidence, as well he knew. "I'll figure out who the remainin' victim is, you know."

He smiled. "Not this one, you won't."

Something in the way he said it gave her pause. "Is it Acton?" she asked, almost before she recognized the thought.

"No," he replied, and was telling the truth. "I wouldn't put you through it, even if he was on the list. You are one of my favorite people, did you know?"

She leaned forward again. "Then *please* let me convince you to change your mind. I am goin' to find out about the last victim and put a stop to it; you don't want to end your career as the subject of such a story."

"No," he agreed with bitter irony. "I am more suited to incite from the sidelines, and then run from the responsibility of what I have done."

Doyle decided she'd done as much as she could, and it only remained to lay the whole before Acton and let him decide what to do. Gently, she asked, "Do you have someone who is takin' care of you at home?"

He took a deep breath. "Yes. Better than I deserve. It's a hard thing, dying."

"Aye, that," she agreed somberly, remembering her mother's ordeal—incomprehensible to imagine having to face it without faith. Rising to leave, she gathered her coat around her. "I'll remember you in my prayers, if you have no objection."

"Not at all," he smiled. "If anyone can convince God that he exists, it is you."

CHAPTER 44

*D*OYLE WAS THOUGHTFUL AS SHE WALKED TOWARD THE MET; IT had occurred to her that all her crises seemed to be resolving themselves in a very satisfactory manner, and all at once. Williams was not a turncoat; Savoie did not seem inclined to serve as Solonik's henchman; Masterson could no longer serve that role even if she wanted to; and the vigilante killer was Maguire—something she probably should have figured out long ago. All in all, there seemed to be unmitigated good news, particularly if she was pregnant again. Now, her only task was to find out who the last victim was, and she had a sneaking suspicion—from the way Maguire'd raised it—that it was someone she knew. So—if one followed the thinking, someone she knew had gotten away with murder. Who?

She absently responded to the desk sergeant's respectful greeting as she came through the lobby doors. The last murderer on the list could easily be Williams—Williams had dispatched his uncle the evil-doer; presumably with Acton's help. But it was hard to imagine how Maguire would have discovered such a thing. No—more likely it was a crime the CID had investigated, so that it had come to Maguire's attention in the first place. And besides, Maguire would have approved of Williams's actions anyway—after all, Williams was a vigilante, himself. Maguire was more credulous—and soft-hearted—

but in the end, he'd also turned to vigilantism. When he realized he'd been using his influence to champion cold-blooded killers, the remorse and guilt must have been overwhelming. The fuse had then been lit by the terrible realization that he'd aided and abetted a pedophile, and in an attempt to atone for all past sins, he'd tried to mete out a rough justice, however belated.

When she came to the lifts in the lobby, a PC held the door for her and she stepped in, smiling her thanks. *The difference between me and them—Acton, Williams, and Maguire,* Doyle realized, *is that I believe in an ultimate justice, and so I am not so enraged or frustrated when earthly justice falls short. I have neither the desire nor the expertise to take the place of God.*

"Have a nice day, Officer Doyle," offered the PC when she stepped out at her floor.

"Thank you." *No doubt he'd tell his mates tonight at the pub that he'd shared a lift with her,* but it didn't rankle as much as it had in the past. *We all need the assurance that right makes might,* she thought; *it's a long wait 'til heaven.*

With this improved attitude, Doyle voluntarily ducked her head into Munoz's cubicle on the way to her own. "How was your weekend, Munoz?"

"Miserable. I'm to take the veil."

Doyle considered this pronouncement. "You'd be quite the nun, Munoz. They'd have to dedicate a twenty-four-hour confessional booth to you alone."

With a twist of her swivel chair, Munoz turned to face Doyle. "Help me, then; Acton must know some eligible men. And you know what I mean by eligible."

Rich, thought Doyle correctly. "I will ask him, Munoz. I will, I promise." She thought about it. "What if it's a choice between someone unexciting but with lots of money who would adore you, versus excitement and less of the other two?"

"I will make those types of assessments," Munoz replied. "Just get me some names."

"Will do," Doyle agreed, and briefly toyed with the idea of Sir Stephen, but then decided Munoz shouldn't be hooked up with a pretender to the throne, so to speak; Acton had enough troubles. And even Munoz didn't deserve the likes of Sir Stephen.

To be courteous, Munoz asked Doyle about her weekend.

"Fraught with peril," Doyle replied. "We visited Acton's mother."

The other girl arched an amused brow. "Did you? What's she like?"

"A harridan. Hates me from my Irish insides out."

Munoz laughed in appreciation. "She's one to talk; there was that scandal about Acton's father, after all."

Doyle's antennae quivered and she pretended that she knew. "His disappearance, you mean?"

"DCI Drake said it was generally thought she did away with him; the insurance wouldn't pay."

Saints, thought Doyle in abject dismay. Was it *true*, then?

"Ask Acton if he knows any eligible men whose mothers are dead already," Munoz said thoughtfully. "That would be ideal."

"Amen to that," said Doyle fervently, and turned back toward her cubicle. She'd just settled in to look through the updates on her files when Williams rang in. Lifting her mobile, she answered, "Are you callin' in with a report, like a good underling?"

But as it turned out, indeed he was. "I thought I'd swing by the *London World News* to review the archives—the old coverage of the mother's murder."

"And check in on Masterson in the meantime," she added in admiration. "You are a *trump*, Thomas."

He lowered his voice. "Apparently, earlier today there were shouting matches in her office and the owners of the paper are meeting with the publisher. I'll see what else I can find out."

"Excellent sleuthin', if I may say so." No need to tell him that this was no longer breaking news; he had gone to all the effort, after all.

"I don't think she's here; after I do the research, I may try to track her down to see if she's drowning her sorrows and would like a sympathetic ear."

"Remember that you are no longer to be sacrificin' your virtue on that particular altar, me boyo."

"Yes, ma'am." He rang off.

So—this corroborated what Maguire had reported; Masterson was in disgrace and getting the sack, thanks be to God. It had occurred to her, after Acton's phone call to Previ, that even if Masterson had the goods on Acton, the powers-that-be might not allow the story to run. Doyle knew such things happened—even the mighty press could be stifled. Still, it was hard to stare disaster in the face, and it was an enormous relief to know that Acton's plan seemed to be working. She then realized that Williams was on a sleeveless errand, and rang him up again.

"Hey."

"Hey, yourself. What's up?"

"Thomas, about the research . . ." She belatedly realized she wasn't certain what she wanted to tell him.

"What is it? Do you have a lead?"

She offered hesitantly, "More than that; I think I've solved it—but it's tricky and I need some advice from Acton."

There was a small silence and she grimaced—didn't handle that very well; it was Williams who had been helping her out like he was a first-year peeler, every step of the way.

"He's tied up on the Wexton Prison case, can I substitute?"

She tried to make amends. "Your advice is excellent, Thomas. It's the identity of the suspect that creates the problem."

"Oh, I see; a political issue?"

"Sort of," she hedged. Williams's feelings wouldn't be hurt with that excuse, and it really was political, in a way.

"Are you there?"

"Sorry," she said. "I wish I knew what to do."

"To recap, you think you know who the killer is, but you can't move on it for some reason."

"Yes. And meanwhile I'm worried he's going to murder one more former killer before he's done."

There was a pause. "That's some detective work, DS Doyle."

"Thank you, DI Williams. I'm not sure it will amount to anythin'; I'm sorry I'm bein' so mysterious."

"So everything's on hold?"

"Yes," she said slowly. "Let me see what Acton wants to do."

Doyle rang off, and then decided to call Acton on his private line, even though she knew he was interviewing suspects in the prison corruption investigation; apparently at least one judge was involved, and so Acton had been called in to handle yet another politically delicate case. He answered immediately, as he always did when she used the private line. "Kathleen."

"Are you hip-deep in anythin'?"

"I'm interviewing personnel."

A code of silence had been erected around the rumors of judicial graft, and she hoped he could unearth something helpful. "I won't keep you then. I'll be needin' your advice on the vigilante case."

There was a small pause. "You've solved the case?"

She smiled in surprise. "Faith, am I that transparent?"

"To me, you are. If you need me now, I can spare an hour."

"No, it can wait."

"Right, then; I'll leave for home soon."

She hesitated. "I may be a bit late—I have some shoppin' to do." This, in the event he checked her GPS and wondered what she was doing at the bookstore; she was not one for books.

"Don't be too late; you need your rest."

She smiled into the mobile and rang off. Hopefully Acton

would know what to do with Maguire; there was precious little evidence to support a prosecution there, also.

The rest of the afternoon passed uneventfully as Doyle tried to come up with the parameters for a search with respect to the other crimes Maguire had covered; she had a half-formed idea in the back of her mind that if she could identify Maguire's next victim, she could dissuade him from the last murder on the list. It would probably be another sensational case with a sympathetic killer—a domestic abuse victim? Or perhaps another hero of the community? She tapped the eraser end of a pencil on the desk as she thought about it, and checked the time. In another twenty minutes or so, she'd pack up and wander over to the bookstore. With any luck, she'd dissuade Savoie from carrying out Solonik's evil plan, and send him home none the wiser that she'd shot his brother dead. All in all, it would be the capper to a good day's work.

CHAPTER 45

*H*E WAITED, AND WHILE HE WAITED HE ADMIRED THE VIEW, BEING *careful to stand back so as not to be seen. It was dark early at this time of year, and the lamps were lit on the street below. The alarm system had been a challenge; it was intricate and customized, one of the best he'd seen. He did not mind; he was a patient man.*

He heard the lift land at the floor, and he turned his head, listening, although the sound was barely perceptible. He had always had exceptional hearing. He had to.

Softly, he stepped over to his position and waited, balanced on the balls of his feet. A key card was placed in the slot and he drew a breath and held it; it was always the first few seconds that were crucial. The door opened and Acton stepped in, then turned to the wall to switch on the light.

He stepped behind Acton and let him feel the barrel of the gun at his head. "Do not move. I am a friend to your wife, and I must speak to you. Do not set off the alarm."

Acton had frozen at the first movement. He now said slowly, "Right, then."

"I will not take your gun, but you must not reach for it; understood?"

"I am unarmed."

This falsehood was unworthy of such a one, and he made a derisive noise of disapproval.

"I beg your pardon—I will not draw. May I move, now?"

He stepped back. "Yes. Slowly."

Acton turned and looked at him, carefully lowering his hands.

"Do you know who I am?"

"Yes," Acton said. "Where is my wife?"

"She is at work. She does not know we are cahoots."

There was a small silence while they measured each other, and he allowed Acton to recover from the surprise. This was important; if things happened too quickly, men became nervous. This one was also tall, like the blond man. She needed a man closer to her height—she was not so tall.

"How do you know my wife?"

"She was fighting un violeur, but she was going to lose."

Acton had an involuntary reaction; a slight movement in his facial muscles he could not control. So; he did not like to hear this about his wife.

"I took care of this problem for her."

"Merci," said Acton.

He smiled. This was a courtesy, to use his language, and it was appreciated.

"Why do you help my wife?"

He shrugged, and quoted what she had said to the tall blond man. "Believe it or not, she is a friend." He paused and added regretfully, "Nothing more; she is not that kind."

"No," agreed Acton.

"She has another problem, that one." He added, gently scolding, "I think that you do not keep track of her as you should."

There was a small pause, and then Acton bowed his head in acknowledgment. "No doubt."

"Solonik is after her—he is the wolf wearing the clothes from the lambs. He asked that I bring her to him—to meet."

Acton listened and said nothing.

Watching him in return, he observed, "Your wife, she was not afraid of him. She says that Solonik is taking your goat."

Again, there was a small pause before Acton nodded in agreement. "That does sound like something she would say."

He shrugged a shoulder. "She is a comic, that one."

"Yes." Acton smiled slightly in return.

"She says Solonik is having la revanche, but does not want you to see that it is him."

"I see."

This seemed too measured a reaction, in light of the nature of the disclosure, and so he explained plainly, "The woman at the newspaper— Solonik sent her to your bed."

Acton nodded. "Yes."

So—he already knew of this. This was interesting; perhaps his wife had told him of the photos—although she did not seem the type to confront him. She would be a sad little bird, instead. He continued, "Solonik asked me to do terrible things—and take photographs. When I do not do them, he will find someone else."

"Then he must die," said Acton.

"Yes." As it turned out, Acton was an easy man to speak to.

"Name your price."

He looked at Acton thoughtfully for a moment. "This wife of yours; you tire of her—yes? There are many other women; perhaps you will set her aside."

There it was again; the involuntary movement of the face. "No."

He conceded with good grace, and named a sum, instead. He could see, now that he had met him, that Acton wanted his wife, although she did not seem to his taste. It had been a chance, only, and he was a patient man. Although he would not want Acton angry at him; he measured men for a living, and this was not one to cross.

"Shall I pay you now?"

He was sorry to put an end to this pleasant conversation, but the time had come to address that which was unpleasant. "I must ask you for information, first."

Acton's posture shifted slightly. "I'm afraid I cannot share any official—"

He shook his head impatiently. "No; not that kind of information. I would like to know what happened to my brother."

Acton was silent.

"I think you know who I mean; you brought him into your office. He thought you did not guess, but I think to myself—why would such a man take such an interest in one such as him? So I think you knew."

Acton said only, "What information would you like about him?"

"I believe he last came here, to this flat; but your wife says you did not kill him." He tilted his head. "I believe her, because she does not make a good liar."

"No, she doesn't," Acton agreed.

"But I think she knows more than she says."

Acton contemplated him gravely for a moment. "Yes; she knows who killed him, but she does not wish to cause you pain."

So—it was true that Emile was dead. This was not unexpected, but was not welcome news, nevertheless. He took a breath. "You will tell me what you know, if you please. I would like to know what happened to my brother."

Acton bowed his head and said without emotion, "Your brother was a man who preferred the company of men."

This was not a surprise. "Yes."

"There was another policeman who pursued your brother, but your brother was no longer interested. The other came to deliver evidence to me—evidence of correspondence between Rourke and Solonik. Your brother was here, also, and there was a quarrel—"

He lifted his brows in surprise. "They fought here? In your home?"

Acton explained, "I was not here, but my wife was." He paused, and offered in apology, "I had to hush it up; my wife would have been involved in the scandal."

"Of course," he said slowly. "I understand this."

"Please accept my condolences for your loss."

He nodded, absently, and then focused, lowering his brows. "You will tell me who killed him—who this other policeman was."

Acton lifted a hand in apology. "Surely you see that I cannot."

There was a small silence. "If it was your brother, you would wish me to say."

"I would," Acton agreed. "But you would not tell me, either."

Dropping his gaze to the floor, he pretended to shrug in concession. "Perhaps not." It did not matter; it would not be so very difficult to discover the name of the policeman who had delivered such evidence.

"May I fetch your funds, now?"

He nodded, and followed the other through a door to the back of the flat.

Acton asked, "How did you get past the alarm?"

He shrugged. "I would rather not say." He watched his host deactivate another alarm and open a wall safe, so that he could plainly see what was inside. There were rows of weapons, and Acton paused and met his eyes for a moment. "If you are available for a project, I could use some assistance."

His gaze rested thoughtfully on the cache of weapons in the safe. "Tell me of this."

"Someone is not telling me the truth at the Home Office; someone who can be influenced by outside interests." Acton pulled a stack of bills out of a small strongbox, and casually handed him the stack without counting them.

"This is so? It is a shame that no one can be trusted in the government, in these times. It is the same in my country. They are knockers, I think."

"Perhaps," said Acton, shutting the safe, "we can speak again soon."

"Done," he said. "But first, I would have one more thing from you."

Acton waited, showing no concern.

"I have too much information for you to be easy, so you must swear on the soul of your wife that you will not come after me."

"I swear it," said Acton immediately. "I owe you a debt I can never repay." He offered his hand.

He appreciated the handshake and felt generous. "There is a flaw in the third redundancy," he disclosed, referring to the alarm system. "The electromagnetic pulse is intermittent."

"Merci," said Acton.

CHAPTER 46

*D*OYLE IDLY WANDERED DOWN THE AISLE FOR THE THIRD OR fourth time, so bored that she actually was tempted to buy a book. Annoying, it was, that she had no way to check with Savoie to see if he'd been called away by some other, more pressing skullduggery. Just as she was checking the time on her mobile, he appeared at the end of the aisle, his pale eyes upon hers and his hands in his pockets. "Greetin's," she offered with false heartiness. "Are you here for your pound o' flesh?"

In an unexpected gesture, he reached to take her hand. "Ah—we would be good together, little bird. You will change your mind?"

Resisting an urge to snatch her hand away, she replied, "We would be like chalk and cheese, my friend."

He cocked his head as he puzzled it out. "Very different."

"Yes; and I would spend all my days prayin' for your poor soul."

He laughed aloud at this, the sound a little harsh, as though he did not laugh often. He was in a festive mood, she saw. "I will speak to Solonik; I will tell him to leave you alone."

Doyle stared at him in surprise. "And he will? Just like that?"

"*Mais oui*," he said easily, and relinquished her hand.

She harbored an uneasy suspicion that this casual reassurance deliberately omitted her better half. "Will he leave Acton alone, too?"

"*Bien sûr.*"

Doyle took this to be an affirmation, but was understandably skeptical of this unlooked-for turn of events. "Why would you help me, if I have no money?"

"I help myself," he corrected her with a thin smile. "I have interests, you remember."

Recalling his involvement in the contraband rig, she wisely refrained from asking any more questions—she shouldn't withhold that type of information from Acton, so it was better if she didn't know any of the illicit particulars.

Savoie regarded her, a trace of amusement still lingering in his gaze. "Solonik telephoned me this day—he is very unhappy."

With some surprise, she stared at him. "Surely he's not allowed to make calls in prison?"

He smiled at her as though she were a very amusing child, and did not deign to reply. "He says Acton is upsetting his plans. Acton is taking the newspaper woman's goat, is he not?"

With great satisfaction, Doyle affirmed, "Indeed he is. He is cookin' her goose."

He laughed aloud again. "Then you have no more troubles."

With all sincerity, she thanked him. "I appreciate it so very much; you have saved me in more ways than one."

His eyes gleamed. "I am one of your saints, then."

"Oh, I don't know if heaven is ready for the likes of you, Philippe."

"That is good; I am not ready for heaven." Leaning in, he kissed her gently.

She stood still and acquiesced, although she could feel herself blushing furiously and hoped there were no security cameras capturing this marital lapse. But the kiss was chaste and brief, and then he pulled away and lifted a plain card out of his pocket. On it was penned an international telephone number next to a hand-sketch of a goat. "If you wish to speak to me, call this number and follow instructions. But tell no one else of it, if you please."

Looking at it, she nodded. "Will you go back home?"

"Perhaps, perhaps not; I may stay here for a time."

This raised a twinge of alarm within her breast, and she felt she should warn him, "I can't help you if you run into trouble, and I can't ask Acton to help you."

He was amused for some reason, but said gravely, "I understand."

They regarded each other for a moment, and she thought of her baby, and how much easier everything seemed, all of a sudden. "Please stay in contact, if you'd like. I will always stand your friend."

He held her chin between his thumb and forefinger and shook it slightly. "Try very hard to stay out of trouble."

"Done," she teased, and he released her.

CHAPTER 47

*D*OYLE CHECKED THE TIME AS SHE CAME UP THE LIFT TO THE flat. She was not later than her usual, despite all that had been accomplished on this tumultuous day. She was hungry, which was to the good—perhaps she wouldn't lose her appetite, this time. Leastways, no one was poisoning her, which was a step up from the last time.

As she entered, Acton looked up from across the room where he sat at his desk. She knew straightaway that he had been drinking, and felt a frozen moment of fear. Although if there was bad news he would not be drinking so heavily; instead he would stay alert and focused—he only overdid it after the crisis had passed.

She crossed over to him, and he lifted his head to receive her kiss. His laptop was open on the desk, displaying her location on a GPS monitor. Laying a finger on the screen, she pointed to the indicator. "Look, here I am."

He smiled and took her hand. "You had a good day?"

"Very good indeed; I have a million things to be tellin' you."

"I am at your disposal."

But she knelt down before him, still holding his hand. "What's happened?" she asked gently, looking up into his face. "Should I start barricadin' the door?"

He loosened his hand to stroke her head. "Sorry—I don't mean to upset you. I kept telling myself that I wouldn't pour another glass, and then I did."

She was getting mixed messages, and couldn't decide why this was. "Should I leave you to it, then? You know I don't mind."

"No. Stay with me, I want to look at you." Obligingly, she rested her head against his knee, and he stroked her hair for a few moments. "You have solved the case?"

Without preamble, she told him, "It's Kevin Maguire, from the paper. It's dyin', he is, and he's tryin' to right past wrongs."

There was a pause, while Acton's hand rested on her head. "It fits. Have we any evidence?"

"None." Best not to mention she'd had a nice little chat with the murderer this fine day. "But I think we can set up a trap and seizure, if I can figure out who the next victim is."

There was a small silence. "You are certain he is the killer?"

"I am." Warily, she lifted her head to eye him. "Remember, you are not to take matters into your own hands, Michael. I can catch him; I have one of my feelin's, I do."

"Fair enough," he replied mildly.

She laid her head down again. "Williams was reconnoiterin' over at the *World News*, and says that Masterson was sacked."

"Yes, she was. And apparently, she was in such a temper that the suggestion of mental imbalance had immediate credence."

Doyle wasn't certain what "credence" meant, but she understood the gist. "Well, thank the saints and holy martyrs. And a good riddance—you can do much better than her, Michael."

But he didn't chuckle in response, instead fingering her hair absently. "I will bring some pressure to bear so that she does not attempt to tell her tales elsewhere, or sue the paper."

Doyle hadn't thought of this, as she worried about only one

crisis at a time. Fortunately, Acton was good at crisis multitasking. "*Do* you have pressure to bear?"

"Yes," he replied, and offered nothing more.

She was all admiration. "Is there *anythin'* you don't know?"

"Apparently so."

A bit surprised by the nuance in his tone, she glanced up at him, but he did not elaborate, as his hand moved from her hair to gently lift her chin. "Your face is so beautiful." He brushed her cheekbone with a thumb.

She knew where this was leading, but desperately needed sustenance. "Hold that thought, Michael—d'you mind if I make somethin' to eat? Then we can pick up where we left off."

Standing a bit unsteadily, he accompanied her into the kitchen, and paused at the sink to splash water on his face and lean on his arms, trying to gather himself. She wished he would tell her what was bothering him, but knew better than to ask him again directly; he would tell her only if he wanted, and apparently, he didn't want to.

Since she didn't feel ambitious, she decided to put together a ham and butter sandwich, which required neither time nor expertise. Her slightly-more-sober husband came over to stand behind her, stroking her arms as she buttered the bread. "The bruises have all faded—from the night you were attacked."

"Finally; this skin of mine is a blessin' and a curse."

He put his arms around her waist and rested his chin on her shoulder. "That's just it—you are so appealing. It is at the same time a blessing and a curse."

"You need to work on your compliments, Michael," she noted in a dry tone. He smelt of scotch.

"Men want to take care of you."

She hoped they were not wandering into the subject of Williams, and said merely, "I'm not so very helpless, my friend."

"No—in fact, I think you try to protect me. I had not realized it before, but it explains a great deal."

She paused in her sandwich-making and grasped his hands at her waist. "Of course I do, Michael. I love, love, love you and I don't want you to be unhappy." She paused and leaned her head back so that her face rested against his. "As you are now."

"Can you guess," he said softly, kissing her neck, "what would make me happy?"

With a smile, she turned to face him. She knew his heart wasn't in it, but he was going to make an effort and so she would play along—if she was needed to render aid and comfort, the pitiful sandwich could wait.

He ran his mouth along her collarbone and she clung to him as he lifted her onto the counter and began to unfasten her trousers. Here is something new, she thought with interest as she carefully slid the butter knife away from the immediate area. The session in the tack room had apparently inspired a new trend; next he'd be wanting to have at it in the morgue, or something.

Later, they sat before the fire, eating the sandwiches, with Acton's mood much improved. The remedy, Doyle thought with satisfaction; works every time—a shame I can't bottle it up and sell it. Reminded of her promise to Munoz, she licked her fingers and ventured, "I told Munoz that I would ask you if you knew of any eligible men."

Leaning back on his hands, he gazed at her, amused. "Eligible, meaning without the common sense to run in the opposite direction."

"Exactly." He gave her a look and she began to laugh, because it truly was funny. "I just need to tell her that I asked, is all."

"How about Williams? It would take his mind off waiting to outlive me."

"Michael," she admonished, gently punching him on the

shoulder. "Don't be givin' the few men in *my* quiver over to Munoz, for heaven's sake. Besides, Munoz has already made an unsuccessful run."

"Williams resisted? Good man."

Best not to mention Williams's other little liaison—that one would probably not sit so well with Acton. "I won't poke fun at Williams; he had my back on this vigilante case, and it was much appreciated."

Suddenly serious, Acton straightened up to take her hand in his, and ducked his head for a moment, gathering his thoughts. "Perhaps in the future, you will not hesitate to tell me if you encounter a problem, Kathleen. I won't berate you—I promise; I only want to know so that I can help."

Oh-oh, she thought in a panic—which of my many transgressions has he unearthed? "You make me very uneasy, Michael," she hedged. "What's afoot?"

"Nothing," he said gently. "I just wanted to say."

This was not exactly true, and she was quiet, feeling guilty.

"I would forgive you anything, you know."

She lifted a corner of her mouth. "That's perhaps not the wisest thing to be sayin' to one's wife, Michael."

"Yes; especially one as charming as you. But it is the truth, nevertheless."

She knit her brow, suddenly. "Does this work both ways? Am I to know the next time you are smokin' with a brasser for all the world to think that you are cheatin' on me?"

There was a small silence; he was startled by her outburst, and small blame to him—she was startled, herself. "I'm sorry I'm soundin' like an archwife, Michael. Apparently, that still rankles."

His arms came around her, and he rested his cheek on her head. "No, you are exactly right—forgive me. It should work both ways, but there are times I must alone decide what is best for the both of us. I must reserve that right."

She sighed; he was right—it was probably best she did not

know the details about some of his doings. "Aye, then," she conceded. "This marriage business is a rare crack, isn't it?"

"Yes," he agreed. "It is. And I must make a better effort at it."

Wickedly, she teased, "I don't know—any more effortin' and I'll be worn to a thread."

"Just so," he replied, and ran a well-satisfied hand up her arm—proud of it, he was. "I will take you to out to dinner tomorrow night. Where would you like to go?"

Quirking her mouth, she gave him a look of extreme skepticism. "Saints, Michael; just as though we were an ordinary mister and missus?"

"We can do it if we put our minds to it." He bent his head to murmur against her neck. "Will you wear your dress?"

Very pleased by this show of husbandly interest, she teased, "And where will I be puttin' my gun? I can't very well put it in my bosom—there's no place to hide it."

With gentle pressure, he pushed her so that she lay back down on the rug. "Let me search for a good place."

Giggling, she acquiesced. Apparently, her worries that she'd served her purpose—and that now his fixation on her would dissipate—were without foundation. Or at least for the next twenty minutes or so.

CHAPTER 48

"VERY NICE, MADAM, IF I MAY SAY SO."

Reynolds stood to one side, his hands clasped behind his back as Doyle critically examined her reflection in the mirror. Acton had just come home and had promptly gone in to shower, so she'd asked Reynolds for advice about earrings, and was tentatively pleased with the end result; the black knit dress clung to her slender figure and set off the whiteness of her skin against her auburn hair. "D'you think the skirt's too short?" It seemed very strange to show such an expanse of pale leg.

"Lord Acton will not think so."

The servant had not betrayed by the flicker of an eyelash his reaction to the fact that the grocery list she'd left on the counter featured a pregnancy test, which was hopefully a good omen, and not a sign that he intended to resign straight-away.

She heard the intercom buzz, and then Reynolds's voice as he went to answer it. A moment later he stood at the entry to the bedroom and announced, "There is a detective down-stairs who asked for Lord Acton, and then when I said he was unavailable, asked for a word with you, madam."

"Downstairs?" It could only be Williams, and she wondered

what he needed as she crossed to the kitchen intercom—perhaps he had more information on Masterson. "Hey."

"Doyle? It's Samuels."

This was a surprise, but it was probably something important, if he was coming after-hours like this. "Oh—oh, hallo, Samuels. Acton is showerin', I'm afraid. Can I help?"

"Would you mind coming on down for a moment? I have something I'd rather not leave with the concierge."

This was untrue, and gave her pause. "Oh? What sort of thing?"

He lowered his voice. "It has to do with Solonik."

This was true, and she immediately entertained the unwelcome thought that—no matter what Savoie had promised—Solonik was going forward with his vengeance plan. "Right; I'll be down directly."

Reynolds offered, "Shall I accompany you, madam?"

But she harbored a burgeoning fear that her doings with Solonik were about to be exposed to Acton, and so she mustered up an easy smile. "No—he's a friend from work and I'll just say hallo."

Trying to hide her anxiety, Doyle descended in the lift and walked out to see Samuels in the vestibule near the revolving glass door, ashen of face as he clutched a padded mailing envelope. Her heart sank; he was emanating guilt and anxiety—Samuels, who had been asking too many questions about Acton. He did not seem ambitious enough to be the conspiratorial type, but then again, you never knew. She decided it would be best to pretend she did not know what was afoot—if she had any trouble, after all, the concierge was close to hand. With a friendly smile, she approached him, balancing carefully on her heels. "Hallo, Samuels. What's up?"

A sheen of perspiration reflected off his brow as he glanced at the security desk. "Come out to my car, I need to show you something."

She wasn't certain if this was true, but had a ready excuse. "I can't—I'm gettin' ready to go out. What's this about Solonik?"

In response, he stepped close and pressed the envelope next to her side. "Keep quiet and come with me—I have a gun."

This was true, and Doyle's eyes flew to his in astonishment as he took her arm and firmly steered her toward the revolving door. For a moment, she debated putting up a fight here—where help was at hand—as opposed to going along and hoping to catch him off guard, or even talk him out of it. It was not an easy decision, what with the gun barrel aimed against her in the approximate location of the baby. "Samuels," she said as calmly as she was able. "You can't be serious—what ails you? Have you been drinkin'?"

"Come along—quickly. If you cooperate, I won't hurt you."

"Where are we going?" She leaned back, but he had her arm in an iron grip and pulled her along to the sidewalk outside. Stalling, she asked in a meek tone, "Can I take off my shoes? I'm not used to walkin' in them."

"We won't be walking long; I've got a car up ahead, in the alley."

This did not bode well, and she realized she'd have to make a stand rather than get into a car with him—best to allow him to think she was frightened and docile, and then take her chance when the moment of truth came. "Samuels; I'm Lady Acton, for heaven's sake—you canno' just be stealin' me off the street."

"No talking—and stay over here, next to the building." Nervously, he glanced around them, but the street was quiet on this weekday evening; the ground still wet from a recent shower. And now that she had a good look, she realized there was something strange about his pallor—something not right. "Are you on drugs or somethin', my friend? Because you're not acting rationally."

"Rationally," he corrected in annoyance. "Stay quiet; and once we get in the car you'll lie down—I can't take the chance someone will recognize you."

"All right—all right; don't be pullin', I'm comin'." She feigned a stumble and took the opportunity to slip out of her shoes, hopping along to keep up. At least she had a weapon of sorts, now. "I wish you'd tell me what this is all about, Samuels—Acton will be furious."

"No—Acton will be stymied."

As his hurried steps echoed along the quiet street, Doyle silently kept up, the damp pavement cold against her feet as she tried to decide what would be best to do. It was miserably ironic that this was the one time she was not wearing her ankle holster—*stupid* dress.

After another nervous glance behind them, Samuels abruptly turned into a side street, but then stopped so short that she bumped into him. Before them was Williams, approaching up the narrow sidewalk and seemingly unconcerned, his hands in his pockets.

"Hallo, Williams," said Samuels, and pressed the gun barrel against Doyle meaningfully.

"Hallo, Williams," she dutifully repeated.

Williams stopped in surprise and looked up at them. "Hallo; where are you two off to?"

"We're going to the coffeehouse to talk over some evidence," said Samuels, indicating the envelope.

Williams's gaze rested on Doyle's, and she slid her eyes sidelong. Go call Acton, she thought. Go get help; I'll stall him.

"You forgot your coat, Doyle," said Williams.

"I'm quite all right, we're just goin' down to the corner—are you comin' to see Acton? I think he's expectin' you." This said with a great deal of meaning.

But Williams was nothing if not stubborn. "First, let me lend you my coat."

Williams began to shrug out of his coat, but Samuels was

not to be diverted by whatever the other man had in mind, and immediately abandoned all pretense, yanking Doyle before him like a shield. "Don't move, or I swear I'll shoot her."

Williams slowly raised his hands to each side and said reasonably, "Samuels, it's *Doyle*. You can't shoot Doyle; if you need a hostage, take me."

Samuels swallowed hard and glanced up, gauging where the CCTV cameras were. "Where is your car?"

"Across the way," said Williams, indicating behind him.

"Right—I'll take her in your car. Give me your keys and your mobile."

"Let her go," said Williams, who made no move to comply. "I'll drive you wherever you want to go and say nothing to anyone."

"You're not well," added Doyle. "C'mon, Samuels; *please* rethink this."

Samuels gave Doyle a slight yank, just for emphasis. "Do you think I'm an idiot? You're my last chance at staying alive. Now, do what I ask."

"Samuels," Doyle carefully turned one of the shoes around in her hand. "You *do* sound like an idiot; no one is tryin' to kill you."

Samuels made a derisive, agitated sound that was not at all in keeping with his normally easy-going demeanor. "Don't you know what happened to Solonik today?"

"Solonik is *dead?*" She turned her head to stare at him, so astonished that she dropped one of her shoes.

"Not a good end." Samuels took a ragged breath. "And I'm not waiting around to be next—someone is staking my flat."

Doyle could not like the implication. "For heaven's sake, Samuels—Acton did not kill Solonik. Let's all go back and forget this ever happened." Tensing her hand on the shoe, she met Williams's gaze for a quick moment, trying to convey that she was about to make a move and that he should get ready.

But this plan was interrupted by a passerby, who hailed them from across the narrow street. "Excuse me?"

Wary, Samuels pressed the gun into Doyle's ribs and they turned to face a businessman, dressed in a fine suit of clothes and approaching rather apologetically, carrying an umbrella and a briefcase. "I'm sorry to interrupt, but aren't you that policewoman who jumped off the bridge? Would you mind if I took a snap? My wife will never believe it."

"Stay back—she's—she's not well," directed Samuels as he held out a cautioning hand. The movement brought the packing envelope away from Doyle's side for a moment, and after deciding that there was no time like the present, she jerked up her shoe, trying to aim the heel toward her captor's eyes and, at the same time, twisting away from the envelope.

Several things then happened in rapid succession; with a curse, Samuels flinched away from her heel, and Williams lunged, calling out, "Get down!" Doyle, however, was not about to go down to the ground in a short skirt, and wound up sandwiched between the grappling men, getting an arm free so as to shove her palm under Samuels's chin whilst they all fell against the brick wall with a thud.

"Everyone, freeze." Suddenly Acton stood beside them, holding a gun barrel against Samuels's temple. "Kathleen, step away."

"He has a gun," Doyle advised, not certain whether she should untangle herself whilst Samuels still held it.

"Drop it." There was an ominous click as a bullet was loaded into the firing chamber of Acton's weapon.

Gasping for breath and grey-faced, Samuels dropped the envelope from shaking fingers and slowly sank to the ground as Doyle and Williams stepped away from him. Acton bent to pat him down with his free hand, his face a grim mask. His hair was damp and he was in his shirtsleeves, which only served as a measure of his agitation—Acton's appearance was always impeccable. "Report."

Williams made to speak, but Doyle interrupted, conscious of the witness who had halted in surprise a few steps away, and continued to watch as events unfolded. "Perhaps not just now."

"I say," said the passerby in alarm. "I think he's having some sort of seizure."

It was true; Samuels had slumped over, his eyes rolling back in his head and his jaw clenching. Acton and Williams crouched over him, Acton loosening his collar and flipping up an eyelid. "Call an ambulance," he directed Williams. "And then take my wife to the flat and wait there."

Williams hesitated. "Should I—"

"Do as I ask," said Acton in a tone that brooked no argument, and Williams promptly pulled his mobile, glancing up to note the cross streets.

The businessman stepped forward to address Acton in a deferential tone. "Am I needed? I was just on my way home."

Acton glanced up at him. "You'll be needed to make a statement, I'm afraid." Then, to Williams, "Go."

Williams took Doyle's arm, but Doyle had frozen in confusion. When the passerby had leaned over, she'd glimpsed a neck tattoo beneath the starched collar, and realized with a jolt of surprise that he was Gerry Lestrade who—if she could keep her cast of villains straight—was Savoie's other brother. She was strongly reminded that Acton did not believe in coincidences, and so ventured, "Might I have a word, Michael?"

Sirens could be heard approaching in the distance as Acton rose to take her aside. "Quickly, then."

There was nothing for it—she would have to warn him, and take her lumps. She swallowed. "I believe this man is not a casual passerby. I believe he is affiliated with Savoie, so please be careful."

He stared at her for a moment, and she had the feeling he was surprised but not necessarily as alarmed as he should have been. "I see."

"Be careful," she said again, although Acton surely must have drawn his own conclusions.

"Go," he directed. "I'll be there shortly."

"Are you angry?" she asked in a tentative tone, unable to stand the suspense.

"Not at you." He leaned to kiss her forehead. "Go."

CHAPTER 49

DOYLE AND WILLIAMS SAT QUIETLY ON THE LEATHER SOFA, waiting for Acton. Doyle had been carefully wrapped in a blanket by Reynolds, who was now brewing coffee, pale of lip and emanating guilt and remorse. Doyle could only imagine the scene that had transpired when Acton had stepped out of the shower and wondered where his wife was.

Williams, glumly seated beside her, was not faring much better than Reynolds. "I'm going to get the sack."

"No, you're not." She paused. "Don't tell him about Masterson, though."

"I had no idea he would do such a desperate thing—Samuels, of all people."

She knit her brow. "Then why were you stakin' him?"

"I wasn't—Acton asked me to go over to his flat tonight, to see if he was there. He must have known about what happened to Solonik, and was aware that Samuels had a connection."

"Yes—we think Samuels was feedin' him information about Acton."

"Not a surprise." Williams watched Reynolds move about in the kitchen and then noted in a neutral tone, "At least that means I'm off the hook as a suspect."

Ah—she saw that the memory still smarted, and she was

quick to reassure. "Recall that I never believed it was you who was the back-stabber."

"Oh yes, you did."

She corrected herself. "Well, I realized almost immediately it wasn't you. You have to admit I had good reason—you were consortin' with the enemy, an' all."

But it appeared he wasn't going to let her wriggle off the hook so easily. "If the tables were turned, I never would have doubted you."

"Whist, Thomas; recall you once accused me of bein' a brasser, tryin' to seduce Acton for capital gain."

"I was in insulin shock at the time," he explained, annoyed. "That hardly counts."

"Let's call it even, then." She paused while Reynolds served the coffee, and after a quick internal debate, decided that since she was traumatized, and the baby was the size of a mustard seed, a little cup of coffee would not be outside the line.

Williams took a sip and then clicked her cup with his own. "Excellent use of a shoe, DS Doyle."

She demurred, "I truly was in no danger—he wanted me as a hostage, is all."

"Were you going out? You look bang-up. Or you did, anyway."

"May I offer sandwiches, perhaps?" Reynolds hovered, giving off just a hint of disapproval.

Why, I believe I am being chaperoned, Doyle thought in amusement. "No thanks, Reynolds. We're waitin' to be chewed out, so we're not hungry."

"I understand completely," said the servant heavily, with a glance toward the door.

"Make sure the new vase is not close to hand," she cautioned.

Any further commiseration was halted by the appearance of Acton himself, whose gaze rested on Doyle immediately as he came through the door. "Are you all right?"

"I am," she replied, then amended, "I have lost a shoe."

"What is the protocol?" asked Williams, who had risen to his feet.

Acton took a warm jacket out of the hall closet, and considered this question as he pulled it on. "It seems we've had the tragic death of an off-duty policeman. Perhaps not unexpected; we shall see if he had a history of drug abuse, or a preexisting condition."

Yes; no doubt such a thing would come to light—although whether it was true or not was another matter. There was no question it would be best to keep this little contretemps—and the reasons for it—away from the light of day. "There will be CCTV feed," Doyle reminded him.

"No—I don't think there will," Acton replied without concern. Then, to Williams, "You may go; I will have a debriefing tomorrow."

"May I prepare a light supper?" asked Reynolds.

"No; you may go, also."

Both men took their leave with no further ado, and Doyle watched them go, thinking that she was lucky there was little she could do to earn her husband's disapproval. "Please don't be sackin' people, left and right, Michael—I was an idiot, and I'm that ashamed to call myself a banner."

He struggled with it for a moment, but in the end, could not contain himself. "You left the flat to speak to a man who you know is trouble, and you did not take your mobile or your weapon."

Poor Acton—he must have been beside himself, and she couldn't very well tell him why she was so eager to meet with Samuels alone. "I'm an idiot," she repeated, and hung her head like a good penitent. "Thank the holy saints DC Samuels had some sort of seizure." She glanced up at him from under her lashes.

"I did not kill him," he said immediately, and it was the truth.

This was a relief, although it went without saying that the man would have sealed his own fate had he indeed kidnapped the fair Doyle, and it was just as well Acton wasn't given an opportunity to wreak his own revenge. Cradling her cup, she observed in wonder, "So just like that, Solonik and Samuels are both dead. Faith, it's almost as though the turf war is still goin' on, in a strange way. At least this time you are not behind the killin's, Michael—which shows remarkable restraint, all in all. I am very proud of you."

He ran a hand, gently, over her head. "I want nothing more," he said slowly, "than to keep you safe. And happy."

There seemed to be an odd nuance beneath the words, and she was moved to take his hand and say with all sincerity, "You always make me happy, Michael—please don't think it's dependent on your tryin' to be someone you are not; I would forgive you anythin', too."

"Let's not test it, shall we?"

"When's the next time we're due for Trestles?" she teased.

He mustered up a chuckle, leaning in so that his forehead rested against hers, his hair still damp.

Rather stricken by this delayed reaction to the dire events, she assured him, "Believe me, Michael, I have learned my lesson—no more walkin' like a lamb into an ambush." She thought of her meetings with Solonik and Savoie, and could only thank God fasting that he knew nothing about those particular misdeeds. "I have repented of my wayward ways, my hand on my heart."

"I am glad to hear it."

He hadn't moved, and taking his hands in hers, she asked, "How are you? I can't tell and it's frustratin'; please put me out of my misery."

She felt him draw in a breath. "I am as well as can be expected."

"I am a trial to my poor husband," she lamented.

"It has not escaped my notice," he replied softly against her head, "that you would have no trials at all, had you not thrown in your lot with me."

"Whist—I'm a bundle o' bad luck."

"Shall we share a fruit pie?"

She raised her head with a smile. "You're scarin' me, Michael. Who are you, and what have you done with the Chief Inspector?"

He lifted her hand to kiss the palm. "I am determined to keep you well fed, this time."

"All right. Do your worst." He put an arm around her and she leaned her head on his shoulder as they made their way into the kitchen. "This is exactly what I deserve for dressin' up. It's against the natural order, is what it is."

"Nonsense; you are breathtaking."

"Knocker; you'd think I was breathtakin' in a hopsack."

"Or out of one." He kissed the top of her head.

"I see how it is," she teased. "Despite all your fine talk of food."

"Hush." He pulled out a kitchen chair. "Sit."

"You're not to be hushin' me, husband; it does you no good a'tall."

"I know; I can barely face down the neighbors when I see them in the lobby."

Scandalized, she hit him with a napkin.